Quintin Jardine gave up the life of a political spin doctor for the more morally acceptable world of murder and mayhem. Happily married, he hides from critics and creditors in secret locations in Scotland and Spain, but can be tracked down through his website: www.quintinjardine.com.

Praise for Quintin Jardine's novels:

'A triumph. I am first in the queue for the next one' *Scotland on Sunday*

'Remarkably assured . . . a *tour de force*' *New York Times*

'The perfect mix for a highly charged, fast-moving crime thriller' *Glasgow Herald*

'[Quintin Jardine] sells more crime fiction in Scotland than John Grisham and people queue around the block to buy his latest book' *The Australian*

'There is a whole world here, the tense narratives all come to the boil at the same time in a spectacular climax' *Shots* magazine

'Engrossing, believable characters . . . captures Edinburgh beautifully . . . it all adds up to a very good read' *Edinburgh Evening News*

'A complex story combined with robust characterisation; a murder/mystery novel of our time that will keep you hooked to the very last page' *The Scots Magazine*

Quintin Jardine

A RUSH OF BLOOD

headline

First published in 2010 by
HEADLINE PUBLISHING GROUP

First published in paperback in 2011 by
HEADLINE PUBLISHING GROUP

1

Cataloguing in Publication Data is available from the British Library

978 0 7553 5766 6

Typeset in Electra by Avon DataSet Ltd,
Bidford-on-Avon, Warwickshire

Printed in the UK by CPI Mackays, Chatham, ME5 8TD

Headline's policy is to use papers that are natural, renewable and
recyclable products and made from wood grown in sustainable forests.
The logging and manufacturing processes are expected to conform
to the environmental regulations of the country of origin.

HEADLINE PUBLISHING GROUP
An Hachette UK Company
338 Euston Road
London NW1 3BH

www.headline.co.uk
www.hachette.co.uk

This is for Mike Jecks, time traveller, author, all around good guy, and the only genuine morris dancer (no, that is not rhyming slang) I have ever met, with thanks to Jane and the kids for letting him spend so much of his time in the fourteenth century.

Acknowledgements

The author's thanks go to Richard Kweicinski, for his expert advice on what would be a fair price to pay for a brothel.

The man knelt on the crest of the hilltop, facing the full moon as it bathed the city below in a light that would have been the purest silver, but for the distortion of the sodium street lighting. He had always loved that skyline. He thought of others he had seen on his travels, New York, Sydney, Chicago, Singapore, each one distinctively spectacular, but none of them blessed with the majesty bestowed by the best part of a millennium of growth, of unplanned evolution.

The best times in his life, he had known them all there; he thought of his youth and of the suspicion that he, after all, might just be immortal, unquenchable, unbeatable. Prince of the city? No, even back then, before he had come to the height of his powers, he had felt like a king. He had laughed there, he had fought there, he had loved there, and on two occasions he had cried there, cried tears of pure joy. He smiled at the recollection, and it stiffened his resolve.

'Do it,' he whispered. 'Set them free.'

One

'Are you sure he's dead?' Detective Chief Superintendent Mario McGuire asked, as he looked at the crumpled form, lying on the frozen hilltop.

Neil McIlhenney sighed. 'Always with the rhetoric, even at this time of the morning. I reckon he must be, unless his brains have wireless capability, seeing as how most of them are spread over that cairn.' He nodded towards the pile of stones that marked the summit. 'It's a bizarre situation; I doubt if even the boss has seen one like it. Given that it's minus five degrees at the moment, according to the readout in my car, and that today's forecast is for minus two, at best, we're going to have to figure out how to thaw the stuff, to get it off.'

'Boiling water?'

'Jesus,' the detective superintendent chuckled, 'how did you ever get to be head of CID? We're at the top of Arthur's Seat. Where are you going to plug the kettle in?'

'Primus stove? Or maybe we could light a wee fire.' McGuire stamped his feet. 'Christ knows, we need one.' He paused. 'And now, are you going to tell me why our force's two highest-ranking detectives are standing here, at seven thirty in the morning, freezing our nuts off over the body of one of the most obvious and effective suicides I have ever seen?'

'I thought I'd leave that to Ian, give him his moment of glory.' McIlhenney beckoned to a uniformed officer who was standing a few yards away, as if waiting to be called. 'Sergeant McCall, explain.'

The middle-aged man stepped towards them. 'Look at his hand, sir,' he said. 'Right hand.'

'Forget the "sir", Ian,' the DCS growled. 'We were all plods together, remember?' He dropped to one knee beside the body, and took a small torch from the pocket of his heavy, fleece-lined leather jacket. Dawn was on its way, but the light was still poor and a mist hung around them like a screen.

The man was facedown, his legs twisted beneath him, as if he had been kneeling when he died. He was dressed in a dark suit; even covered with a layer of frost, it looked expensive, tailored rather than off the peg. 'No coat,' McGuire murmured. 'Don't suppose he was bothered about freezing to death.' His right arm was thrown out in front of him, still holding a sawn-off shotgun by its pistol grip. Taking care to avoid the head, the top half of which was missing completely, the detective focused the beam of his flashlight on the hand. He leaned closer, peering at a tattoo, depicting a knight on horseback, brandishing a sword, in white against a red background.

'How many of those do you know in Edinburgh?' asked McCall.

'Just the one,' the head of CID conceded. 'Tomas Zaliukas . . . or Tommy Zale, as people used to call him when he was a young gang-banger. He was very proud of that tattoo. Still, it isn't his copyright . . .' He paused.

'There's a Lexus four-by-four in the car park at the foot of the hill,' said the sergeant. 'The keys are still in the ignition, so the owner wasn't bothered about it being nicked. I've checked; it's registered to Lietuvos Leisure Limited, the holding company for Zale's boozers.'

'Did you search him?'

'And have Arthur Dorward chew me out for compromising the scene?'

McIlhenney grinned. 'No, best not to risk that.'

McGuire looked at him, as he stood up. 'Have we got a forensic team on its way?'

'Yes. And the duty doc.'

'This does put a different complexion on it, I'll grant you. "Known to the police" is an inadequate phrase for our Tomas, from the stories you and I know of his early career . . . from our own experience of him, for that matter; and you know what I'm talking about. Who'd ever have thought he'd wind up like this, though. What do you reckon, Neil? Could he have had some help?'

'Anything's possible,' the superintendent replied, 'but it would have taken a lot of help to get the job done this way. Tomas was a pretty chunky guy. Then there's the matter of his team; he always had plenty of people on call.'

'Maybe he wasn't paying them enough,' the DCS suggested. 'They could have been bunged not to answer the phone, or even to do the job themselves.'

'I can't see it, Mario. All his close associates, all the

managers of his pubs, his clubs, and those massage parlours were Lithuanians, like him, a real clan.' His gaze switched to McCall. 'Can you remember, Ian, were there many tracks in the frost when you came up here?'

'Only two sets that I could see, one human, the other canine, left by Mr Oxley, the insomniac dog-walker who found him, and his pal Muttley . . . I wish I'd a pound for every dog with that name. But the frost's been hard all night, and for the last couple of days. Zaliukas must have left some footprints himself coming up here, but they've been covered over since then.'

'Arthur Dorward will find them, and any others that might be there,' McIlhenney declared.

'I heard that, and don't be so bloody sure,' said a voice behind them. 'Crime scenes are not improved by having the Glimmer Twins stomp all over them in their size twelve wellies.'

The two detectives turned to see a man crest the hilltop, red hair escaping from his black woollen hat. 'Ah, but we don't think this is a crime scene, Arthur,' McGuire countered, 'not in the way you mean.'

'Then what the fuck am I doing here, pray . . . sir?'

'Same as usual. We want you to confirm that we're right, and to tell us all you can about what happened here.'

Detective Inspector Dorward, head of what had been the city's forensic squad, before its absorption into a national scientific service, stepped towards them, carefully, making sure that he stepped on nothing but frosty grass. 'And what is here then?' He was carrying a lamp, much bigger than McGuire's.

He shone it on the remains. 'Jesus Christ Almighty!' he exclaimed, with a small, involuntary jump. 'This is not what you'd call a cry for help. Do you know who he is?'

'From the tattoo on his hand,' said McIlhenney, 'the Lithuanian national crest, we reckon it's Tomas Zaliukas.'

Dorward's eyebrows rose. 'Is it, indeed? In that case, you two might like to prepare yourself for the humbling experience of being wrong for once in your lives. He must still have a few enemies from the old days.'

The head of CID chuckled. 'You reckon? Arthur, this man put a sawn-off in his mouth and pulled the trigger. You have your whole team crawl over this scene and see if you can tell us different . . . but you won't.'

'Maybe so,' said the inspector, stubbornly, 'but . . .' He stopped and looked directly at the senior officers. 'Listen, you two; global gangster culture's a bit of a hobby of mine, as you must know.'

'Only too well,' McGuire agreed. 'You're always rattling on about it.'

'So much so that I've signed up to do a PhD on the subject at Edinburgh University. Part of my thesis is going to focus on cause of death among criminals: those who die of natural causes, the majority, those who're killed by rivals, the second largest group, and those who're executed by the state, a small minority. We're agreed that Zaliukas was a gangster, yes?'

'He might have taken on a legitimate front later on, but in his younger days, sure, pure hoodlum.'

'Suspected of a couple of killings, but never charged.'

'Killings, serious assaults, extortion, the story went, but

never any witnesses or trace evidence that we could tie to him
. . . apart from one incident that was nipped in the bud. He
hasn't had his hands dirty for years, though.'

'Maybe not, but his personality hasn't changed. Research
shows that people like him have strong psychopathic
tendencies. This includes a disregard for life, even their own.
This is evident in the modern generation, in the street gang
world. A lot of these kids regard death as an occupational
hazard. It's nothing new, really; look at gang culture in other
eras and in other countries, and you'll find the same thing. But
my studies show that what gangsters do not do is top themselves.
Go back over the years and you'll find that the suicide rate
among people like . . . people like Tommy Zale, is way below
the national average. Frank Nitti, Al Capone's sidekick, is the
only prominent figure who went out that way. There was
another killed himself, supposedly, around that time, but there's
a good chance that he was actually done by the cops.'

'Fair enough, Arthur,' McIlhenney protested, 'but if this is a
gangland killing, like you're suggesting, why would it be set out
to look like a suicide? Chances are that when the post-
mortem's done they'll find that Zaliukas had cancer and knew
it.' He smiled. 'A brain tumour possibly, so you'll need to figure
out how to get that frozen grey matter off those rocks for
examination.'

Dorward threw him a disdainful look. 'And why the hell
would I want to do that? I'll just send the rocks down to the
morgue with the rest of him and let it thaw out in the warm.
Now go on, the pair of you, before you do any more damage
with those bloody great feet of yours.'

6

Two

'Do you miss it?' Bob Skinner asked, as he adjusted his tie, checking in the mirrored wardrobe door that the knot was satisfactorily wide. 'Time for a trim,' he thought, noting the fact that his steel-grey hair, which he had allowed to grow longer during the winter, was beginning to touch his ears.

She looked up at him in surprise, from the dressing-table stool. 'Miss what?'

'Everything: all the trappings of power that you lost along with your majority in Parliament; the civil service private secretary, the official transport, the First Minister's official residence.'

Aileen laughed. 'And the key to the executive washroom? Do I miss it? The car at the door whenever I needed it; that was nice. Lena McElhone as my PS; yes, but she'd have been moving on anyway, within the service. As it was, she'd delayed her promotion by a year to stay with me. The tied house that went with the job? Absolutely not. I don't miss an Edinburgh base; I love it here in Gullane, plus there's still my flat in Glasgow for when I'm in my constituency. The truth is, I never liked it when we stayed there; the place gave me the creeps.

I'm not saying it was haunted, but all those Scottish Secretaries, and First Ministers that had used it. That's why I had the mattress changed, and all the linen, when I took over. The idea of sleeping in the same bed as Tommy Murtagh had been in.' She shuddered. 'Yuk! Despicable wee man. Or Bruce Anderson for that matter.'

'Ach, Bruce is OK.'

'My God,' she exclaimed. 'I never thought I'd hear you say that.'

'He is, though, now that he's given up politics for good, and lost all that anger he had bottled up within him.'

'Is he still seeing the Duke of Lanark's daughter?'

'Anthea Walters? Not even professionally. He's passed her on to another drug counsellor. When the judge gave her a suspended prison sentence for heroin possession, it was conditional on her staying in rehab for the full two years. No, Bruce is a different man altogether to the guy I fell out with.'

'The archbishop likes him,' she conceded 'so I suppose he must be.'

'Jim Gainer likes everybody; he has the gift of bringing out the best in people.'

'He'd be struggling with Tommy Murtagh. I wonder what he's doing now; he's dropped off my radar completely.'

Bob smiled. 'If you put your mind to it, you wouldn't be long in guessing what he's up to. Like many a fallen politician, he's a public affairs consultant, a lobbyist. While you were First Minister he kept a low profile, but now the Nationalists are in power, I hear that he's more out in the open.'

'How do you know all this? That's not your world.'

He picked her navy blue jacket from the bed as she stood, and held it for her as she slipped it on. 'Honey,' he said, 'I'm the chief constable. Everything is my world. Plus he has priority; I keep half an eye on the little bastard. He tried to ruin your career, and mine. I won't forget that, ever.'

'I bet he was jumping for joy when the Nats won the by-election for Ainsley Glover's seat and took over the Scottish Government.'

'I'm sure he was, but he had to do it privately. It was his own party that had lost out.'

'Mmm,' Aileen murmured. She led the way out of the bedroom, past the children's rooms, from which sounds of awakening were coming, and downstairs, into the kitchen. 'You want toast?' she asked.

'When do I ever? Cereal'll do as usual.' He filled the kettle and switched it on, dropped a tea bag into each of two matching mugs, then served himself a bowl of Special K.

'You know what?' his wife remarked, as she waited for the toaster to pop. 'I'm not so sure we did lose out.'

Half-smiling, he raised an eyebrow. 'Go on.'

'Well, if you think back six months or so, when I sacked my coalition partners because they were useless, and formed a minority administration, you'll remember that most of the Scottish media thought I'd lost the plot. When the opposition won the by-election, became the largest single party in the chamber, challenged me and won, they were absolutely convinced that I had. But what's happened since then? The economic shit-storm has got worse . . . as I was told by the Prime Minister last summer that it would . . . and there's no short-term answer. So now I'm leader of the Scottish opposition, and I get to stand up at First Minister's questions and bat my successor all around the chamber for his failures in tackling an impossible job that's made all the harder by financial constraints imposed from London by my own party. I know that power and the responsibility of government is what we're all about, but there are times when it's better not to be in the firing line.'

His eyes narrowed slightly as he filled the two mugs. 'Are you saying that you planned this whole thing?' he asked.

She winked at him. 'From about half an hour after Ainsley Glover died and his seat became vacant. I knew we had no chance of winning that by-election. If I'd still been in the coalition, it wouldn't have made much difference, because the Nats won't share power with anyone, so . . .'

'You set yourself up for the chop?'

'Ever so slightly. Now go and check the bookies and see who's favourite to win the election next time.'

'Have you always been this devious?'

'Bob, I'm a politician.'

He laughed, incredulously. 'Sure, but for the last four months I've been beating myself up because I thought it was me who talked you into leaving the coalition.'

'As if you could.'

'So you're actually just where you want to be.'

'Yes, and not just politically. I've got a new husband, a new family, and a hell of a lot more time to spend with them than I'd have if I was still First Minister.'

'And after the next election?'

'That's another thing about politicians; very few of us ever think that far ahead.' She took her mug from him and sipped it cautiously. 'Right now, I'm thinking no further into the future than First Minister's questions at lunchtime.'

'I might come and sit in the public gallery,' Bob suggested.

'And have the TV cameras pick you out again? You didn't like it last time that happened.'

'But neither did the First Minister. He kept glowering up at me.'

'That was for the cameras too; we had a laugh about it afterwards. He and I get on fine on a personal level. You've met him. What do you think?'

'Clive Graham? On the same personal level? I like him too. On a political level, he's pro-police, and that's fine with me.'

Aileen sipped her tea again, found it cooler, and drank some more. 'And is everything else fine with you, Chief Constable Skinner?'

He smiled at her, from the eyes. 'I've never been happier, my love. I got quite misty-eyed when Jim Gainer blessed our union.'

'So your daughter noticed. I didn't, though; my own vision was a bit blurry at the time. But I didn't mean at home. You're six months into your new job. Are you fine with that?'

He slipped his empty cereal bowl into the dishwasher, tossed what was left of his tea into the sink, put his mug on the rack, and closed the machine. 'Truthfully, I'm enjoying it far more than I thought I would. I've got a team around me that's pretty much hand-picked, and I can do the job the way I want to, spreading myself around without getting tied down by paperwork and meetings. Brian Mackie's the perfect deputy from that point of view, and Maggie Rose is settling in as well as I knew she would as assistant chief. With them, and those two monsters that run CID reporting directly to me . . . I reckon I've got the best team in the country. With them to lean on, any idiot could do my job. So yeah, I'm fine.'

'But restless?'

He frowned at her. 'What makes you say that?'

'The idea that you could even contemplate taking the time to come and watch me this lunchtime.'

'I was kidding. Honest.' He hesitated. 'If I seem fidgety, it's probably because everything's going too well. Since that fuss last August, there's been barely a ripple on the surface of Greater Edinburgh.'

'See, you are doing a great job.'

'Nobody's that great. I really don't like it when it's as quiet as it's been. It usually means we're missing something.'

'Nah! You've scared the bad guys shitless; that's all there is to it.'

'If only.' He glanced at his watch. 'Come on, we'd better say "So long" to the kids and be on our way, or we'll catch the worst of the traffic.'

'That's all right,' she chuckled. 'You're the chief, you can put your blue light on the roof.'

Three

'This is going to sound terrible,' the woman began, 'but what's your name again?'

Her companion, propped up on his left elbow, grinned down at her. 'Sauce,' he said.

'No,' she chuckled, 'my memory's not that bad. I meant your real name. It was noisy in that Indigo place last night; I couldn't hear you properly when you told me.'

'It's Harold,' he murmured, as if it was a confession. 'Harold Haddock. Hence the nickname, get it?'

'Have they always called you "Sauce"?'

'From my first day at nursery school.'

'Nobody ever calls you Harold, or Harry?'

'Most people don't even know that's my name.'

'I'll call you Harry, then, from now on . . . unless you hate it, that is.'

He slid his free hand under the duvet and fondled her left breast, tracing his thumb round the areola. 'You can call me anything you like.'

'Harry it is, then.'

'Fine. Now it's your turn to own up. Why do they call you "Cheeky", Ms Davis?'

'It's my name.'

'No more than mine's "Sauce". Come on, what's it short for?'

She pouted. 'Not telling you.'

'Why not?'

'Because I hate it.'

'It can't be that bad.'

'It is.'

'Let me guess.' He knitted his brow. 'How about "Rumpelstiltzkin"?'

She laughed. 'Don't be daft.'

'OK, let's try "Chiquitita". How about that?'

Her eyes widened. 'How did you . . . Here, did you look in my bag at my driving licence while I was asleep?'

'No,' he protested. 'It was a guess, honest.'

'Clever boy, eh. If you guessed that you must be able to work out the rest. My mum was a big Abba fan. She saddled me with it. When I was wee my grandma called me "Cheeky" and it stuck.'

'Hey, it could have been worse,' Sauce pointed out. 'It might have been "Waterloo". Imagine being called after a battle, or a railway station in London. And as for "Fernando", that definitely would not have worked.'

'You won't tell anyone else though, will you? How about I keep calling you "Sauce", and you keep calling me "Cheeky"?'

'That's a deal.'

She slid closer to him. 'It's nice this, finding out things about each other.'

He nodded. 'I know lots about you already, though.'

'Apart from my real name, you mean?'

'Sure. For a start, you're not a real blonde.'

'And you're the only guy who's ever found that out the same night I met him.' She reached for him. 'Whereas you, you're ginger all the way down.' She drew a deep breath. 'Or up, as the case may be.' She paused, frowning slightly. 'I mean that, you know. This is not typical behaviour for me. I've always been a hard nut to crack, yet here I am back at your place and doing the deed . . .' she glanced at her wristwatch, all she was wearing apart from a fine gold neck chain, '. . . less than twelve hours after we met. I should feel like a hooker, but I don't. Maybe I'm a mug, though.'

Gently, he smoothed her hair back from her forehead. 'No,' he said, solemnly, 'you're not . . . you're neither. This may sound like a line, coming from a guy, but this is not what I do either. I won't say I'm a puritan, I've had a few girlfriends, but I've always been a "one step at a time" sort of bloke. I could not believe that it was me coming on to you last night, but I just couldn't help myself. I've never known anything like this, or anybody like you.'

'And you seem to be finding out more about me all the time. Go on, then, what else have you discovered?'

'You're not from Edinburgh.'

'How do you know that?'

'Because you said it was your first time at Indigo. It's the best club in town. A girl your age, if she was local, would have been there before now.'

'All true. And what age am I then?'

'Not so easy. Twenty?'

'Thank you, kind sir. Actually I'm twenty-two. And you?'

'Just turned twenty-five.'

She felt his bicep. 'And strong with it.'

'I work out, plus I play a lot of golf.'

'Are you any good at golf?'

'Category One.'

'What does that mean?'

'It means good.'

'So, you're an ace at outdoor sports as well as indoor. That's something I've found out about you. Any more about me?'

'One last thing. You've got lousy taste in friends.'

She frowned. 'Why do you say that?'

'Because the one who took you to Indigo must be a right slapper, if she pulled, then buggered off and left you on your own.'

'I can look after myself.'

'I've heard a few girls say that, even after they've found out different.'

Cheeky drew herself up, until they were eye to eye. 'And where have you heard them?' she asked, quietly.

'In my job. I'm a police officer, a detective constable.' He watched her face closely, looking for the reaction that he had seen too often before.

The only change in her expression was a coy smile, so faint that it only just touched the corners of her mouth. 'Mmm,' she whispered. 'Are you indeed?'

'Does that make any difference?'

'Should it?'

'It does with some women.'

'Not with this one. I don't choose who I fuck on the basis of their occupation.' She pulled him, drawing him with her as she lay down once more. 'As I'm about to prove,' she whispered. 'Unless,' she added, 'you've got to go to work, or make some other sort of sharp exit.'

'Not that sharp; we were late the other night and the overtime budget's strapped. I don't start till midday.'

'You weren't working last night, were you?'

'No danger. I was there with Jack . . . my sergeant . . . and his girlfriend. Strictly off duty. Indigo's a popular hang-out for cops, because it's well run and there's never any trouble.'

'Jack. Was he the big tall guy?'

'That's him; Jack McGurk.'

'His girlfriend looked nice.'

'She is; they haven't been together long.'

'Neither have we.'

'So that means we are together,' Sauce ventured.

She rolled him on to his back. 'What do you think?' she hissed. 'Not getting cold feet, are you?'

'I promise you, Cheeky,' he replied, 'at this moment, not one single part of me is cold.'

Four

'Are you ready for your command group meeting, Chief?' asked Gerry Crossley. 'Will I call everybody in?'

Skinner nodded to his office manager. 'Yes, I'd better get on with it.' He tossed aside the copy of the *Saltire* that he had been reading, landing it neatly on top of the pile on his coffee table. 'That bloody traffic's getting worse, you know. I've just been reading about how tough the recession is, but it seems that more people than ever are going to work in the morning. Do you find that?'

'It's hard to tell. The work on the new tram system's having such an effect.'

The chief constable snorted. 'Hah! One of the craziest decisions the City of Edinburgh ever made, in my private opinion, pouring incalculable amounts of money into a transportation system that was outmoded fifty years ago. I'm glad I pay my council tax in East Lothian.' He stood up, behind his desk, and moved towards the informal seating. 'Ask ACC Steele to come in first,' he said. 'I want five minutes with her before the rest join us.'

He was glancing at the *Scotsman* when he heard a soft

knock on the half-opened door. 'Mags,' he exclaimed, as the newcomer stepped into his room. His eyebrows rose. 'In uniform, this early in the morning?'

'I'm going round the divisional HQs within the city this morning,' Margaret Rose Steele explained, as she took a seat at the coffee table. 'I was off for so long that some of them must have forgotten what I look like.'

'Fat chance. You could have been off for longer, you know. You were entitled to more maternity leave than you took, and the job would have waited for you. There's no overtime at our level, you know.'

'How about job-sharing?' For the merest instant, a hint of alarm showed in his eyes. She laughed. 'Don't worry. I'm still living in the real world. Bob, I came back to work this early because I had to. My illness, losing Stevie, having the baby: if I'd stayed away any longer I might have forgotten who I was before it all happened, and who I still am. I'm a police officer, with ambitions that I want to fulfil and a command level job has been one of them for a long time.'

'And have you settled in? That's what I wanted to ask you. Is everything OK? Do you have all the support you need?'

The ACC nodded. 'Everything's fine. You've been great, Brian Mackie's been great, David Mackenzie's the picture of efficiency.'

'How about domestically? Is there any way we can help there?'

'Again, I'm handling it fine. My sister's given up any thought of going back to Australia. She's living with me permanently, working from home and looking after Stephanie. I go home at lunchtime whenever I can, and on the odd occasion that Bet has a presentation, or a meeting, I bring the baby into the office. That's all the domestic life I want for the moment. I'm not ready for socialising . . . although I did say I'd look in on the Central Division dance on Friday, if only for half an hour or so. Are you and Aileen going?'

Skinner hesitated for a moment. 'I am,' he began, 'but unaccompanied. It might come with the territory for me, but not for my wife. The fact is, Mags, given the size of our force, there are a hell of a lot of social functions through the year. My predecessor regarded it as his duty to go to each and every one, and somehow the organisers got the idea that an invitation was expected. They also came to expect him to put his hand in his pocket for a round of drinks. Cost him several thousand over the years. Maybe you'd put the word around all the divisions, discreetly, mind, that the new incumbent will not take it out on any organisers who leave him off the guest list, and that any who don't can expect him to turn up in uniform, and loom over the proceedings like a rain cloud. If I want to go to an event I'll buy a ticket or chip into the kitty like everybody else.'

'Will do. Does that go for Brian and me too?'

'Of course, if that's how you want to play it. I'm not thinking of myself alone here, you understand. I'm as sociable as the next guy, but given Aileen's position, there's always going to be someone at these dos who has a few drinks and tries to talk politics. Sure, she could see them off, but why the hell should she have to?'

'Why indeed?' Maggie agreed. She smiled. 'I hope you don't mind me saying this, Bob, but she's really good for you.'

'I don't mind a bit, 'cos you're right. She found my soft centre right away. Third time lucky, no mistake. I was devastated when Myra died, but there was angst there amidst the bliss. Sarah and me? Sure, we'd the hots for each other at the start, plus at that point in our lives we each needed someone, but it was never quite right. We were very different personalities, and there was a culture clash there from the start. But at least we liked each other enough to part amicably. With Aileen, though . . . sometimes I just can't believe I'm this happy.'

'Then long may it last.'

Bob's mouth fell open. 'Aw, Jesus,' he exclaimed, 'listen to me. What a clown! You're the last person who should be hearing this.'

'No,' she said, firmly, 'I'm the very person, because I've had the same experience. I've lost Stevie, yes, but do you think that makes me wish I'd never met him? The opposite: it makes me all the happier that I did. The truth, Bob, is that you and Aileen are both going to die, and barring accidents . . . literally . . . one of you is going to die before the other. You're in the same boat as Stevie and me, as every other lifetime partners on the planet, and I'm here to tell you to grab every good moment you can.'

He threw his head back. 'I've never thought of it that way, you know,' he sighed. 'You're right, of course. We are on the same journey.' He looked at her. 'You've got an extra passenger too, the wee one, wee Stephanie.'

'So . . . ?'

'Hey, I've already got four of those, even if one of them is grown up, and one's adopted.'

21

'But Aileen hasn't.'

'She's got her career.'

'So have I.'

'Kids aren't on her agenda.'

'They weren't on mine either, as you know very well. Maybe I should bring Stephanie out to see you at the weekend, and you should ask Aileen again after that.'

He shook his head, smiling. 'Wonders of the world, Maggie Rose Steele, advocate for motherhood. You do that, Mags; you and your sister come for lunch on Sunday, about one o'clock. Bring wee Goldilocks and watch us trying to keep our three bears in check.'

The chief constable rose from his chair, stepped across to his desk, and pressed a button, his signal to Gerry Crossley that he was ready for the other participants in his routine morning meeting. After a few minutes they filed in, led by Brian Mackie, the tall, bald, deputy chief. He was followed by the command corridor adjutant, Superintendent David Mackenzie, his uniform immaculate, as it always was, and by the massive, dark-haired Mario McGuire, jacketless, wearing a pale blue shirt and black cords.

'Should we turn down the heating?' Skinner asked him.

'Early morning call,' the head of CID replied, an explanation that was understood immediately.

'Ah, you got dressed in the dark. Man, you look frozen.'

'To the marrow, Chief. I'll tell you about it in a minute.'

The group joined Steele at the chief constable's meeting table, while Skinner pulled his leather swivel chair from behind his desk and rolled it across the floor. 'Morning, all,' he began. 'Let's go through the day. ACC Steele is on a tour of the city, she tells me. Mags, do the divisional commanders know you're coming?'

'Yes, although I haven't tied myself down to a specific time with each of them.'

'Fair enough, since it's your first visit in your new post, but I'd suggest that as a general rule you're a bit less courteous than that. Everywhere you go today you'll see tidy desks and full out-trays. That's fine, but is it the norm? Remember when I was deputy and I used to drop in occasionally, just to say "hello"?'

'Of course.'

'Can you ever remember me calling you to tell you that I was coming and to put the kettle on?'

'Now you mention it, no.'

'Exactly. I rush to say here that your desk was always neat and your out-tray was always bigger than your in-tray, but you were the exception rather than the rule, and that's one reason why you're sitting here today. I was at a do with Aileen a few weeks ago and I met one of the Police Board members there. She gave me this nice smug smile and told me that it was time we had a woman at chief officer rank. I told her . . . fairly abruptly, I'm afraid . . . that any organisation that allows gender bias or tokenism of any kind to influence its promotion policy is doomed to failure, sooner rather than later.'

'Was Aileen within earshot?' asked Brian Mackie. 'I seem to remember her party doing something like that not too long ago.'

The chief constable nodded. 'Oh yes, she was there, and she

backed me up. She told the woman that the only positive discrimination she believes in is in favour of talent.'

Steele frowned. 'So what are you saying to me, Bob?'

'I'm getting round to saying that there will be one or two of your colleagues who will mutter behind your back that you are where you are because you're female. They're irrelevant, although anyone who says it to your face, you should refer to me. The rest, the great majority, are your friends and know your qualities; but there lies another difficulty. You don't have pals at the office, not in our service.' He looked round the group. 'All of you are my friends outside this building, in my private life, but here you're colleagues and your performance is measured in exactly the same way as every other member of this force. Mags, you're now in line command of many people who outranked you only a couple of years ago. Some of them you like, some you don't, but treat them all the same. You have to be that wee bit aloof; your authority has to be clear to them and to others. If any of them are reluctant to call you "Ma'am" in front of junior officers, deal with it, for this is a disciplined service and your rank requires it. What they call you in the privacy of their own offices is for you to determine.'

'Got it.'

'I know you have. It might lead to some awkward moments . . . hell, no, it will . . . but it's the next step to being a chief constable,' he glanced around, taking in Mackie, McGuire and Mackenzie, 'for all of you. So,' he smiled, 'no more scheduled visits to your divisions.'

His gaze locked on Mackie. 'Brian, what's on your plate?'

The deputy rolled his eyes. 'The joint working party with the local authorities, fire and rescue and the ambulance service on traffic management; ten thirty, Edinburgh City Chambers, and I know from experience that it'll go on all day.'

'You better leave now,' Skinner growled, 'if you want to get there on time. Speaking as a commuter, I'm fucking hacked off with it.'

'Any message for them?'

'Yeah, tell them from me that presiding over an unfolding disaster does not count as any sort of management in my book. Tell them they should suspend all work on the trams in the city centre, and switch to laying the line from the western end inwards. That might give some people a bit of respite, or at least share the grief. Tell them that the chief constable will not have gridlock in the city and that if this fucking project falls further behind schedule, I will arrest the senior managers and have them shot!' He sighed. 'Failing that, just do your best to get people to work on time.'

'I take it you were held up this morning,' said Mackie.

'You take it right. Seriously, it's one thing for me to be late for the office, but it's another for ambulances and fire appliances to be stood still in traffic. That's where the focus has to lie.'

'I'll emphasise that. I was planning to say that our traffic cars are going to crack down on improper use of bus lanes. Emergency vehicles, top priority, taxis and scheduled buses second; I'm also going to suggest that city tour buses and private hire coaches should be banned from using them.'

'Can we do that?'

'We can amend the regulations.'

'How will that help rush-hour motorists?'

Mackie allowed himself a thin smile. 'It won't,' he said. 'Sorry, Bob.'

'Bugger. Anything else?'

'One thing.' The DCC glanced at Mackenzie. 'David flagged it up for me. The Serious Crime and Drug Enforcement Agency is on the lookout for a new deputy director, and from what he's heard there's a degree of urgency about it.'

'Interested?'

'Absolutely not.'

'Quite right, but if the director's job comes up and you fancy it . . .'

'I'm happy where I am . . . unless that was an unsubtle hint.'

'Far from it. But you'd be perfect for the job.'

'I'll settle for imperfection for now. However, there's a second job on offer; national drugs co-ordinator, open to chief inspectors and above.'

Skinner's eyes settled on Mackenzie. 'David. You've got drugs squad experience, and you were damn good at it. Fancy it?'

The superintendent's eyebrows came together. 'There was a time when I might have, Chief, but even then I wouldn't have been right for it. I'm a recovering addict myself; my problem might have been alcohol, but still, that's an environment I'm better off avoiding.'

'That's good. I'm selfish; we need you here.' He paused, then turned to the head of CID.

'Mario: what was that wake-up call about?'

McGuire grinned. 'It was to a suicide, would you believe?'

'Eh? What did you do to the guy who called you out to that?'

'The guy was McIlhenney. He was called before me, by Ian McCall.'

Skinner leaned back in his chair. 'Right, Ian's a sensible guy. So do I take it that death wasn't self-inflicted?'

'No. Subject to forensics and the post-mortem report, it almost certainly was. What gives us an interest is the identity of the dead man: Tomas Zaliukas.'

The chief constable gasped in surprise. 'The Lithuanian? Tommy Zale? What did he do?'

'He climbed Arthur's Seat at some point last night and shot himself, with a sawn-off.' The DCS opened his mouth and touched his palate with the first two fingers of his right hand. Beside him, Maggie Steele shuddered. 'McCall saw that tattoo on the back of his hand, and knew who he was. We left Dorward and his team to gather him all together.'

Skinner closed his eyes, as if he was picturing the event. 'Tomas always saw himself as a hard man. Not without cause, I must say; he even took a swing at me once, when he was a young gang-banger. I'd to hit him four times to convince him to stop; only Lennie Plenderleith ever did better than that.'

'Did you do him for assault?'

'There was nobody else around at the time; no witnesses on either side.' He chuckled. 'Besides, it would have been awkward; I broke his cheekbone.' He thought for a few seconds. 'Yes,' he continued, 'it fits. I can see that if Tomas decided to do himself in, it wouldn't be any overdose, it would be done in the most macho way he could imagine. I wonder why he chose Arthur's Seat.'

McGuire's eyes glinted. 'If he'd done it at home, his wife would have been annoyed at the mess.'

'Are you sure he was sporting one of those?' the chief constable asked. 'I heard a whisper at the golf club at the weekend from a surveyor who works with his property side that Regine had taken the kids and left.'

'Where did he hear that? Paulie and I were in Indigo last Monday and she was there, as usual.'

'From Tomas himself; last Friday.'

'Do you know where she is now? I suppose we'll have to get in touch with her.'

'No, I don't. She's French, though, so I guess that might be a good place to start. Do you know their story?' he asked, looking around the table, at four shaken heads. 'They're quite a couple; well matched. They met when Tommy was down-market; he'd been involved in a couple of low-grade rackets, protection, fencing stolen fags and alcohol, a dodgy security company, usual things. But he'd started his move upwards, into his first couple of pubs, the kind with go-go dancers, before they gave them poles. Regine was a proper dancer; she applied for a job. When Tomas asked her to audition, and told her what was required, she told him she wasn't a stripper, and walked out. A couple of days later, he met her in the street, apologised, and offered her a job managing a place he'd just bought. And they went on from there.'

'You must go back a bit with Zaliukas, Bob,' Brian Mackie commented.

Skinner nodded. 'Yes indeed. I remember him from the time when he first pitched up in Edinburgh, back in the late eighties. He was only a kid, not much more than twenty; it was just before the collapse of the Soviet Union. He was a merchant seaman, on a Lithuanian vessel; he jumped ship down in Leith, walked into the first Catholic church he could find and asked for sanctuary, would you believe. He got it too, in a way; the parish priest took to him and helped him get leave to remain in Britain. Not that the Lithuanian regime of that time gave a shit about one wee sailor. It was too busy clinging to power by its toenails. Tommy was still cautious, though; he decided that he needed more effective back-up than the priest who'd helped him out, so he went to work for Tony Manson, driving him, running errands, doing security at some of his massage parlours. He was a gopher, really.'

He paused, reflecting. 'He fancied himself, though, and when his country finally got its independence, Tomas brought some of his old mates across, and set up his own team. That's when he got the tattoo, by the way, to show that he was the boss. Manson was OK with the new operation. If you remember, Tony didn't like too many people close to him, and in truth with big Lennie Plenderleith as his right-hand man he didn't need them either. He made a habit of contracting stuff out, and the Lithuanian boys came in very handy for that. If somebody had crossed him and he wanted to keep Lennie out of it, he'd give the discipline job to Tommy Zale . . . as most people called him then. I also know for a fact that a couple of times Tony took on contracts for associates of his in Newcastle and in London, and passed the work on to those boys; cash down and a bonus on completion.'

'No chance of a prosecution?' Steele asked.

'It was a while afterwards before I found out, but anyway, there was no chance of any physical evidence. I had inquiries made in both cities, and the people involved were being treated as missing, no more. No bodies were ever found, but there must have been proof of some sort that the jobs had been done for Manson to have paid out.'

'Unless your source was spinning you a tale,' Mackie suggested.

'No chance. My source is unimpeachable; he had no reason to lie to me, nothing to gain, nothing to lose. The stories showed what the Lithuanians were capable of in those days. They didn't just work for Manson either. They freelanced, they did security work, unlicensed but more or less legitimate, they fenced stolen goods, and once a couple of them were fingered as team members on an armed robbery put together by Jackie Charles. Again, though, it couldn't be proved.'

He smiled, and his eyes seemed to focus on a point back in the past. 'I was a DCI at the time, and Alf Stein was head of CID. He told me to sort it out. That was all the instruction he gave me. I went to see Tommy, one on one, and we had a wee chat. I leaned on him, and told him that I was not going to have hooligans with guns running around on my patch, and that if he didn't bring his people into line I would show him what hard really meant. He thought it was a challenge; found out it was a promise.'

The chief constable paused. 'He got the message, though. He knew that if he kept on the way he was going, I'd see him in the jail, so gradually he changed. He focused on the security business, and if he was still fencing, I never heard about it. He bought a pub in Leith, then another in Slateford. When the transfer of the licences came up before the board, I was asked to comment on his suitability. I took a chance; I gave him the nod. Having done that, I kept a bloody close eye on them. They did well; both had been pretty scruffy, but Tommy invested money in them and took them upmarket. Sure, he had the go-go girls at lunchtime and in the evenings, but they were top-end talent, no sexual simulation, and definitely no interaction with the customers. He installed two of his boys as managers, and employed his own firm to handle security, so there was no trouble. That was a big change; before he took over, our uniforms were never out of those places.'

'And now when they go in, they're off duty,' said Mackie.

'That's right,' Skinner concurred. 'Tomas set up his company then, moved the pubs into them and started to expand. The next place he bought was a rundown disco down at Abbeyhill. That's where Regine took over as manager; between them they did another complete makeover, and turned it into the most popular nightspot in the city, a club, instead of a disco. She's managed it ever since, and supervised all the other places.'

'Indigo,' said McGuire. 'Yes, Paula and I go there quite often.'

'She doesn't mind, given who owns it?'

The head of CID stared at him, his eyebrows rising. 'Why should she?' he asked, slowly.

'Ah well,' Skinner smiled. 'That's another story I heard on this grapevine of mine. The way it went, although Tomas was concentrating mainly on what he called his "entertainment division", he couldn't quite kill off some of his old Tommy Zale habits. One day, Paula's dad, your Uncle Beppe, had a visit from him in his office. Tommy told him that the Viareggio family had a very nice, broad-based business, with great growth potential and that he'd like a piece of it. Beppe thanked him very politely, but said that he didn't need or want any outside investors. Tommy told him that wasn't quite what he had in mind, and gave him a couple of days to think it over. As we both know, Papa Viareggio, your grandad, would have chucked him out the window, second floor or not, but Beppe wasn't cut from that cloth. He crapped himself and went running to Paula.' He paused. 'With me so far?'

Impassive, McGuire nodded.

'Good. As always, Paula knew what to do. Next day, Tommy was in his own office, when two fucking monsters came in unannounced, having walked right through the two bodyguards outside. They showed him warrant cards, which identified them as police. One of them didn't say anything, but the other, a guy with black curly hair and a wicked smile, told Tommy that he'd just done something incredibly fucking stupid by threatening his uncle, and that any repetition would have the most severe consequences. Beppe never had any more trouble; in fact he never heard a word from Zaliukas again.'

'And where did you hear all this?' the DCS asked quietly. 'Has our pal Neil been indiscreet around the dinner table?'

'Hah!' Skinner laughed out loud. 'You should know him better than that. No, I heard the tale from none other than

Tommy Zale himself. Priceless: the silly bugger thought I'd sent you to warn him off! He called me within the hour and asked if he could come and see me. He began by apologising for what he said was a complete misunderstanding, and for not making it clear to Mr Viareggio that his visit was simply to see whether they might have had any business interests in common. At first I hadn't the faintest fucking idea what he was talking about, but I let him go on, and kept my face straight as I pieced it together. When he was done, I gave him the glare and asked him if he'd taken the warning to heart. He assured me that he had, but that it hadn't been necessary.'

'And yet you never said anything to us? Or even thought about it?'

'Oh, but I thought about it, boyo,' the chief constable told him. 'I almost had the pair of you on the carpet for using the job to sort out a family matter. But when I considered it some more, I decided that if you had come to me and reported an attempted extortion, as you should have, I'd have told you to do exactly what you did. I knew who you two were at that point, but I didn't know a lot about you. After that, I made it my business to find out, and by Christ, look where both of you are now.'

McGuire smiled. 'In that case it's probably just as well that McIlhenney talked me out of beating the shite out of him and throwing him in the dock.'

'That was a good career move on his part, I'll concede . . . and on Tomas Zaliukas's, when he threw himself on my mercy. He was desperate to convince me that he was entirely legit, and by that time, apart from the odd wee aberration like his silly threat to Beppe, I reckon he probably was. I'm quite certain that nothing illegal ever happened in any of his pubs, not with his knowledge at any rate. He went on to acquire a dozen pub and club licences across Edinburgh, and a few more in the counties around it. They were all spotless.'

'No drugs going through any of them?' asked Mackie, his tone sceptical. 'Not even the discos?'

'Nope. There were warning signs in all the toilets of his clubs, and the managers all had firm instructions; anyone caught smoking hash or popping pills on the premises was chucked out and barred. Anyone caught snorting coke or injecting was detained and handed over to us. It was the same with anyone pushing any sort of drug, but they were usually carrying a few lumps and bumps by the time we arrived.'

'Those principles still apply,' McGuire confirmed. 'The notices are still there in the bogs in Indigo . . . and in any of Zaliukas's pubs that I've been in. He welcomes cops in all of them, and because we go there, the places are clean in every respect, and there's no chance of any of the new young hooligans going into any of them looking for protection money. As for Paula, I don't think she knows that the place is owned by the same guy who scared her dad, if she even remembers that incident. But come to think of it, I've never seen Zaliukas in any of his own places.'

'You don't, very often,' said Skinner. 'Tomas has kept a low profile for some years now.' He glanced at his deputy. 'As for the drugs thing, Brian, not even in the wildness of his youth was he ever into that. Tony Manson wouldn't have allowed it. He was a funny bugger, that one. I know that he dealt drugs himself; it was one of many things we couldn't pin on him. But I always had the feeling that he did it so that he could control it in his territory. He didn't leech on the users either; back then it was reckoned that Edinburgh had the cheapest smack in Scotland.'

'Are you saying he was benevolent?' Steele murmured.

'I'm saying that if there can be such a thing as a responsible drug baron, he was. He realised that if he didn't feed the demand, someone else would, somebody who didn't care at all about the addicts, only about the money that could be screwed out of them. Manson didn't really approve of the business, and he reasoned that made him the best person to run it. This strange morality of his led him to make sure that none of his closest associates, the people he liked most, were involved in it in any way. Lennie Plenderleith never was, and neither were Tommy Zale and his Lithuanian crew. He ran quality control himself, he subcontracted distribution to other people. They hired the dealers, and Tony had Dougie Terry . . . Remember him? The guy we called the Comedian? . . . keep an eye on them to make sure no liberties were being taken. If we'd been running the trade we couldn't have done it better than he did. When Tomas started to break into the pub business, it was easy for him to make his places drug-free from the start, because Manson spread the word that they were off limits. By the time Tony died, Zaliukas was strong enough to make it stick himself.'

'You sound,' said Mackie, 'that you wish Manson was still around.'

'I do, in a way. Since he met his end, the business he ran

with discipline and with the understanding that it's bad practice to bleed your customers dry has been taken over by people with no morality at all. Fortunately they tend to be stupid and we knock them down pretty quick, but when we do that, in the process we create a business opportunity, and the whole cycle begins again. It's like that bloke who had to push a rock uphill for all eternity.'

'Sisyphus,' Mackenzie volunteered.

'You can get injections for that,' the chief constable retorted. He looked up at the wall clock. 'You people should be getting on with your day.' As his colleagues stood, he added, 'My highlight, incidentally, will be lunch in Oloroso with my daughter, to celebrate her appointment as a partner in Curle Anthony and Jarvis. She called me last night to give me the good news. The even better news is that she's paying.'

'Congratulations,' Steele exclaimed.

'Thanks, Mags, but it was all her own work.' As the others headed for the door, he put a hand on McGuire's shoulder. 'Stay for a minute, Mario, please. Sit yourself back down.'

When Skinner resumed his seat he saw that the head of CID was smiling. 'What's tickling you?' he asked.

'I'm thinking of what you said about Papa Viareggio. You were wrong. He wouldn't have done anything to Zale himself; he'd have done what Paula did, more or less. She came to me and asked me to see to the guy as I thought best. He, though, he'd have called somebody else, and Zale would have had that hand with the tattoo nailed to a tree, maybe about ten feet off the ground. I remember when I was about eight or nine, this very old man came over from Italy for a visit. He was Papa's uncle, Patrizio, and he was fucking ferocious. He wasn't all that big, but he never smiled, and there was something about his eyes that chilled me; there was no twinkle in them, all darkness. He was, and remains, the scariest man I've ever met, and from what Papa told me when I was a bit older, my great-grandfather was just like him.'

'Jimmy Proud, my predecessor, knew your grandad well,' said the chief. 'He liked him, but he reckoned that he'd evolved from a long line of brigands, and that you have a lot of his blood in your veins. He was right, and it's brought you to where you are now.'

'I'll settle for that,' the DCS confessed, 'although I'm still surprised by it. When I was a detective constable, detective sergeant was the height of my ambition. I never dreamed I'd get any higher.' He nodded towards the ceiling. 'Thanks, Papa.' He paused. 'What did you want to talk about, boss?'

'Zaliukas. I'm still thinking about him. That incident with Beppe could have shaken the last of the cowboy out of him; indeed I thought it had. He built his leisure chain still further, he went into property development, taking old, derelict buildings and restoring them; he won a lot of respect in the business community. There was even a feature on him in *Insider* magazine. He was about to be up there with the big boys . . . and then he went and got himself kicked off the ladder. You know how, of course?'

'Sure,' said McGuire. 'He bought Tony Manson's massage parlours, from his estate, after his death. And when word of that got around, it reminded every one of those establishment figures who were just about to accept him of what he was and where he'd come from. He was back on the outside.' He looked at Skinner. 'Did you know that Beppe was offered those, by the selling solicitor?'

'No, I didn't.'

'The daft sod was interested, but Nana Viareggio, my mother, and Paula all vetoed it. After that, Tomas Zaliukas bought them. Why, do you think? You're right, it did cut across what he'd been doing up till then.'

'I believe,' the chief replied, 'that he honestly thought they'd fit into the leisure business that he was creating. If he did, big mistake, Tomas. It wasn't like buying an old pub and giving it a makeover. The customer base of those places was never going to change. There was a naivety about Zaliukas; he was a family man by this time, happy with Regine and Aimée, the first of his daughters. He may well have thought that there was a market for massage parlours, saunas, and general pampering. He may have thought that was what these places really did, even though he'd worked for Manson and seen them close up.'

'Or maybe he just thought he could be anonymous,' McGuire suggested. 'I heard he set up another company to buy the places.'

'Maybe, but whatever his motives were he wound up owning a chain of brothels, pure and simple. From being a fast-rising young tycoon, be became "the pimp" behind his back. Sure, he did spend money on the facilities, and he did employ a couple of people who actually were qualified masseurs, of both genders. But the same customers still went in there, with maybe an added twist. He had women turning up and booking the males, looking for the same special services. He had gay blokes going in expecting a hand job from them. Most of his new staff walked out; most but not all. So he gave in to the inevitable, and he ran the places as they'd always been run, on the borderline of legality, clean, but seedy, left alone because they bring prostitutes in off the street. I wonder if that had anything to do with Regine leaving,' he mused.

'Whether it had or not,' said the head of CID, 'his death isn't something for us to follow up. The aftermath will be for Zaliukas's lawyers. The man blew his brains out, unassisted; that's how it was. Dorward's people won't find a scrap of evidence that says anything different.'

'But he still has to be identified,' Skinner pointed out. 'From what you've said, he isn't recognisable, and there won't be enough left for a dental match-up either. His tattoo isn't going to satisfy a court.'

'We'll get DNA from his car, or from his house, and we'll match it to the body. That'll do it.'

'You're probably right,' the chief granted. 'But the thing is,' he continued, 'I want us to investigate it. Unless the post-mortem shows up a credible reason, I'd like to know what it was that drove Tomas to do something as out of character as taking his own life. What's the responsible division? Arthur's Seat? Central, yes. I'd like you to have Becky Stallings and her team do some digging. They don't necessarily have to go looking for Regine, but they should talk to his team, the people who worked for him, talk to everyone who had regular dealings with him. Find out if anything had happened lately, anything serious enough to make him do something as drastic as this.'

'Is that really our business? We all have to prioritise, boss.'

'It's a sudden death, from gunshot wounds. We're required to make a report to the fiscal, so that he can decide how to categorise it. That makes it our business; let's just spend a bit more time on this than we normally would on a suicide.'

'Even if it leads us nowhere?'

'Even if . . .' he stopped abruptly. 'My friend,' he went on, 'I might be wearing the chief constable's epaulettes, but I'm still a detective, and I will be till I die. All my career, I've found success by following my instincts. This time they're telling me there's something not right here.'

Five

Maggie Steele looked up at the façade of the divisional headquarters building in Torphichen Place. She had left her car in its secure park, but preferred to make her entrance boldly by the front door rather than casually by the back. She knew that word of her arrival would have been spread by the gate officer, but that made no difference. She remembered Skinner's advice at the morning briefing, and wanted to gauge reaction as she walked into her old office for the first time as an ACC.

The grey stone pile was not impressive. It was an old structure, and if it had been purpose built, then it had been for an era long left behind by modern policing. Any newcomers looking at it would have been forgiven for doubting its fitness for purpose before ever stepping inside; indeed they would have been right. It was small, it was cramped, and it was yards away from the complex Haymarket road junction, making vehicle access a nightmare at the peak periods which seemed to be extending to fill most of the day. It was always a shade too hot or a shade too cold. There was nothing about it that did not need improvement.

And yet Maggie loved the place. Much of her police career had been spent there, in uniform and in CID. Its faults had been no hindrance to her rise through the ranks, and it had been the scene of the most unexpected yet uplifting turnaround in her personal life. It was where she and Stevie Steele had made their great discovery. Newly out of her unsuccessful marriage to Mario McGuire, she had been in charge of the Central CID office and Stevie had been her DI. They had known each other for years as friends and colleagues. He had carried a reputation as something of a playboy, more because he had been attractive to women than from any headlong pursuit on his part, but it had meant nothing to her. He had been a nice guy and a good cop and that had been it. Until one night, one completely unexpected night when she had looked at him and everything, all her assumptions, all her certainties even, had been turned upside down. They became lovers, she fell pregnant, they were married, it was all unbelievable . . . indeed, if not for Stephanie, she might have believed that she had imagined it all. Not too good to be true, but too good to last.

Life, she reflected, standing in that cold drab street, where the sun rarely shone in winter, is a series of judgement calls. We cross the road through traffic how many times a day? We flick how many switches that might be live, but are not? We drive through how many green lights trusting that we are not about to be T-boned by a skidding truck? Stevie's fatal miss-call was to rush though a door in a cottage in Northumberland; the wrong door.

By that time she had known of her illness, and had been

faced with a life-threatening judgement of her own: to carry on with her pregnancy until Stephanie was almost full term, or to have her delivered weeks early, on the edge of viability, so that she could have surgery. In the aftermath of Stevie's death, she had taken the gamble, put the egg before the chicken and delayed her vital operation. Since the end of her follow-up treatment, her regular scans had been clear, and her consultant was smiling. Most of all, though, her baby was perfect, and every time she looked at her, she could see her father.

She shuddered, not only from the cold, and stepped towards the door entrance to the Divisional building. The door was pulled open before she reached it, by a veteran officer. 'Good morning, ma'am,' said PC Charlie Johnston, looking far more neat and tidy than she had ever seen him, 'and welcome.'

'Thank you, Constable,' she said as she stepped inside, with a brief, formal nod, thinking, *Bob was right. No more advance warning of visits.*

Superintendent Mary Chambers, in uniform, was waiting for her in the public area. She repeated Johnston's 'Good morning ma'am' in a voice loud enough to be heard by the sergeant and two constables who were standing, almost at attention, behind the counter. 'Jesus,' Steele asked herself, mentally, 'when Bob Skinner walked in here unannounced in my time, what did he see?'

'And to you, Superintendent,' she replied, feeling that she wanted to loosen up, but knowing that she had to maintain the formality. Chambers half-turned, stretching out an arm as if to escort her. Just then, the door at the back of the public office swung open, and Neil McIlhenney stepped through, slipping a waxed cotton jacket over his suit. 'Hi, Mags,' he said with a cheery smile, and carried on his way.

Quickly, Steele headed in the direction from which he had come, leading the way upstairs, to what had been her office less than a year before. As she had expected, her former desk was neat; the files in the out-tray were stacked much higher than the in-tray. She hung her cap on the stand and slumped into a chair. 'Bloody hell, Mary,' she exclaimed, 'I feel like a schools inspector.'

The superintendent laughed. 'Want a coffee?'

'Tea, if you have it.'

'No problem.'

Steele watched as Chambers switched on her kettle, and found a mug and a tea bag as it came to the boil. 'How goes?' she asked, as Chambers finished brewing up.

'Job or personal?'

'Job.' She took the mug as it was passed to her, handle first. 'Thanks.'

'Official report?'

'No, I'd need that in print. Just you and me.'

'Well, the highlight of my month is that Charlie Johnston's two weeks off retiring. He's a nice guy, but a throwback. He's the original plodder after whom we've all come to be named, and he's been filling in his time, drawing his pay and waiting for his pension from the day he joined the force.'

'He's reliable, though. He doesn't make mistakes. His problem is that while he does everything by the book, he does it all very slowly.'

'Tell me about it,' Chambers grunted. 'He seems to have an effect on time itself. If he'd boiled that kettle it would have taken ten minutes.'

Steele laughed. 'True. Mind you he does have one virtue that you'll miss. He knows everything. Nothing goes past Charlie, not a single fact, or piece of gossip, about what's going on in the office. When I was here, if there was something that I couldn't quite pin down, I always asked Charlie, and he always came up with an answer. Has he said what he's going to do when he retires?'

'He's been talking about applying for a security job in one of the museums or art galleries.'

'Tell him that I'll give him a reference if he does. Tell him also that if he fancies the idea of being re-employed as a civilian clerk, he should give me a call and I'll see what opportunities are available.'

'What?' the superintendent exclaimed. 'Do you want the paper trail to grind to a halt?'

'Alan Royston, the force media manager, has a vacancy. While Charlie has a nose for gossip, he never gives anything away. He might be a good guy to have mixing with journalists.' She sipped her tea. 'OK, Charlie's departure's the highlight. What about the rest?'

'We've been quiet. There's been an increase in call-outs for shop-lifting, a by-product of the economic slump, I suppose, but otherwise we're not over-stretched.'

'Got everything you need?'

'Apart from a new building, you mean? That apart, for the moment we're fine.' She paused. 'Ach,' she resumed, 'I go on about this place, we all do, but it works. We do a decent job here, so we can go on with it for a while.'

'Don't be too quick to tell me that, or anyone else in the command corridor. Do that and you'll stay a low investment priority. Complain, Mary, complain.'

Chambers smiled. 'If you insist. Charlie Johnson says that the gents' toilets are what he'll miss least about this place.'

'That's a surprise; he's spent a good part of his career in there. But act on it; ask the guys, and if they agree, drop me a memo. If we refurbish the gents', the ladies' will be done at the same time, automatically. From what I remember, they're not too fresh either. Right,' she said, 'that's what you need. Now, is there anything you want to ask me?'

She waited. 'Well,' the superintendent replied, finally, 'there's the job, this job, the one I'm in. I'm still only acting divisional commander, and I'm way down the list for promotion to chief super. What's my situation?'

'That's with Brian Mackie and the boss, but do you want it permanently? You have the option of going back to CID.'

'I'd be a spare wheel there, in this division at any rate. Becky Stallings may only be a DI, but she's bloody good; besides, with the new structure, and her reporting to Neil McIlhenney, my old job doesn't seem to be there any more. So for now, if there's a chance, I'd like to stay here.'

'In that case, I'll fix it. You're right in that I can't swing an early promotion, but I'll speak to the chief, and tell him I want you here.'

Chambers looked at her gratefully. 'Thanks, Maggie. I

appreciate that; I've been feeling in limbo lately, at work at any rate.'

Steele looked at her. 'I wouldn't be doing it if I didn't believe it was best for all of us; you, me and the force.' Her expression softened. 'Going back to CID, how's young Sauce getting on? He's been an unofficial protégé of mine ever since he was the rawest of probationers, under the warm and comforting wing of PC Johnston.' She shook her head. 'I still can't get over my predecessor putting a rookie at risk by sending him out with Charlie.'

'From what I see, and hear, he's doing bloody well. Jack McGurk told me the other day that the lad keeps him on his toes, and Jack's a hard guy to please.'

'That's good to hear. It doesn't surprise me, though; that kid's got "high-flyer" written all over him.' She grinned, then performed one of her trademark switches of subject. 'You've been in limbo at work, you said. Should I read anything into that, away from the office?'

For a few moments, Mary Chambers' plain square face took on an expression that might almost have been described as coy. 'Well,' she began, 'you know my relationship broke up a wee while back?'

'Yes, I was sorry to hear it. I thought it was pretty stable.'

The superintendent shrugged her shoulders. 'It had run its course. It was mostly my fault. Cop's disease; I got so wrapped up in the job that I was never really at home, and my other half finally got fed up with it and found other interests.'

'I know that one,' Steele admitted. 'It was what happened to Mario and me. So how are things now?'

'Getting better. I've met somebody, somebody new.'

'Good for you. Is it public knowledge yet?'

Chambers shook her head. 'No, not yet. It will be soon, though; I'm planning to do something really reckless, and take her to the divisional dance on Friday. It'll ensure a lively evening, if nothing else.'

'I'll look forward to meeting her.'

'Are you going to be there?'

'For a while. So's the chief, each of us unaccompanied.'

The other woman looked alarmed. 'Is he? Oh my God, I'm not sure I'm brave enough for that.'

'Don't be daft,' Steele declared. 'One thing about Bob Skinner: he's as liberal as they come . . . apart from where his daughter's concerned, and there isn't a cat's chance in hell it's her you're taking to the ball.'

Six

'This is a great day,' said Bob, as he slid into his seat in the rooftop restaurant, and the waiter who had shown him to the table withdrew. 'It's barely ten years since we were sweating over your Highers results, and here you are with a partnership in one of the biggest law firms in Britain.'

'Size matters, Pops,' Alexis Skinner replied, with a grin. 'In business law, at any rate. When I graduated, I seem to remember you wondering whether I might have been better joining a smaller practice. If I had I'd still be at least three years away from where I am now, and the money wouldn't have been nearly as good.'

'It was still a gamble, though.'

'I was betting on myself. Yes, I might have stayed sub-merged in the talent pool, and never made it beyond senior assistant. Yes, I might have been a bigger fish in a smaller river, but if I'd settled for that, I'd always have been casting envious glances out to sea. Also, I'd have been doing broad-based work; I'd have been a general legal labourer, if you like, a bit of conveyancing, a bit of family law, a bit of litigation. In a big firm you can specialise, focus on what you're best at . . . and

I'm best at corporate law.' She picked up the menu, then looked up at him again. 'I could argue that I've followed your example.'

'What do you mean?'

'I mean that you could have been a chief constable years ago, if you'd been prepared to go to Dumfries, or Inverness, or Penrith, or Portishead. But you didn't; you stayed in Edinburgh, where you could specialise in crime and where you could eventually carry that specialism into the top job, as you have done. You didn't just do that either; along the way you've trained a whole line of cops in your own image, people like Maggie, Mario, Neil . . .' She stopped short. 'You know what I mean.'

'I know what you mean, and I also noted the name you left off that list . . . Andy Martin. Have you heard from him lately?'

'No,' said Alex, firmly. 'I didn't expect to, and I certainly won't be in touch with him.'

'Good; there would only be grief in it for you.'

'I know it. Have you seen him since . . . since he and I managed to embarrass you?'

'Not once; his chief constable always turns up at our association meetings when I'm there. He only goes when it's just deputies involved. However I did hear that Karen had her new baby.'

'What is it?'

'A boy.' He seemed to wince. 'They've called him Robert, would you believe.'

'Yes, I'd believe it. Did you acknowledge the birth? I mean did you send them a card, or a gift for the wee one?'

'I sent Karen exactly the same thing I gave Danielle when she was born, an investment bond. Why should one kid be deprived because his dad is an idiot?'

'And why should you be deprived, Pops?' she asked, while studying the menu.

'What do you mean?'

'Andy was your closest friend. To my knowledge, he has never in his life said a word against you, and yet you've shunned him, twice, because of me.'

'True, and while I've been known to give people a second chance, a third is out of the question.'

She shook her head, but cut off her retort as the waiter returned, pad in hand. They gave their orders, and Alex chose a bottle of Martin Codax, a Spanish albarino that she knew her father liked.

'Pops, you don't need to be doing this,' said Alex as the young man headed for the kitchen. 'What happened was my fault rather than Andy's. I was the one who left the curtains open and let those bloody photographs be taken. They never saw the light of day anyway; the court made sure of that.'

'They were shown to me by a journalist, and that was enough. DCC Martin is a non-person for me, and for you, for that matter, since Karen's let him off with a yellow card.'

'Exactly, she has, but you've suspended him from your life, *sine die*.' She smiled, to ease the tension that had developed between them. 'Do you know what they call Andy in your force, Pops? Lord Voldemort . . . he who cannot be named. Yet it needn't be like that.'

He shrugged. 'But it is. Am I a rational man, our kid?'

'Yes, of course.'

'No, only mostly yes. If someone hurts you avoidably, I get all irrational. It's the way I am, and it's how it is with Andy and me. Now, please; let's change the subject. How's your new pad suiting you?'

'Excellent. I miss my flat beside the Water of Leith, but I couldn't refuse the offer I got for it, not in the current market, and the new place was a steal. I would say I've traded up; living next door to the Parliament can't be bad. I've always fancied a penthouse, so a duplex . . . that's even better. I'm going to give Aileen a key, so she can nip in and have a quiet scream if things get too much for her.'

'Do you miss the neighbours?'

'Griff and Spring Montell?' She wrinkled her nose in a gesture that was unmistakably dismissive. 'Can't say that I do. Detective Constable Montell: let's say he had his uses, as an escort when I needed one, but he was bang out of order in not mentioning ever that he'd left an ex-wife and a couple of kids behind him in South Africa. She wasn't even officially ex when we first . . . met, so to speak. He's definitely off the list. As for his sister, I never really got to know her; we'd nothing in common, you might say.'

'I might indeed,' he chuckled. 'No snags since you moved in?'

'None at all, and the view . . . well, you've seen it; it's fabulous, all across the Holyrood Park, and Salisbury Crags.' She frowned, for an instant. 'By the way, was something happening up there this morning? I couldn't see very clearly because the fog was still hanging around, but there seemed to be screens up, right on the top of Arthur's Seat. Have you heard anything?'

Bob nodded. 'Suicide,' he told her. 'But it was very messy; not something we want to be talking about over lunch . . . or at all, for that matter.'

As he spoke, the wine waiter arrived; he presented the bottle, then opened it and waited for Alex to give it her approval. She nodded, then watched as it was poured. 'What would Mum say,' she asked, 'if she was still around to see this?'

Her father smiled, and his eyes went somewhere else, more than twenty years back in time. 'I can tell you exactly,' he whispered. 'She'd have said, "I'd prefer red." A woman with views that were never left unspoken; and d'you know what?' He focused once more. 'I'm looking at her image right now.'

'Indeed?' she challenged. 'There are those, Andy first among them, who would say that you're looking in a mirror, and so am I.'

Seven

'What are we doing here, Jack?' DC Haddock asked his companion, as he slid his car into a residents' parking space in North Castle Street, switched off the engine and displayed a card bearing the force crest and reading 'Police business'. 'This is supposed to be a suicide and we're CID: uniforms should be doing this, surely.'

'SOW,' DS McGurk replied, as he unfolded his towering frame out of the passenger seat, looking bulkier than was usual, in a fur-lined leather jacket.

'What's that when it's at home?'

'Senior Officers' Whims. We're here because Becky Stallings told us. She told us because Neil McIlhenney told her. He told her . . . either because it was his idea or because he got told himself, the latter I reckon, since I don't see him volunteering us for this job. That leaves Mario McGuire, but he's of the same mind as big Neil. There's only one man who's going to tell him what to do and that's the chief himself.'

'Is he subject to whims?'

'Oh yes. I was his exec for a wee while, so I know that for sure. If the boss has an itch about something, it has to be scratched.'

'So what do we do? All the DI said was to make inquiries.'

'That means we do what we think best, and that is, what we bloody well like.' He looked at a brass plate fixed to a fence outside a tall, terraced building, faced with grey stone, like much of central Edinburgh. 'This is it,' he said. 'Lietuvos Leisure Limited. Lietuvos Developments Limited. The dead man's companies. I wonder what the hell the word means.'

'I looked it up,' Haddock volunteered. 'Dead simple; it's Lithuanian for Lithuania. The late Mr Zaliukas seems to have been quite a nationalist, for all he lived here for more than half his life. What with this, and his tattoo . . .' He paused. 'We're sure the body is him, are we? If the crest on his hand is all we have for ID . . . well, there could have been others like it in the Lithuanian community, couldn't there?'

'For a start, Sauce, the morgue told me that the body was carrying Zaliukas's wallet, wearing his watch and had his car key in its pocket. The shirt it was wearing is monogrammed with the initials "T Z". As for the tattoo, my old boss Dan Pringle once told me a story about Zaliukas. In the early days of his gang, back in the nineties, one of his guys got a bit uppity, saw himself as a rival. So he had the same national crest put on his own right hand. Tomas decided to make a point of his own; he removed the imitation himself, at the wrist, with a chainsaw.'

'Jesus! Did the poor sod die?'

'No. They put a tourniquet on and got him to the Royal in time. We were called, but the guy swore it was an accident; he said that he'd been lopping a tree and had slipped. As soon as he got out of hospital, he went back to Lithuania. Come on, let's get inside; it's fucking freezing out here.'

The Lietuvos office was in the basement level of the building. Seeing lights inside, the two detectives walked down the few steps from the pavement, only to find that the door was locked. McGurk pressed a button above the letter box. 'Here,' he muttered, as they waited, 'I forgot to ask. Did you score last night?'

Despite the cold, Haddock felt himself flush. 'Mind your own damn business, Jack,' he retorted. 'I don't have to ask whether you did. You and Lisanne were all over each other.'

The big sergeant shrugged. 'It's allowed. She's moving in with me. That was a right stunner you pulled, though. Are you seeing her again?'

'You'll find out on Friday, at the dance.'

As he spoke, the door opened. A frowning woman, on the lower edge of middle age, looked up at them. 'What is it?' she demanded, brusquely. 'This is a private office. We do not see salesmen here.'

'We're not selling,' McGurk told her, 'and although we might look like them, we're not Jehovah's Witnesses either. People usually call us "The Polis": CID.' He showed her his warrant card. 'Now are you going to let us into the warm, please.'

The guardian relented, she opened the door and let them step inside, into a small reception area with a desk and a door behind it: the sergeant had to duck to avoid the lintel. 'What is wrong?' she asked. 'Has there been trouble at one of the pubs? Have we had a break-in? I'm sure if there had been, the manager would have reported it to us.'

'No, that's not it. Who's in charge here?'

'Mr Tomas Zaliukas, but he's not in at the moment.'

'Has he been in at all today?'

'No, he hasn't; I was expecting him, but he hasn't arrived yet.'

'Has he called in to say where he is?'

'No, but he wouldn't. He doesn't tell me of his every movement.'

'In his absence, who's in charge? You? Mrs . . .'

'Mrs Gerulaitis. No, not me; I am secretary to Mr Zaliukas and to my husband, Valdas. He is Mr Zaliukas's deputy, and so if anyone is in charge in his absence, it is him.'

'Good,' said McGurk, patiently. 'Is he here now?'

'Yes, but he is busy.'

'So are we, but it's necessary. We'll be as quick as we can, I promise you, but we need to speak to him.'

The woman frowned. 'Very well, I'll tell him.'

'Thank you.' The sergeant sighed.

'OK, OK!' she snapped. 'Wait, will you, while I see if he is available.'

'Thank God you get a drink quicker than this in Zaliukas's pubs,' Haddock muttered, as she disappeared through the door at the rear of the reception area. He wandered across to a low table in the bay window of the office; the few glossy magazines that were scattered upon it were all in a language that he assumed was Lithuanian. There were no chairs, apart from that behind the desk; the comfort of visitors was not a priority.

Happily their wait was short. The door reopened, and a man appeared, tall, but still dwarfed by McGurk. He wore a two-piece, single-breasted suit with a pinstripe that seemed to emphasise his lean build. His hairline was receding, and a few grey hairs showed, to match the dandruff that lay on his shoulders like a gentle fall of snow. 'Gentlemen,' he said, managing to smile yet look concerned at the same time. 'Valdas Gerulaitis. What's the problem?'

'DS McGurk, and DC Haddock. I hope there is no problem, but we reckon we have some bad news for you. Can we go somewhere private?'

'Sure. Come on through to ma office.' The man's accent was more Scottish than that of his wife, and his tone was friendlier. He led the way along a narrow corridor and into a room at the rear of the building with a view of a car park, bounded by a high, wire-topped wall.

McGurk pointed to the barricade, as he and Haddock took the seats they were offered. 'Do you really need that?' he asked.

'It works,' Gerulaitis replied, as he sank into the chair behind his desk. 'We haven't had a break-in since I had it put there.'

'Did you have many before?'

'A couple; we never lost anything other than a couple of DVD recorders, but it was a nuisance. The wide boys think because we own licensed premises we store booze here. Naturally, we don't, nor do we keep cash; why should we when the banks still have night safes. Nevertheless . . .' He shook his head, presumably at the stupidity of the city's petty criminals. 'You guys want a coffee?' he offered. 'I'll get my wife . . .'

'We're fine, thanks,' said the sergeant, glad to have seen the back of the woman. 'You're a director of the companies, sir, yes?'

'No, the directors are Mr and Mrs Zaliukas. I look after the figures. I trained as a bookkeeper in Lithuania, before I came over here to join Tomas.'

'And that's all you've ever done for him?'

Gerulaitis smiled again, this time with a raised eyebrow. 'That's all. My talents are financial, not physical. Tomas is my cousin, so I know what you're getting at; but all I'll say is that if he ever was involved in the sort of activities there used to be talk about, he'd have known better than to involve me.'

'What do you do here?' Haddock asked. 'What does Lietuvos Leisure own?'

'It has pubs and clubs, plus a couple of restaurants; it's a successful, growing business. The other company's very profitable too: Lietuvos Developments Limited, that handles our property activities.' He opened a drawer, took out a brochure and tossed it across the desk. 'That's some of its portfolio. Mind you,' he added, 'we're sitting on our hands, like every other developer right now, waiting for the market to get its balls back.'

The young DC picked up the document and glanced at it. 'And the massage parlours?' he said, quietly.

Gerulaitis shook his head. 'They have nothing to do with me, and their acquisition wasn't funded by either of the companies.'

'So legally, who or what owns them?'

Suddenly he seemed a little less friendly. 'I'm not at liberty to tell you that, Detective,' he said.

Haddock grinned. 'That's Detective Constable, sir; you're making us sound like LAPD. If we were interested, which I'm not saying we are, we could find out in no time from the property register.'

'Then you'll have to do that, or ask Tomas's lawyers.'

'Who would they be?'

'The same as this company, I suppose, although I don't know for sure . . . Curle Anthony and Jarvis, that's who we deal with.' Suddenly, all humour left his face. 'Wait a minute,' he said. 'The obvious thing would be for you to ask Tomas himself, not come questioning me. What's up? Has he been arrested?'

'No, sir.' McGurk looked at him solemnly. 'I can assure you that he hasn't. When did you see him last?'

'Yesterday; he was here till after six, apart from a break in the afternoon when he went out. After that Laima . . . that's my wife . . . and me went to eat in Portofino, one of our restaurants. The manager's just hired a new chef, and we wanted to check him out. Tomas was supposed to be coming with us, but at the last minute he told us to go on our own. I guessed he might still be upset.'

'About what?'

'His wife left him. She took the girls too.'

'Was it sudden, her departure?'

'She was supposed to be coming last night as well, when the arrangement was made.' Gerulaitis leaned back in his chair. 'But look, why are you asking this?'

'We're trying to establish his state of mind, sir.'

'His state of mind?'

'Yes, how did he seem yesterday?'

'A bit edgy, after Regine did her runner. A bit moody, but

that's typical Tomas.' He frowned. 'A bit like the old days,' he added quietly.

'What do you mean, like the old days?'

'When Tomas was younger, he was very volatile, unpredictable. As he's got older, that's disappeared, and he's got a lot more controlled. But now you make me think about it, that's how he was yesterday.' Gerulaitis leaned forward, he frowned, and for the first time he seemed impatient. 'But come on, gentlemen, out with it. What the fuck is this visit about?'

'A body was found this morning, sir,' Haddock told him, 'right up on top of Arthur's Seat. Male.'

The Lithuanian's face paled, instantly. 'Are you saying it was Tomas?' he whispered.

'We think it was, but identification isn't straightforward. Cause of death appears to have been a contact wound inflicted by a sawn-off shotgun, so . . .'

'Jesus Christ.' Gerulaitis's mouth fell open; he covered it with his right hand.

'Do you know if your cousin had a sawn-off?'

'No, but it wouldn't surprise me if he had.' The man recovered some of his composure. 'Was there a tattoo?' he asked.

McGurk nodded. 'Yes. Lithuanian national crest, back of his hand.'

'Then it's Tomas; nobody else would have one.'

'Probably not, but still . . .' He paused. 'Did he have any other distinguishing marks that you know of?'

'There was another tattoo.' Gerulaitis tapped his right arm, just below the shoulder. 'Just there; his wife's name, entwined through a heart. Was it there?'

'I can't tell you,' the sergeant admitted. 'We haven't seen the body, or any photographs. Easily checked though. Do you know where Mrs Zale . . . sorry, Mrs Zaliukas, is? We have to find her; if I'm right in assuming they're not divorced, she's next of kin.'

'No, and Tomas said he didn't know either. My wife and I are not close to them as a couple. I know Regine is French, and that she comes from a place south of Bordeaux . . . I leave remembering place names to Laima; I'm lousy at it . . . but not a lot more about her than that.'

'How will she live? What will she do for money?'

'No problem there. With dividends, she takes a hundred and fifty thousand a year out of the companies. She has her own bank account, so access to cash won't be a problem for her.'

Haddock glanced at McGurk. 'We should be able to trace her through her withdrawals, Sarge. Which bank is it, sir?' he asked the Lithuanian.

'We're with what used to be Bank of Scotland, but Regine had her own arrangements. You'd better ask the lawyers.'

'We'll do that. Do you have a contact there?'

'The man I deal with is called Willie Conn.'

'Thanks. We'll pay him a visit. Meantime, since you're a blood relative, we have an unpleasant task for you. Your cousin has to be formally identified.'

Gerulaitis shuddered. 'Maybe Laima should do it. She never liked him; it'd serve her right.'

Eight

Detective Constable Griffin Montell leaned back in his chair, linked his fingers behind his head and let out a sigh so loud that it was almost a bellow. 'Hey,' he said, to the room in general, 'do you ever feel that when some people go missing we should simply say, "Thanks, God, for that one," rather than open a bloody file on them?'

DC Alice Cowan glanced at him across their facing desk, frowned, and continued with the witness statement that she was keying into her computer. Detective Sergeant Ray Wilding swung round in his chair. 'Got anyone particular in mind?' he asked.

Montell sat upright once more and slapped the folder in the centre of his desk, between two piles. 'This guy here,' he replied. 'Maurice Glazier; reported missing almost two years ago, in April. He's got a record as long as my . . . It goes all the way back to when he was eight years old. He's such a boon to society that it took six months for his partner to report him missing, yet here we are spending police time trying to find him.'

'And have we?'

'What?'

'Found him.'

'Not a trace.'

'No, and we won't either.'

'Are you saying he's dead?'

'Hell no, I'm saying that he's done a runner and doesn't want to be found.'

'You know the guy?' Montell's accent pointed straight to his South African origins.

'Wee Moash?' Wilding chuckled. 'Sure. Everybody who's been around for a certain length of time knows wee Moash. The only reason his record started when he was eight is because that's the age of responsibility in Scotland. "Habitual" or "recidivist" aren't good enough words to describe him. His criminality's genetic, it's in his DNA. He was born a thief, simple as that. His girlfriend probably took so long to report him missing because she thought he was in the nick, or with his other woman. He had two, one in Granton and the other up near the Old Town.'

Montell nodded. 'Spot on there. That's what her statement says; that he was quite often away for a few months, for either of those reasons.' He laughed. 'She also said that she finally reported him missing after she decided he'd never have stayed away from his greyhound that long.'

Wilding nodded. 'That's probably true. Who made the report?'

'Sadie Greengrass, of Dowie Road.'

'That's Granton Woman. Who looked into it?'

'Tarvil Singh.'

'What did he do?'

'He interviewed a woman called Maxine Foster, of Neuk Drive.'

'That's Lochview Woman. I've lifted Moash from that address myself. What did she say?'

'A mirror image of the other one's statement.' He beamed. 'I suppose she didn't report it because she wasn't left holding the greyhound.'

'We know he's not in jail, do we?' asked Alice Cowan, interested at last.

'Tarvil's better than that,' Montell told her. 'After he spoke to the Foster woman he went straight to the Crown Office and checked that out. He also made inquiries south of the border. Glazier wasn't in custody anywhere in Britain, and if he'd been charged since then we'd know, because he's flagged as missing. Cold trail; nowhere else to go.'

'So,' said Wilding, 'any theories?'

'Maybe he's dead,' Cowan suggested. She ran her fingers through her short-cropped hair; several months earlier she had dyed it blond for an undercover operation, and had stuck to the style. 'Maybe he stole from the wrong bloke and got caught in the act.'

'No,' the sergeant declared, firmly, 'I don't buy that. Wee Moash never steals anything big enough to get him killed for it. He also never gets caught with his hand in the till, pocket or anything else. He's a pretty good thief; all his arrests, as an adult at any rate, have come when he was stopped with stolen gear on him or when it was traced back to him. When that happened he always pleaded guilty, got the minimum sentence, did his time or paid his fine and went back to work. Christ knows how many thefts he's actually pulled off.'

Montell frowned. 'And he's lived in Edinburgh all his life?'

'Apart from a few spells locked up in other places, yes.'

'So why should he vanish, if he's not dead? There's no clue in either woman's statement.'

'Well,' Wilding drawled, slowly, 'there is a wee bit of background that's not in your file. Let's see; the last Moash sighting was what month, six months before April, October, yes?'

'That's right.'

'Mmm. In that case . . . in that month, there was a suspicious death investigation under way. I wasn't involved in it, I was doing something else, but Stevie Steele was, and I heard from him that wee Moash had got himself involved on the periphery. It turned out that he found the guy's body, stole his coat, then phoned the death in anonymously, only Tarvil Singh recognised his voice when he heard the tape. He co-operated in a meaningful way, and the property was recovered, so he wasn't charged. But . . .' He paused, scratching his chin.

'But what?' Cowan demanded, impatiently.

'At the time it wasn't clear whether the death was murder or suicide. Stevie knew that Moash couldn't kill anybody, but he put the frighteners on him anyway, to get a statement out of him. I reckon the wee man was scared that in the absence of anyone else, we might come back to him, so he did a runner.'

'And are we still looking for him in that connection?' Montell asked.

'No, of course not. His file wouldn't be in that pile of yours if we were. Anyway, that thing was cleared up pretty quickly. So no, we have no reason to give a bugger about where he is, other than the fact that it's our job. So, Griff, if I were you I wouldn't waste any more time worrying about it. I'd get back into your stack of missing person cold cases to see if you can trace somebody who is worth finding.'

'Amen to that.'

The DC had barely placed the Glazier papers on the heap by his right hand when Wilding's phone rang. 'CID,' he said as he put it to his ear.

'It's Kathy at the front desk, Ray,' a woman told him. 'Is DI Pye there? I've got a call that I think is for CID.'

'Sammy's on a course, I'm afraid. That leaves me in command, or so he laughingly said. Who's the caller?'

'It's the doctors' surgery along at Ocean Terminal.'

'One of the docs?'

'No, it's the practice manager; her name's Taylor. It's about a girl they've had brought in. They think . . .'

'Let her tell me, Kath,' he interrupted. 'Put her through.' He listened, until he heard a change in the background noise on the line. 'Miss Taylor,' he began, 'DS Wilding, what can I do for you?'

'It's Mrs; Mrs Rita Taylor. We've got someone here, a young woman, we think she may have been assaulted in some way.'

'What does she say?'

'Nothing.'

'Is she unconscious?'

'No, but she's in a deeply confused state. She can't even tell us her name.'

'You said she's young. How young?'

'Obviously we can't be sure, but looking at her, I'd say she's in her mid-teens.'

'Who brought her in?'

'A delivery driver. He told our receptionist that she stepped off the pavement in front of his van, just up the road from the surgery. He stopped in time, thank goodness. He said he thought she was drunk, and got out to give her a piece of his mind, but realised very quickly that wasn't it.'

'Is he still there?' Wilding asked.

'No, he had to get on with his rounds and so he left.'

'That's a pity. We'd have liked to talk to him.'

'Why?'

'Who's to say he was telling the truth?' He paused. 'But that can stick to the wall for now. Let's concentrate on the woman. You said you think she's been assaulted. Is she cut, bruised? Has she been knocked about?'

'No, but the doctor who took a look at her thinks she may have been sexually assaulted. He doesn't want to conduct a detailed examination without your presence, because she isn't in a state to give consent. He is fairly certain, though, that she's taken a drug or possibly been given one.'

'Date rape?'

'That thought has occurred to us.'

'We'll be right along,' said the sergeant.

'Can you send a female officer?' Mrs Taylor asked.

'In a case like this, that's automatic. We'll attend shortly.'

As he hung up he was aware that both DCs were looking at him. Quickly, he filled them in on the half of the conversation that they had been unable to hear. 'Get your coat, Alice,' he told Cowan, as he stood. 'You're needed on this. You mind the store, Griff.'

'If you say so, Ray.'

There was hesitation in his voice and Wilding caught it. 'But?'

'When I was in South Africa, I worked for a spell on a dedicated sex crimes unit. I'm actually trained in the area.'

'How long were you on it?'

'Two years.'

'OK, if you want it, I'm happy to let you handle it.'

'Who's in charge?' asked Cowan, with a hint of belligerence.

'For fuck's sake, Alice,' the sergeant snapped. 'I am. You're colleagues, of the same rank; work together. Get along there, find out what this thing is all about, then report back to me.'

Nine

As he looked down at the body, Valdas Gerulaitis started to shake, so violently that dandruff began to fall from his shoulders like tiny snowflakes. Jack McGurk took him by the elbow. 'Steady, sir,' he said. 'Just concentrate on the arm, and the back of the right hand; that's all we need you to look at. Ignore the rest of it.' He knew that he was asking the impossible; a towel had been placed over the head, but it did little to conceal the truth, that most of it was missing.

It may have been the sergeant's words, or it may have been embarrassment over his weakness, but the Lithuanian recovered his composure. 'Yes, yes,' he whispered, as he stooped slightly to peer at the small, but intricate, tattoo on the dead man's right deltoid, but only for a few seconds before straightening again. 'That's Tomas. I don't need to look at the other one to tell you. I was with him when he had it done. He dared me to have one as well. I hate needles but I couldn't lose face, so I did.' He turned his back on the trolley, his nostrils narrowing as if to fight off the antiseptic odour. 'Can we get out of here?' he asked.

'Sure,' said McGurk. He nodded to the attendant, and led

the way back into the anteroom, with its curtained window, through which the viewing would have been done in circumstances that did not require a closer inspection. A little old man was waiting there; he was so small that his students in Edinburgh University's pathology division were known to call him 'Master Yoda' behind his back, and occasionally plain 'Master' to his face.

'Your cousin?' Professor Joe Hutchinson asked.

Gerulaitis grimaced. 'Yes.'

'I'm sorry.' He paused, awkwardly. 'I know that sounds inadequate, but one thing I've learned in a long career is that there's no consolation for family members in this place.' He craned his neck to look up at the skyscraper-like McGurk. 'What do you want me to tell you, Sergeant?' he asked.

'Your findings will do, Professor.'

'That's not difficult. In shorthand, death was caused by the total destruction of the brain and cranium, the result of contact gunshot wounds. It was instantaneous.' He glanced at Gerulaitis. 'You couldn't do it any quicker,' he added, for his benefit.

'And?'

'You want me to spell it out, Jack? Man, this is as obvious and determined a suicide as I've ever seen. There are no marks on the body that offer even the faint possibility that Mr Zaliukas was restrained, or tied up, or anything else. I assume that the lab is doing residue testing on his clothing, as we're doing on his hands.'

'Of course.'

'Then you'll find without doubt that he fired the gun. I

know nothing about Mr Zaliukas, about his background, his business or anything else, but the fact that CID are handling this matter and asking these questions points me in a certain direction. Well, my boy, whatever madcap theory you are pursuing, you can nip it in the bud. This is suicide, and that is what I would say under oath, absolutely and unequivocally.' He frowned. 'Come on, Sergeant,' he said. 'You weren't expecting me to say anything else, were you?'

Mindful of Gerulaitis's presence, McGurk fought off the urge to smile. 'No,' he admitted, 'but we have to be thorough. You, of all people, must realise that.'

'Oh yes,' the tiny pathologist conceded. 'I know how the Force works . . . as my students will tell you.'

Ten

'How was your dad?' asked Pippa Clifton.

Alex Skinner threw her secretary a cool glance across her new work space. 'My dad was fine, thank you. Why do you ask?'

'No reason . . . other than the fact I've always thought he's dishy. He reminds me a bit of that guy on the telly; you know the one I mean, he's on everything. He plays a judge, and a policeman, and . . .'

'Excuse me, woman, are you looking for a smack in the mouth? The chap of whom you speak is about fifteen years older than my dad, and chubby with it, these days.'

'They can do wonders with make-up,' Pippa chirped on. 'He must be really pleased, your dad, about you being made a partner. My mum was astonished when I told her.'

'That's comforting to know. In that case I'm sure your dear mother will be the first to appreciate that because I'm a partner my time is now even more valuable, so unless you've got something work-related to tell me or ask me, please bugger off back to your desk.'

'I have, actually. There's one of your dad's finest in reception, asking to see you.'

Alex frowned. 'About what?'

'He didn't say. He came in asking for Mr Conn; when he was told he'd retired, he asked for whoever's taken over his clients.'

'What's his name?'

'Detective Constable Haddock, would you believe? Like that chap out of Tintin.'

Alex's eyebrows rose slightly. She had heard of DC Haddock, the one with the nickname, from Maggie Steele. 'Pippa,' she began, 'must all the people in your wee life relate to TV actors or cartoon characters? Go fetch him please, but tell him he's got two minutes unless it's something I can bill out to a client, in which case he has as long as I reckon his interest is worth.'

She waited, more aware than ever of the fact that virtually every minute of her working life was meant to be spent on fee-earning matters. Her new office, slightly larger than a toilet cubicle, was close to reception and so Pippa returned within a minute, leading a tall, slim young man with a fresh face, ginger hair and ears that were never going to be ignored. 'This is Ms Skinner,' she told him. 'She's taken over from Mr Conn.'

Alex noted the change in the detective constable's expression at the mention of her name, and the look of caution that seemed to come into his eyes. She stood as he entered. Pippa closed the door behind her as she left. 'Take a seat,' she said. 'You're the one they call "Sauce", aren't you?'

Haddock grinned, instantly at ease. 'That's me,' he confirmed. 'And you're the one they call the chief constable's daughter.'

She nodded. 'Something which gets you no special favours,' she declared, but with a smile. 'What brings you here?'

'Are the Lietuvos companies among the clients you've taken over from Mr Conn?' he asked.

'They are, but I've been involved with them before, so they're not new to me. Before you say anything else, I'd better tell you that whatever you might have heard about their owner, or whatever you might believe about him, I cannot discuss any aspect of my business dealings with him.'

'Not even if the companies were dodgy?'

She shot him a look that was part of her genetic inheritance from her father; he seemed to sit a little straighter in his chair. 'Sauce,' she said, slowly, 'if the companies were dodgy, we wouldn't be acting for them, so I hope you're not going to suggest that they are. If this firm had a motto it would be "Probity", and we'd nail it over the door.'

'No,' he assured her, hastily. 'I'm sorry; that was a throwaway line. The businesses aren't under investigation, I promise you.'

'But their owner is?'

'Not exactly, Ms Skinner . . .'

'Alex.'

'Alex. His death is.'

'Mr Zaliukas is dead?'

'I'm afraid so.'

Her cop's daughter's mind focused, instantly. 'And you're CID? How did he die?'

'He killed himself. Our inspector's been into his house, using keys that were found on the body. She found his computer still switched on. There was a note on the screen. It said, "I couldn't live without Regine and the girls." Not much room for doubt, but I'd a phone call from my sergeant while I was waiting in your reception area telling me that suicide's been confirmed at autopsy, and that he's been formally identified.'

She hesitated. 'It wasn't up Arthur's Seat, was it? My father told me at lunch that there had been a suicide up there. He said it was messy; he didn't want to tell me any more. Was that it? Was that Mr Zaliukas?'

'I'm afraid so. And yes, it was very messy; that's why it took us so long to get the formal identification done.'

'Poor guy. Mind you, it doesn't change the nature of my relationship with the Lietuvos group. Mr Zaliukas may be dead, but it's the business that's my client. With that in mind, what did you want to ask me?'

'We could start with the last time you saw him.'

'I've never seen him. I've handled work relating to the company in the past, as an associate of the firm, but Mr Conn always met with the principals, Mr Zaliukas and his wife. He and I had a meeting scheduled for Friday morning.'

'To discuss what?'

She frowned. 'Problem number one. I can't discuss my communication with my client.'

'Can you help me just a bit?'

She heard his plea. 'I can tell you that the meeting was routine; it was set up purely for the two of us to meet, so that he could decide for himself that he was happy to work with me in the future. I can probably tell you also that there is no crisis within the companies, of which I'm aware. We may be in a recession, but people aren't sitting at home worrying about it. They're still going out to pubs and clubs, so the leisure side of the business remains on a sound footing.'

'How about the other side, the development arm?'

'That's OK too. Lietuvos Developments constructs and refurbishes commercial property, some for sale, some for rental. Management anticipated a downturn a couple of years ago, and postponed several potential projects until it's blown over. Meantime, the rental properties are all occupied by tenants with sound covenants . . . that's to say, they're all good risks . . . so income is well in excess of existing borrowing. I can tell you all that because it's in the current corporate brochure. That was produced two months ago, and the text was certified as accurate by Mr Conn.'

'I've seen that. What about the share ownership? That's public information; it would help if you could tell me about it, save me looking it up.'

'Sure. I'm under no constraint there; that's public information. Each company has one hundred issued shares of one pound each, half owned by Mr Tomas Zaliukas and the other half by his wife.'

'That's changed a bit.'

'True. Very true; his half is now owned by the estate of the late Mr Tomas Zaliukas.'

'Who inherits?' Haddock asked.

'I don't know,' Alex admitted. 'I'll need to get back to you on that. Mr Zaliukas's family matters are handled by a different division of the firm. I'll speak to the partner in charge and tell you what I can.'

'Would he . . .'

'She, Sauce.'

'Sorry. Would she know where Mrs Zaliukas is? We've been told that she left him last week, and obviously we need to contact her.'

'That's not obvious to me, I'm afraid. We're his legal representatives, you've informed us of his death, and you don't need her for identification purposes, since that's been done. It's for us to take it from here. She shouldn't be upset any more than necessary.'

Haddock shook his head. 'I'll still need to talk to her . . . or someone will. We'll need to ask her about her husband's state of mind if nothing else. If she has any information, the fiscal will want to know about it.'

'I'm sure he'd agree with me that it would be OK for her to provide it in statement form, through this firm.' She paused, to consider the point. 'Let's not argue about it at this stage, Sauce. We'll contact Mrs Zaliukas and we'll tell her that you want to interview her. If she agrees, fine; if not . . . we'll do it my way, or you can try having me leaned on by someone higher up the tree, but I'll tell you now, you'll have to go to the very top.'

He rolled his eyes, and smiled. 'It won't be me that does that,' he said.

'It wouldn't work anyway.' She looked at him across her desk, her hands on the arms of her chair. 'If that's all . . .' she began.

Haddock stayed seated. 'What about Mr Zaliukas's other business?' he said. 'The massage parlours.'

'Curle Anthony and Jarvis has nothing to do with those,'

Alex replied, firmly. 'Mr Conn was very firm on that point when he was here, and he stressed it to me when we did our client handover.'

'Do you know who does run it?'

'As far as I know, Mr Valdas Gerulaitis looked after it for him, but that's only hearsay from Willie.'

'And he owned the properties directly?'

'I don't know for sure, but I doubt it. His other businesses are incorporated.' Alex sighed. 'All I can tell you is this, and again it's second-hand, from Mr Conn. A few years ago, when the properties came on the market, Mr Zaliukas came to him and asked him for advice that he wasn't prepared to give. Our client wasn't happy. In fact he was so unhappy that I think my predecessor might have been a wee bit scared.'

'Scared of losing his business, you mean.'

'No, scared of losing something more personal. That's only my impression, mind, from the way he was when he told me about it. Anyway, to mollify him, Willie sent him to another firm, one that has a big criminal practice, and other expertise, and to a particular lawyer, a man called Ken Green. The firm's called Grey Green. You may have heard of it.'

'I've dealt with them, and him. Not close up, but I know who he is. He acted for a kid we arrested for murder last summer.'

'Then go and renew the acquaintance. I'll get back to you as soon as I can, on Mrs Zaliukas and on the will.'

Eleven

'What's eating you today?' Griff Montell asked Alice Cowan as she locked their borrowed car. The freezing temperature made his breath hang in the air.

'What the hell are you talking about?' she challenged as they headed for the medical centre, a hundred yards away on the street corner. 'Why should anything be eating me?'

'I'm talking about that crap back in the office about who's in charge. That and the fact you've been frosting me for a while now. Have you run out of civil words?'

'No!' she snapped. And then her face cracked into an involuntary smile as she realised how contradictory her reply had sounded. 'It's you who's been distant with me, Griff. That's more like the truth.'

Montell was forced on to the back foot. 'No I haven't,' he said, defensively.

'Oh no? You asked me out on a date a couple of months ago; we had a decent time and we did it again a couple of weeks later. Since then, nothing. Was I boring? Do I turn you off? Do you like your women with less meat on their bones? Have I got BO? Or have you found a better option?

Whatever, it would be nice to know so that I can do something about it.'

He stopped, at the kerbside. 'None of the above,' he told her. 'You're good company, you're attractive, you smell nice and my reaction to you is entirely positive. And I'm not seeing anyone else either. I just . . . I just wanted to pause for thought, that was all.'

'You're not still carrying a torch for your ex-wife, are you? Or maybe for Alex Skinner?'

'I miss my kids,' he replied, 'but not their mother. As for Alex, she was a neighbour and she was a friend, end of story. No bridges back there.' He stopped. 'Alice, we can't have this conversation now; we have a job to do.'

'True,' she conceded, 'but it's not over.'

They crossed the street and approached the surgery. A woman was waiting in the reception area. Her body language radiated impatience; Cowan guessed she had been watching them approach, and had seen them pause.

'Police?' she asked.

Montell nodded, introducing himself and his colleague.

'At last!' hung in the air, but remained unspoken. 'Rita Taylor, practice manager,' was her clipped response. 'I spoke to your sergeant. Hopefully, you're fully briefed.'

'Yes, we are,' said Cowan. 'Where is the girl?'

Mrs Taylor turned towards a corridor that led out of the reception and waiting area. 'She's in a consulting room. A practice nurse is with her.'

'And the doctor who did the initial examination?'

'With another patient at the moment. But there's not much

she could add to what I've told you at this stage. Nurse Chetty's competent, I promise you.'

'Let's see her then.'

The detectives followed her into the corridor, to the second door on their left, which opened into a windowless cubicle, furnished with a sink with lever taps, a small desk, two chairs, and an examination table. The young woman who lay on its paper coverlet was dishevelled. Dark roots showed under blond hair that looked lank and in need of a wash. She was wrapped in a blanket, from which her feet protruded, clad in dirty grey carpet slippers.

'Was she wearing those when she was brought in?' Montell asked.

The small, brown-complexioned nurse who stood beside the table nodded. 'Yes. Them and a light cotton dress, that was all. She was freezing; not far off being hypothermic. We've warmed her as best we can.'

'But she's still not responsive?'

'No more so than when she was brought in.'

'Was she carrying anything? A bag, any sort of identification?'

'No.'

'Damn it.' He glanced at Cowan. 'We'll need to wait until she can tell us herself who she is.'

She looked at Nurse Chetty. 'Now you've had more time to look at her, any idea what she's taken?'

'Not heroin,' she said firmly. 'I'm sure of that; I've seen plenty of those in my career. She's not drunk; there's alcohol involved but it's just boosted the effect of whatever else is in her system.'

As she spoke, the girl gasped, and whimpered, sounds rather than words, which turned into a squeal. Cowan sat on the edge of the examination table and touched her face. 'It's OK,' she soothed. 'You're safe.' The girl showed no sign of understanding, yet the gesture seemed to calm her.

'GHB,' Montell murmured.

'What?' his colleague exclaimed.

'Gamma hydroxyl butyrate, if you want it the hard way. I've seen its effects when I worked this area in South Africa. It's one of the most common date rape drugs, and easily obtainable, because any arsehole with a chemistry set can put it together. It's illegal to make or possess it and it's not commercially produced. This girl's hallucinating; she's semi-conscious. Those are symptoms of overdose. How's her heart rate?' he asked.

'Very slow,' said the nurse.

'Yeah. If it was ketamine, it would probably be higher than normal.'

'How long does it take to wear off, in your experience?'

Montell raised his eyebrows. 'Mixed with alcohol, it could be a couple of days.'

'Do you know how to treat an overdose?' The question came from behind him. He had forgotten that Mrs Taylor was still in the room.

'The doctors I worked with used to rehydrate, that's after they'd pumped the stomach.' He paused. 'You might want to do both, and then she should definitely be examined for sexual activity, forced or otherwise, as soon as possible. You should get that doctor along here as soon as you can.'

The practice manager nodded and left. 'You'd better get her undressed,' Montell told the nurse, 'and give her what treatment you can. I'll step outside while you do that. Alice . . .'

'I know,' said Cowan, calmly. 'I'll stay here to help, and yes, to look for signs of physical abuse.'

'Of course.'

'Any thoughts?' she asked, as he took hold of the door handle.

'The time of day,' Montell replied. 'It's still only the afternoon, and this girl's been wandering the streets in Leith. Date rape is what it says; it happens during social interaction. At lunchtime? I don't buy that. Then there's the way she's dressed, and the amount of the stuff she's got in her system.' He opened the door. 'You help the nurse, I'll do some thinking about this.'

Twelve

As he stood in the entrance of the law office in Drumsheugh Gardens, waiting for the receptionist to finish her filing and acknowledge his presence, Sauce Haddock experienced a moment of uncertainty. Jack McGurk had sent him to Curle Anthony and Jarvis on his own, in the knowledge that he would be well received, but might Grey Green be a different matter?

He knew from remarks dropped by colleagues, both uniformed and CID, that Ken Green was not regarded as a friend of the police, rather as a thorn in their side, or even, as Charlie Johnston had once put it, 'shite on ma shoe'. His own acquaintance with the man, brief and at a couple removed though it had been, had been enough to mark the man down as abrasive. As the tight-suited clerk finally deigned to look in his direction, there was a moment when Sauce almost turned and headed back into the street.

But it passed. He showed his warrant card to the woman. 'DC Haddock, CID. I called fifteen minutes ago; Mr Green's expecting me.'

'Is he?' she replied, not about to take his word. 'Let me check.' She turned her back on him and picked up a phone.

'Gladys,' he heard her begin. The rest was indistinct, but he passed the test. The guardian of the firm faced him once more. 'Yes,' she said, no more friendly than before, 'he is. His secretary will be down to collect you.'

Like a parcel, Sauce brooded. What a difference between this snooty cow and Alex Skinner's PA. She'd been a right tasty lass, and friendly with it. But no sooner had her face appeared in his mind's eye than it was replaced by another, that of Cheeky Davis. He realised that it had been all of ten minutes since he had thought of her. He smiled, looking forward to their date in the Drum, in George Street, that evening.

'Mr Haddock.' The voice from the half-landing of the panelled stairway brought him back to real time. He looked up, and as he did so he noted that for all its colourful name, the firm of Grey Green did not appear to favour the appointment of bright young things. 'If you'll come with me, Mr Green is waiting.'

He took the steps two at a time until he had reached her, then let her lead him for the rest of the way. Double doors led into Green's office. The lawyer stayed seated as Haddock entered, his back to a window overlooking the wedge-shaped gardens. He made no offer of a chair, but the young detective took one nonetheless.

His host, mid-forties, dark-haired, clean-shaven, in a navy blue suit, three-piece, and striped shirt, eyed him up. 'So what do you want from me, son?' he asked, in a tone that said, I'm humouring you, for now. 'Have we met?' he continued. 'If we have, I don't recall it.'

'We were in the same room once,' Haddock replied, 'but neither of us had anything to say to the other.'

'And what do you have to say, or ask, now?'

'Did you represent Tomas Zaliukas, occasionally known as Tommy Zale?'

'I do represent him, yes,' the lawyer replied, cautiously.

'No, you did. He's dead. He killed himself early this morning.'

Green blinked, once, then again. 'You're joking,' he exclaimed. It seemed to Haddock, in the light that shone from a tall lamp beside the desk, that his face was a few shades paler than before.

'That's not in my job description, sir. He put a shotgun in his mouth and pulled the trigger.'

'God!' The solicitor shook his head, violently. 'Jesus!' Haddock sat silent, giving him the opportunity to invoke the Holy Ghost if he chose. 'What made him do that?' he added, eventually.

'That's what we're trying to establish, sir.'

'There's no chance that he was . . . ?'

'No. Suicide is all we're looking at. When did you last see him?'

'About three months ago, the last time we had a licence up for renewal.'

'Did he mention any worries he might have had?'

'Tomas Zaliukas didn't have worries. He gave them to other people.'

Haddock was surprised. 'Are you saying that your client was less than upright?'

'I'm saying nothing for the record, either police or Daily, but come on, son, we both know where Tomas came from.'

'Mr Zaliukas had no criminal convictions.'

'All my clients are innocent, son, but they're not always the sort of people you'd want your mother to meet.'

'You represented him in relation to his massage parlour businesses, yes?'

'I looked after the licensing of them.'

'Did Valdas Gerulaitis have anything to do with them?'

'He might have, he might not; I don't know.'

'Are you able to tell me about the history of your relationship?'

'I don't see why not, not now. You better write this down. It's complicated.' Haddock nodded, and took out a notebook. 'Tomas came to me a few years back,' the solicitor continued. 'He told me that he'd been offered eight massage parlours by the executors of the recently deceased Tony Manson, but that when he'd asked Curle Anthony and Jarvis to advise him on the purchase, they'd given him the bum's rush, but suggested that I might take a more liberal view of that sector. I did, I negotiated the deal for him and I handled the conveyancing and the transfer of the licences. If you don't know, the council requires these businesses to have public entertainment licences.'

'Yes, I know that. So, Mr Zaliukas bought the premises in his own name?'

'No, they were bought through a company that I had set up for him.'

'Which he owned.'

Green smiled. 'The company was formed and registered in Uruguay.'

'Uruguay?' the young detective exclaimed. 'In South America?'

'That's the only one I know of, son. It has a very accommodating climate for this sort of transaction, even now that the G8 countries are starting to get tough with that sort of thing.'

'I see. What's the company called?'

'It's registered as Lituania SAFI. That stands for Sociedad Anonima Financeria de Inversion, and it's the way a Uruguayan offshore company is described. The law there means that the shareholders in the business can stay anonymous, and so can its directors, or director, for you only need one.'

'Mr Zaliukas was the director, I take it.'

The solicitor nodded. 'Yes, but not the only shareholder. In law, there must be at least two.'

'Who's the other?'

'Regine, Tommy's wife,' he replied.

'So she was involved in the massage parlours too?'

Green's brow knitted, for a second or two, as if he was considering the point. 'Yes . . . but she didn't know it,' he added quickly. 'He just used her name.'

'Did she ever find out?'

'No idea.'

'She left him last week.'

'Then maybe she did.'

Haddock paused, considering everything he had just been

told. 'Am I wrong, Mr Green, but isn't that set-up a hell of a complicated way of owning eight massage parlours?'

'It might seem so,' the lawyer conceded, 'but it doesn't cost very much to administer, and there are two advantages, which I don't want you to note down. One is that the company pays virtually no tax. The other, and more significant, is that if the policy of the council and of your force ever changed, and there was a determined investigation of the other activities that might or might not go on in these places, it would be bloody near impossible to convict anyone of living on the earnings of prostitution. OK, that's the view of a defence lawyer,' he admitted, 'but I think you'll find that the Crown Office would agree with me, and so would the court if it tried it on.'

'Academic now, in Zaliukas's case at any rate. But what about the money? Didn't that come from the other businesses?'

Green shook his head. 'No, and CAJ will confirm that. Tommy told me it was all his. In truth, it wasn't all that much. The executor was instructed by the sole beneficiary of Manson's will to sell the places for no more than the property value; he didn't want any money from the value of the businesses.'

'Who was that?'

Green looked at him in surprise. 'You don't know?' He smiled. 'Ah, but you're only a lad, right enough. His name's Lennie Plenderleith, currently doing life in Shotts Prison for a couple of murders, and put there by your chief constable, Bob Skinner.'

Thirteen

'I need you to tell me everything you can remember about the van driver who brought the girl in,' Griff Montell told the practice receptionist. Since stepping out of the consulting room, he had spoken to Rita Taylor, again, and two of her colleagues, without moving a step closer to identifying the man. Finally, it had occurred to Mrs Taylor that he should really be speaking to Sally Ross, who, she had said, was on the front desk at the time and who had probably seen more of him than anyone else.

'Well, where is she?' he had asked, his patience strained.

'Oh, she's gone for a dental appointment.' Mrs Ross had saved the day by walking through the entrance door at that very moment.

'He was tall,' she replied. 'How tall are you?'

'Six three.'

'Right, he wasn't as tall as you, but I'd say still a bit over six feet. He had a moustache, dark like his hair, and he'd a big chin.'

'Age?'

'Hard to say, but older than you; probably over forty.'

'Complexion?'

The petite, golden-haired receptionist seemed surprised by the question. 'Normal, I'd have said; his skin looked all right to me.'

The DC smiled. 'I didn't mean that, Mrs Ross. What was his ethnic origin?'

'Ah. He was white; he had quite a pale face, although he was one of those men who always look as if they need a shave . . . in fact maybe he didn't have a moustache; I'm not sure now. That might have made me think he did. He was Scottish, of course; maybe not from Edinburgh, but Scottish.'

'That's good. How about the rest? Spectacles?'

'No. He was heavily built, thick chest, bit of a tummy on him. It hung over the belt of his jeans.'

'What else was he wearing?'

'A check shirt, mostly red on a white background, and one of those sleeveless quilted things. What do you call them? Puffer jackets. That's it. Blue, unzipped. His whole appearance, he reminded me of somebody, and I've just realised who it is. Desperate Dan.'

It was Montell's turn to look bewildered. 'Who?'

Mrs Ross stared at him, then chuckled. 'Of course, you're not Scots, are you, so you didn't grow up with him, like us. Desperate Dan's a cartoon character in the *Dandy* comic, a great big cowboy. That's who the van driver looked like.'

'When he brought her in, did he speak to you first?'

'Yes. He told me that he'd almost knocked her down when she'd staggered in front of his van, that he hadn't hit her, but that she still needed attention. He said she was ill, not drunk.'

'What did you think?'

'She was barely able to stand, her eyes were all over the place and we couldn't get a word out of her. My first thought when he half-carried her through that door was that she was totally plastered.'

'And Nurse Chetty confirmed later that she had taken alcohol.'

'Did she? I didn't know that.'

'No reason why you should. Sorry, I was thinking aloud, that's all.' He frowned. 'What happened after that, Mrs Ross, after he'd told you what had happened?'

'I came round from behind the desk, and got the girl into a seat, then I called for Sonya Chetty.'

'And the man?'

'He stood there and watched.'

'For how long?'

'Hardly any time. As soon as I'd taken charge of the girl, and called for Sonya, he said that he had to get on with his deliveries, and he left.'

'I don't suppose you got a look through the window at his van, did you?'

'No, but when he went out the door, he turned right, and there isn't much of a view to that side.'

'OK. That's just about it, Mrs Ross. Only one more thing. When this happened, was the waiting area busy?'

'No, it was empty. You've only got me as a witness, I'm afraid. Me and the driver, that is.'

Which could be a problem, he thought, as he thanked her and walked back towards the consulting room. Alice Cowan was waiting in the corridor, just outside the door, with another woman, short and stocky, with greying hair. 'This is Dr McNulty,' his colleague told him. 'She's just completed the examination.'

'What's the score?' Montell asked as he shook the doctor's hand. 'How's she doing?'

'She's going to be all right, but I'm going to send her to the Royal. She needs to be kept under observation for a couple of days, and I'd imagine you're going to need to talk to her when she's able. We've got nowhere else to send her anyway; we don't know where she lives, or anything else about her.'

The woman looked up at him. 'You were right about her, Detective Constable. Whatever was in her stomach's been absorbed into her bloodstream, but she has taken a drug, or more likely had it administered to her, along with alcohol. It might have been flunitrazepam, or Rohypnol, to give its commercial name, but it probably was GHB. Given to her for the usual reason as well. There's no indication of forcible intercourse, not physically forcible at any rate, no violent rape, but she has been sexually active recently, and probably quite frequently. I'd suggest that you take her underwear for lab testing. Whoever's done this to her has signed his name, good and proper.'

'We'd want her clothing automatically, Doc, in a case like this.'

'Sorry, of course you would,' Dr McNulty conceded. 'I've had it put in sterile bags for you.'

'Thanks. Anything else you have to tell us?'

'Two things. First I don't believe this is a one-off experience.

This girl has all the hallmarks of a regular drug user, she's under-nourished, she's dehydrated, and she's physically weak. The first thing I'd look for in someone like her is heroin use, but I don't see any sign of that . . . no needle marks, or any such. Blood tests will confirm this, and I've taken some for you, but I believe that she's been on this drug over an extended period.'

'And the other?' Cowan asked.

The doctor hesitated. 'Understand,' she said eventually, 'this isn't a medical opinion. It's subjective, but looking at her features, I don't think this girl's Scottish, or British at all. She's had some dental work, so maybe a specialist could give you a more informed view than mine, but me, I'd say this kid's eastern European.'

'If you're right, I hope she speaks English when we get to interview her.'

'Should one of us go with her in the ambulance?'

'Not unless you want to sit looking at her for a day or so, till she gets her wits back. I'll handle her admission from here. I'll let you know what ward she's in and you can send somebody up to keep an eye on her.'

'Thanks, Doctor,' said Montell. He took a card from his pocket and handed it to her. 'Those are my numbers, office and mobile . . . although I'll stay at my desk till I hear from you.'

He let Cowan lead the way outside, through the waiting area, which had gained a few patients, and into the cold dark evening outside. 'What do you think?' he asked her as they reached their car.

'The phrase "sex slave" comes to mind,' she muttered, grimly, as she slid behind the wheel. 'Looks to me as if some sicko bastard's been keeping her under the influence of that stuff and using her as a toy.'

'So how did she escape?'

'Maybe she didn't. Maybe the sicko bastard was the so-called van driver, having a crisis of conscience.'

'That's possible.'

'Should we put a public appeal out for him, do you think?'

'We should do something, even if it's only to have the media ask him to get in touch with us.'

'How about a description?'

'We might even be able to issue an artist's impression.' He grinned as he told her of his interview of Sally Ross.

'Nice one,' she laughed, as she started the engine. She made to engage gear, then stopped. 'Do you want to carry on with that heart to heart we were having earlier?'

'No,' he replied. Her expression tightened, not quite imperceptibly. 'Instead,' he went on, 'how about we pick up where I left off a couple of weeks ago? Ray Wilding told me that he and Becky are going to her divisional dance on Friday. Would you fancy the two of us joining them? It's an open event.'

'Let me think about it.' She steered the car out into the traffic. 'Right,' she said, 'I've thought about it. OK.'

Fourteen

'Uruguay?' DI Becky Stallings exclaimed.

'That's what the man said, boss.' Haddock grinned. 'I don't suppose . . .'

'No, you don't. If the need for a trip out there did arise, you are right at the back of the queue.' She glanced at McGurk. 'As for you, Jack, you're too tall ever to be comfortable on a plane, so . . .' The Londoner frowned. 'Where is bleedin' Uruguay anyway?'

'East coast of South America,' Haddock volunteered. 'Jammed in between Argentina to the south and Brazil to the north.'

'Hardly a day trip, in that case. Just as well this is an i-dotter.'

'A what?' McGurk drawled.

'An i-dotter, a t-crosser, a routine inquiry allowing us simply to tell the procurator fiscal that Tomas Zaliukas partially decapitated himself while the balance of his mind was disturbed.'

'Ah, but the problem is,' the sergeant pointed out, 'we can't tell him that with any authority. Professor Joe says that he was in perfect physical health, apart from the bit of him that's still spread over the hilltop. Also, I've discovered that he hasn't been near his GP in seven years, since he and Valdas Gerulaitis had inoculations for a foreign trip.'

'I wonder where they were going.'

McGurk looked at Haddock. 'That's barely relevant is it, Sauce?'

'Probably not. It's just that he set up the offshore company around that time, and Mr Gerulaitis told us that he had nothing to do with that part of his cousin's business. Yet Alex Skinner said that her predecessor, Conn, thought that he did.'

'Interesting. What did Green say?'

'He didn't know.'

'Still . . .'

'Let's not over-complicate things,' Stallings told them. 'That's not really relevant, is it? You two put a report together now, saying suicide, motive unknown, and I'll email it to Mr McIlhenney.'

'But what about the money?'

'What effing money, Sauce?'

'The money to pay for the massage parlours. Shouldn't we find out where that came from?'

'There's no one left to tell us that,' she countered, 'except maybe the widow.'

'Or maybe Gerulaitis. Or this man Plenderleith; his lawyers might still hold the detail of the transaction.'

'DC Haddock,' Stallings told him firmly, 'just do that report.'

'Boss, I've got a date.'

'Then the quicker you're done, the less late you'll be. If she really fancies you, she'll wait.'

The young man sighed. 'Very good, ma'am.' He looked across at McGurk. 'I'll do notes of my interviews with Alex Skinner and Mr Green, Jack, yes?'

'You do that. I'll write up mine and summarise everything.' He paused. 'By the way,' he added, 'it's lucky for you that cunning Ken was cooperative, otherwise you and I would be having a discussion about an excess of initiative.'

'I saved time, didn't I, by going straight along there to see him? If I hadn't taken the chance, it could have been a couple of days before we'd got to see him. Anyway, he was OK, nothing like the slippery bastard they say he is.'

The DS chuckled. 'You wait till the first time you come up against your new best friend in the witness box. Then you'll see what he's really like. Go on, get on with it; you've got a hot blonde waiting somewhere.'

Haddock nodded and bent over his keyboard, but he had barely typed half a page before his mobile played the opening bars of Bon Jovi's 'Living on a Prayer'. 'Bugger,' he whispered. He picked it up; the number on the outer screen was vaguely familiar. He flipped it open. 'Sauce,' he said.

'Do you always answer like that, Detective Constable?' Alex Skinner asked.

'Unless I know it's the chief on the line,' he replied.

She laughed. 'I've got some information for you. I've spoken to my colleague in our personal client department, and I can give you the details of Mr Zaliukas's will.'

'Thanks.' He grabbed his notebook and a pen. 'Go on.'

'It's pretty simple in outline. His property and all its contents, investments, cash, and valuables, all pass to Mrs

Regine Zaliukas. His holdings in Lietuvos Leisure Limited and Lietuvos Developments Limited are to be vested in a trust fund for the benefit of Mrs Zaliukas and their children. That's it, almost. There's one other item; his shares in something called Lituania SAFI, of which this firm has no knowledge, but which looks like an offshore company of some sort, is to be transferred to a Mrs Laima Gerulaitis.'

'Her?' Haddock exclaimed. 'Why the hell would he do that?'

'Who is she?' Alex asked.

'His cousin's wife. According to him, she didn't like Zaliukas.'

'What's this company anyway? Can you tell me? My partner's going to need to know.'

'It owns the massage parlours. As it was explained to me, it's a liability shelter. The directors and shareholders are guaranteed secrecy under Uruguayan law.'

'Jesus! That's pure Ken Green.'

'But legal, yes?'

'So far. It gives you an insight to Mr Zaliukas, though, and reminds me of one of my dad's personal aphorisms: you can take the man out of the gang, but you can't take the gangster out of the man.'

'Seems not. Who's the executor?'

'Mrs Zaliukas.'

'That's no surprise. Now, what about the lady . . . the widow, I suppose? Can we interview her, or will you give us her state-ment? It's no big deal either way, to be honest. We're probably in the process of wrapping this thing up even without it.'

'Just as well, for we haven't been able to get in touch with her. We have a mobile number for her, but she's not answering at the moment. When we raise her, I'll let you know.'

'We could get the French police to trace her.'

'They wouldn't know where to start, and anyway my partner would rather you didn't. She knows Mrs Zaliukas and would prefer to break the news herself.'

'Fair enough. I'm cool with that. Anything else?'

'Just one small point. The clause in the will transferring the offshore holding to Mrs Gerulaitis . . . that was inserted only yesterday afternoon. That might indicate that my late client's suicide wasn't a complete spur-of-the-moment thing.'

Haddock smiled. 'Hey, Alex,' he said, 'I'm supposed to be the detective here.'

Fifteen

'How are you doing?' Bob Skinner asked his wife. 'I'm ready to head home if you are. Gerry's gone already.'

'I'm almost done,' she told him. 'If you leave now, by the time you get here I will be.'

'How's your day been?' he asked. 'How did First Minister's questions go?'

'Are you telling me you didn't even watch it on television?'

'I couldn't. I got tied up in a meeting, then I had to leave to meet Alex.'

'You were better off with her. It was pretty dull today, no flashpoints. The BBC political editor's going to say that we boxed a draw, but the truth is there wasn't a blow struck on either side. How about you?'

'Nice lunch. My kid's got an extra glow about her. It'll last for a while, and then she'll work out what her next ambition is and set off in pursuit of that.'

'Marriage and children, maybe.'

'That's well below the horizon.'

'The right guy will turn up one day, you'll see.'

'As long as he's not a cop . . .'

'Bob! That business with Andy is history; get over it.'

'I am over it. As for forgetting it, no danger. Now go on, finish off what you're doing and I'll pick you up in front of the Parliament building in fifteen minutes or so. Wait inside for me, though. It looks colder than ever out there.'

He hung up, stood, and slipped on his jacket. He was almost at his door, when there was a soft knock and it opened. 'Got a minute?' Neil McIlhenney asked.

'Yes, but only the one. What is it?'

'Tomas Zaliukas. I've just had a report from Becky Stallings. She wants me to sign it off to be passed to the fiscal. You started this off, so I thought I'd better run it past you.'

'What does it say?'

'Read it for yourself.' The superintendent handed him a printout of Stallings' email.

Skinner glanced through it, then read it for a second time, more closely. 'No doubt about the suicide, then.'

'No. The note on the computer more or less caps it. Plus, when we did a full search of the house we found a floorboard in Zaliukas's study that had been taken up. There was a box of shotgun ammo hidden between the joists, and it wasn't full.'

'And the note points to the motive.'

'That's right; depression, over Regine leaving him.'

'You know me and guesses, my friend. I've never minded following them up, but I bloody hate including them in submissions to the Crown Office. Young Haddock's note says Alex told him that he made a material change to his will yesterday, Tuesday. One day later, that will's in effect. In it, he left everything else to the wife and kids, except those massage parlour properties. Why not?'

'They're brothels, Bob.'

'And Regine could have sold them if she wanted out of that business. But he left them to his cousin's wife. Why? Could he have been screwing her?'

'According to McGurk and Haddock, even the cousin must have to pluck up his courage to do that.'

'OK, there has to be another reason, as yet unknown, so this report is incomplete. On top of that, there's Ken Green; I hate it when that bastard's involved. I hate it even more when he suddenly starts being cooperative with a raw young DC.' He handed the report back to McIlhenney. 'Don't let Stallings submit this to the fiscal, not yet. We're not done.'

'But what else can we do?'

The chief constable smiled. 'There's these two seagulls, out in Gullane. Every day in the winter, when the weather's frosty, like it is just now, they appear on the green . . . us Motherwell boys don't have lawns . . . in front of our house, and they drum their feet on the ground, pit-pat, pit-pat, pit-pat, just like that, until their food supply sticks its head out to see what all the fucking noise is about. That's what we can do, Neil. You tell Becky and her boys to get back out there and drum up some worms.'

Sixteen

'The worst moment in a girl's life,' said Cheeky, 'is when she's sitting on her own in a pub, thinking that she's been stood up. If you hadn't sent me that text . . .'

'. . . you'd have been out of here. I know,' Sauce sighed.

She laughed, a soft tinkling sound, yet it cut through all the background noise of a bar that was not completely full, but still busy for a midweek evening. 'No,' she told him, 'but I'd have been hammered by the time you arrived.'

He looked at her as he settled into his chair, setting a white wine on the table before her then pressing a wedge of lime into his Sol beer with his thumb. She was dazzling; her teeth sparkled as she smiled, her shortish blond hair was perfectly haphazard, and her make-up helped to emphasise the blueness of her eyes. 'Come on, Cheeky,' he replied, 'admit it. You've never been stood up in your life.'

She beamed. 'OK,' she admitted, 'I wasn't speaking from personal experience. Have you? Ever been stood up, I mean?'

'Find me a guy that hasn't. I've had my share. I wasn't even certain that you'd be here tonight.'

She raised an eyebrow. 'Do I strike you as a "fuck 'em and chuck 'em" girl?'

'No, but my sad experiences with women have left me taking nothing for granted.'

'What's your worst one?'

He whistled. 'Out of so many?' He scratched his head. 'I learned early on not to arrange to meet in places where a lot of people would see you being dissed.'

She glanced around. 'You took a chance on this one.'

'Maybe, but you're not the sort of woman a guy would arrange to meet outside McDonald's, or on the Waverley Station concourse.'

She winked. 'I'll take that as a compliment, rather than just you trying to talk your way into my knickers . . . again. Now come on, spill some beans.'

'Well,' he began, 'my most publicly humiliating experience wasn't a stand-up in the conventional sense of the word. I was at Indigo one night, with some mates, and I asked this girl up to dance. When we were done she stayed up for another, and a third: I thought I might be in there. Then she said to me, "Just you wait there," and headed off through the crowd. I mean I thought she'd gone for her coat, so I did what I was told. I stood there for a couple of minutes, then five, then ten, right up until I saw her back out on the floor with one of my pals, putting a fucking lip lock on him, and realised that the rest of the team were stood up at the bar laughing their rocks off at me.'

'What a slapper! What did you do?'

'I told them that none of them would ever park safely in Edinburgh again.'

'You abused your police powers?' she gasped in mock condemnation.

'Nah. I wish I could have, but the traffic wardens are separate from us. Speaking of parking—' he added.

'I didn't bring my car,' she told him, before he could finish. 'Going by what I saw this morning, I reckoned it would be impossible to park at your place, so I caught the train.'

'Where do you live anyway?' he asked. 'You never told me.'

'You never asked. I've got a wee house out in South Gyle.'

'On your own?'

'No, with my husband and two kids! And he's an all-in wrestler.' She paused. 'Yes, Sauce, I live on my own. Like I said, it's a wee house, no bigger than your flat, and not in nearly as lively a part of the city.'

'It'll be new if it's out there.'

'Fairly. I'm only the second owner.'

'You did well to get a mortgage. If I wasn't a cop, I'd have been struggling.'

'Accountants are a good risk too.'

'You're an accountant?'

'Yup. I don't have my full CA qualification yet, but I've got my degree.'

'Where do you work?'

'I'm on my second year of a training contract with a firm called Deacon and Queen.'

'Never heard of them.'

'Maybe not, but they're top five. Name me half a dozen accountancy firms you have heard of.'

He smiled. 'You have a point. So how come you didn't have to go tearing in there this morning?'

'I'm on an audit team, out with a client just now. I sent them a text saying that I had a domestic situation. That wasn't exactly a lie, was it?'

'No, I'd have bought that.'

'So how was your day, when eventually you got there?'

Sauce shrugged his shoulders. 'I suppose I could call it routine. I spent it on a sudden death investigation. You want to talk bizarre coincidence? The victim was the guy who owned Indigo. I just finished the report. That's why I was a bit late.'

'How sudden was it?'

'As sudden as they get. Suicide by swallowing a sawn-off shotgun.' He winced. 'Shit, I'm sorry; I shouldn't have told you that.'

She screwed up her face. 'Yuk! OK on an empty stomach, but only just. What a mess it must have been.'

'Happily I didn't get to see it. All I've had to do is the follow-up, trying to establish why he did it.'

'And did you?'

'I talked to his cousin, to a nice lawyer and to a dodgy lawyer, but no, not really. The guy's wife left him last week, and took the kids; that's the only motive we've got.'

'Maybe it was an accident,' Cheeky suggested. 'Maybe he was just playing with the thing and it went off.'

'On top of Arthur's Seat, in the ball-freezing cold? No, we're sure that killing himself had been on his mind, because he changed his will just before he did it.'

'To take his wife out of the picture?'

Sauce shook his head. 'No. She and the kids get the lot, apart from some pieces of not very desirable property that he seems to have decided at the last minute to leave to his cousin's wife.'

She frowned. 'Things like that are awful sad,' she murmured, sipping her wine.

'I suppose,' he conceded. 'It's best not to think about the emotional side of an investigation; the physical can be hard enough. Mind you, sometimes you can't avoid it; if it's a colleague, say . . .'

They sat silent for a while, as if they were reflecting on their first serious discussion.

'Those properties,' said Cheeky, finally moving on, 'they must be really crap.'

'Oh, they are. Not nice at all.'

'I wonder why he decided to leave them to that woman, then.'

'So do we. Maybe it's because she's a crap person.'

'You've met her?'

'Jack and I did, this afternoon. Not very nice at all.'

She reached across and squeezed his arm. 'Never mind, Sauce. Cheer up, you're finished with all that, you said, so what are you doing tomorrow? What's your working day like? Mine's pretty predictable.'

'That's the attraction of CID, I suppose. We never know what's next, unless we're on a specialist unit. Maybe you could join us when you finish your training. There's a dedicated fraud unit that covers the whole of Scotland. They recruit accountants for that.'

'Show me the money, love. That would be the problem.'

'I'm sure. Police pay's all right, but it would be nice to climb the ladder as fast as I can. At the moment I'm right at the bottom. But you were wrong when you said that job was finished. I had a text from Jack just as I was coming through the door. We signed off on the report, sure, but the bosses have kicked it back.'

'Why?' Cheeky asked, casually. 'Have they got a down on you and him?'

'Not that I know of. No, it's . . .' He stopped.

Cheeky held up her hands. 'Don't tell me! Don't tell me! I don't want to know.'

'Ach,' he chuckled, 'it's OK. It's probably just that this guy was a bit of a hoodlum in his youth, so the high heid yins are being ultra thorough.'

'They can do that on their own time,' she declared. 'This is ours. Let me get you another beer, then . . . what do you want to do?'

'A meal, I thought. What do you like?'

She reached to the left, to the side of her chair that he could not see, and held up a bag, an overnight bag. 'What do I like or what do I want? I like pizza and I want . . . the biggest takeaway we can get from Papa John's, or Mamma's, which-ever's nearest to your place. Then no more shop talk, just all that pepperoni, and you and me. Does that sound like a deal?'

'It works for me . . . and forget the second beer.'

She drained her glass and eased her long legs out of her chair. 'Then let's get the show on the road, for I warn you now, Sauce, I can't call in late two days on the trot.'

Seventeen

'The brass neck these bastards have got,' Detective Sergeant Lisa McDermid exclaimed, shielding her eyes with a mitten-clad hand against the low sunshine of the crisp, clear early morning.

'A crude technique, I'll grant you,' said DI George Regan, looking massive in the well-worn Crombie overcoat that he had inherited from an uncle a few weeks before, 'but there's nothing new about a ram raid.'

'I've never seen one.'

'Not even when you were in uniform?'

'No.'

'Simple but effective. Get a truck, an old Land Rover, any sort of chunky vehicle and stick it through the front door of the target premises. Entry achieved, you help yourself. This place is a classic target; a golf pro shop, nice big double doors, just one step up from ground level.'

'But it's alarmed. They were pretty reckless, trying it on.'

'No; they were professional. That's no deterrent to these characters. They're in and out like a fiddler's elbow, and in a rural area like this one . . .' He called to a uniformed sergeant, standing a few yards away. 'Kenny, what was our response time? Do you know?'

'Twenty-five minutes. Our nearest car was in Dunbar.'

'There you are, then,' Regan told the DS. 'The owner of the business got here before we did, and he was in bed in Dirleton when this happened. The alarm company's monitoring centre called him first, then us. Me, I like old-fashioned alarms, with bells or sirens that make lots of fucking noise and waken the neighbours. Remotely monitored things like this one don't; those casings up there are empty, just for show. Sometimes they'll put sirens on the inside, the thinking being that burglars will be scared off.' He grunted. 'Scared off, my arse. Waste of time and money.'

'A siren wouldn't have done much good here,' McDermid pointed out. 'Witches' Hill Golf and Country Club; it's not quite in the middle of nowhere, but isolated enough. There isn't a house in sight. Besides, do we want neighbours having a go and getting their heads bashed in with baseball bats?'

'Come on, Lisa,' the DI retorted. 'Not many people are actually that brave, but they do call us with vehicle descriptions, registration numbers and so on. The bastards who did this are clean away. The socos will take all the fucking fingerprints they like, but it won't do us any good. This is a shop. Hundreds of people will have left their dabs all over it. I remember a break-in a few years ago in a store in Fountain-bridge, where they came up with prints that matched two well-known blaggers. Bingo, we thought. It took us a week to trace them, and no wonder; when the shop was done they'd been on holiday in Gran Canaria. They'd been in the place as legit customers. Our best chance here is if the stuff they've nicked shows up online, but they'll not be daft enough to do that. Likely it'll be sold privately, word of mouth, at a knock-down, but still for enough to make the job worthwhile.'

'Do we know what's been taken?'

As she spoke, a man, lean and white-haired, of medium height, stepped from the violated premises and stood in the shattered doorway. 'We're about to find out,' Regan said. 'What's the damage, Mr Fairley?'

'Clubs,' the golf pro told him. 'They've cleaned me out of all my high-end stock. The trade-ins and the cheaper starter sets are still there, but the Callaways, the Titleists, the Taylor-Mades, the Pings, they're all gone; irons, woods, and all the putters and the specialist stuff, the rescue clubs and lob wedges. They've taken the best of the balls too.'

'Any idea of the total value?'

Alasdair Fairley frowned. 'Net?' Regan nodded. 'I can get you an exact figure off the computer, but with the stock I was holding, in the region of eighty thousand.'

'And they'll shift it for about twenty-five, if they sell direct, yes?'

'You probably know more about it than me, but that sounds about right.'

'But couldn't we trace it in use?' McDermid asked. 'Through golf courses and the like.'

Fairley frowned at her. 'You're not suggesting that a PGA professional would *handle* stolen golf clubs, are you?'

'No, not at all,' she said, hastily, quelling his outrage. 'I meant couldn't we carry out spot checks on golfers to see what they're using?'

The pro looked at Regan, one golfer to another, as if to say, 'Will you tell her or will I?'

The DI picked up the prompt. 'Lisa,' he explained, 'golf clubs don't have bar codes, or serial numbers of anything permanent to identify an individual item. So once Mr Fairley's own sticker has been removed, that's it for tracing them. More than that, once a club's been used, it's changed in some small way. So even if we were to do anything as fascist as to walk on to every golf course in Scotland and ask players to show us their equipment, it wouldn't do us a blind bit of good. But we're not going to do that. Why not? Because the chief constable's a golfer. So's the deputy chief. So's the chair of the local council. So are most of the judges on the Supreme Court bench, and so, for that matter, am I!'

'So what are we going to do?' she demanded.

'You're going to circulate the information nationally, and Mr Fairley here's going to claim on his insurance.'

'And maybe look at installing CCTV,' said the victim.

'That's the cheap option,' Regan told him. 'You could do that, outside and in, but . . . These people have had a look at this place before they did the job, as any good thief would do. If you'd had cameras, they'd have masked out number plates, worn masks and put the things out of commission as soon as they could. No, the only way you can improve security is by spending a hell of a lot of money on steel roller grilles to make this place impregnable.'

'I only own the stock, not the shop itself. The Marquis of

Kinture does; it's his club. I doubt if he'd fork out for that.'

'In that case, do what you can to make it difficult to get in, and hold less stock in future.'

'I expect my insurer will limit my cover from now on, so I'll have to do that anyway.' He paused. 'How long will it be before I can start clearing up the mess?' he asked. 'I'll also need to arrange for the place to be made secure. Plus, I should be opening the shop now. I'll have members turning up soon.'

'When it's this cold?' McDermid exclaimed.

'You really don't know golf, Sergeant, do you?' Alasdair Fairley smiled, for the first time.

'You might as well start now,' Regan told him. 'I'll tell our socos, when they get here, just to look for tyre and footprints, not to bother with fingerprints. We can get on our way once they arrive, Lisa. We've got no more to do here. Meantime, I might go and take a look at the course. I've never been here before, and I've heard it's pretty good.'

'Call me when you have a free day,' said Fairley. 'If we're quiet you can play it, on the house.'

'Thanks. I'll take you up on that.' He wandered away from the pro shop, towards the first tee. He was peering down the first fairway, through the thinning mist, when his mobile sounded. He checked the number, but it showed 'Private'.

'Yes?' he answered cautiously.

'George.'

'Ah, it's you, Fred.'

For some reason, Detective Chief Inspector Graham Leggatt, senior CID officer in East and Midlothian, was known to close colleagues and friends as 'Fred'. He always had been, and it was rumoured that not even he knew why. 'What have you got there?' he asked.

'I don't want to be pessimistic,' the DI replied, 'but you can mark this one up for the unsolved column. It was a well-planned job, simple and well-executed. Eighty grand's worth of untraceable gear's disappeared into the black economy. I don't remember anything as pro as this in the time I've been on this patch.'

'There hasn't been. I'll tell you how well planned it was.' There was a pause. Regan heard a slurping sound. Fred Leggatt was famous for drinking tea in industrial quantities. 'We have three patrol cars in East Lothian through the night, best case. When this job was pulled, they were all en route to calls. Every one of them was false, and when we checked, we found that everyone was made on a different untraceable pay-and-go mobile. How about that for planning?'

'Gallus bastards,' Regan chuckled.

'Indeed. Much as I dislike the idea of putting Mario McGuire off his breakfast, I'll need to pass this up the line.'

Eighteen

'Jesus, Sauce,' Jack McGurk laughed, 'your eyes are like piss holes in the snow. Is this girl a vampire? Has she been draining your lifeblood?'

'With respect, Sergeant,' Haddock retorted, 'mind your own business. Better still, shut the fuck up. I never said a word when you and Lisanne got together, even though I seem to recall you practically crawling in here a couple of times.'

'He has a point,' said Becky Stallings. 'Cut the boy some slack. All his wet dreams seem to have come true. Now,' she continued, 'as I let you know last night, that job we thought was over has been chucked back to us for further attention. The problem I have is that I don't know what else we can do.'

'We could ask the French police to find Zaliukas's wife for us,' the young DC suggested. 'That's assuming she is in France.'

'Her lawyer may have contacted her already, as Alex Skinner said she would. Even if she hasn't, this is a civil matter, not criminal. If CID calls France and asks for help in tracing her, it might send out the wrong signals. She might wind up being arrested.'

'We could look closer at his companies. Maybe they're not as sound as Gerulaitis claims.'

'That's more like it. Pull the last three years' accounts from Companies' House and have a look. You know who they bank with, or so you told me, so have a word with his manager. And what about these massage parlours, or saunas, or whatever the hell they are? From what you said they're all run independently by managers, but Zaliukas must have had regular contact with them. Talk to some of them, see what they say.'

'What will we be looking for?' McGurk asked.

'Ideally, we'll be looking for someone who tells us that Zaliukas confided in him recently that he was deeply distressed, that he was missing his wife more than he could stand, and that he couldn't go on. We'll be looking for any fucking thing that lets me throw this back at Neil McIlhenney with "Mission accomplished" stamped all over it.'

Nineteen

'Twin,' Mario McGuire asked. 'Are you free?'

'Sure,' said Neil McIlhenney, and hung up. He was certain that more people within the force, and maybe across Edinburgh, thought of them as the original Glimmer Twins than there were those who recognised it as the nickname adopted by Mick Jagger and Keith Richards more than forty years earlier. It had been bestowed upon them, by Paula Viareggio, one night in the Café Royal bar, when they were in the first half of their twenties, when he had been engaged to Olive Clarey, and when the torch that Paula carried for her cousin Mario was still hidden in her handbag.

He left his office and walked the few yards to the one with 'Head of CID' on the door. 'Whassup?' he asked as he slumped into a seat. 'Are you narked because the report on Tomas Zaliukas isn't signed off yet?'

'No, not especially. If the chief constable wants us to dig deeper, so be it. No, this is something else. There was a burglary overnight at the pro shop at Witches' Hill golf club. A ram raid; they took out the main door with a vehicle then helped themselves to eighty grand's worth of golf gear.'

'Witches' Hill? That's in East Lothian, isn't it, up behind Aberlady? Outside Edinburgh; not my area.'

'Maybe not, but you're my *de facto* deputy, and I want to bounce this off you. This isn't the only job of this sort that's been pulled recently. Two weeks ago the shop at the Mayfield course in Broxburn was done in exactly the same way. Then and now, they were long gone and out of town before uniform could respond to the alarm call. The places were well chosen. They're isolated, and they could get their wheels right up to the premises. We're nowhere near catching anyone for Broxburn and Fred Leggatt isn't holding out any hope of a result for today's either.'

'I suppose we have to assume it's the same team,' McIlhenney murmured.

'We might even be able to prove it is, if they've left tyre marks, but there's something else. On each occasion our responses were hindered. All our available cars in each area were heading for calls that turned out to be bogus. We've traced the originating numbers and in each case, the calls were made from a cheap, disposable mobile.'

'Bought where?'

'Dunno yet. That's our only line of inquiry for now, but there's every fuckin' chance that they were stolen too.'

'How many cars are we talking about?'

'In East Lothian, three, in West Lothian, five; all diverted to places far away from the crime scenes.'

The superintendent frowned. 'That isn't a hell of a lot, is it, when you spell it out.'

'Tell me about it,' McGuire snorted. 'Remember that

exchange I had with NYPD? One of the stats I picked up is that they have over three thousand patrol vehicles in a smaller geographical area.'

'And ten times the tax-paying population to fund them, and a hell of a lot more I'll bet than ten times the number of incident reports. The world is as it is, Mario; we all have to live within our means.'

'But how do we do that? For I know for certain that this team will not stop at two jobs. And how long will it take for other clever bastards to get in on the idea? We've got the potential for a significant crime wave here.'

'Then we'll have to nail them as fast as we can,' McIlhenney responded, 'before the media catch on and they start to build a criminal fan club. But this isn't just a CID job.'

'I know. That's why I'm going to raise it at the boss's daily meeting . . .' he glanced at his watch, '. . . in ten minutes. I've got a fair idea how that'll develop, so I'd like you to keep yourself handy for a follow-up session with me and Mags, later on this morning.'

Twenty

'Have either of you had word from the hospital yet about your mystery girl's condition?' Ray Wilding asked.

'I've just checked,' Alice Cowan replied. 'She's stable, and more lucid, but she's not responding to questions yet. The doctor in charge says we needn't even try to interview her before this afternoon.'

'That leaves you sat on your hands. Has the press office issued your public appeal yet?'

'Yes, they put it out first thing this morning. It'll be in the *Evening News*, and on broadcast media by lunchtime.'

Wilding frowned. 'Couldn't they have done it last night?' he grumbled.

'Alan Royston said it was too late to catch anything. He's been around long enough to know what he's doing, so I didn't argue.'

The DS grunted. 'Not everyone would agree with that. I've got a pal who works on local radio; he'd have put it on air straight away if he'd been given it. How did you word it?'

'I didn't; Griff drafted it.'

'I put in as much as we want used,' Montell offered. 'Young girl, dyed blond, reasonably well nourished, possibly eastern European, brought into surgery after being found dazed and incoherent in the street nearby. Anxious to trace anyone with any knowledge of her, in particular the Good Samaritan van driver who brought her in, and maybe saved her life. OK,' he said, 'the last part may be an exaggeration, but it's headline material.'

'As in "Good Samaritan lifesaver vanishes", you mean? Next thing you know the red-tops will be inviting the punters to buy him a pint when he's found. There's no mention of possible sexual assault, I notice.'

'Are you kidding, Ray? Even if the guy is absolutely genuine, it's odds against him coming forward. If I'd included that, there would be absolutely no chance.'

'Yeah, granted,' Wilding conceded.

'One thing we have got, though, is a quick response from the lab. I hadn't expected anything much today, but I've just had an email. Nothing firm yet, but interesting nonetheless. Apart from her slippers, all the girl was wearing was her cotton dress, a bra, and pants. She didn't wash her knickers very often, and wasn't too worried about getting stripped for action either, for they've found semen stains on both garments, from more than one donor. They're not going into numbers yet, but either this girl was gang-banged, or . . .'

'She's on the game,' Alice Cowan declared. 'Now there's a surprise,' she added, her voice heavy with irony.

'In that case,' said Wilding, 'maybe some of the local girls will know who she is. Go ask some questions.'

'Now?' Cowan challenged. 'Where are we going to find prostitutes at this time of day?'

'The massage parlour girls you won't find that easily, but there's someone else you might ask. Have you ever heard of Joanne Virtue, Alice?'

The DC frowned. 'I can't say that I have. Who's she?'

'Big Joanne is the nearest thing we have to an oracle down here in Leith. She used to be a hooker herself, although she's out of that life now.'

'I take it Virtue was her work name,' Montell said.

'Nope,' the sergeant chuckled, 'it's the one on her birth certificate. When she was on the street, they used to call her the Big Easy. Life throws up some oddities, and she's one of them. Joanne's never been an informer as such, as in grass, but if something happened that she thought was wrong, she'd tell us about it. Ask her if she's heard about any new talent, maybe not being treated right, and see what she says.'

'Where do we find her?'

'At work, probably. After she passed on her street corner to a younger model, she managed a massage parlour for a while, for a wee hood called Kenny Bass. But she moved on from that. Last I heard she'd got herself a job as a receptionist with a funeral undertaker. Makes sense when you think about it. Who better to make that first, sympathetic impression on the newly bereaved than a retired whore with a heart of gold?'

Twenty-one

'If all customers were as soundly based as the two Lietuvos companies, Detective Constable,' said Andrew John, 'the banking sector would never have run into difficulties. Guys like me would still be carrying our bonuses home in bloody wheelbarrows, instead of praying that we can get out of here with our pension funds still intact.

'In the old days, Tomas Zaliukas was the sort of customer we didn't want. Cash rich, sure-footed in the licensed premises he bought and always with the knack of picking the right area on the property development side. We made money out of lending in those days, but Tomas never needed to borrow much, not in the long term.

'Today, guys like him are like gold dust: loads of cash on deposit, property assets that are worth four times our exposure with him, and income to service his loans umpteen times over.'

Haddock let out an involuntary sigh, then hoped that it had not carried across the desk. 'Still,' he said, 'you'll keep the business.'

'I can only hope so. For all that he was always on about his roots, Tomas had more sense than to go anywhere near the Lithuanian banks. His cousin might take a different line.'

'It won't be his decision,' the young detective commented, then paused as he realised what he had let slip.

'You mean Gerulaitis won't inherit anything? That means it all goes to Regine?'

'Please, Mr John,' Haddock begged, 'forget I said that. I shouldn't have.'

'That's all right, it's gone already. I'll give you one in return. I'd rather have one Regine than a hundred Valdases.'

'Why do you say that?'

'Because she exudes integrity. Valdas, on the other hand, is one of those guys . . . Let's just say that if I was forced to invite him for dinner, we'd be keeping all the good stuff well out of sight. Under Tommy's eye, he was fine, but Tomas never let him out of his sight either. He told me as much; he said once that when the kids were babies, and Regine had her hands full, Valdas asked him if he could manage Indigo, for a change of scenery. He fobbed him off by telling him he was too valuable where he was, and paid him off with a pay rise, but the real reason was that if he had put him in there, he'd have to employ an accountant just to make sure he didn't bleed the place dry.'

'Do you think he could have been up to something and Mr Zaliukas found out?'

'I don't, because even Valdas is bright enough to have known that he wouldn't get away with it. Tomas was better than that; he had some nose for business. He took me with him once to look at a pub he was thinking about buying. It was unofficial, of course; we went in as punters on a Friday night and spent a couple of hours there. When we came out, Tommy told me straight off what the place should be doing in profit and what it was actually doing, in other words, what the staff were ripping out of it. When he put his auditors in to do due diligence on the place, they found that he'd been spot on, both times.'

'So that's why his pubs make so much money; because he could spot all the scams?'

Andrew John frowned; his left eye twitched. 'Yes. That and . . .' He looked Haddock in the eye. 'You're not going to hear this, any more than I heard what you said about Tomas's will, right.'

'Absolutely, sir.'

'OK, we all know what Tomas got up to when he was younger, don't we?'

Haddock nodded.

'So did you ever ask yourself, when he went legit, what happened to his boys, the "associates" he brought over from Lithuania?'

'Well,' the DC replied, 'I didn't, because it was before my time.'

'Let me tell you. They went into the pubs, but later when he bought the massage parlours, most of them became managers and the licensees of record. In other words, they never went away, and they were as close to Tomas as they'd ever been. If you look at all the years he's been in the pub business, you could probably identify the few people who've ever been caught stealing from him just by cross-referencing the names of his bar staff with admissions to A and E.'

'Wow!' the young detective exclaimed. 'Didn't that make you uncomfortable about having him as a customer?'

The banker smiled. 'No, it made me very careful always to spell out every clause and condition of every deal we ever did.'

'Those places,' Haddock ventured. 'Do you know where the money came from to buy them? The lawyer involved was vague on the subject.'

'It was kosher,' John replied at once. 'Tomas paid himself a dividend from Lietuvos and that's where it went. As for Ken Green, he'd have asked no questions; that's the way he is.'

'Can you tell me how much?'

'I can find out. So can you, by pulling the accounts for the right year, but I can probably do it quicker. But tell me. Why do you want to know? Tomas shot himself, didn't he?'

'For sure.'

'But you don't know why?'

'No.'

'Why do you need to?'

'Because someone way, way above my pay grade does.'

'If that's who I think it is, say no more. I'll call you when I've got that figure for you.'

Twenty-two

Griff Montell looked at the forty-something woman in the chair opposite him, and tried to imagine her standing on a street corner, garish blond dye job, red shiny boots, bum-freezer jacket and short skirt maximising the legs that were still her best feature.

He failed, abysmally. Joanne Virtue's hair was a lustrous brown, and he could tell that every visit to her salon of choice cost her plenty. Her suit had come, if not from Harvey Nichols, then from one of those designer sections on the first floor of John Lewis, where his sister did her clothes shopping. Her face was full of angles, from the sharpness of her chin to her dark, tick-shaped eyebrows, but the smile with which she had greeted them had been kind, and her eyes were expressive.

At that moment, they were expressing anger. 'Let me get this right,' she said, quietly, as if she did not want her voice to carry any further than the plush, velvet-draped reception room in which they were sitting, 'you have come to my place of work to ask me about a part of my life that I've left behind me. Thank God we've got no clients here the now.' Her accent was Scottish, but even the South African could tell that it had originated in Glasgow, not Edinburgh.

'This is an urgent investigation, Miss Virtue,' Alice Cowan retorted. 'We've got a girl in trouble. We can do this interview down in our office if you'd prefer it.'

Instantly, the woman's eyes turned icy cold. 'You listen to me, kid,' she whispered. 'If you ever threaten me again, I'll pick up the phone and I'll call Neil McIlhenney. I hear he's gone up in the world since I saw him last, so you'll know who he is, for sure. "So what?" you might be thinking, he's a nice guy. But he's got another side that you wouldn't want to see. There's history between Neil and me . . . not that kind, before you jump to the wrong conclusion . . . and I'd only have to ask him the once to have you cut off at the fucking knees.'

Cowan looked at her colleague. 'Griff . . .' she began, but he held up a hand.

'Alice,' he said, 'I think we should listen to the lady. Miss Virtue, I apologise for disturbing you here, but it's necessary. We have a kid in the Royal in her teens, still drugged out of her skull after twenty-four hours and unable to tell us what happened to her. However, we do know that it involved several men and that she was horizontal at the time. It may have been a domestic incident, but . . .'

'How old is she?'

'Sixteen, maybe, possibly less. We know nothing about her, but we're told she may be east European. She's been fed GHB and booze, probably over a period.'

Joanne Virtue's strong features twisted into a grimace. 'Then whoever did it needs sorting out. You want my guess, she's been brought here, either with the promise of a good job, or she's just been kidnapped, and she was being broken in.'

'Have you heard of that sort of thing happening in Edinburgh?' asked Cowan, seemingly chastened.

'No, but I've been out of that life for a bit. For a short while, I managed a massage parlour, but I . . .' she paused, as if she was considering exactly what she had done '. . . I made a complete break from what I'd been.'

'Would it be worth us talking to the owner?'

'The guy I worked for doesnae own it any more. The last thing I heard about that place was that he'd sold it: that he'd been pressured into selling it, even.'

'Pressured by whom?'

'By a Lithuanian guy; one of that lot runs it now. But the word was that a bloke called Tommy Zale was behind him.'

'Never heard of him,' said Montell.

'He owned pubs and the like. That wasnae his real name, it was something longer. There was a piece about him in the *Saltire* this morning. He was found dead yesterday morning; "no suspicious circumstances" according to your outfit. The Lithuanians have been taking over the massage parlour business in Edinburgh for years.' She laughed, quietly, briefly. 'Sorry, the public entertainment business, according to the Licensing Court. I never saw it in print anywhere, but they're supposed tae control it all. If somebody's been running girls into Edinburgh, then it's either that lot, or they'll be as keen as you are to find out who it is.' She paused. 'Where did you find this lass?'

'She was brought into a surgery near Ocean Terminal.'

'Mmm. There's a massage parlour not far from that. If I were you, I'd be asking there about her.'

Twenty-three

'We are not alone,' Mario McGuire announced.

Maggie Steele and Neil McIlhenney looked at each other across the small conference table in the head of CID's office. 'I've always thought there were other beings out there,' said the detective superintendent, laconically, 'but I didn't expect contact to be made in my lifetime. What about you, Scully? What do you think?'

'You must stop watching that sci-fi stuff,' the ACC retorted.

'Indeed,' McGuire continued. 'I fed information on our two raids to the national intelligence centre in Paisley, and had an interesting response. Over the last six months, there have been similar, no, pretty much identical robberies at golf clubs in Seamill, in Ayrshire, in Blairgowrie, on Tayside, in Cumbernauld, near Glasgow, and on Loch Lomondside . . . not the big club, another one.'

Steele's eyebrows rose. 'Nobody thought to issue a national alert? What is the SCDEA for?'

'They're short-handed through there, but that will be done now, they promise. The guy I spoke to in the intelligence unit told me that the new deputy director's been appointed . . .'

'That's lightning fast; the boss only mentioned the vacancy yesterday.'

'I know, but they've short-circuited the usual procedures. The director's just gone off on long-term sick leave, so they need someone in post, like now; whoever the new appointee is, he'll be running the show from the off.'

'Your contact didn't tell you who it is, did he?'

'He didn't know.'

Steele laughed. 'So much for intelligence. But back to the topic. We have a determined, professional outfit in action all across Scotland, running rings round us all. They've hit us twice, probably knowing how exposed we are rurally. We have to assume that they're going to do it again. So what do we do?'

'I've been thinking about that,' McIlhenney said. 'How about we have CID teams in place to respond instantly to any alarm calls from golf pro shops?'

'Jesus, Neil,' McGuire hissed. 'Budgets, budgets; they'd be sat on their hands all night, across the whole of our county area. Mags, can you make extra patrol teams available?'

'Budgets, Mario, budgets.'

'Can you divert patrol teams from the city?'

'We're stretched there too.'

'Dead end, then.'

She nodded. 'However,' she began, 'there is one tactic that's occurred to me. Do you know, or can you find out, the time elapsed between the last false alarm call logged in by our communications centre and the alerts from each golf club that's been done?'

'I know already. Ten minutes in the first case, eleven last night.'

'OK. Then how about, if we have police emergency calls during the night in quick succession, taking all of our cars out of play, be it three in East Lothian, four in West, whatever, we delay the response to the last of those calls by fifteen minutes. If we have an alarm warning within that time, the third car heads like shit off a shovel for the location.'

'But what if these calls are genuine?' McIlhenney exclaimed. 'What if some guy really is beating his wife to death?'

'It's a hell of a chance to take, I'll grant you. But statistically, how many calls do we get during the night out in the counties? Damn few. And in quick succession?'

'Statistics won't stop someone from bleeding to death.'

McGuire nodded. 'I agree. It would be a risk, Mags. And I suppose I could have a few CID on stand-by, let's say one unit in Edinburgh, one in Dalkeith and one in Livingston. But we'd need to get the OK from the boss to holding back responses.'

'Would we?' she posed. 'What about allowing him deniability?' The words hung heavily in the air. For almost a minute no one spoke.

'No, Maggie,' said the head of CID, at last. 'If we pulled something like this without telling him, and it went disastrously wrong, you know that friendship would go out the window. He said as much yesterday. He'd have our guts, all of us. And at the end of the day, he'd carry the can anyway, whether he knew or not. We've got to tell him. I might be the junior officer round this table, but I'm putting my foot down on this one. It's a matter of loyalty.'

Steele leaned back in her chair, staring him down, but he held her gaze. And then she laughed. 'Absolutely,' she exclaimed. 'Consider that a test, and you've passed. I was only wondering whether you two were still the reckless buggers I used to know.'

'Thanks very much,' McIlhenney growled.

'Ah, don't take it to heart, man,' she chided. 'Have you lost your sense of humour as well? I've already spoken to Bob, before I came along here. He says, "Do it, and do it from tonight." Is that OK with you,' she asked, 'or do you want it in writing?'

Twenty-four

'How did you get on with the banker?' Becky Stallings asked, watching Haddock from the doorway of her small office, as he hung his coat on the stand in the corner of the CID room.

'Fine, boss,' he replied, casually, as he took his seat. 'I thought bank managers were all stuffy beggars, but Mr John's not like that. He was very helpful.'

'Hey,' Jack McGurk laughed, 'we should send you out on your own more often. Yesterday you had that fucking weasel Ken Green eating out of your hand, and today you've got a banker being nice to you. When you say he was helpful, does that mean he told you the time for free?'

'He told me a damn sight more than that.' He glanced at Stallings. 'Boss, if you were hoping that Zaliukas had money worries we didn't know about, you can forget it. The man was both cash-rich and asset-rich: minted, end of story.' He paused. 'Mr John liked him, too; he didn't say so straight out, but he told me some stories about him that made me think they'd got on. He was wary of him, though.'

'In what way?' the DI asked.

Haddock frowned, searching for the words to explain himself. 'The feeling I have,' he began, 'is that Zaliukas was regarded by a lot of people as someone who'd been a seriously wide guy in his youth, but who'd managed to leave all that behind and reinvent himself as a successful, respectable law-abiding businessman, and that when he bought those eight massage parlours, it was no more than a good property deal. Am I right?'

Stallings nodded. 'I never met the man, but yes, that's the picture that I've formed from what the bosses have said about him.'

'Well, from what Mr John told me, I have a feeling that he didn't change as much as they thought. Everything I've heard, from what Alex Skinner said about Willie Conn, her predecessor, from Andrew John himself, and even something I didn't hear, just a feeling I picked up from Ken Green, makes me feel that the people who actually knew him, and worked with him, still regarded him as a man who shouldn't be messed with.'

'Are you saying that he was involved in organised crime all along?'

'No, I'm not saying that. But we do know that he once ran a gang of Lithuanian hard men, and that he placed a lot of those guys in the legitimate businesses that he acquired or built up over the years.'

'Apart from Indigo,' McGurk cautioned. 'As I understand it, his wife ran that place from the start.'

'She's been gone for a week or so,' Haddock pointed out. 'I wonder who's been running it since she left.'

'Dunno. Valdas Gerulaitis maybe?'

'No danger. Tomas didn't trust him. According to Mr John, Valdas once asked if he could have that job, but his cousin told him that he was too valuable at the centre of the business. The truth was he kept him there so that he could keep an eye on him. I reckon he kept an eye on everything. I reckon that his leisure company is as profitable as you've probably found out by now that it is, Jack, from those annual accounts that are lying on your desk, because there was virtually none of the pilfering that's endemic in that industry. Why? Because Zaliukas could spot it whenever and wherever it happened and anyone he caught wound up in the Royal.'

'I suppose you can prove that,' the DS challenged.

'I'm told that I can, if I want to, just by trawling the admissions record.'

'This from your friendly banker?' asked McGurk. Haddock was silent. 'So what did you give him in return?'

The detective constable's face reddened. 'Nothing on purpose,' he replied. 'I let slip that Valdas isn't going to inherit any of the Lietuvos businesses, that Mrs Zaliukas and the kids are.'

'Oh shit!' McGurk whispered.

'I'm sorry, Jack,' said the young man. 'It was an accident; and Mr John can be trusted. No harm will come of it.'

'That's not what I meant, Sauce. If Gerulaitis is bent, will Regine be at risk when he finds that out? That's what I'm wondering.'

'I doubt it; he wouldn't have been expecting them to come to him. But it could explain why Tomas left his interest in the massage parlours to his wife, though . . . indirectly, it goes to Valdas. A wee sweetener, maybe; a loyalty bonus.'

'You think you've had a great morning, Sauce, don't you?' Stallings chuckled.

'I wouldn't say that, boss.'

'Just as well, for neither would I. I send you out to find something that will let us consign this investigation to the bin, once and for all, and you come back with an even clearer picture of a man who's rich, successful and completely in control, the unlikeliest of suicides.'

'I don't think he was a suicide,' Haddock told her, bluntly. 'I don't think he killed himself.'

'Aw, Jesus,' McGurk guffawed. 'Sauce, get a grip. I know you're a detective, that's your job, but sometimes you have to admit to yourself that there's fuck all to detect! I've seen what's left of Tomas Zaliukas. So has Neil McIlhenney, so has Mario McGuire and so has Professor Joe Hutchinson, the most eminent forensic pathologist in Scotland. Every one of us believes that Zale blew his own fucking head off. Maybe you and I should go along to the mortuary right now, so that you can take a good look for yourself.'

'Somebody doesn't.' The murmur was so quiet that it failed to carry across the room.

'What?'

'I said that someone doesn't believe it. Why else would our report have been kicked back last night?'

'The chief can be a stickler,' McGurk countered, 'but he hasn't seen the body either.'

'Then maybe we should take him with us next time we go

to the morgue. How about you give him a call and ask him if he wants to come? D'you fancy that, Sarge?'

'I'd do it in a second if I thought it would help get your head out the clouds.'

'Boys, boys, boys, boys, boys!' Becky Stallings called out, as the two glared at each other. 'Sauce,' she said, 'you're entitled to your opinion, but you're outvoted . . . or you would be if this was a democracy. It's not, and that's why we're still chasing this fucking rabbit. Jack, I agree with you. From everything I've heard, any fiscal would sign this off as self-inflicted. But all we can do right now is follow current orders, continue to investigate, and complete as full a background report on the victim as we can pull together. When we re-submit it, as we will when I decide we should, it'll offer no conclusions. It'll say that all lines of inquiry have been exhausted, and let Him Upstairs make of that what he will. Agreed?' She stopped abruptly. 'What the hell am I saying? Yes it's agreed, because it's what I say will happen.' She looked at McGurk. 'Jack, have you finished going through those accounts?'

'Yes, and they're like Sauce said: the companies, Leisure and Developments, are both rock solid. The auditors' reports are glowing.'

'And there's no link to the massage parlour business?'

'None that I can see.'

'I know where the purchase money came from,' Haddock offered. 'Zaliukas took a dividend; all above board. I had a call from Mr John while I was on my way back here confirming the amount: a quarter of a million.'

'Thanks for that,' said the DS. 'There is something

interesting about that side of our man's life, though. I've been checking with the city council's licensing people. It seems that the purchase from the Manson estate was just the start; since then Lituania SAFI's been expanding its holdings, buying up similar premises, then leasing them to individuals who take over the licences. There are fifteen of these places in the city. Guess how many Zaliukas's company owns now, Becky?'

'Tell me.'

'Twelve, all leased to people with Lithuanian names. They read like a fucking football team. The company seems to have been working towards a monopoly. I've spoken to the owners of the other three, the ones it doesn't have. They've all had approaches within the last six months from the same bloke.'

'Who?'

'Ken Green.'

'These approaches; were they proper?'

'From what I've been told, yes. All he asked was if they'd be interested in selling. Incidentally, all three owners were at pains to tell me that they do not provide additional services, so to speak.'

'Did you believe that?'

'Sure. It would be too easy for us to check, so why should they lie? The media assume that all private massage parlours are brothels, but it's not true. There are people who only want their backs rubbed.'

'Mmm,' Stallings mused. 'Maybe the theory about Zaliukas wanting to change the places he bought wasn't true after all.'

'No maybe about it, surely? If he'd ever intended to legitimise the businesses, he'd have bought them through

Lietuvos Leisure, would he not? Anyway, back to these three; one of them was fairly recent, so there's been no follow-up, but in the other two cases, each owner had a visit a few weeks after from another man. No threats were made; it was all friendly. Chunky offers were made for the businesses, and they were told they'd stay on the table till they were ready to accept.'

'Who made these offers? Who was the friendly visitor? Do we know? Was it Zaliukas?'

'No. It was Valdas.'

'Was it, by God,' the inspector hissed.

'He'd only have been doing that with Zaliukas's approval,' Haddock declared.

'Maybe yes, maybe no,' said McGurk. 'But we do know for sure that he lied to us about his involvement. We also know, Sauce, that your pal Ken Green only volunteered as much as you knew already. They both need follow-up visits, but we'll do it together this time.'

'Do that,' Stallings agreed, 'but first, check out some of these places. It seems that we've got an ethnic group operating under a very clever and well put together front. The head's been cut off; let's see if we can find out how the body's reacted.'

Twenty-five

'Alex,' Veronica Drake exclaimed, 'I have other clients, of whom two are in extreme personal difficulty at the moment and requiring my attention. They're where my priorities lie. I'm sorry for Regine Zaliukas and her kids, but I've never met the woman. If she chooses to go away for a few days, she's not going to tell me about it, and if she goes to a place with a lousy mobile signal, or leaves her phone switched off, that's her problem, not mine.'

'Fine,' Alex shot back, 'that's your perspective. Mine is that I've got two companies whose owner and chief executive has just died without leaving any guidance as to who should succeed him. In total, the businesses have a full-time payroll of eighty-four employees, let alone the casual bar staff, and I don't have a mandate to run them myself.'

'What about the other directors?'

'There is only one other director, Ronnie, and that's Regine Zaliukas. You might not feel it's urgent that she knows about her husband's death, but I bloody well do.'

Drake shrugged her padded shoulders. 'OK, if you're telling me that it's a corporate matter, over to you. You find the woman.' She took a slim folder from her desk and handed it over. 'Those are her papers, with all her details, including her contact number. If you get stuck I'm sure your father could make a couple of calls for you. I wish I had that luxury.'

Resisting the urge to wrap the documents around her partner's ears, Alex took them from her and stalked back to her own tiny office. 'Bitch!' she hissed as she slid behind her desk. She opened the file and flicked through the few documents that it held; photocopies of Regine's birth and marriage certificates and of her French passport, a letter from a French bank in a place called Nérac, confirming the details of a euro account in her name.

The note of her mobile number was the last in the file. It made Alex wonder how hard her partner had tried to contact the woman, but she put the question to one side to be raised later, if necessary.

She picked up the paper and keyed in the eleven digits, then waited. The tone, when it sounded, was European, a long, single beep, confirming her assumption that Regine Zaliukas was not in the United Kingdom, and indicating, encouragingly, that her mobile was switched on. It rang several times, then just as she expected to be picked up by voicemail . . .

- 'Hello?' English, but in a French accent.

How did she know I was calling from Britain, Alex wondered, since CAJ's number is always hidden?

'Mrs Zaliukas?'

'Yes, this is Regine.' She sounded fluent; her accent was not noticeably Scottish.

'My name is Alex Skinner. I'm a partner in Curle Anthony

144

and Jarvis, and I've just taken over responsibility for the Lietuvos companies from Mr Conn, who's retired.'

'My husband told me this was happening,' the woman replied, coolly. 'You're the chief constable's daughter, aren't you? Tomas laughed when he told me that. He said if anything would make Edinburgh people regard him as respectable, that would. I told him that maybe you wouldn't want to work for him.'

'Any client acceptable to Mr Conn will be acceptable to me,' Alex told her. 'Mrs Zaliukas, where are you? We've been trying to reach you since yesterday, but only getting your voicemail.'

For the first time, she detected a degree of anxiety, in that Regine Zaliukas hesitated. 'At this moment,' she began, eventually, 'I am sitting in my car, in the car park of E. LeClerc, a French supermarket. The children and I have been away for a few days.'

'Where are you staying?'

'We are in my parents' house; one hundred and five Rue St Cauzimis, Mezin, in Lot et Garonne.'

'Are your kids with you right now?'

'No.' The woman paused. 'They're being looked after. Listen, why are you asking me this?'

Alex took the plunge. 'Mrs Zaliukas, I'm afraid I have some dreadful news. Your husband was found dead yesterday morning, in Edinburgh.'

A great gasp of breath sounded clearly down the line, followed by a long period of silence. 'Dead?' she said at last, in a quavering voice. 'Tomas? Dead? How?'

'The police believe that he took his own life. He was shot.'

'He . . . They . . . They think that, the police?'

'Not just them. They've already done a post-mortem and that's what the pathologist says too. Mrs Zaliukas, Regine, I'm sorry to have to break it like this, but our view was that it was better for you to hear from us, your lawyers, than to have men in uniform turning up at your door, possibly when your children were there.'

'Yes.' The voice was whisper quiet, but more controlled. 'I appreciate that, thank you.'

'The police in Edinburgh would like to interview you, about your husband's state of mind. I've told them that you might prefer to communicate with them through us.'

'Yes, I would prefer that. But I can tell you now, that when last I spoke to Tomas, let me see, it would be on Sunday, he was fine.'

'You were estranged, though?'

'Whoever told you that?' she exclaimed. 'No, I decided to bring the children over here for a few days, that was all. When both of them are higher up the school it will not be so easy. I was almost ready to go back.' Pause. 'Not now, though. I believe I will stay here for a little longer. This is a huge shock; my family is in France. I need its support.'

'I understand that but, Mrs Zaliukas, there is the question of your husband's companies. They now belong entirely to you and your children. Someone has to run them. If you don't want to do it, you need to appoint a chief executive. Since Mr Gerulaitis is already there . . .'

'No, no. Not Valdas, not him; not for one second. You, Miss Skinner, could you do it?'

'I couldn't be a director,' Alex told her. 'I'm not allowed to. But I could administer the business on a temporary basis, on your behalf, with your authority.'

'Then I'll give you that authority right now.'

'It has to be written.'

'There will be a letter in the post this afternoon, or better, faxed to your office. I can do that, can't I?'

'Yes, you're already a director of both companies. But are you sure? You've never met me.'

'If you are a partner in that firm, you must be up to the job. And I share Tomas's view. Who better to represent my interests than the chief constable's daughter?'

Twenty-six

'How quickly can you get an interpreter?' Wilding and Montell heard Cowan ask as they came back into the CID office. 'OK,' she said, firmly, a few seconds later, 'do it. The force will pick up the tab.'

The DS frowned. 'Was that our money you were spending, Alice?'

'Don't worry,' she assured him. 'The DI wouldn't have any problems with it if he was here. While you two gourmets were at the sandwich shop, I had a call from the Royal. Our girl's started to respond. Her name's Anna, and she's hungry; that's all they've got from her so far, but one of the nurses there is Polish, and she says that she's speaking Russian. When they ask her questions in English, all they get are blank looks, and they say she's still way too wandered to be putting it on.'

'Who were you speaking to just now? The Polish nurse?'

'No, one of the administrators. They have non-English speakers admitted quite often, so it's something they have to deal with. They have a list of people they can call on at short notice. They guy I spoke to says he can get a Russian translator from the university; she should be there by the time we are.'

'Shouldn't we go to that massage parlour place first?' Montell suggested.

'Why would we do that? We were going there to question the manager about the girl. Now we can question her about him . . . if that's where she came from.'

'True,' Wilding agreed. 'How about I go along for a look at this massage parlour place?'

Cowan glared at him. 'If it turns out that our girl has been held there, I want to be the one that kicks the door in, waving a search warrant. If you pull rank on this, Ray, I will be in a very serious huff.'

He chuckled. 'Anything but that! OK, you two head off to the Royal. See if you get any sense out of this lass; that's the first priority, right enough.'

'Can we take ten to eat our sandwiches?' Montell asked. He delved into a large paper bag that he was carrying and handed a film-wrapped baguette to Cowan. 'Corned beef and pickle,' he told her. 'That OK? They didn't have any pastrami left.'

'That'll do, I suppose.' She grinned at him. 'First thing you've got right today.'

Twenty-seven

'You know, son,' Ken Green drawled, frowning at Haddock across his desk, 'I was being nice to you yesterday when I agreed to see you, but I have a busy practice, and limited free time, so this is pushing it.'

'Your cooperation is appreciated, sir,' said Jack McGurk. 'That said, there are times in this job when I feel like a dentist.'

'Oh aye? Why's that?'

'It's because getting information from so-called cooperative people can be like drawing teeth. You'd have been much nicer to my colleague yesterday if you'd told him everything about your client's involvement in the massage parlour business.'

'The boy asked me questions . . .'

Haddock leaned forward. 'Excuse me, sir,' he began, 'but am I right in thinking that it's best for someone in your profession to have decent relations with the police?'

'Yes, you probably are.'

A look came into the DC's eyes, a look that neither of the two men in the room had ever seen before. 'In that case, sir,' he went on, his tone low and even, 'you should be aware of this. The next time you call me "son", or "the boy", you'll be making an enemy for life. If that doesn't seem like much of a threat to you, think on this; all things being equal, in twenty years' time you'll still be in the lawyering game, doing pretty much what you do now. And I'll still be a police officer, still lifting your clients. But chances are I'll be a bit further up the ladder. Maybe I'll be a DS, like my colleague here, or maybe we'll both be a notch or two higher. But even if I'm not, even if I'm still a humble detective constable, I will make it my business to shit on you at every opportunity. Can we be clear about that?'

Green glared at him, but Haddock held his gaze, unblinking, until the solicitor looked away. 'That can cut both ways,' he growled. 'Wait till the day I get you in the witness box.'

'I'm sure there will be a few of those. I repeat. Are we clear?'

'We're clear.' The reply was almost a snarl.

'Good.' The DC glanced at his sergeant. 'Sorry, Jack, I had to get that off my chest.'

'You beat me to it by about half a second, Sauce. Now, Mr Green, to business and to what you failed to volunteer to us yesterday. Since you helped Mr Zaliukas set up his offshore company, and buy the former Manson premises, he's continued to make acquisitions in that sector. Four more, in fact. Were you involved in those transactions?'

The lawyer sighed. 'I was. My client instructed me to make formal offers to the owners of the premises in each case.'

'We know where Tommy got the money for the first buys, but where did the cash for these come from?'

'From the operating profits of the first eight businesses.'

'With bank support?'

'No; they were all straight cash buys.'

'The sales went ahead, so we know that deals were done, but were all your offers accepted immediately?'

'One was accepted on the spot, one a little later. There was negotiation on the other two, but terms were agreed.'

'And was that negotiation carried out by you, or was a third party involved, possibly a man called Valdas Gerulaitis, Zaliukas's cousin?'

'I've got no knowledge of that. All I know is that in each case I was contacted by the seller, who said that he was now willing to deal.'

'Were you aware that one of these places, in Polwarth, caught fire, and another, in Lauriston, was flooded out, not long before the sales happened?'

'Of course not.'

McGurk smiled. 'Neither were we, to be honest, until I asked a few questions of my colleagues in fire and rescue earlier on today. Did you know that another initially reluctant seller, a guy called Kenny Bass, was the victim of a hit and run accident not long before you and he came to terms?'

'I've no knowledge of any of that stuff. Look,' he protested, 'Tomas ran his pubs and clubs like clockwork, but as far as I know he kept his hands well off the other places.'

'What do you know about Gerulaitis?'

'Nothing!' He hesitated. 'Well, I know he was Tomas's cousin, and I know that when Tomas went to Uruguay to set up the company, he took him with him for . . . well, for company.'

'Were you there too?' Haddock asked.

'No. That wasn't necessary; I made all the arrangements through an agent.'

'Since yesterday, have you had any instructions about the running of these businesses?'

Green shrugged. 'Who's to give me instructions? Regine, I suppose, but that's hardly going to be at the top of her to-do list right now.'

'Not necessarily Mrs Zaliukas,' said McGurk.

The lawyer's eyes narrowed. 'What do you mean by that?' he challenged. 'Who else would Tomas have left his piece of the company to?'

'I'm not free to tell you that, but I do know that it isn't her, or their children. All I will say is that while you might have been able to maintain your innocence before, you might find it more difficult from now on.'

Twenty-eight

'I preferred the old Royal,' Alice Cowan volunteered, as she tucked the parking slip into her pocket.

'Before my time in Edinburgh,' Montell reminded her. 'What sort of a building was it?'

'You mean "is"; it's still there. It's being redeveloped. Victorian. Ancient. Something like Gormenghast, if you know your Mervyn Peake. It was a shambles of a place, a nightmare to get about, with its own resident cockroach population that they could never quite eradicate, big old-fashioned wards with little or no privacy, just about everything a hospital shouldn't be . . . and yet people loved it, and they associated with it in a way they never will with this new place.'

'Parking must have been a nightmare.'

'Not as bad as you'd think, and not as expensive as it is here either.'

'Claim it on expenses.'

She gave him one of her rare, warm smiles; sometimes he thought they were rationed to a set number per day, or even per week. As he looked at her, he found himself wondering whether she smiled in bed, and resolved to find out. 'Too damn right,' she said, knocking him off his guard for a second.

'Where is the girl?' he asked, snapping himself back to the professional present.

'Ward two zero seven. General medicine, second floor.'

'You seem to know your way around.'

'A cousin of mine was in here last year, in the same ward.' Alice led the way into the building, and straight in until they came to the main stairway. 'Over there,' she said, when they reached the second level.

'Where do we find her?' Montell muttered.

'Dunno.' She paused then pointed towards a young woman PC, in uniform, who stood at the entrance to the ward. 'But she might give us a clue. Hiya, Kylie,' she greeted her, as they approached.

The girl looked round, startled. 'Alice,' she exclaimed. 'Are you here for the kid?'

Cowan nodded, then glanced sideways at her companion. 'Yes. Do you know Griff Montell? Griff, PC Kylie Knight.'

'How do,' she said, as she shook hands with the burly South African, thinking, no, but I'd like to. 'I'm glad to see the pair of you. I'm bored out my scone just standing here. Waste of time, too. The lassie isn't going anywhere. She's just glad they're feeding her. Has she been charged with anything?'

'No.'

'What? Not even possession? Then what the . . .' pause, '. . . am I doing here?'

'We think she's a victim of a sex crime. The story we have is that she was found in the street. We thought she might have escaped from somewhere. You were here in case somebody came after her.'

'Well, nobody did,' Knight replied, still a little reproachful. 'Can I go, now the CID posse's arrived?'

'Humour us, Kylie,' said Montell. 'Look after our horses while we interview her, then we'll know if we still need cover here. Where is she, anyway?'

Knight half-turned, indicating a door behind her. 'She's in that side room. The interpreter arrived about five minutes ago; she's in the nurses' station with the charge nurse. Ah,' pause, 'she's seen you.'

The detectives looked into the ward, to see a male, blue-clad nurse approaching, followed by a small woman, in a dark trouser suit. 'I'm Russell Cairns,' the man announced, 'and this is Mrs McStay, from university.'

'Lyudmila McStay,' the interpreter added, in explanation. 'I acquired the surname ten years ago.'

'DCs Cowan and Montell,' the former replied. 'We were called yesterday when our girl was brought into the surgery. How is she now?' she asked Cairns.

'She's OK for you to talk to. We want to keep her for at least another day, though, to let the drug clear her system. We've identified it as GHB, for sure.'

'So have we,' Montell told him. 'Our lab's also working on other samples.'

Cairns winced. 'I won't ask. We've also tested for the whole range of sexually transmitted diseases, including HIV; happily she's come up clear, so far, but it'll take weeks for us to be absolutely certain. Come on, let's look in on her.' He led the way past PC Knight and into the small side room. The window looked south, letting the weak afternoon sunshine brighten the scene. The girl the detectives had last seen the day before lay on the only bed in the ward, propped up on cushions with an empty plate on her lap, a bag of sugar sweets on her side table, and a can of Irn Bru in her hand. Her hair had been washed and brushed, and some colour had come back to her cheeks, making her look even younger and far prettier than before. She smiled at the nurse as he stepped up to her, but when she looked beyond him, at Cowan and Montell, it was without the faintest flicker of recognition.

Mrs McStay went to the foot of the bed. 'We've already had a chat,' she told the officers, 'but only to establish that her name is Anna Romanova, and that she's fifteen years old.'

'Fifteen?' Cowan hissed.

'That's what she told me, and I don't doubt it.'

'Does she know why we're here?'

'No, and it's pretty obvious she doesn't even know who you are.'

'Then tell her please.'

They listened as the interpreter spoke to her, in her own language. Halfway through, a frown appeared on her face, and by the time she was finished it had turned to a look of pure fear, reflected by the tone of her voice, unmistakable to them, even in an alien tongue.

'She says have you come to send her back?'

'Tell her, if you can,' Montell replied, 'that we've come to look after her. Her best interests are all we're interested in. Ask her where she's from.'

As Mrs McStay explained what he had said, Anna seemed to calm down, but the frown remained. When she replied, a conversation developed, and continued for some time.

'I've made her understand,' the translator told them when it was over, 'that you two are on her side, that you're not going to put her in prison. I've anticipated some of your questions, and established a little more. Anna is Russian, but only ethnically. She says that she is from Estonia . . . that's quite believable; a quarter of the population are of Russian descent . . . that she was born there, and so were her parents. They were killed in a train accident when she was eight; there was nobody to look after her, other than her grandmother, her father's mother, who was too old to take her on, so she wound up in an orphanage called St Olaf's, run by the Russian Orthodox church . . . although from what she says, it wasn't very Christian in its practices. She also speaks Estonian, by the way, but it's been very much her second language all her life.'

'That's all good,' Cowan declared. 'We can check that out. Estonia's in the European Union; it means she isn't an illegal. She can be taken into care here, and maybe even fostered, if she doesn't want to go back to her orphanage.'

'Stay objective, Alice,' Montell murmured. 'There's other issues here. Ask her how she got here, Mrs McStay.'

The woman sat on the bed beside Anna and took her hand as she spoke, and as she listened to what the girl had to say. When she was finished she looked up at the officers. 'She says that she and her friends Ivana and Nadia, two other girls from the orphanage, one her own age, the other a year younger, were approached in the street in Tallin by a man. She says that he was friendly; he bought them ice cream, and asked them where they were from. They told him, and then he asked them if they were happy there. When all three said that they were not, he asked them if they would like to go on an adventure with him. He said that his business was to find girls to work in big houses in Britain, for wages beyond their dreams and for a life like a movie star. Naturally enough, the girls all said yes. Why would they not, poor little things, after years of being treated like Cinderellas by bloody awful nuns. So they met the man next day in the same place; he collected them in a big van, Anna says, with no windows but with lots of seats, for it wasn't just them, there were six others, ethnic Estonian girls.'

'Orphans too?'

'I don't think so; she said they were a year or two older than her and her friends and they were . . . these aren't the words she used, but it's what she meant . . . more worldly.'

'When did this happen?' Cowan asked.

'At the end of October, so she's been here for about three months.'

'And where did they go?'

'She doesn't know. All she knows is that they drove for a long time, until they came, as she says, to a place where they could hear lots of seagulls. There, all nine girls were put into what she described as a big shed.'

'A big shed,' Montell repeated. 'Could that have been a freight container?'

Mrs McStay nodded agreement. 'I think it must have been. The man told them,' she went on, 'that the next part had to be secret, and that they had to stay there. He said that it wouldn't be long; gave them plenty of food and water, and lamps that worked on batteries, then they were closed in. There was noise, she says, they were lifted and then driven again; then . . . and this is the way she put it . . . it got bumpy. One of the girls was very sick. From what she told me next, they were only at sea for one night. A couple of the other girls had watches, so they knew what time it was, at least what time it was where they had come from.'

'And when they docked?'

'That's as far as we'd got.'

'Let's pause for a bit,' said Russell Cairns. 'She's getting anxious.' He pointed to the plate on Anna's lap, and she nodded vigorously. 'She's also as hungry as a rugby pack; I'll get her some more sandwiches.'

As they waited, the detectives and the interpreter stood by the window, leaving Anna sipping at her Irn Bru, and smiling occasionally in their direction, as if she was finally beginning to believe that she was safe. 'We need to know everything she can tell us,' Montell murmured to Mrs McStay. 'How she got to Edinburgh, and an idea of how long it took. That might give us a clue to where they were brought in.'

'Yes,' Cowan confirmed, 'and more than that. From what she says we've got eight other kids out there, possibly being subjected to the same sort of abuse she has. We need to trace them too, fast, and we need to find the scumbag who's behind it all. I really want to meet him.'

'Me too,' her colleague growled, as the charge nurse came back into the room.

'Prawn mayonnaise,' he announced. 'That's all we've got left.'

Mrs McStay translated for Anna, who managed to nod, shrug and grin at the same time, making it as clear as if she had spoken that she had no idea what prawns were but did not care, as long as they were edible.

They waited until she was finished, before the interpreter went back to the bed and resumed her questioning. At first the girl answered quickly, and freely, until her face seemed to darken, and her eyes twisted with pain as she spoke, as if that had come back with the memory of what she was describing. Then, suddenly, from out of nowhere, she put her hand to her mouth and giggled.

Lyudmila McStay was grim-faced as she turned back towards the detectives. 'I think she's told me all she has to tell now. They were driven off the ferry, she said; the truck went into a park, and they were let out.'

'To avoid any search by customs, I suppose,' Cowan murmured.

'That's not something she would know, is it? All she says is that they were transferred into another closed van by the man from Tallin and another man, a fat man, and driven again, for three hours, she says, until they stopped. Again, she knows the time from the older girl with the watch.'

'Three hours,' Montell mused. 'What does that tell us?'

'Depends on where they stopped, doesn't it?' Cowan pointed out. 'If it was Edinburgh, then it tells us they landed at Newcastle.'

'And sailed from?'

'Almost certainly Holland; from what she's saying she was on a roll-on, roll-off ferry, a passenger vessel. All the other routes to Newcastle are freight only, where they'd have been lifted off by a crane.'

'How come you know so much?'

Alice winked at him. 'I was in Special Branch, wasn't I?'

'Where did they stop, Mrs McStay?' Montell asked. 'Does she have any idea?'

'Not a clue. But from what she says . . . She told me that when they stopped, and the van was opened, they were in a place beside a wood. She says there were caravans, but they were all empty. Over the tops of the trees they could see a line of huge windmills.'

'Windmills? Soutra, perhaps?'

She thought about it for a few seconds. 'Yes, that's a possibility, I would say. When they got out, there were cars waiting for them, four, with drivers. The man from Tallin . . . that was the last time she saw him . . . told them that these people would take them to the houses where they would be working, that they would be given clothes there and fed. Anna and her two friends from the orphanage all went in the same car, with a man whose name was Linas, a big rough fellow, she says, with his hair cut like a German; I think she means that he had a crew cut. The other two girls were dropped off on the way, and she and this Linas man ended up at a place in the city, near the sea, she said. He took her into a basement flat, by her description, with lots of rooms. It was hot even though it had been cold outside, and there were several women about. One of them gave her new clothes to wear, and she dyed her hair, making it fair from dark. But she didn't stay there. Linas took her upstairs to another house, the flat above, where it was just the two of them. He gave her some food ... pizza, she remembers ... and something to drink that made her feel dizzy. Then he told her to take her clothes off, and ...' Mrs McStay drew in a deep breath, then let it go. Garlic bread for lunch, Montell thought. '... he raped her. The poor little kid,' she whispered to them, as if Anna could have understood her had she heard. 'She didn't know what was happening to her, and I don't think she does yet. She simply talks about him "doing the thing", not just him, but other men who came to the house. She doesn't appear to have been beaten, ever, or threatened, not that she can recall. She was simply kept drugged and used. But she's very vague about it. She says that all her memories of that time are hidden in a mist. I hope it never clears.' She looked at Alice Cowan. 'Is that all?' she asked. 'For I don't think I can take any more of this.'

'How did she get out? It would be useful to know that ... and the name, of course.'

The interpreter took the girl's hand once more, and spoke to her, softly. Her replies seemed to the onlookers to be hesitant, but finally she nodded and was finished.

'All she can remember,' said Mrs McStay, 'is of another man coming to the house, and looking into her bedroom. But this man didn't "do the thing" with her. Instead there was shouting, and noise; these are very confused recollections, you understand. Then she was outside, with the man, she thinks, but isn't sure, although she does remember that it was very cold. After that she was in another house, as she puts it, with more people, kind people and then, finally, she was here. She likes it here, she says.' There was another pause, during which the woman's eyes seemed to mist over. 'She wants to know, though, when is she going to work in the big house, like Uncle V promised.'

'Uncle V?' said Montell.

'That was what the man in Tallin told them to call him. But one of the other girls, one of the older ones, had another name for him. That was why Anna giggled earlier. She called him the Snowman, because his shoulders were covered in white flecks from his hair, covered in dandruff.'

Twenty-nine

'Let me get this straight, kid,' said Bob Skinner slowly, into his mobile. 'You are now running Lietuvos Leisure and Lietuvos Developments. Is that what you've just told me?'

'That's how it is. Regine Zaliukas and her children own both companies now, or will when probate's completed on the will. She's executor of the estate, and as such she has the power to appoint an administrator to run them on its behalf. And she's appointed me. I thought she was kidding at first, but she wasn't.'

'Have you told your boss?'

'Mitchell Laidlaw? Of course I've told him, and I've checked with Ronnie Drake.'

'How did they react?'

Alex laughed. 'Mitch's first reaction was to rub his hands at the thought of all that fee income; then he told me to get on with it, for a couple of weeks, until Regine's had time to come to terms with her husband's death, and consider the future more calmly. Ronnie's seriously pissed off that Regine didn't ask her to take it on. Well, screw her. If she'd shown more enthusiasm about contacting Regine in the first place, she

165

probably would have wound up in the frame. I told her as much too.'

'Christ, Alex, listen to you. A partner for a day and you're making waves.'

'Like hell I am. I'm making a point. Ronnie Drake's a spare wheel in this firm; it's just as well she's not long for it.'

'What do you mean?'

'The private client department's being hived off; in other words, we're getting rid of it. Don't worry,' she added, 'I'm not giving away any secrets. Our press people announced it this morning. The management board has been wanting to do it for a while. Willie Conn was the last of the opponents, and now he's gone . . .'

'Mitch hasn't said a word to me,' Bob grumbled, 'and I'm a private client.'

'He will, though; meantime he asked me to tell you. You'll be getting a letter as well.'

'So I've got to look for a new lawyer?'

'No. A very few key clients are being invited to stay on, and you're one of them. This is office politics, Pops, part of my new world. But enough of it: I'm still waiting for you to tell me that you're pleased for me.'

'About what?'

'About this new appointment,' Alex exclaimed, exasperated.

'I'm not sure that I am. The late owner was a known, if unconvicted, hoodlum. I thought he'd left that behind him, but now I'm not so sure. He died a sudden and violent death, which is under police investigation as we speak, for all that I told you yesterday it was a suicide. Now you want me to be pleased because my daughter's taking control of his businesses?'

'Pops, these companies are absolutely kosher.'

'I don't doubt it. But what about the people who work for them? You know nothing about them at all. This sidekick of his, Gerulaitis. How's he going to take it when you swan in there and tell him that he answers to you from now on?'

'He's going to take it like a gentleman; in about half an hour, give or take a few minutes. I've fixed a meeting with him in his office.'

'And if he doesn't?'

'Then he'd better be checking his contract of employment, for if he refuses to accept me, or to cooperate with me, I'll have no choice but to fire him.'

Bob frowned. 'Listen, love,' he said, quietly, 'I know you've never traded on my name, and that you can get quite spiky when it's brought up, but just this once . . . Since Gerulaitis is Tomas Zaliukas's cousin, you can be sure he'll know all about me. I want you to promise me that you will make certain that this bloke knows exactly who you are, and that he knows your name's no coincidence.'

'Father,' she replied, severely, 'you are being melodramatic. But, since I was put on earth to fill your life with light and joy, I'll do what you ask; just this once.'

'Good. You've made an ageing man happy.' He sighed. 'Now, Regine. She says she's staying in France?'

'Yes, for the moment. There's nothing she can add to your investigation, other than to confirm that her husband seemed perfectly normal last time they spoke. But she also told me that the idea she'd left her husband is all balls. She was taking a short break in France with her kids, that's all. I've left a message to that effect with Sauce Haddock's DI, though she didn't seem overjoyed to get it.'

'Hers not to reason why,' the chief constable murmured. 'There's the small matter of a funeral,' he continued.

'Which can't happen until you lot release the body,' his daughter pointed out.

'As soon as I give the nod to the report to the fiscal, he'll be able to OK it.'

'And when will that be?'

'When I'm convinced there are no worms left down there. Yours enigmatically, Robert Morgan Skinner. Bye, kid.' He snapped his mobile shut, ending the call.

Thirty

Neil McIlhenney's eyebrows almost formed a single dark line as he looked at Ray Wilding. 'Sunshine,' he said, quietly, 'you're quite high up the list for promotion to inspector. That's why I've been happy to leave you in charge here while Sammy does his stint at the police training college. But if I find you've left me out of the loop about anything else, I will become distinctly unhappy.' He took an A4 sheet from his pocket and held it in the air. 'I get a call in my office from a journo who's got my direct number. He asks me how we're getting on with identifying the mystery girl. "What fucking mystery girl?" I say to him, and he directs me to one of our own media releases that I've never fucking heard of, let alone seen. I had to stonewall him, and now I'm having to come down here to sort it out. You know the rules; anything issued by our press office that affects my patch is copied to me by the originator. Alan Royston's already had his balls kicked, and now it's your turn.'

The sergeant folded in the face of the detective superintendent's rare show of anger. 'I'm sorry, boss,' he said. 'There was a push to get it out last night, so I guess I forgot about that. When they issued it this morning, well . . . Sorry,' he repeated.

McIlhenney nodded. 'OK, point made, apology accepted. I know it wasn't your mistake, Ray, that it was one of your troops, but it's your can, and I respect you for not trying to duck out of carrying it. I'll leave you to kick whatever arse requires it. But,' he continued, 'you said you tried to have this issued last night. Why wasn't it?'

'Royston said there was no point, that it was too late.'

'Too late to try to identify a girl whose parents might be sitting at home worrying themselves to death about where she is? Did he really say that?'

'Apparently so. But from what I hear, if her parents are chewing their knuckles anywhere, it's in Russia.'

'Russia?' McIlhenney's frown returned as he considered the implications of the revelation. 'You've been asking around, I take it?'

'Yes. Griff and Alice did a trawl. They even went to see Joanne Virtue.'

'The Big Easy? She's out of that game now, though.' He grinned, fleetingly. 'People used to go to her to get laid; now it's to get laid to rest. She's working in an undertakers.'

'How did you know that?'

'I gave her a reference.'

'Mmm. You'll be getting yourself talked about, sir. Griff told me that when Alice got a bit hoity with her, your name came up. Joanne nailed her to the wall with it.'

The superintendent nodded. 'With my blessing. Joanne knows where some bodies are buried, figuratively speaking, of course. She did us a big favour once, and it will not be forgotten. Could she help?'

'No, not really. Montell and Cowan were going to check one place out, but they got called up to the Royal to see the kid. She's back in the land of the living. They're with her now.'

'I hope she stays there. Let me know how it pans out. Meantime I'm heading back up to Fettes to speak to someone about Mr Royston's sense of urgency.'

Thirty-one

What an unpleasant woman, Alex Skinner thought as she was shown into Valdas Gerulaitis's office. *I can see why her husband's cousin chose to leave her a string of brothels.*

Her husband was much more affable. 'Miss Skinner,' he greeted her. 'Our new lawyer, I'm told. That's a familiar surname around Edinburgh.'

'For the avoidance of doubt,' she said, taking the first opportunity to keep her promise, 'he's my father. It hasn't kept me completely out of trouble, but he is a pretty formidable insurance policy for a single girl to have.'

'I'm sure, from what I've heard of him. My late cousin, Tomas, spoke of him occasionally, with great respect.' He slapped his palms on his desk as they both sat. 'Now, what can I do for you? I can't spare too much time. It's a wee bit daunting to be landed with the job of running two companies.'

'That's what I've come to discuss, Mr Gerulaitis,' she replied. She laid her briefcase on the desk, opened it and took out two documents. 'That,' she said, sliding the first across the desk 'is a notarised copy of Mr Zaliukas's will. There are a couple of matters that concern you indirectly, but I want to draw your attention to the disposition of the two Lietuvos companies. Under its terms, these pass to Mrs Zaliukas and her children; they now own the businesses, one hundred per cent.' She handed him the second document. 'And this is a copy of a faxed letter from Mrs Zaliukas, in her capacity as executor of her late husband's estate, appointing me interim administrator of them both.'

Gerulaitis's eyes widened. As he read, his mouth dropped further and further open, until it gaped. 'Wha . . . what does this mean?' he stammered.

'For you, nothing. You continue in your present position; "financial controller" is your title, I believe. But every decision that affects the companies materially will be taken by me.' Pause. 'I know this is a shock to you, but I'd ask you to respect Mrs Zaliukas's wishes and cooperate with me.'

The man recovered his composure. 'Of course,' he said, quietly. 'I'll have to think about it, though, longer term.'

'Sure, but bear in mind that I only expect to be here in the short term. In due course, Mrs Zaliukas will want to appoint a permanent chief executive. That might be you, it might not; it'll be her choice. In the meantime, I'd be grateful if you could provide me with a set of keys for these premises, and a note of the alarm code, in case I want to drop in when you're not here. Then I'll leave you to read the rest of the will. As I said, there's something else in there that I expect will be of great interest to you.'

Thirty-two

'What'll happen to her, Alice?' Griff Montell asked.

The two detectives had driven in silence since leaving the Royal Infirmary. The South African had exploded with anger as soon as they had stepped out of the building and Cowan had left him to cool off in his own time.

'Something good, I hope,' she replied.

'Sure,' he snapped, bitterly. 'I can see her now being passed around from pillar to post, nobody wanting to take responsibility for her, until eventually she's shipped back to her orphanage in Estonia.'

'No,' said Cowan, firmly, as they drove through Seafield. 'That's not going to happen, because we're not going to let it. She might be a European Union citizen, but she's entered the country illegally, without a passport.'

'Maybe we'll find she has one.'

'Bollocks, a fifteen-year-old orphan with a passport? Don't be daft. That makes her our business, that and the fact that she's a victim of crime. First, obviously, we'll check her story out, with the orphanage in Tallin; it'll stand up, I'm sure. Mrs McStay will be calling there even now to confirm that a girl called Anna Romanova is missing, and to get the full names of the other two. Once we have those details, I'll report the circumstances to the social work department. They'll go to the sheriff and get child protection orders on all three girls.'

'What good will that do?'

'It'll make them what they'd call wards of court in England, and it'll give us instant powers to care for the other two when we find them. With a bit of luck, we'll be able to keep them safe under social work supervision at least until they turn sixteen, and can make their own decisions about their lives.'

Montell scowled. 'They're just kids, Alice. What a mess to be in.'

'I'd never have guessed you were such a softie. You must miss your own, right enough.'

'That's why I never talk about them,' he said, quietly. 'It would make it worse. Alex Skinner has a major down on me because I never told her about them, but that's why.'

'Then explain to her . . . if you're still interested in her, that is.'

'I'm not, in the way you mean, and I never was. Alex was more of a pal than anything else. She and I used to call me her handbag, a useful accessory.'

'Is that how you see me?' Alice asked, steering through the junction at the foot of Constitution Street.

'I'd like to think that we're pals.' Hesitation. 'The truth is that I'm scared off anything more than that. Once bitten, gnawed, savaged . . . several times shy.'

'What happened, Griff, with your wife?'

He stared at the road ahead. 'She left me; walked out with

no warning. I got home from work one night, she was gone, the kids were gone, most of the furniture was gone, and our joint account was cleaned out.'

'Another guy, I take it.'

'Funny thing is, I could probably have taken that. No, Maura left me for another woman. I went a little bit crazy when I found out; after I calmed down I hired a lawyer and petitioned the court for custody of the kids.'

'What are their names?'

'Shaun, he's six, and Daisy, she's four. I argued that it was bad for them to be brought up by a same sex couple. The female judge called me a homophobe and gave Maura permanent custody, with control over my visiting rights. She also awarded maintenance that left me with hardly a fucking rand for myself; I'd to take a second job to survive. So I left. My sister was planning to move to Scotland, so I asked if I could join her. We hadn't been close for years . . . Maura never liked her . . . but she agreed. Spring's a good sort; we get on fine, sharing a place. We give each other our own space. That's important.'

'I'm sure. How did you manage to switch jobs? Was it easy? I've sometimes thought of moving myself.'

'My boss was sympathetic to me, and he helped fix up the transfer to this force, even though I had to drop a rank to get it.'

'You were a DS there?'

'Yeah, the equivalent, and on the up. By now, Ray Wilding's Springbok doppelgänger would have been calling me "sir".'

'Regrets, then.'

'Only over the kids. I like it here, and financially it's better.

Maura's lawyer advised her to go to court here to get an enforceable maintenance order. It blew up in her face, for the Scottish court awarded generous maintenance for the kids, but not a penny to her. Now I can breathe again.'

'You should get a promotion here soon from the sound of it.' Alice glanced sideways at him and smiled. 'I'm sorry I was such a wuss yesterday, with all that "Who's in charge?" crap.'

'Don't be. I'm happy. Besides, you'll probably make sergeant before I do.'

'I don't think so.' She frowned. 'Not after I got kicked out of Special Branch.'

'I never knew that,' Montell exclaimed. 'What happened?'

'Long story,' she replied, 'for another time. But it was my fault.' Pause. 'Life'll work out, Griff. You'll see.'

'Maybe. I'll tell you one thing though, for sure, just between the two of us. I wasn't a homophobe before it happened, but I fucking well am now!'

'I wouldn't share that with too many other people,' Cowan advised. 'Political correctness is everything in this world, and even more so for cops. If we're caught being prejudiced in any way, we are down the fucking toilet.' As she spoke, she took a sharp left turn off Commercial Street. 'Breck Street,' she announced. 'Number seventy-seven. The Softest Touch massage parlour. Can you see a sign?'

Montell nodded. 'Just up there on the right. You can park right in front of it. God,' he cracked his knuckles, 'I'm looking forward to meeting this man Linas.' As he spoke, his eyes narrowed. 'Alice,' he murmured, as she drew to a halt at their destination, 'what the hell are those two doing here?'

His partner followed the direction of his glance, and saw, heading in their direction, a lean, towering figure alongside a younger, smaller, but still tall individual with reddish hair.

'Jack?' the South African began as he stepped out of the car.

McGurk and Haddock stopped in their tracks. 'Where are you going?' the sergeant asked.

'Right here, the massage parlour.'

'Same here. What are you after?'

'A Lithuania arsehole called Linas something or other. We want him for rape, sex with a minor, false imprisonment, people trafficking and, with any luck, resisting arrest. Did you hear about the girl we found yesterday?'

'I heard something about it this morning on the radio,' Haddock replied. 'Unidentified, possibly east European, yes?'

'That's right. We've identified her now, and we've heard her story.'

'And you really think this guy will still be hanging around if he's behind what happened to her?' said McGurk.

Montell's eyes gleamed. 'We can only hope.'

'I doubt it. We're here because we've been checking on all the massage parlours owned by a guy called Tomas Zaliukas. He shot himself yesterday morning, on top of Arthur's Seat.'

'I read about that in this morning's *Saltire*,' Cowan volunteered. 'That was him? The guy who owned Indigo, and a lot of other places?'

'Including twelve of these knocking shops. Your girl, Griff. She's been trafficked, you said?'

'Trafficked, drugged, used and abused. That's her story and we believe it. According to the charge nurse in her ward she only knows two English words, "fuck" and "pizza". We believe that she's one of a consignment of nine girls, brought over from Estonia about three months ago. What have you found in the other places?'

'That's the strange thing. We've found "closed till further notice" signs on all of them. We asked some of the neighbours. As near as we can find out, they were all working as usual till yesterday morning.'

'Anna . . . that's our kid . . . was taken into a surgery near here yesterday afternoon,' said Cowan.

'After Zaliukas shot himself,' Haddock murmured. 'I wonder if someone guessed we'd be looking into his affairs and, knowing there were trafficked girls in some of them, decided to get them out of sight.'

'That's a reasonable theory, Sauce,' his sergeant agreed. 'And I've got a fair idea who that might have been. One Valdas Gerulaitis.'

Montell's brow furrowed. 'Valdas? Describe him, Jack.'

'Lithuanian, tallish, lean, dark hair, greying and receding, well dressed, bookkeeper by profession but crook by nature. Married to a horrible wee dragon of a woman who's just inherited a half share in these bloody places.'

'Anything else?'

McGurk considered the question for a few seconds. 'Yeah,' he said, 'one other thing, now you force me to recall it. Major dandruff problem.'

'The Snowman,' Cowan exclaimed. 'That was what the girls called the guy who kidnapped them for that very reason. And he told them to call him Uncle V.'

'Oh my,' Haddock chuckled. 'Has he got some talking to do.'

'Sure, but there's one anomaly,' Montell pointed out. 'The guy who took Anna into the surgery didn't look a bit like your Snowman, or like we're told Linas looks, but from what she said, he actually took her out of the place where she was kept.'

'The massage parlour,' said McGurk.

'No. She says that she was in a house above it. Since this is a tenement building, we take that to mean a flat.'

'Well, let's check the lot out and worry about who's who afterwards. If this Linas lived above the store, you never know, he might still be there.' Pause. 'I suppose I should call for uniform back-up.'

Although Montell was the junior officer, there was a sense, even if unspoken, that he had taken command of the situation. He shook his head. 'No, Jack,' he murmured. 'If he is there, that would just spook him. Besides,' he added, 'this bastard is mine, all mine.'

Thirty-three

'We don't like to drop the guy in it, Chief,' Mario McGuire insisted, 'but I agree with Neil. We may have lost hours in this investigation because Alan Royston took the easy way out last night. If he'd done what he was asked by Alice Cowan when she asked him we'd have got some media exposure, on air and online, straight away.'

'So deal with it,' said Skinner.

The head of CID was taken aback by Skinner's reluctance; his dark eyebrows twitched slightly. 'If he was police staff, I would have. But he's not, he's a civilian and as such he's not subject to my discipline.'

'Exactly. He's a specialist, an adviser.'

'And in this case his advice has been crap.'

'But still, that's what he is; he doesn't have the executive power to override the wishes of any police officer. Cowan could have insisted on the release going out last night, but she didn't.'

'She's a DC, boss. Even if she knew she could have called his bluff, she'd have thought twice about doing it.'

'In which case she should have gone to Sammy Pye . . . OK, he's on a course . . . to Ray Wilding. It's down to her.'

McGuire shook his head. 'With respect, sir . . .' he began.

The chief constable laughed. 'With respect,' he repeated. 'The polite way of telling a senior officer that he's talking bollocks. Go on, chum, spit it out.'

'OK, Alice is a good soldier, as you well know. But she got herself in a hole in Special Branch a wee while ago, and I for one will forgive her reluctance to take the chance of digging another one. If she'd leaned on Royston, he'd taken umbrage and come to me, and I'd taken his side . . . No, it's my view that at best the man's judgement was off the mark; at worst, his staff had all gone home for the evening and he just couldn't be arsed staying on to issue Alice's release himself. Either way, it's my view that he should be chinned about it. If you tell me to do the chinning myself, I will, but . . .'

Skinner raised a hand, as if in surrender. 'Yes, I get the drift. That would leave him open to be on any line manager's carpet when there was a disagreement, but his contract says that he reports to me or my deputy.' He paused, considering. 'I could give this to Brian Mackie to deal with, but I won't. It's down to me.' He looked the head of CID in the eye. 'You know why I'm reluctant, Mario, don't you?'

'I think so, but I'm not going to say it, in case I'm wrong.'

''Ckin' hell, you're turning into a diplomat. OK, a few years ago, there were professional issues between me and Royston, when I was deputy chief. I thought about bulleting him then, but there were personal issues between us as well, so I backed off, in case my motives were called into question. After that, any judgement calls involving him I always passed upstairs to Sir James Proud. But I'm in his chair now, so I don't have that option. I'll deal with it; I'll call him in right now in fact.'

'Thanks, boss. It's not as if it's a sacking offence . . .'

'Hell, no, not even an official warning, just a slightly awkward conversation, that's all. As it happens, I need to talk to him about something else, an interesting idea that Maggie's had and passed on to me.'

'My breath is bated,' McGuire chuckled. 'I'll clear off, then. By the way,' he asked as he stood, 'how is the old chief doing? Have you heard from him lately?'

Skinner nodded. 'I sure have. He's bought a house in Gullane, less than a mile away from mine. He's even talking about taking up golf. He tells me that the Marquis of Kinture has offered him honorary membership at Witches' Hill. The two of them sit on a company board together.'

'Maybe somebody will offer him cheap golf clubs, if he hangs around the right pub.'

'I don't see Jimmy Proud hanging around any pubs, although when he moves out our way, I may introduce him to a couple. Speaking of Witches' Hill, are we set to go on that operation Maggie cleared with me?'

'Sure. You never know, we might even get a result.'

Skinner frowned. 'It's not often I get pessimistic, Mario,' he said, 'but these are well-organised bastards. We'll do well to keep pace with them, far less be one step ahead.'

Thirty-four

'The sign is just the same as the other six we've been to so far,' said Sauce Haddock, peering at the door of the Softest Touch massage parlour. He put his finger on a brass button on its facing and held it there. The buzz inside was loud enough for the four detectives to hear it clearly, but there was nothing else, no sound of movement, no sign of light through the frosted glass panels.

'There could be somebody hiding inside, though,' Alice Cowan suggested.

'There could,' Jack McGurk agreed, 'but since your girl Anna told you that she wasn't held here, I don't see us having grounds to force an entry.'

'On the other hand,' Griff Montell growled. Next to the massage parlour, there was a heavy green-painted entrance door, with six tenants' names and doorbells displayed at the side, above a speaker. 'Flat 1a,' he read. 'L. Jankauskas.' He chose flat 3b and pressed its button. When no reply came after half a minute he went to the next. His third choice, flat 2a, F. Bryan, was the lucky one. 'Izzat you, Benny?' a young male voice asked.

'No,' said McGurk, heavily, 'it's the polis; we need in, but not for you. Open the door then stay in your flat.'

F. Bryan thought for all of two seconds; there was a tone from the speaker, and the door swung open at Montell's touch. He led the way up to the first floor of the four-storey block, where he saw two doors, facing each other, number 1a on the right.

'Will we knock?' asked Cowan.

'Allow me,' said McGurk. 'I'm good at knocking.' He raised his right foot and slammed the sole of his heavy shoe directly on to the Yale lock. The frame splintered, and the door swung open.

Again Montell headed the charge, silently, with no warning shouts, into a narrow hallway, with four doors off. Each one was open, but nobody emerged to greet them. There were two bedrooms to the right. Both empty, the South African saw as he looked in; the bed in the first was made up, but in the other it was dishevelled, its sheet crumpled and filthy, and a duvet was tossed on the floor.

The house was rank. He sniffed; it stank of sweat, of stale food, and of something else.

'Griff.' Sauce Haddock's voice was quiet, but his tone was laden as he stood in the doorway to the left.

Automatically, Cowan and McGurk stood aside to let him through. He reached the young DC and followed his gaze. In the centre of the main living area, a man lay on his back. He wore a grey thermal vest and jeans, and the ridged soles of his Timberland boots faced them. He had a close-cropped crew cut; his head was shaved at the sides, and his neck lay at an angle that told the whole story of what had happened to him. 'German hair,' Montell murmured, remembering Anna's translated description.

Linas Jankauskas's eyes were wide open, staring upwards, not at the police officers, as they stood around him, but at the ceiling. Not that he saw it, though; Alice Cowan reckoned that it had been a few hours more than a full day since he had seen anything at all.

'Who did this?' Haddock whispered as Montell knelt beside the body.

'Desperate Dan,' Cowan replied.

'Eh?'

'The so-called van driver, who took Anna into the surgery for medical care. That's how the receptionist described him.'

'Then she was spot on,' McGurk murmured, as he contemplated the victim. 'This Linas was a powerful-looking guy. There isn't a mark on his face, but his neck's broken. Whoever did this to him must be the strongest fucking cowboy in the world.'

'We'd better call Ray,' said Montell as he stood.

'Why Ray?'

'It's our division, Jack.'

'Maybe so,' the sergeant agreed, 'but we've got an interest in this too. This death links directly into an investigation we have under way. You call Ray Wilding, fine, and I'll call Becky Stallings. They can put their heads together, and when they do, you can bet they wind up running to Neil McIlhenney. But,' he concluded, 'we'll make those calls from outside. We've had eight great big coppers' feet trampling all over this crime scene, so let's tiptoe very carefully out of here before we contaminate it any more. I seriously do not want that grumpy old sod Arthur Dorward getting mad at me.'

Thirty-five

'You wanted to see me, Bob?' The force media manager stood in Skinner's doorway. Behind him, Gerry Crossley, who had been signed off for the day, was putting on his coat. 'Will it take long?' he added. 'I have a meeting this evening, and I'll have to be off soon.'

The chief constable felt his hackles, always sensitive, begin to rise, but he forced them back down and smiled. 'No,' he replied. 'Shouldn't take a minute. Come on in.'

He waited, standing, as the slim, moustached, forty-something Alan Royston took a seat. 'I won't offer you a drink, if you're in a hurry,' he said, as he slid into his own. 'Two things,' he began. 'First, we've got a PC retiring in a couple of weeks, a man called Charlie Johnston. You won't have heard of him, I don't suppose. Charlie's a real time-server, always careful to keep his head below the radar. He and I joined the force in the same month, and he hasn't taken a step forward since. That said, Maggie Steele has got it into her head that he might make a very useful addition to the civilian staff in the press office, once he hands in his warrant card. I'm inclined to agree with her. I know Charlie's strength . . . you'll note I used the singular . . . as well as his weaknesses. So, if he's up for it, and I'm sure he will be, I'd like you to take him on; an initial six-month probationary period, to be safe, but I'm sure you'll find him an asset.'

Royston fidgeted in his chair. 'I'll take your word for it, Bob, if HR are happy.'

Once again, Skinner bridled, but his smile stayed in place. 'I won't be asking Human Resources, Alan,' he chuckled. 'I'll be telling them. We'll keep it within budget by rotating one of your police staff back into the mainstream.'

The media manager shrugged. 'If you say so, fine. Now, if that's all . . .'

The chief held up a hand. 'Two things, I said. That press release you issued this morning, about the unknown girl we were trying to identify.' Royston nodded. 'You'll be glad to hear we've made progress; we know who she is, where she's from, and how she got here. It's an ugly story, and I'm going to crap on the guys responsible from a great height.'

'That's good to know, Bob. Do you want me to issue another release saying that she's been identified?'

'No, because we're still interested in the guy who dumped her at the doctor's. No, my concern is this. I've got some fairly pissed-off CID officers who said that you were asked to issue our public appeal last night but declined to do so, on the grounds that nobody would have used it until this morning.'

The media manager's features tightened. 'That was my judgement,' he said, curtly. 'It was late in the evening, and nobody was dead. The morning papers were pretty much made up by then; they couldn't have used it.'

'Well, I'm afraid I don't agree with it, Alan,' said Skinner. 'I know a guy called Spike Thomson who'd have had it on radio by ten. One phone call by me to June Crampsey at the *Saltire* and she'd have squeezed it in. Another phone call to the *Scotsman* saying that she was carrying it and so would they. Wrap a bit of colour round it and the tabloids would have jumped in too. Sure, we identified the kid anyway, but there's still our mystery man, and we have reason to believe that he may be important.'

Royston glared across the desk. 'Chief Constable, if you're saying that you don't have confidence in my judgement . . . well, I think we both know why.'

Skinner set his forced bonhomie aside. 'Chum,' he said quietly, leaning forward, 'if I had let personal issues get in the way of the job, you'd have been long gone. It was my faith in your judgement that kept you here. You fucked up last night, and you know it. I'm telling you, don't let it happen again.'

'It won't,' the man retorted.

'Good. Enough said.'

'Not quite. It won't happen again because I'm leaving.'

'Aw, for fuck's sake, Alan,' the chief exclaimed, 'don't be so thin-skinned. If everyone I chewed out did that there'd be no bugger left here.'

'It's not that. I've been head-hunted, Bob, offered another position, and I'm minded to accept it. That's what my meeting this evening's about.'

'When did this happen?' asked Skinner, taken aback.

'Earlier this afternoon, so no, it didn't have any bearing on my fuck-up, as you put it. I apologise for that, as I wouldn't like us to part on bad terms.'

'What is this job? Who's offered it?'

Royston shook his head. 'I can't answer either of those questions, Bob, not at this stage. Listen,' he added, 'it's not you that's making me leave. Don't think that for a minute. I just feel stale here, that's all; it's time to go.'

'I see. Is there anything I can say to . . .' Before he could complete the question, his phone rang. He snatched it up. 'Yes!' he barked, before his expression softened almost instantly. 'Neil, what's up?'

Royston watched him as he listened to McIlhenney, as his frown deepened, until his brow was massively furrowed. 'Jesus,' he whispered, eventually. 'Two different threads, tied together. Are you going to the scene?' Pause. 'Then head on down there. Gimme the address and I'll join you.' He snatched up a pen and a pad and scrawled upon it as he listened. 'Got that.' He slammed the phone back in its cradle, then met Royston's gaze. 'That man we were looking for,' he said, 'about the girl: well, we want him even more now.'

Thirty-six

'Becky's on her way, sir,' Ray Wilding told Neil McIlhenney, almost as soon as he had stepped out of his car into the cold Leith evening.

'No, she's not,' the detective superintendent replied. 'I told her to stay away for now. We had four CID officers find the body . . . I assume they're still here.'

'Yes, they're canvassing the neighbours, to see if anybody got sight of this man. DI Dorward and his team are inside.'

'Good, at least they've got something to do. You and I are here, and we're going to be joined by others soon. If Becky had come as well, this would have started to look like a Police Federation picket line.'

'Who else is coming?'

McIlhenney pointed. 'They are,' he said.

The sergeant turned to follow the direction of his finger, and saw the chief constable's black Chrysler ease to a halt on the other side of the street. As Skinner climbed out, so did Mario McGuire from the passenger side.

'Does this mean that Aileen's stuck at the Parliament building?' McIlhenney asked, as they approached.

The chief shook his head. 'No, it's a two-car day: most of them are. We leave a big carbon footprint, I know.' He nodded briefly to Wilding. 'Hi, Ray, how are you doing? Your people, and Becky's, walked right into this one, didn't they just. From what Neil told me, it must have been like a fucking rugby scrum when the four of them went through that door.'

'I know, sir,' the sergeant admitted, 'but big Montell had just come from interviewing the girl victim at the Royal and his blood was up.'

'It's OK,' Skinner told him. 'I have daughters; I'd have been the same as him in that situation. It's probably just as well for everyone except the victim that he was dead when they got in there. Come on; let's take a look inside, see what we've got.'

He led the way into the tenement's common stairway, and up to the flat. A uniformed constable guarded the doorway; he stood just a little straighter as they approached, then stepped aside to let them pass.

The chief constable stepped into the hallway, but went no further. 'Arthur,' he called out, 'how are you doing in there?'

Moments later, Detective Inspector Dorward's head and shoulders appeared round the doorway from the living area, clad in the usual protective tunic. 'As well as can be expected, sir.' He paused. 'Jesus Christ, how many of you are there?' he moaned. 'I haven't got enough tunics for you all. Look, his bedroom's clear; the one nearest the door. Some of you wait in there, please.'

'How do you know it's his bedroom?' Skinner asked.

'All his stuff's there.'

'I suppose.' He turned to his colleagues. 'You three keep

193

Arthur as happy as possible,' he said. 'I'll take a quick look at the victim.'

As the three stepped out of the hallway, he moved to join the DI. Dorward opened his mouth, but he cut him off before he could speak. 'No, Arthur, I'm not wearing a paper suit. My DNA's on file if I leave any behind.' He took care as he walked into the room, watching where he placed his feet, until he reached the dead man. 'Do you know the full story of what happened here?' he asked.

'Aye, Chief. Montell and Cowan told me; I find myself a lot less sympathetic to this lump of meat than I might otherwise have been.'

Skinner leaned over the body. 'Has the doc been yet?'

'No, sir, but I don't need anybody to tell me he's fucking dead, or even what killed him. The pathologists can declare death, and join all the dots later on. I've got no doubt this was done manually, and I don't see any possibility of an accident.'

'No, me neither. Someone's held him and snapped his neck.'

'More than one person, surely.'

'From what I've been told, no.' Pause. 'You are right, though, insofar as we can't say that for sure until the pathologist gives us an exact time of death.' He straightened up. 'I'll get out of your way, Arthur. You're going to find loads of traces here, especially in that other bedroom. I want you to take special care over that. First and foremost we need to prove that the kid was actually kept here. Once we've done that, any of her abusers we can identify from the DNA database is going to be charged with rape, and with luck we will nail some.

You'll also find stocks of GHB, and who knows, maybe other date rape drugs. These were administered to the girl orally; if you can find a glass or cup with traces and her prints on it, also Jankauskas's, that'll help any prosecutions that might follow.'

'Understood.'

The chief constable retraced his steps and joined McGuire, McIlhenney and Wilding in the dead Lithuanian's bedroom. 'Right,' he said, briskly, 'I don't need to tell you guys that we have got some job on our hands. First we need to find this van driver, or whatever the hell he is. OK, I know we can't rule out the possibility that Jankauskas died after he took the girl . . . what was her name again?'

'Anna,' Wilding volunteered. 'Anna Romanova.'

'. . . Anna, out of here, but the autopsy may do that for us. We also can't assume that he acted alone, but Arthur may be able to tell us one way or the other. But we go for this man, big time, computer-generated image if we can get one, the lot.'

'We should get one, sir,' said the sergeant, explaining Sally Ross's cartoon connection.

'Good. Then find her, now, put her together with one of our programmers and see if she can come up with a likeness.' He frowned. 'But that's not all. From what I've been told, there are eight other trafficked girls in this city, and we have to assume that they've all been forced into the sex trade, as Anna was. We need to find them, and we need to keep our fingers crossed that there aren't even more of them out there. That means I want every one of Tomas Zaliukas's massage parlours opened up, and I want it done within an hour.'

'Does that mean we'll need twelve warrants?' McGuire asked.

'Mario, we don't need any fucking warrants. We now have clear evidence that serious crimes are being committed in these places, and that gives us the right to go in there forcefully. While we're doing that, we'll raid the homes of every one of the managers of record, simultaneously, and every one we catch will be arrested on suspicion of involvement in people trafficking.'

He stopped and looked at the Glimmer Twins. 'Isn't it fascinating, guys,' he murmured, 'that on the very day that Tomas Zaliukas took his own life, all this stuff started to blow up?'

'Yes,' McIlhenney conceded. 'It's as if he knew it was going to happen and couldn't face the consequences when it washed over him.'

'Mmm. Looks that way, doesn't it? Too bad he's not around to tell us.' Pause. 'But fortunately, someone else is. Neil,' he said, 'you're in charge of the massage parlour operation. Get the managers' addresses from the city council's licensing office. Pull in uniforms from every city division; use Ray, Becky Stallings and the four officers you have here, and get the job done.' His eyes shone. 'While you're doing that, Mario and I have another job to take care of. We're going to pick up Valdas Gerulaitis, this Snowman as Montell and Cowan say the girl called him, and light a fire under him.'

Thirty-seven

'Yes, I met with him, Pops,' Alex replied. 'I don't think he enjoyed our discussion, but he cooperated. But beyond that, I can't talk about him. You know that.'

'You can't talk about Valdas Gerulaitis, your client. But you can help us trace Valdas Gerulaitis, wanted by the police for trafficking teenage girls from Estonia to Scotland for the purpose of prostitution.'

'What!'

'You heard me. Have you seen today's edition of the *Evening News*? There should have been a piece in it about us trying to identify a young girl who was found drugged in Leith yesterday.'

'Yes. I saw one of the office copies; I read that story.'

'She's one of them. Anna Romanova, a nice kid, according to Griff Montell and Alice Cowan, lured from a convent orphanage in Tallin, thinking she was going to be a housemaid in Scotland. Her description of the shitbag who recruited her matches your client to the very head and shoulders, so they say.'

Sat behind his steering wheel, he listened on his mobile to

his daughter's breathing, on hers. 'What do you need?' she asked, after a few seconds.

'Are you still in the office?'

'Yes.'

'An address, that's all. His phone's ex-directory. There are places we could go to find out, but if you have his home details that would be quicker.'

'One minute.' She was gone for around half that time. 'He lives in Cramond,' she said. 'No street number, just a name. His house is called "Vilnius", and it's in Poacher's Close.'

'I know where that is; not far from Tomas Zaliukas. He was in Gamekeeper's Row, and of course his place had to be called "Lietuvos", hadn't it.'

'Pops, when you arrest this man, will you be holding him?'

'By the balls, as tight as we can, but I don't know for how long.'

'What about his wife?'

'No reason to. Why do you want to know?'

'I'll have to arrange a replacement for Valdas, to take over his book-keeping. Even if you have to release him, I'm going to suspend him. I'll ask the firm's auditors to send me someone along, and I don't want her getting in the way.'

'Do you want me to tell her not to go to the office tomorrow?'

'No, I'll do that myself. If you let me know when you've left the house with Valdas, I'll call her then.'

'Will do. So long.'

He ended the call and slid his gear stick to D. As he drew away from the kerb, he told McGuire of their destination. 'Will he still be there, boss?' the head of CID mused. 'If he's seen the *News* as well, and read about the girl, won't he have realised we'd be after him once she'd started to talk?'

'Could be,' Skinner agreed, 'but he was in his office three hours ago, when he had his meeting with Alex. I reckon if he was going to do a runner, he'd have been gone by then. You heard what I said to Alex; it's no certainty we'll be able to keep him in custody for any longer than a day. He must be confident, and I may know why.'

'Why should he be? Why shouldn't we be able to charge him and have him remanded?'

'Work it out, man,' the chief said as he headed for the western outskirts of the city. 'At this moment, we have the testimony of one girl that Gerulaitis was her procurer. That won't be enough. If we're going to convict him, we'll need corroboration; the word of a fifteen-year-old who's spent the last three months drugged isn't going to be enough on its own. We'll need at least one other girl to back up Anna's identification . . . assuming that she's able to pick him out herself when we stick him in a line-up. Trouble is, at this moment, we only have her. The more I think about it, the fact that he was in his office as usual this afternoon gives me an uncomfortable feeling that when Neil's crews knock down all those doors, they might not find much worthwhile behind them.'

Thirty-eight

'I need every uniform you can spare, Mary,' said DI Becky Stallings. 'Neil McIlhenney told me this comes from the big guv'nor himself. We have five of these places on our patch, and we have to get into them right away. On top of that, three of the managers live close to the premises and we have to pull them in.' She frowned at the superintendent. 'It seems bloody heavy-handed to me, but them's the orders.'

Mary Chambers smiled, grimly. 'Make no mistake, Bob Skinner is heavy-handed, more so than anyone I've ever met, and I spent a good part of my career watching heads being split open in Glasgow, maybe even splitting one or two myself. But his judgement is also the sharpest I've ever seen, so if he says that something needs doing, you don't stand around doubting him, you get on with it. Eight hits to make,' she mused. 'Do we expect resistance?'

'Jack and Sauce say that all the massage parlours they've seen have "Closed" signs on them, so they should be OK. They've already been into the one in Leith and found no surprises. We're to enter the rest, check that they really are empty and secure them for forensic examination, that's all.

The homes are different. Who knows what's going to happen when we knock someone's bleedin' door down? Especially when the guy behind it's a Lithuanian brothel-keeper.'

The superintendent checked the duty roster that lay on her desk. 'Who've you got?' she asked.

'McGurk and Haddock are on their way back here now. I've got one other DC but that's it.'

'OK. I can pull in all my patrols and send three people to each of the parlours. As for picking up the managers, I suggest that you and your DC, and Jack and Sauce, take one each.'

'Fine, but what about the third?'

'I'll do that myself. I'll take Charlie Johnston for back-up.'

'Charlie?'

'I wouldn't trust him to anyone else.'

'I understand that, but still . . .'

'It has to be him, Becky. That's how strapped I am.'

'So be it, then. Neil wants everybody in place by eight o'clock, ready to go on his signal, so that we lift all these guys at the same time . . . that's assuming they're all at home.'

Chambers scowled. 'Eight o'clock,' she muttered. 'That fucks up my social life. I'm supposed to be meeting my other half tonight. Never mind, there'll be another time. At least you don't have that problem.'

'No,' Stallings agreed. 'I know exactly where my other half will be at eight; banging on a Lithuanian's door just like me.'

'You'll be able to compare notes later,' said the superintendent. 'Give me the addresses, and let's get our small army on the march.'

Thirty-nine

'Poacher's Close must be about as secluded as Edinburgh gets,' Mario McGuire remarked, as Skinner approached the right turn that led into the cul-de-sac. 'No through traffic, big plots, only four houses in the whole street; you won't be right on top of your neighbours here, unlike most of the rest of the city.'

'There can be too much seclusion, mate,' the chief replied. He turned into the roadway, and drew to a halt, switching off both engine and lights. 'It's built into most people's psyche. Look at you and Paula; you live in that nice big duplex of yours, you've got neighbours next door, and below you, all the way down to street level. These people live literally under the same roof as you, but how many of them do you know?'

'We know Paul and Edith Applecross, the folk next door, well enough.'

'Oh yes? Do you ever invite them in for supper, or for a drink even?'

'Well, no, but . . .'

'Do you know what her maiden name was? Or how long they've been married?'

'No . . .'

'How about the floors below? There's what, seven of them, four flats on each, twenty-eight households, yes? How many of them would you say you know? Not intimately, just to say "hello" to.'

'Hardly any,' Mario admitted. 'But we never see them, unless we meet them in the lift.'

'No, you don't, do you? Man, for all you know, half a dozen of those flats could be rented out to Vietnamese gangs, and used for growing marijuana under hydroponic lights.'

'Christ, I hope not!'

'Me too,' he chuckled, 'but that's what seclusion is. It's a state of mind rather than a question of location. That said, when Sarah and I lived in that house near to Fettes, I couldn't stand the fucking place. The neighbours were jammed right up against us, and they were nosey bastards. It took us no time to move back out to Gullane . . . at least it took me no time; I never really asked her.'

'How is Sarah, by the way?'

'Single again; she had a boyfriend, but she chucked him. Too bad; Mark and James Andrew liked him. He used to take them to baseball games. My boys have been in the New Yankee Stadium, and it's only been open for a year.'

'Another guy taking your boys out on trips? That didn't give you any problems?'

'Why should it? If anyone had a problem, it was Sarah, although God knows why.'

'She's still happy in New York, though?'

'Yes, she's fine. She's being a proper doctor again, and that's what she wanted. But enough of that; she's enjoying her job now, just as I'm going to enjoy this.' He reached for the handle and was on the point of opening the door, when a fire appliance swung round the corner, missing his car by a matter of inches. 'Jesus Christ,' he roared. 'A few seconds later . . . I'll ram that driver's helmet up his arse!'

'I may assist,' said McGuire 'but where are they headed?' As he spoke, the tender turned into a driveway at the road's end, to the right. The street lighting was poor, but good enough to let him read the names on signs at the entrances to the two nearest properties, and neither was 'Vilnius'.

Simultaneously they leapt out of the car, and began to run. They had gone only a few yards when a second tender roared past them.

'They're going to Gerulaitis's place right enough,' Skinner shouted. He led the way into the driveway, past the sign that bore the name of the Lithuanian capital city. The crew of the second vehicle was deploying as they reached them. 'Where's the fire?' the chief asked, as two firemen ran past him carrying hose ends, looking, he guessed, for the nearest hydrants. If either heard him, he was ignored.

The Gerulaitis home was a large bungalow, with bay windows on either side of the entrance door and dormers above. None showed any sign of fire. 'What's happening?' the slower-moving McGuire exclaimed, as he caught up.

'Plenty, given the speed of those guys with the hoses. Whatever it is, it's round the back.' As he spoke, there was an explosion, mixed with the sound of breaking glass. In the same moment, a red halo seemed to surround the house, framing the lines of its roof.

'What do we do?'

'You stay here. Act as if you're back in uniform; don't let any neighbours in and, just as important, don't let anybody leave the scene.'

He headed round the side of the house, following the last firefighter, just as a third tender arrived, drawing up in the entrance to the driveway. The back garden was fenced off, but there was a gate, which lay open. He stepped through it, feeling a blast of heat as he did, and saw organisation emerging out of chaos. There was a rectangular conservatory built on to the rear of the bungalow, covering most of its width. It was ablaze and its windows had blown out. As he watched, the fire crew split into teams. Two more hydrants must have been found on the other side of the garden wall, for four hoses were concentrated on the blaze, while other fighters, with axes, hacked the remaining glass from the shattered window frames, making a safe passage for their colleagues to advance into the fire.

'Hey, you!' It took a few seconds for Skinner to realise that the cry was directed at him. 'Will you please get the hell out of here,' a white-helmeted man yelled as he walked towards him.

He shook his head, and reached into his jacket for his warrant card. 'Sorry,' he shouted back, above the roar of the flames and the rushing sound of the high-pressure jets, 'I have an interest here; I'm a police officer.'

'I don't care if you're the fucking chief constable,' the man retorted.

'As it happens I am the fucking chief constable.' He brandished the card. 'See? Now back off, for I'm going nowhere. I'll keep out of your way, don't worry,' he glanced at a name on the man's protective clothing, 'Assistant Divisional Officer Hartil.'

'This is a volatile area, sir,' the ADO persisted. 'I can't put you at risk.'

'You're not putting me at risk: I am. Look, I'll stand as far away as I can, but I want to see what's happening.' He walked across to the furthest corner of the garden, beside an ornamental pond. Its surface was frozen; at first the firelight seemed to dance crazily on the ice, but as he watched, it began to fade, as the fire and rescue teams edged their way into the seat of the blaze, bringing it under control. In less than ten minutes the fire that he could see was quenched, although he could still hear the hoses playing indoors, the scene illuminated by lamps that the crew of the third tender had set up on stands on the grass.

After a further five minutes, ADO Hartil emerged from the partly ruined building and came towards him. 'That's it,' he said. 'Under control; my boys and girls are just damping down now, and making sure there's no risk of outbreak anywhere else in the place.'

'Who called you?' Skinner asked.

'The place has a monitored alarm system, fire as well as intruder. Usual routine; they phone the householder first, then if he doesn't reply, the keyholder and us.'

'Which means that the place was empty?'

'Usually that would be the case. Unfortunately, not this time. Did you say that you have an interest in the people who live here?'

'In the husband, yes. My colleague and I came here to arrest him.'

'Did he and his wife live here alone, or were there other occupants?'

'My understanding is they have no kids. That's all I can say. I've never met him, but my understanding is that he was around six feet tall, dark-haired. Wife, smaller, dumpy; both in their mid-forties.'

'I'm afraid that's not going to help us identify what's in there, either of them.'

'Shit. They're both dead?'

'Very. You want to see?'

'No, but I'll have to.'

'Hold on then, till I get you some boots from our appliance.'

'Make that two sets, please, and ask my colleague to join us. He's round the front.'

He waited by the pond, gazing at the house. On impulse, he took out his mobile, and pressed the last number he had called. 'Pops,' his daughter answered quickly. 'Do you have him in custody?'

'No,' he replied, 'that wasn't possible. I'm at his house, though; there's been a fire.'

'My God! Bad?'

'Don't look for him to be in the office tomorrow.'

'You mean he's been injured?'

'Injured to a crisp, from what the fire chief's been saying. I'll give you the full story later. I have to go now.'

He ended the call as Hartil approached, with Mario McGuire, and two pairs of thigh-length waders. The police officers struggled into them, leaving their shoes behind on the edge of the pond, then followed the ADO towards the wrecked house.

They paused at the entrance to the conservatory; it had been reduced to a bizarre, windowless skeleton, with its UPVC frame buckled by the heat, and in part collapsed. 'Everything in here was lost,' said Hartil. 'All this garden furniture's supposed to be fire retardant now, but no fucking way was this lot. It went up like kindling, once the fire burned or blasted its way through from the big dining kitchen inside. That's where we think it started. The householders seem to have been trapped in there.' He shone a torch on a double-width doorway. Only the frame was left, and behind it, on the floor, they saw two forms, blackened, buckled, but still recognisably human. Skinner looked at them, and shuddered. He opened his mouth as if to speak, but no sound emerged.

The firefighter allowed the chief time to compose himself. 'Obviously,' he continued, when he judged he was ready, 'it's too early to say for sure, but it looks as if they were caught between the advance of the fire and here. This must have been their only escape route, but it must have been locked. Poor bastards were trapped; their best hope was that the smoke got them before the flames reached them. Usually that's what happens in a house fire, but not always.'

'I don't suppose you have any idea yet how it started?' Skinner whispered.

'No, it's way too early even to take a guess. It's down to our investigators to work that out.'

'I'd like our people to be involved.'

'Of course. Are you saying you suspect this might be arson, sir?'

'In this investigation, Mr Hartil, I'm ruling absolutely nothing in and nothing out. What state's the rest of the house in?'

'Not as bad as it might have been. The fire travelled up the way as well, obviously, but we contained it before it compromised the structure of the building.'

'That's good. I want this place secured, and I'd like your people to mop up as best they can. Tomorrow morning, your forensic people and mine are going to be going through this with the finest toothed comb they've got.'

Forty

'What's gonnae happen, ma'am?' Charlie Johnston asked, as they stood in the small Stockbridge terrace, looking across the street towards the double upper colony house that was the address of record for the manager of the massage parlour in Raeburn Place.

Mary Chambers checked her watch. 'In about four minutes,' she told the veteran, 'Detective Superintendent McIlhenney's going to come on radio and give us the go. When that happens we go straight up those steps and invite Mr Arturus Luksa to accompany us back to Torphichen Place.'

'Dae we cuff him?'

'That'll depend on his attitude.'

'The punters'll no like this, ye ken,' Johnston sighed mournfully. 'All the massage places bein' shut.'

'Does that mean you approve of prostitution, Charlie?'

'That hardly matters, ma'am, does it; whether a tired old plod's for it or agin it. There's been hoors in Edinburgh since the first ships came intae Leith . . . maybe before that . . . and there always will be. Better indoors than up against the rough-cast walls, that's all Ah've got to say about it.' She saw him frown, his face yellow in the sodium lights. 'But when it involves druggin' fifteen-year-olds and puttin' them on the game, that's another story.'

'Where did you hear that?' she demanded.

McIlhenney had decided that the uniforms involved in the arrest need not be told the full story behind the raids, in case it led to an excess of zeal. 'The priority, Mary,' he had said, 'is to bring them all in quietly and in one piece.'

Johnston smiled, his head tilted slightly. 'I pick things up, ma'am, that's all. I suppose that's why I had a call from the ACC this afternoon. See these houses,' he carried on, in one of the least subtle changes of subject she had ever heard, 'they call them colonies. D'ye ken why that is?'

The superintendent knew that a thirty-year veteran with a secure pension was not about to answer any question that he chose not to, so she gave up. 'Can't say I do, Charlie,' she replied.

'It's because of the way they were designed, in a sort of beehive style. They were built by a cooperative, for working people, in the second half of the nineteenth century, and intae the twentieth. There's over two thousand of them across the city. Folk go on about Edinburgh bein' the Old Town and the New Town, but they forget about these. Bloody brilliant, they—'

The crackling of the radio stopped him in mid-sentence. 'All units move,' ordered a voice, metallic but unmistakably that of Neil McIlhenney. The two officers reacted immediately.

'There's a light on upstairs,' Chambers pointed out.

'Do ye think he's got a girl up there?' Johnston asked.

'We'll soon find out.' She led the way briskly up the flight of stone stairs that led to the beehive house, the PC in her wake. He was panting as she rang the doorbell.

The door was opened by a woman, pretty, petite, dark-haired, expertly made up and clad in a red sheath dress. 'You're early,' she began. 'I wasn't expecting . . .' Her voice tailed off as she saw the uniforms.

The superintendent noted a wedding ring. 'Mrs Luksa?'

'Yes. What can I do for you?' Her voice was assertive, just short of aggressive. Both officers knew instinctively that she'd greeted police at her door before.

'Is your husband in?'

'Yes, but he's busy. He's upstairs putting our son to bed. We're going out: I thought you were the babysitter.'

'Ask him to come down, please.'

'No! Look, it's not convenient. Go away; come back in the morning.' She made to shut the door in their faces, but Chambers slammed her meaty right shoulder into in, knocking it wide open and sending the smaller woman flying.

As she hit the floor, a man appeared, dressed in a white shirt, open-necked, dark trousers, and black patent shoes, bounding down the stairway at the back of the hall. 'Arturus Luksa?' the superintendent shouted.

They expected him to go to his wife's aid, but instead he turned at the foot of the stair and disappeared through a door.

'He'll get away,' Chambers shouted.

'No, ma'am, there's only one door in these places.'

They followed him, the senior, yet younger, officer in the lead, into a small, well-equipped kitchen, just as Luksa closed a drawer and turned to face them, a twelve-inch knife in his hand. 'You bastards!' he hissed. 'You come into my home, but you don't leave it!' He lunged at Chambers, thrusting the blade not at her chest, but above her stab vest, at her throat.

She froze, seeing her death coming at her.

Later she realised that everything must have happened inside two seconds. Charlie Johnston moved alongside her, drawing and extending his baton, and in the same movement lashing it across Luksa's wrist and, at the very instant its tip pierced the superintendent's skin, sending the blade flying, so hard that it bounced off the tiled wall on to the work surface. It was spinning crazily as he whipped his weapon on to the forehand and cracked it into the side of the attacker's knee.

The Lithuanian fell to the floor, screaming and clutching his leg. 'Their fucking footballers do the same every time they get hit,' the PC grunted, as he rolled him on to his face, then sat on his legs and cuffed his hands behind his back. 'Makes me glad I'm a Hibby,' he added as he stood.

Chambers stared at him, feeling a warm trickle of blood running from her wound, down her neck and into her shirt. Her temporary paralysis over, she found that she was shaking. 'Charlie,' she gasped, as she fought for control over her terror and her bladder, 'where did you learn to do that?'

'In thirty years on the job, ma'am, you pick up a few tricks. Pity we're no' still using the old truncheons. This bastard would have had two fractures wi' one o' them.' He smiled at her. 'Do you no' want to sit down?'

'I daren't,' she told him, honestly. 'If I did, it might be a while before I could stand up again.'

As she spoke, they heard a whimpering from the hall. 'Then can I suggest, ma'am,' said the PC, gently, 'that you sit the wife down in the front room, calm her, then verify there really is a kid upstairs and no' another poor wee Estonian lass.'

Silently, she left to follow his advice, as Johnston produced an evidence container from his pocket, another surprise that she noted mentally, picked up the knife carefully, so that he neither left a print nor wiped her blood from the blade, and bagged it.

When she was gone, he hauled Luksa to his feet. 'You might think we've finished our business, son,' he whispered in his ear. 'Well, that depends on you. If you're quiet as a fucking mouse all the way back to our station, Ah might not tell the rest of the lads there what you just tried to do. But just one word out of you, and Ah will. They won't be pleased, ye ken; oh, they will not. We all like Mary, every one of us. We've got this guy McGurk.' He whistled, softly. 'You'll no' believe how fuckin' big he is.'

Forty-one

'What have we got, Neil?' asked Skinner, as he, McGuire and McIlhenney sat around the conference table, each clutching a soft drink can, taken from the fridge in the corner of his room.

'We've got next to nothing, boss. We have ten managers in custody in various offices; the party line seems to be that the places are closed as a mark of respect to Tomas, but they're not saying anything else. We've found none of the eight girls that Anna says were brought to Edinburgh with her, and at first sight there's no evidence in any of the massage parlours that they were ever there. Naturally, the guys deny all knowledge of them.'

'You're one Lithuanian short, aren't you?' McGuire remarked.

'No, we've got a full complement. The eleventh, Arturus Luksa, is on his way here; we've got to handle him differently.'

The chief constable frowned. 'Why?'

'Because he came within an instant of burying a knife in Mary Chambers's throat. He's going to be done for attempted murder. In the circumstances, I didn't think it would be wise to leave him locked up at Torphichen Place.'

'He might not be too safe here either. What happened?'

'From what Mary's been able to tell me, the guy bolted, they cornered him in his own kitchen and he came at her with a blade. She might well have been a goner if Charlie Johnston hadn't knocked it out of his hand, just in time, and subdued the guy.'

'Charlie Johnston?' an incredulous McGuire exclaimed. 'The Charlie Johnston?'

The superintendent nodded. 'The only one we've got. He's spent thirty years on the force trying not to be noticed and now he's going to retire as a hero.'

'Is Mary OK?'

'She's got a cut on her throat; it's superficial, although it was very close to an artery, according to the doctor who patched her up. Charlie really did save her life.'

'Then he's in for a big fat commendation for bravery,' Skinner declared. 'And if he takes the job he's being offered in the press office, I might stick him a couple of points up the salary scale as well.'

'What's Royston going to say about having him on his team?' McIlhenney asked.

'Fuck all, because it won't be his team.'

'Jesus, boss, you didn't fire him, did you?'

Skinner snorted. 'No, he fired us. He says he's been head-hunted, and he's taking it; a new challenge, all that crap.'

'What's better than here? Strathclyde, I suppose.'

'He wouldn't tell me, and I didn't press him, but there's no vacancy there. It could be commercial, or local government. The truth is, I don't give a bugger. I'll let him go right away and put a sound pair of hands in there from the uniform side . . . Ian McCall maybe . . . to hold the fort until we can find a professional replacement.'

'What about your night?' the detective superintendent inquired. 'Where's Gerulaitis? Have you got him locked up here too?'

The chief constable and the head of CID exchanged glances. 'He's cooling his heels, you might say,' McGuire volunteered. 'In the morgue: him and his wife. While we were going to pick him up, they were dying in a house fire.'

'Jesus. Not accidental, surely?'

'Man, I can understand why you sound sceptical, given the circumstances. So are we, but the first fire and rescue investigator on the scene went straight to a wine cooler, a mini-fridge thing, and focused on that. Her first thought is that the fire started there, and that it could well have been an accident. The couple appeared to have been trapped in the kitchen, with only one way out, and that door was locked. When the fire people found what was left of it, and the frame, there was no key in it.'

'It's been a bad week for the Lietuvos group,' McIlhenney murmured. 'A suicide and a fatal accident. What's next?' As Skinner glared at him, out of the chief's sight McGuire raised his eyebrows and put a finger to his lips. 'What?' he protested.

'As of this afternoon, Neil, my daughter is running those companies, temporarily.'

'But not the massage parlours?'

'No.'

'So don't worry. There's no problem with the pubs or the development business.'

'What makes you so sure?'

'Logic, and you'll say the same if you look at it objectively. You know what I think? Zaliukas didn't know Gerulaitis was running the girls. When he found out . . .'

'He was so upset that he shot himself? The Tomas I know would have killed Valdas, not himself.' Skinner frowned. 'There has to be something behind it, yes. According to what Regine told Alex, it had nothing to do with her, but I still haven't a fucking clue what it is. Unexplained suicides happen, accidents happen, and somebody wins the lottery every week. Those are facts, and you have to acknowledge them. But what I do not believe is that twelve massage parlour managers shut down their knocking shops as a mark of respect for a man who didn't even want to be seen as owning them.'

'Let's interview some of the women who work there,' McGuire proposed, 'and find out what they say.'

Skinner nodded. 'Do that for sure, but there's another card we can play. This man who nearly killed Mary Chambers. He's looking at an attempted murder charge. With a police officer involved? That's a potential life sentence with a high tariff. It might make him more inclined to cooperate.'

It was McIlhenney's turn to glare. 'You're not thinking about doing a deal with him, are you?'

The chief constable shrugged. 'Needs must. Let him sleep on his predicament, Neil. I'll have a word with him in the morning. Just the two of us; a quiet wee chat.'

Forty-two

'There's no possibility of Alex being in danger, is there?' Aileen asked.

'No,' Bob replied, perched on his stool at the breakfast bar, with a glass of dark red wine in his hand, 'I don't believe so, or by now I'd have done two things: I'd have insisted that she move out here with us, and I'd have called Mitch Laidlaw and asked him to get her out of it. Neil was right; if these two deaths are linked to Zaliukas's business life then it's to those massage parlours. Still,' he murmured, 'Mitch is a shrewd guy, and he values the reputation of his firm more than anything else. Sooner or later the press are going to start digging into Tomas's entire career, and without the law of defamation to restrain them, since you can't libel the dead, they're going to print some garish stuff. It's going to leave a bad smell around town, so I wouldn't be surprised if he resigns the account, legitimate or not, and tells the widow Regine to find another administrator.'

'That'll disappoint Alex. When I spoke to her earlier she was quite taken by her new role.'

'Oh, I know she is. But I also know that she was shaken

when I told her that Gerulaitis and his wife were dead . . . not because she felt at risk herself, simply because she'd met them both a few hours before, and then to think of them like . . .' He shuddered.

Aileen reached out and touched his arm. 'Bad, was it?'

He nodded. 'There are aspects of our job that can be pretty hard to take, but when you see the things that the fire and rescue people . . . women as well as men now . . . have to deal with.'

'You don't need to be doing that sort of stuff now, you know,' she pointed out.

Bob chuckled. 'You mean I could lead from the back? No, I don't think so. When you persuaded me to go for the chief's job, or when I persuaded myself . . . to be honest I can't remember which it was now . . . it was on the basis that nothing was going to change. My dear friend and soon to be near neighbour Sir James did things his way. Jimmy would have parted with his lunch on the spot if he'd seen what Mario and I had to look at earlier on, but he was a great chief constable nonetheless, the best this city's ever had. I'll handle it the way I think I can do it best, and if I can be half as good as he was, that'll still be pretty damn good.'

'Love, you're not getting any younger. You look knackered. That last birthday, the one you wouldn't let anyone mention . . .'

'What your birth certificate says and what your body says do not always coincide. Given the day I've had I'm entitled to look beat up, but I don't look any worse than any of my officers, least of all Mary Chambers, who almost lost her life tonight.'

'Yes, how is she? Do you know?'

'I looked in at Torphichen Place on the way home,' he replied. 'She says she's OK, and she looks it . . . but she hasn't had the nightmares yet.'

'Does she have anyone to hold her hand in the dark?'

'I don't think so, not right now. There's someone new, I believe, but not in residence, not a bidey-in.' He refilled both of their glasses, killing the bottle of Shiraz, pushed himself off his stool and slid an arm round her shoulder. 'Come on,' he said, and led her through into the garden room. 'Speaking of holding hands in the dark,' he murmured, as they settled into the sofa that faced the moonlit Firth of Forth, 'my mind goes back to something that somebody said to me yesterday.'

'About what?'

'About you. About us.'

Aileen pressed herself against him. 'Sounds intriguing.'

'Maybe. Or maybe you'll pour that Aussie red over my head. You and me, my love, have we ever really sat down and talked about having a family of our own?'

He heard her sudden intake of breath. 'We've discussed it,' she whispered.

'In a roundabout way, I agree, and what you've said is that we've both got high-pressure jobs, and I've made some joke about having loads of kids as it is. But have you ever said to me, "I don't want to have a baby, ever?" Have you?'

'No. I've never put it as directly as that.'

'Well, do it now. As who-the-hell-was-it said, tell me what you want, what you really . . .'

'. . . really want?' She finished the line, then sat up straight and turned to look him in the eye. 'You know what they say about politicians?' she asked, then continued without giving him the chance to reply. 'That we're all devious and deceitful, and that's on our good days. I try not to be, Bob, honestly I do, and I believe that in my public life I succeed. But at home, a new wife, a new stepmum with a new family, sometimes that's not so easy. The fact is, I've been meaning to start this conversation myself for a while, and it's my fault that it's taken Maggie Steele . . . I'm sure that's who you meant . . . for it to happen. I should have raised the subject about three months ago, in fact, for that's how long I've been off the pill.'

He laid his head back and gazed at the ceiling, silently, his face impassive.

'I'm sorry,' she said, quietly. 'It was rotten of me, totally irresponsible; it's just that . . . the first time I saw Maggie's baby, I got incredibly broody. Until then I didn't appreciate what the word meant. I'll go back on it,' she declared. 'Right now, I'll go back on it.'

He looked back towards her, cupped her face in his left hand, and kissed her. 'No,' he whispered, 'no, you will not. I love you like crazy, my purpose in life is to make you happy, and if that's what you want, I can only do my feeble best to make it happen.' He grinned. 'As you pointed out, I am getting on a bit.'

They sat in silence for a while looking out on the great river. 'Bob,' she whispered, eventually, 'leading from the front is good. I suppose that's what I do in my job. But I don't take physical risks like you've done in the past. Will you promise me at least that those days are gone?'

'As much as I can. I won't charge any more barricades, I promise.'

'That's as much as I can expect out of you, I suppose. I don't know why, but I find myself thinking of that woman you mentioned, Regine, the Lithuanian man's widow, and how she must feel.'

'Yes,' said Bob, 'I've been thinking about her too, strangely enough. I'm not entirely sure how she is feeling, and that's what I find intriguing. She told Alex that she'd been about ready to come back to Edinburgh. Yet now he's dead, she doesn't seem to want to come near the place.'

'But when Alex spoke to her, it was to break the news of her husband's death. The woman would be in shock, in no state to make decisions.'

'She was in a fit state to decide on the spot to keep her husband's businesses out of cousin Valdas's hands, and to appoint her lawyer to run them in her stead . . . a young lawyer she's never even met. I've met Regine myself a few times over the years; in Indigo, and once at a business dinner she attended with Tomas. She's a very together lady . . . and there's something else. She loved that club more than any of their other places, yet she doesn't want to come back to make sure it's OK. She doesn't even seem to want to come back to bury her husband.'

'She will, Bob, she will. Give her a couple of days. Right now . . .' she took his hand and stood, drawing him with her, '. . . how about we find out how feeble your best really is?' She winked at him, provocatively. 'Or are you too tired?'

Forty-three

George Regan wiped the last trace of shaving gel from a corner of his moustache, and buttoned his shirt. He fixed his tie, looking in the mirror when he was finished to check that the knot was to his satisfaction, then stepped back into the bedroom from the shower room.

'Fastidious bugger, aren't you,' said Jen, not unkindly, tying the green dressing gown which hung loosely about her shoulders.

'One of us has to be,' he retorted, casually . . . then snapped his mouth shut, as if that might pull his words back in, but they were gone, out there in the air beyond recall, doing their insidious damage.

'I'm sorry,' she replied, quietly. 'I'm sorry I can't be as lively as you want. I'm sorry if I've let myself slip. But I do try, George.'

He put his arms around her. 'I know you do, love, and I shouldn't have said that. I'm not getting at you, honest. The fact is, I'm worried sick about you. I see you fading away, day by day, and it's gutting me. I've been hoping that my new job and the move to Longniddry would help, but it hasn't, has it?'

'It will do.' She pulled away from him, brushing strands of grey-streaked, lustreless hair from her forehead. 'Let me go, now, and I'll make your breakfast.'

He watched her as she left, not quite shuffling but on the way there. Jen was still two years short of forty, but, he thought, if she was ever to be put in a police line-up for a witness, they would have to look for women pushing fifty to accompany her. It had almost happened too; there had been a shoplifting incident in the local co-op that had taken a bit of string-pulling by Neil McIlhenney, at area manager level, to make go away.

Five years earlier, losing a child had been the worst thing George had ever imagined. What he had not ever imagined was that it would happen to Jen and him. But it had, and it had taken half of their lives too. Fastidious? Yes, he was, and he had become so; it was his conscious way of cutting himself off from the man who had suffered all that pain. He tried hard to see someone else in the mirror . . . yet he never quite succeeded, for all the cotton-rich shirts, the silk blend suits and the inherited Crombie overcoats.

Jen had gone in the opposite direction. In the aftermath of their son's death he had suggested that they might try for another child; her fury had been so terrifying that he had never thought to hint at it again. Since then she had withdrawn more and more; she was a soul cast adrift, and her physical being seemed to be disintegrating a little more each day. Their lost boy was a taboo subject, for all that his presence hung around her like a shroud. There was no possibility of another child because they never had sex; the last time had been months before, and then she had been so rigid that he had stopped halfway through. He wanted to help her, but she seemed to have moved beyond his emotional reach, and no more counselling was going to do any good.

She was at her best when she was busy. Jen herself might have gone to the dogs, but the house was as pristine as George. She fed him well too. When he joined her in the kitchen, the kettle was boiling, the toaster was loaded and she stood cracking two eggs into the frying pan. He went to help her, but she told him to sit down, so he did, at the kitchen table, switching on the radio as he passed.

It was tuned to Forth Two; Jen's day-time companions were Bob Malcolm and Spike Thomson. 'And now Forth news,' a female voice announced. 'Police in Edinburgh are remaining tight-lipped about a series of raids carried out across the city yesterday evening, believed to be related to the sex trade. This follows the discovery in Leith yesterday afternoon of the body of massage parlour manager Linas Jankauskas. Detective Chief Superintendent Mario McGuire, head of CID, later confirmed that his death is being treated as murder.'

Indeed? Regan thought. *Makes me all the happier I'm out here in my nice county backwater.*

'Edinburgh fire and rescue officers confirmed late last night that two people, believed to be husband and wife, died last night in a fire in a house in Cramond. Investigators are provisionally linking the tragedy to faulty wiring on a kitchen appliance.'

'Did you hear that?' he asked Jen, as she buttered his toast . . . all she ever had for breakfast was tea and a yoghurt. 'I'm going to check every plug in this kitchen.'

'You needn't bother,' she replied. 'I do that all the time. Everything's perfectly fine.'

'That's good to know.' She laid his breakfast before him, on a tray. 'What are you doing today?'

'Oh, just the usual. This house takes a lot of looking after, you know.'

'And so do you, love. Why don't you get on the bus, go up to town like you used to? Hit the shops, give the credit card a battering. Look what's happened since you stopped going to M&S and Debenhams; the whole economy's fucked.'

She smiled, kindly; she had always been kind. 'I think it's taken more than me to do that,' she said. 'If it'll make you happy, I'll see if I can get an appointment at the hairdresser.'

That would make me very happy, George thought, but before he had a chance to say so, his mobile sounded. He picked it up, instantly fearful that he was about to be called into Edinburgh to help with Operation Whatever-the-hell-it-was, but when he checked the number he saw that the caller was within the county.

'Regan,' he answered, curious.

'Detective Inspector,' a man said. 'This is Andrew Fairley, Witches' Hill golf club. Sorry to be on so early, but something else has happened. It's . . . ah, I'm still trying to take it in. I'd be grateful if you could come to the club, as soon as you can.'

Forty-four

'Ah'm a masseuse, mister, that's all,' Maxine Frost insisted, standing in front of her fireplace, cigarette in hand. 'If you got my name and address from the massage parlour, you'll know that.'

'Mrs Frost,' Jack McGurk told her, 'we're not bothered about what you do at work. If you say you're a masseuse we'll take your word for it, without even asking who or what you massage, or what with. We want to know about other people who might have been in business at your place, specifically teenage girls, not Scottish, from eastern Europe.'

'I don't know what you're on about.'

'We're on about kids who were lured away from their home in Estonia and put to work in brothels in Edinburgh,' Sauce Haddock snapped. 'Is that specific enough for you?'

'I don't work in a brothel. I'm a masseuse.'

'Where did you train?'

'College.'

'Do you have a certificate?'

'You don't get certificates. It was a night class.'

'I'll bet it was,' said McGurk. 'How many people work at your place?'

'I dinnae ken. We work shifts. We set our own hours, like. We're self-employed.'

'Is that so? What's your tax reference number? Come on, tell us; one call to the Inland Revenue and we can find out.'

'Aw, come on,' the woman protested. 'This is polis harassment.'

'Absolutely, Mrs Frost,' Haddock agreed, cheerful once more. 'Now are you going to talk to us, because my sergeant here's Plymouth Brethren, and he'd really love to make that call.'

'Ah'll bet he would, the bastard. He looks just like one o' them too. Kent it as soon as Ah clapped eyes on him.' Pause. 'OK, there was a girl that didnae speak English. She came in about three months ago.'

'What age, do you reckon?' the DC asked.

'Sixteen or seventeen, eighteen tops. But if you're sayin' she was forced on the game, you'd be wrong. I didnae see her every day like, but she settled in pretty quick. She had her regulars after a few weeks. There's one guy used tae come in and ask for Miss Head; ye can gather from that she was versatile. We wound up callin' him Mr Head.'

'Where can we find her?'

'She stayed wi' Marius, the manager, as far as Ah kent. He's got a big flat, down Scotland Street. Ah was at a party there one night; nice place.'

'How big?' McGurk murmured.

'Like Ah said, big,' Mrs Frost retorted.

'How many could it sleep?'

'As many as ye bloody like, just aboot. It's got four bedrooms. Why?'

'Do you know if she was the only girl who stayed there?'

'How the fuck would Ah?'

'Fair enough,' the DS conceded. 'When did you see her last?'

'Three days ago. Mr Head was in. The same night Ah got the call frae Marius, telling me the place wis shuttin' for a while.'

'Is that all he said?'

'Aye. It was sudden, like. Ah finished about ten, and Ah was barely home when he phoned us.'

'Wait a minute,' Haddock interrupted. 'Did you say that was three nights ago? Tuesday?'

'Aye.'

'Did Marius say why it was closing?'

'No. Ah asked him, like, but he telt me to mind my own fuckin' business if I wanted tae get back there.'

'Did he say when that would be, when you would be back?'

'A few days, maybe a week; that was all.'

'OK.' The DC looked up at his sergeant, who nodded.

'That's all you can tell us, Mrs Frost?' he asked.

'That's it. Now will you please fuck off back tae your prayer meeting?'

McGurk grinned. 'I hope you've got another merry quip for the tax man when he comes calling,' he chuckled, as he headed for the door.

'Marius,' he muttered, when they were back on Dalry Road. 'He was the guy that Becky lifted, wasn't he?'

'That's right. He came along quietly,' she said, 'and even invited them to have a look round. No girl there last night or she'd have found her.'

'No.' The sergeant frowned, dark and menacing. 'He came quietly . . . unlike that bastard that put the nick in Mary Chambers' throat. I'd like to know where he is right now.'

'You and our entire station,' Haddock agreed. 'I'm not surprised they moved him. I heard it was a headquarters car that picked him up.'

McGurk whistled. 'In that case he'll have to take his chances with the Twins. He may wind up wishing that he'd stayed with us.'

'They wouldn't, would they?'

'No, but I'll bet they scare the shite out of him anyway.'

The young DC pondered Arturus Luksa's predicament for a few moments. 'There was something else in there,' he continued. 'Did you pick it up?'

'What?'

'Maxine said that she got her call from Marius three nights ago, right?'

'Yes, agreed. So?'

'So when did Zaliukas kill himself?'

The DS's eyes widened. 'A few hours later; you observant young sod. So what do we read into that? Tomas Zaliukas shut down the massage parlour operation, and then he went out and killed himself?'

'That's one possibility, but what if it was someone else gave the order?'

'Who, Valdas?'

'That's the obvious assumption. Too bad we won't be able to ask him.'

McGurk shrugged his shoulders. 'Personally, I find it hard to grieve about that, especially since we've got eleven massage parlour managers in custody who know the answer to the question.' He started to walk back towards Haymarket. 'Whatever, Sauce, that's above our pay grade. All we can do is get back to the office, feed in what we've picked up, and maybe suggest that forensics take a look at the Marius guy's place in Scotland Street, to see if there's any evidence of the Estonian girls having been kept there, and if we're lucky, evidence of where they've gone, or rather, been taken. But what it all amounts to is a singular lack of progress for all the effort of the last twelve hours or so.'

'There probably is no more,' Sauce muttered gloomily. 'These girls will be scattered all over the place by now.'

'Speaking of girls and sex,' said McGurk, as the monument on the distant road junction came in to view, 'you look fresher this morning.'

'Weekend coming up, Jack,' the young DC replied, 'starting with the disco tonight. We've got to save our strength for that.'

Forty-five

Detective Inspector Regan's mind was still at home as he eased his car up the driveway that led to the pro shop and club house at Witches' Hill, sticking close to the ten miles per hour speed limit. The morning was bright and, if not exactly warm, much less cold than the previous few days had been, and so he was not surprised to see that the car park was almost half full, even as early as ten past nine.

He slid into the first empty bay, then headed for the shop. Three figures waited outside; the tall, slim Fairley, an older man, dressed for golf in tartan slacks, a crested sweater over a polo neck and a flat cap, and another, in a powered wheelchair.

'Hello, George,' the second man called out as he approached.

Regan peered at him, and blinked. He had rarely seen Sir James Proud in anything other than uniform. 'Good morning, Chief,' he replied.

'Not the chief any more, son,' Bob Skinner's predecessor pointed out.

'Ah, but it's a bit like being President in America,' the DI countered. 'You keep the title for life.'

'But not the salary, unfortunately.'

You must be doing all right if you can afford to be a member here. He kept the thought to himself.

'Have you met the Marquis of Kinture?' Sir James continued.

'No, sir,' said Regan, adding mentally, *he doesn't drink in my local.*

The man in the wheelchair extended a hand, and they shook. 'Inspector,' he grunted.

They might never have met, but following his transfer to East Lothian, Regan had made a point of reading up on the county's movers and shakers. He knew Kinture's story: latest of an ancient and titled family, a top-class golfer before being crippled in an accident, he had channelled his love for the game into the creation of a world-class course on a piece of otherwise useless land on his estate. After a colourful beginning, Witches' Hill had matured to a level that had led to its being discussed as the venue for a European Tour event.

'Good to meet you, sir,' he replied. He was puzzled. Had Fairley asked him to come along for a lecture on rural crime prevention from Proud Jimmy and his mate?

'We're getting in the way here,' the retired chief declared, putting an end to that supposition. 'We'll clear off and leave you and Andrew to it.'

'Is he playing?' Regan asked as they left, Proud lengthening his stride to keep pace with the wheelchair.

'The Marquis, obviously not,' Fairley replied. 'Sir James is. He and Lady Proud are in a mixed foursomes tie in about half an hour.'

'I didn't know he was a golfer.'

'Between you and me, he isn't, not yet, but he's had a couple of lessons and he's got the makings.'

'Like his successor?'

'Not quite. I hear that Mr Skinner's playing off seven just now; that makes him the biggest bandit in East Lothian.' Fairley smiled. 'That reminds me; we had another of your lot out here a few months back,' he added, 'playing against us in a winter league game. A lad called Haddock; he gave our club champion a dog licence.'

'Eh?'

'Beat him seven and six. I wish he'd join here; he'd walk into our team.'

'He won't be doing that on a DC's pay, Andrew. Now, what's the problem? Did our people leave a mess behind yesterday?'

The pro shook his head. 'No. I'd rather that than what's happened. You're not going to believe this: I've been bloody well done again.'

'What?' Regan gasped.

'No kidding. I got a local firm in yesterday to fix the damage from the previous night's robbery, and to make the place secure. They did what they could, but all they could manage short-term was a temporary door, with wired glass. As well as that I asked the alarm people to come in and repair the system. That was buggered when the sensors were ripped off the door frame; somehow it shorted out the control box. They couldn't fit it in yesterday, but they promised me they'd do it today. Fucking brilliant, that. I got in this morning and found the replacement door jemmied open. Yesterday it was golf clubs; today it was all my clothing.'

'The lot?'

'Well no, not quite. They left everything that had the Witches' Hill crest on it, but they've still got away with about forty grand's worth of designer stock, men's and ladies'. They took my shoes as well: FootJoys, Adidas, all gone.' Fairley frowned. 'I'm wondering if it was the builders, George. Or maybe a leak from the alarm company that the place wasn't covered.'

'We'll check them both out, Andrew, I promise you, but I don't hold out hope of a result from either of those. Alarm companies' information security is always very tight. As for your builders, if they're local . . . Unless they had a casual on yesterday, someone they don't know, I can't see that either. You know what I mean; shite, own doorstep, etc.' He walked over to the door and examined it; splintered frame, top and bottom, opened expertly with a minimum of force. 'No, whoever did this had a shopping list, and he was smart enough to leave anything that would be easy to trace. Just like yesterday's team. In fact,' pause, 'I'm going to get our technicians back here to see if they can find and match any tyre tracks. I wouldn't be surprised if what we've got here is a repeat performance.'

Forty-six

Mario McGuire winced, his disposable tunic rustling as he stepped into the ruined house, joining two people who stood beside what was still recognisable as an Aga cooker. 'Do they all smell as bad as this the day after?' he muttered.

'This is mild,' Frances Kerr told him. 'At some scenes we'd still be wearing breathing apparatus the day after.'

'How did you get into this business?' the head of CID asked.

'I chose it,' she replied, 'out of necessity. I was a firefighter, station officer rank, but I hurt my right shoulder at an incident. It left me with a permanent weakness that would have made me a liability on operational duty. Normally that would have been it, but the fire service is very aware of the need to be seen as an equal opportunity employer. That might be why I was offered the chance to retrain for this side.'

'Crap,' said ADO Hartil, cheerfully. 'You have to do a pre-entry qualification before you get anywhere near training as an investigator. Frances was top of the class by a mile.'

'Shut up, Joey,' she told him. 'Don't build me up before I've found anything definite.'

McGuire glanced at her. 'What have you found so far, then?'

'Nothing beyond first impressions last night.' She pointed to a burned-out metal box that sat against the wall next to the door that had led into the big dining kitchen from the hall. 'That was a wine cooler,' she said. 'Its cable was frayed right through, as if it had been trapped under one of its feet at some point. That thing on the wall next to it was a rail. There's what's left of some kind of fabric around the cable, leading to the possibility that a tea towel fell on to it, and was ignited. Whatever it was, that's where the fire started. The place was carpeted, the flames would have spread very quickly along the floor, and in a kitchen there's all sorts of stuff to fuel it. The exit into the hall would have been cut off right away, and that would have left the door to the conservatory as the only escape route.' She moved towards it, stopping halfway beside a pile of black cinders. 'This was a table. I found two plates, wine glasses, a bottle, and cutlery among its remains. The plates had food burned into them, and there was a casserole dish in the oven with what was left of a moussaka. It looks as if Mr and Mrs Gerulaitis were at their dinner when the fire started, probably behind them.'

'Wouldn't they have smelled the smoke right away?'

'I'm not sure there would have been a lot of smoke, not at the start. But as I said, the fire would have spread very quickly. Whatever alerted them, the only way out was that door, that locked door. We found the key eventually,' she added, 'in a kitchen drawer.'

'So why didn't they find it? That part of the floor was tiled. Couldn't they have reached it?'

'Panic, Chief Superintendent,' said Joey Hartil. 'That's what people do when they're trapped by a serious fire. Panic's a major cause of death in these situations. It makes people overlook the obvious, it makes them jump out of high windows when they'd have been all right if they'd stayed calm and waited for us.'

'So the poor bastards were caught between a locked door and a hot place.'

'Colourfully put,' Frances Kerr conceded, 'and accurate, until they were eventually consumed by the hot place. That's my theory, anyway; it's what the scene's telling me.'

'Gerulaitis wasn't a wee bloke. Couldn't they have smashed their way out?'

The investigator shook her head. 'Obviously not, not without one of your rams, at any rate. This is a well-built house; its doors and windows were designed with security in mind. If they'd been able to reach the window beyond the food prep area, they might have got out that way. But they couldn't, poor people.'

McGuire frowned. 'Earlier on you said you hadn't reached any definite conclusions, but you sound pretty certain to me.'

'Och, I am, really. We've just got one or two more things to do and then I'll be able to turn in a report.'

'Such as?'

'I need to go over the outlying areas of the fire, that's one. Then there's the dogs.' She looked at Hartil. 'How are we getting on with that, Joey?'

'We should have them this afternoon.'

'What bloody dogs?' the head of CID asked, puzzled.

'The Central Scotland brigade has a couple of dogs,' Kerr explained. 'They're specially trained to sniff out accelerants at fire scenes. We'll run them through here as a matter of routine, to save us having to do it later when the insurance assessors arrive on the scene. Those boys are worse than juries; they want everything beyond even an unreasonable doubt before they pay out.'

'That's all? You'll be able to give me a formal report by the end of the day?'

'Yes.' She gazed at McGuire, her brow furrowed. 'But why you? You're CID, top man in CID at that.'

'Let's just say,' he replied, 'that we've got a file on Mr Gerulaitis that needs closing.'

'Understood, but this is an accidental death.'

'Understood also.' He grinned. 'Maybe I've been a cop for too long, Ms Kerr; but when I encounter an accident that's as damn convenient as this one, my nerves start to jangle.'

'Let me put them at ease, then, as soon as I can.'

'You do that. Meantime, I'm going to attend the post-mortems on the pair of them, if only to make sure that they really were Valdas and his wife. I'm a bit of an unreasonable doubt man myself.'

Forty-seven

'OK, George,' Neil McIlhenney sighed, 'since Mario's out, I'll speak to Arthur Dorward and ask him to send a couple of people out to join you. Meantime, don't let any more vehicles near that shop.'

'I won't. The members don't drive up to it anyway; they use the car park, then walk to the clubhouse. The only contaminating tyre tracks they're liable to find will be from a wheelchair. I've just met His Grace, or whatever you call a marquis.'

'I think "My Lord" usually cuts the mustard with them. I'm not surprised he was on the scene; he must be spitting bullets. We'd better look out for him to be on the phone to the boss; the two of them are pals.'

'He doesn't need to,' Regan sighed. 'He was able to bite the ear of the old boss, in person.'

'Sir James?'

'None other. He was with him. But as it happened, they were both pretty reasonable, given the circs. It doesn't stop me feeling like a tosser, though.'

'Nah, George, nobody's going to blame you apart from

yourself. If you're right and it's the same team, they've put one over on all of us. We'll learn and it won't happen again. If it's somebody else, it'll be a local opportunist and you'll nail him.'

'It happened on my patch, though.'

'Forget it. You're CID, not crime prevention. The guy who should be kicking himself is your man Fairley, for not moving his stock into the main clubhouse till the shop was properly secured.'

McIlhenney hung up, then called Arthur Dorward at the police lab, told him what had happened, and asked for specialist technicians to be sent to the scene. That done, he walked along to Maggie Steele's office, arriving just as she returned from the chief constable's morning meeting.

'I can guess why you're here,' she said, as he held the door open for her. 'You want to know whether we had any false alarm calls last night.'

'I'll bet we didn't,' he replied. He told her what had happened at Witches' Hill. 'Poor old George Regan. He got along there and found Lord Kinture and Proud Jimmy waiting for him. He's checking out the local possibilities, but I agree with his view that it's the same crew come back for what they left the night before.'

Steele winced. 'Word can't have filtered back to Bob or he'd have mentioned it, for sure.' Pause. 'Neil, do you reckon this is worth feeding to the Serious Crime Agency?'

'I've thought about that,' the detective superintendent admitted, 'then decided against it. This isn't serious crime, and it isn't even organised in the accepted sense. It's just a clever, opportunist team, operating across Scotland. I reckon it's best dealt with by CID in the various forces pooling information, so that we can all be on the alert for a sudden unusual burst of 999 calls, and also for signs of the stolen gear appearing on the market . . . unless most of it's been moved on already.'

'I'll bet it hasn't. If they're as clever as all that,' she pointed out, 'they'll have a disposal plan worked out. First thing we should do is assess the total value of everything they've stolen. Let me have a list of all the robberies, with contact points for each. I'll ask David Mackenzie to pull everything together and see what we've got. It could be,' she ventured, 'they're thinking about moving it in one lot.'

McIlhenney frowned, doubtfully. 'Dunno about that, Mags. The only way to shift that amount of specialist gear would be to open a pro shop of your own.'

Forty-eight

The interview room was in the basement and so it had no windows. Its only illumination came from a low-energy bulb, its walls were bare and the radiator that was its only source of heat had been switched off. Arturus Luksa was shivering as he sat at the small table; it, and two chairs, were its only furniture. He stared up at the tall, grey-maned figure who had just entered the room and ordered his uniformed guard to leave them alone. The man was in shirtsleeves, as he was, but looked altogether warmer, as he settled himself into the chair opposite the Lithuanian.

'I want a lawyer,' Luksa declared, trying to force defiance into an expression that until then had looked uncertain. 'I want Ken Green.'

'This is Scotland, not England,' the newcomer snapped. 'You get a lawyer at our pleasure.' In the pause that followed the prisoner realised how cold pale blue eyes could be. 'At my pleasure. And I have to tell you that I am not fucking pleased. I've got a lady officer with a knife wound in her neck.'

'It was only a little scratch . . . and anyway, I never touch her.'

'Don't insult me, boy,' the man growled, almost bear-like. 'We have your prints and DNA on the weapon, and we have her skin and blood on it. We have witness statements from her and from PC Johnston, the officer who decked you. We also have a recording made over Charlie's open radio of you shouting at Superintendent Chambers as you lunged at her. You are going down, Mr Luksa, for attempt to murder. When we are ready to interview you formally, we'll do that, and you will have a lawyer present. Obviously, Superintendent Chambers won't be handling the interview. That will be done by the head of CID and his deputy, who are, incidentally, every bit as displeased with you as I am. This here, now, is just a chat between you and me. The camera you can see up in the corner there, that's switched off. There's no two-way mirror; they're only for cop shows on the telly. There's no tape recorder, and the lad who was in here with you before has gone for his tea. There's just you and me, Arturus. You're not even handcuffed.' He frowned. 'Fuck me, I've been careless, haven't I? You're probably thinking right now that you could go right through me, out the door and be halfway to fuckin' Lithuania before anyone was any the wiser. And maybe you could. You're a big lad, you're nearly twenty years younger than me. Yes, maybe you could.' The blue eyes fixed on Luksa; suddenly he felt even colder. 'Except nobody ever has, not in all my career on the force, not in all my life. That's one reason why we're here, you see, I actually want you to have a go at me. That means I'll get to restrain you just like my old chum Charlie did. The difference will be that Charlie does everything absolutely by the book, even when it comes to taking down diddies like you.

I don't; never have done.' The man stood. 'So come on, take your shot if you fancy it; I really would like to hurt you, very badly.'

Luksa's eyes fell to the floor, away from that chilling, unblinking gaze. He grasped the sides of his seat, and shook his head, slowly.

The man sat down again. 'You've disappointed me,' he said. 'I thought you had balls. Tomas Zaliukas did; I'll say that for him. He never made it through me either, by the way. I was looking forward to seeing whether you were anything like as tough as him. Too bad . . . for you. I don't take kindly to disappointment, so you'd better not do it twice. I want you to talk to me, Arturus. I want you to tell me about the girls, and I want you to tell me how the massage parlours came to be closed.'

'Why should I do that?'

'Work it out.'

'I help you, you maybe forget about my mistake with the lady?'

'That would be the obvious.'

'I'm sorry, mister. I dunno why I did that.' He smiled, as if it would make a difference. 'They came into my home. I have a temper. Sometimes I'm a nutter.'

'I've met a few of those. So what's it to be?'

'I dunno. Can I trust policeman?'

'That's for you to decide. You can trust any jury in the land to convict you, and any judge to give you at least twelve years. That's a certainty.' Pause. 'Tell me about the girls.'

'What girls?'

The man glared. 'Not a good start, chum. Kids from

Estonia. Young girls. We've confirmed that at least three of them are under sixteen. We know that they were brought in by Valdas Gerulaitis, Tomas Zaliukas's cousin. As far as we can gather, Valdas never did anything that Tomas didn't want him to do, so my assumption is that he was behind it. That disappoints me too, by the way; I trusted Tomas to stay legit, more or less. I never thought he'd have got involved with something as low-life as people trafficking.'

'I don't know about that,' said Luksa. 'Tomas never came near the massage parlours. And I don't know about no girls either.'

'Bollocks, of course you do. Don't lie to me, you're not good enough at it.'

'OK, OK! I hear about them, but they didn't give me one. My place is close to your headquarters; that's why. Too risky, he said.'

'Who said?'

'Valdas.'

'So Valdas was involved with the massage parlour business.'

'We send all the cash to him.'

'Cash?'

'The money we take from the girls.' The interrogator nodded, waiting. 'Look, the way it works,' Luksa continued, leaning forward as if he was imparting a confidence, 'everybody pay to come in; they pay for a massage, twenty quid, that's the minimum, and a sauna, that's another fiver. That goes through the till if it's cash, but usually it's credit cards. What happens with the girls, that's different; cash only.'

'Who sets the price?'

'We do, the managers. Fifty quid a fuck, seventy quid a blow job. Other things . . . a hundred, but that's up to the girls.'

'What's your cut?'

'Straight sex they keep twenty quid, blow job, they keep twenty-five. Anything else, they keep forty per cent.'

'And the rest went to Valdas?'

'Yes.'

'Are the girls happy with that?'

'Who gives a shit whether they happy or not? They go on the street, pimps take them over or you lock them up, or both. With us they're safe. We're licensed, remember.'

'OK, so you've got them over a barrel . . . or maybe over a massage table. But are you happy with it?'

'Me? I do what I'm told.'

'I'm sure you do, Arturus, but let's look at the corporate you, the business as a whole. Were Valdas and Tomas happy with those margins?'

'Valdas never complain to me; Tomas I never see, never hear from. So how would I know?'

'I suppose not. Let's move on then. On Wednesday, every one of your places was closed. As a mark of respect, some of your colleagues in the other places have told us. By the way, those colleagues have all been released on bail; they're home with their families. So go on, tell me; is that what happened, you all got together and decided that's what you should do?'

'No. I get phone call, Tuesday night. Tell me some shit going to hit fan and that we all have to shut down till the smell clears.'

'Tuesday? Are you sure it was Tuesday?'

'Of course I sure. How many days are there in the week?'

'Who called you? Valdas?'

'No, it was Jock.'

'Who the hell is Jock?'

'That not his real name, it's only what we call him. He's Lithuanian. His real name is Jonas; that's like John in our language, so some of us boys, we call him Jock.'

'I don't remember anyone called Jonas on the list of managers that I saw.'

Luksa stared at him. 'He isn't a manager; he's Tomas's own guy.'

'He's a new one on me. Tomas must have kept him close.'

'As close as blood. He's Zaliukas also; he's Tomas's brother.'

'His brother?'

'Yes. His younger brother.'

'How much younger?'

'Maybe ten years. Guy maybe about same age as me and I'm thirty-two.'

'How long has he been in Edinburgh?'

'Not long. He arrived last week; I never heard of him before that.'

'Well, thanks Arturus. You've actually told me something I didn't know.'

Luksa gazed across the table, expectantly. 'When I go,' he ventured, 'will you protect me from Valdas? If he finds out I tell you anything . . . Tomas was a fair guy, but Valdas, he's different.'

'It seems like Gerulaitis hid a lot of stuff behind that false front I've been told about,' the interrogator mused. 'You needn't worry about him,' he said. 'He's no longer your problem. He and his wife are cinders. Anyway,' he stood, his grey hair reflecting the light of the naked bulb, 'you're not going anywhere.'

'But you said . . .' the Lithuanian protested.

'No. As you said . . . can you trust a policeman?'

Forty-nine

'You did leave him in one piece?' Neil McIlhenney ventured.

'Of course,' Skinner grunted. 'His trust in the basic goodness of his fellow man might be damaged beyond repair, but everything else is just as it was when I walked into the room. There was a time when that might not have been the case, but that's all history now. You and Mario are free to interview him whenever you like.'

'Mario's up at the mortuary, for the Gerulaitis autopsies. We'll do it as soon as he gets back.'

'Fine. There aren't too many questions to be asked other than why did you do it? The answer is probably because he knew all about the girls being imported and was scared that he was going to be done for it whether he'd had one at his place or not, but he isn't going to admit that, not yet. Ken Green's his lawyer; he isn't going to say anything with that guy sitting alongside him. You'd better call him, and tell him he has a client in bother. Charge him quick; get him in court this afternoon, so he can be remanded in custody.'

'Will do. What did you get from him? Anything much?'

'Yes, and I'm not sure what to make of it. The "mark of respect" story is cobblers. The managers were all told to close down on Tuesday night.'

McIlhenney nodded. 'Yes, I know. Young Sauce got that from a hooker . . . ouch, sorry, non-PC; a sex worker . . . that he and Jack interviewed.'

'Good for the boy. Maybe he knows what to make of it, for I don't. They were all told to close before Tomas shot himself. Naturally, they all denied any knowledge of trafficked girls . . . all but Luksa, who'd have coughed up anything to get himself off an attempted murder charge. He says he didn't have a girl, but it's a fair bet that all of those who had were told to move them out of there.'

'One of the managers has a flat, McGurk and Haddock found out. It's down in Scotland Street, and from what they were told it was big enough to have housed all the girls, apart from Anna Romanova. I've told them to get a warrant and get in there pronto.'

'Good move.'

'One other thing from the interviews we've done so far . . . not with the managers, but with the local talent who worked there. None of the very few who were willing to talk to us about newcomers from eastern Europe gave any indication that any of the others had been drugged, or abused.'

'Were they being paid?'

'None of them could tell us that either. Where the Estonian girls were involved, the manager took the money. But my guess is that they were, enough to keep them happy.'

'Yes,' Skinner agreed. 'I've got a scenario forming in my

head. From what Luksa said, Valdas was running the massage
parlours . . . that might explain why Tomas left his interest to
Laima. But he got greedy. He worked out that if he replaced
the Edinburgh ladies with cheap, young, foreign imports he'd
have complete control of his workforce and his profits would
go way up. I suspect that's what he was starting to do, but I
don't believe that he'd asked Tommy for the OK first. The way
I see it, Tomas found out.'

'And Valdas killed him?'

'No, no,' he said quickly. 'Tomas shot himself. There's no
doubt about that, none at all. No, something else happened.'
Pause. 'Neil, I want you to do two things. Have Stallings and
her team follow up on this Scotland Street flat and squeeze the
owner hard. If those girls were billeted there as McGurk and
Haddock seem to think they might have been, he's likely to
know where they went.'

'And the second?'

'Ask David Mackenzie, from me, to get in touch with the
Lithuanian equivalent of our Justice Department, and find out
everything they've got on one Jonas Zaliukas, age approx-
imately thirty-two.' The superintendent's eyebrows rose. 'That's
right,' the chief confirmed, 'Tommy had a wee brother. Then
have our people spread that name around town, and go back to
those ten managers we've bailed, and see what they come up
with.'

'Do we want to know anything in particular?'

'Absolutely. It might be worth knowing whether he bears
any passing resemblance to Desperate Dan.'

Fifty

'Is there a pogrom under way, by any chance, Detective Chief Superintendent?' the tiny pathologist asked. 'We seem to be going through the Lithuanian population at a rate of knots.'

'I'll grant you, Joe,' Mario McGuire conceded, 'that God doesn't appear to be on their side this week.'

'Nor mine,' said Professor Hutchinson. 'With the exception of the late Mr Jankauskas, whose neck was broken manually, as cleanly as any hangman could have done it, they have tended to be particularly messy.'

'You can confirm what we thought about Linas?'

'Absolutely. It was very quickly, and very expertly done; no chance that it could have been accidental. There's not a mark on him, not a single bruise.'

'Are we looking for more than one person?'

'All I can tell you is, not on the evidence of my examination.'

'Will your report say any more than that?'

Hutchinson shook his head. 'Very little. He had several things shortly before he died; a raw onion, a pork pie, two bottles of lager, and sexual intercourse. He smoked too much, but used no other drugs that I could find. He was suffering from a small tumour, undetected, I assume, on the frontal lobe of his brain that would have caused him a lot of trouble in the year or two before it killed him. He had poor personal hygiene and his dentist will not notice his passing, not having seen him for several years. Your man was murdered; we wouldn't wish that on anyone, but I can't feel too sorry for him.' He frowned. 'The two I'm working on now, however, they have got to me, particularly the gentleman. In all my career I have never received someone here on two successive days, walking in on Wednesday, and wheeled in last night. It hasn't helped me to remain dispassionate.'

'I can understand that,' said McGuire, sympathetically. 'Can't you get someone else to do the examinations?'

'As dear Sir Magnus, God rest him, used to say, I've started, so I'll finish. Anyway, I'm being assisted by students. While I'm out here talking to you, they're furthering their education.'

'How far have you got?'

'I can give you a cause of death, in each case. If dead people can be lucky, they were. Asphyxiation, caused by the inhalation of thick, toxic smoke; I imagine that the fire and rescue people told you to expect that.'

'Actually they were fairly non-committal.'

'Not like them, but never mind; that's what saw them off, for sure.'

'How about identification? You've taken samples, I'm sure; we may have to match them against personal items from the house. We've been going over what's left of it.'

'Not necessary. Your CID colleagues have been hard at

work; they found dental insurance membership when they looked the place over and your Inspector Stallings reported it to me. I've got their dental records, and they match. There is also the fact that the male victim was wearing Mr Gerulaitis's trousers when he died, to judge by the melted credit cards that we found in the charred wallet in his pocket, once we had prised it out of his incinerated thigh.' Pause. 'Are you going to tell me why your department is so interested in accident victims?'

'Let's just say that we had a special interest in Valdas.'

'And have you found anything to further it?'

'No,' the head of CID admitted, 'but we're still looking.'

'And that's what we're doing,' Joe Hutchinson declared. 'I must get back to my grim workplace and see what my would-be successors have found. One thing I can tell you, though, that may be of mild interest. Wednesday's guest on my table had a very distinctive tattoo at the top of his right arm. Because of the way he was lying, that part of Mr Gerulaitis is reasonably well preserved, and it appears that he had its match, apart from the name at its heart. Both he and his cousin loved their wives, I think, and both visited the same tattooist.'

'Incurable romantics, eh,' McGuire muttered.

'No, Mario,' said the old pathologist. 'There's one event that cures everything.'

Fifty-one

'Should we be doing this?' Aileen asked.

Bob shrugged, and frowned, quizzically. The gesture emphasised the scar on his forehead, just above the bridge of his nose. It was shaped like a slash mark in a web address, and was one of several in his body, although the rest were hidden from sight. Occasionally, a stranger would ask him about it, and he would fob them off with one of a range of stories of childhood falls, or freak sporting injuries. His closest colleagues knew the truth . . . Mackie and McGuire had been there the night he had acquired it . . . but they kept it to themselves. 'I don't see why not,' he told her. 'This might be the senior officers' dining room and I'm at the top table, but it's just another staff canteen. We pay for our meals, and for our guests. Parliament doesn't sit on Fridays, but you're still busy nearly all the time. This is the first chance we've had in weeks to have lunch together, just you and me, no kids. Plus, I'm going to the Torphichen Place do tonight, so we won't be eating together then.'

'But what would the tabloids make of it if they knew?'

'Bugger the tabloids. Anyway, there's nothing for them to make. This facility isn't subsidised.'

'Are you certain?'

He laughed. 'I run this place, don't I? I've made damn sure that all the overhead costs are factored into the prices, including the energy and Maisie's wages. We are not leeching off the council tax payer, I promise you.'

'If you say so.' She shifted in her chair.

'You don't approve of this, do you?' he challenged. 'Go on, admit it; your socialist conscience makes you feel uncomfortable eating in a place that isn't open to everybody.'

She smiled, awkwardly. 'Well . . .'

'Do you think the same thought hasn't occurred to me?' he asked her, quietly. 'It did, years ago, when I reached the rank that opened it to me. I wondered then whether this sort of privilege belonged in the modern police force. Well, now I've reached the position where I could, if I chose, close it down and send all the chief officers and superintendents down to the main canteen, where they can queue up like everybody else and pay a lot less for their grub . . . which they can do anyway, if they choose.' He glanced around. 'I don't see Neil and Mario here; that's probably where they are. But am I going to shut it? No, of course I'm not. This isn't Mao's Red Army; we have a rank structure, and if rank has its privileges, then they're a pretty good incentive to aspiring cops. We all worked our way in here, everybody in this room. One or two unworthy people might have been slipped the key in the past, but those days went even before Jimmy Proud's time.'

'You actually have keys to here?' she exclaimed.

'Don't be daft; that was figurative. There's another thing about this place. There's more shop talked here than there is football. It's a good environment for senior people to discuss policing issues, in private.'

Aileen surveyed their fellow diners. There were a dozen other people in the room, in groups of three and four, all male apart from the only other twosome, Maggie Steele and Mary Chambers, who sat at a table in the furthest corner.

Bob seemed to read her mind. 'And yes,' he said, 'there will be more women here in future, on merit. By the time I leave this post, your gender might be in the majority. Then again they might not, but my point is that there'll be nothing holding them back. We have no glass ceilings; they're all shattered. If you're good enough you'll have the chance to get here; part of my job is talent spotting and when I look at someone all I see is a cop. I'm not concerned with how you urinate, or with your skin tone, or which team you bat for; I'm looking at ability, that's all. Jeez, look at Mary over there; she's a gay woman from Glasgow and here she is at the top table in the Edinburgh force. When I joined, she wouldn't have got within a mile of this place on at least two of those grounds, and maybe all three.'

'How is she, after her escape?' There was a sticking plaster over the wound on the superintendent's neck. 'I didn't expect to see her today.'

'She had the option, I promise you. I spoke to her myself and told her that she could take a week off to recover, longer if she needed it. She told me that a couple of large measures of eighteen-year-old Auchentoshan had done the job.'

'That's good.' She paused, as Maisie set a chicken supreme before her and served Bob his braised beef. 'I'll have a word with her when we've had this.'

'You do that.'

He had no sooner picked up his cutlery, than his phone rang. 'I wish I could ban mobiles in here,' he muttered. 'Unfortunately, we're never actually off duty.' He took it from his jacket pocket, and checked the incoming number. 'Yes, daughter,' he said. 'What's up?'

'Plenty,' Alex replied. 'Have you been leaning on Mitch Laidlaw?'

'There would be no point,' he told her. 'Mitch is so round these days, if I did he'd just roll over and bounce back up again. Why do you ask?'

'Because I've been taken off the Lietuvos account,' she snapped, 'and I can't shake this feeling that you might have had something to do with it.'

'Well I didn't,' he retorted. 'I haven't spoken to Mitch for a while. When you say taken off . . .'

'He called me in this morning, and told me that he'd thought things over and decided that he isn't prepared to have us run the companies indefinitely. He said that if Regine doesn't feel ready or able to come back and take control herself, she should make a permanent appointment as chief executive. Then he called her, with me still in the room, and told her the same thing. He was tactful about it, of course. He explained that it wasn't good practice, and that if she came back and didn't like some of the decisions that had been taken on her behalf it could lead to difficulties, and so on, and so on. He's given her two weeks to do it; in the meantime he's going to handle the business himself.'

'How did she take it?'

'Well enough, according to Mitch; she said that she expected to have somebody in place by that time, once certain obstacles were removed.'

'I wonder what she meant by that.' He frowned as an interpretation struck him. 'Hey,' he murmured, 'when Mitch spoke to her, did he tell her about Valdas and his wife?'

'That was the very first thing he told her.'

'How did she take that?'

'He said she sounded shocked, but not tearful.'

'And the remark about obstacles came after that?'

'Yes.' A small gasp escaped her. 'What are you saying?'

'Nothing, really. Since her husband's suicide my cop's brain's been working overtime, looking for things that aren't there.' He paused, smiling lightly. 'You pissed off, kid, yeah?'

'What do you think? I've just made partner, yet I'm being told . . . OK, not directly, but by implication . . . that I'm not up to the job.'

'That's mince and you know it. You want the straight truth? Mitch beat me to the punch. He read the situation right. A director and a senior employee in those companies have met sudden and unnatural ends within days of each other. Nasty coincidences they may be, but we're now taking a close interest in the other business activities of the two of them, and it's more than likely that our investigation will wash back on to the Lietuvos businesses. If that were to happen, I wouldn't want you involved, so yes, I was getting to the point when I'd have been having a frank discussion with your boss.'

'Behind my back?' Alex exclaimed.

'No, I'd have told you, but whether you liked it or not, I can't hide my feelings. You're best out of this, so you be a good daughter and thank Mitch for me.'

'You can bloody well thank him yourself. I'm ending what's been a great week on a right downer.'

'There'll be other, even better weeks.' Pause. 'Hey,' he asked, 'do you want to end it with a laugh?'

'That depends,' she said, cautiously. 'How?'

'I'm doing a guest appearance at the Central Division disco tonight, seven thirty for eight, in a hotel along at Haymarket. Aileen's opting out on political grounds, so would you like to chum your old man? It's not going to be a late night, not for me at any rate. The troops would be inhibited if I hung around too long, and anyway, these days I can't be seen to put too many over my neck at these affairs.'

'Will Griff Montell be there?'

'I've no idea, but it isn't his division, so . . .'

'Ah, what the hell, suppose he is, he's history as far as I'm concerned. OK. I'm up for it. We'll see how it goes; I might even stick around for longer than you.'

He was about to end the call, when she carried on. 'Oh, by the way,' she said. 'I checked that thing about Zaliukas's will. The new codicil he added didn't replace anything. Before it was added, the holding in Lituania SAFI went to Regine. It seems that he cut her out of that part of her inheritance.'

'Now that's interesting,' her father murmured. 'I wonder why he did that.'

Fifty-two

'Where's that other guy?' Arturus Luksa asked, his elbows on the table. His jacket was creased, and his shirt showed signs of having been worn for too long. He smelled stale, and his chin was dark with stubble.

'He's busy,' Mario McGuire told him. 'Why? Would you like us to get him back?'

'No,' said the prisoner quickly. 'I just like you get my fuckin' lawyer so we can get on with this.'

'Your fuckin' lawyer's on his way,' Neil McIlhenney drawled, 'or at least his office says he is.' He wandered across to the window of the first-floor interview room. 'They said he drives a Jag. I told security to leave a parking space for him, but I don't see any of those out there.'

'How's the lady?'

The superintendent's expression darkened; he glared at Luksa. 'Now, all of a sudden, you care.' He stepped towards the table and sat, facing him. 'Well, since you asked so nicely,' he hissed, 'she's on a life support system; any minute now we could get a call telling us to charge you with murder, not attempted.'

The Lithuanian paled, his eyes widening. 'But I hardly touched her,' he protested.

'What if I told you that you touched her enough to nick an artery, and that it was bleeding inside her throat? What if I told you that she collapsed, and by the time they got her to hospital, she'd almost drowned on her own blood?'

'Naw!'

'You see, you can have all the fuckin' lawyers you like but they won't impress us, or get you any sort of a deal. We're even going to do you for running one of the Estonian girls, whether you had her or not. Hell's teeth, I think we'll do you for trafficking them all, all twelve of them.'

'There was only nine,' Luksa protested.

'And how would you know that? You said you knew nothing about them, you never had one at your place. You know what I think? I reckon it was you, not Valdas, that brought them in. We've got one of the lassies under our protection. She was given a rough time, and right now she thinks we're wonderful; if we ask her she'll identify you like a shot.'

'It was Valdas! Him and Marius.'

McGuire lowered himself into the seat beside McIlhenney. 'Arturus,' he said, slowly, 'right now Valdas is a pork fucking scratching. He and his wife died in a fire in their house last night. He doesn't figure any more. As for this Marius guy, he didn't put a blade in one of our colleagues. We got you, babe, we got you. It'll be a long time before you mount that feisty wee wife of yours again. She'll be an old woman by then . . . mind you, from what PC Johnston told us, she doesn't look like the sort who'll wait around.'

Luksa buried his face in his hands. The head of CID grabbed his wrists and slammed them on to the table.

'You'll look at us when we're talking to you,' he growled. 'Who killed Linas Jankauskas?'

'No' me!' the man wailed, fearfully. 'You not going to do me for that as well.'

'You couldn't have killed him,' McIlhenney chuckled. 'You're a pussy who goes for women rather than men. Plus, you're an idiot, and whoever did Linas was an expert. So come on, who was it?'

'I don't know, honest I don't. It had nothing to do with me.'

'Why was he killed?' McGuire snapped. 'Do you know that?'

'I guess it was because he was freelancing with his girl. He keep her in his own place, he drug her, he fuck her himself, he sell her to punters and he keep nearly all the money. Linas, he was real idiot: he asked for it. If Valdas found out . . . Yes,' Luksa nodded, 'that's it. Valdas found out; he killed him.'

'No, that's not it. We know where Valdas was when Linas was killed.'

'How you be sure?'

'Because he was with us at the time, you clown. Now don't piss us about. We all know it wasn't Valdas, so . . .' He glared at the prisoner. 'Before you answer this, you should consider the situation, and ask yourself how, if that phone rings and we're told the worst about our colleague, how we're going to react . . . or how that other man you saw is going to react. So . . . who do you think killed Linas?'

'I think it may be the new guy.'

'New guy?' McIlhenney fired back. 'What new guy?'

'The guy who told us all to meet him.'

'When?'

'Wednesday, in the morning, day after Jock tells us we're closed for a while. I get a call at home from a man. He says I am to meet him in the Bruntsfield massage parlour, twelve o'clock, and that all the other managers will be there. I ask him who the fuck he thinks he is; he says he has a message for us all from Tomas. Now I don't know at this time that Tomas is dead, but I do know that if Tomas says "Come", you fucking do it.'

'So you went.'

'Too fucking right.'

'Why Bruntsfield?'

'Because it's the biggest place, maybe, I dunno. Anyway, I go and the other guys are there, except Linas. I ask Marius where he is and he says Linas is a fucking idiot, he hasn't turned up. Then this man shows us a piece of paper; it's from Tomas and it's signed by him.'

'How did you know it was genuine?'

'It was written in Lithuanian. The fella was Scottish. It was addressed to all us managers and it said that he has decided to get out of the business and that there's a new owner. When we read it, Marius asks him, "Is that you, the owner?" He says no, but that we should treat him as if he is if we want to stand any chance of keeping our jobs. Then he tells us that we stay closed until he says to open again; he says if anyone asks, we say it's as a mark of respect.'

'This man,' said McGuire. 'What's his name?'

'He didn't tell us, we didn't ask.'

'You didn't ask?'

'No, because when one of the guys says he's going to ask Tomas about this, he tell us that Tomas is dead, and that if we don't believe him we should check the papers in an hour or two. That shut us all up.'

'This was at midday?' McGuire murmured, almost to himself. Luksa nodded.

'The man,' said McIlhenney. 'Describe him.'

'Tough guy.'

'So are we, but you wouldn't be able to trace either of us on that description.'

'He's tall, but not a giant, maybe one metre eighty-five. Heavy built, big chest, thick waist.' He rubbed his face. 'Big chin, dark; maybe needed a shave, like me, or maybe that's how he was.'

'How was he dressed?'

'Jeans, red and white shirt . . . jacket with no sleeves. OK, that's all I remember, other than reading in the paper yesterday that Tomas was dead right enough. That's all I know now, all I can say. Honest. You tell the other man I'm sorry I no' tell him this. And please God, don't let the lady die. I pray for her, honest.'

'You'd better do that,' McGuire rumbled. He glanced out of the window, then grinned. 'Heaven be praised!' he exclaimed. 'Look, Arturus, you've had an answer already.' He pointed, in the direction of a female figure, walking down the slope from the main entrance to the headquarters building. She was stocky, and wore police uniform.

Luksa's mouth dropped open. For a moment, he started out

of his chair, before thinking better of it and subsiding. 'You two are bastards,' he hissed.

'Oh yes,' said McIlhenney, 'we surely are. Now,' he continued, looking at his watch, 'I reckon we've waited long enough for Ken Green. We don't need him here to charge you, and that's what we're going to do, formally, with the attempt to murder Superintendent Mary Chambers, in your house, yesterday evening. You've already been cautioned, and we don't require you to say anything at this stage. You'll appear in Edinburgh Sheriff Court this afternoon, where we'll ask that you be remanded in custody. Mr Green can make his way there, or his firm can send a substitute. Failing that, you can be represented by any other solicitor you choose to instruct, or by someone appointed by the court, if that's what you prefer.' He pressed a button under the table; a few seconds later the door opened and two escort officers entered the room. 'Take him back to his accommodation,' the detective superintendent ordered, 'and have a secure van standing by ready to take him up to Chambers Street. The fiscal's expecting him in the cells there in fifteen minutes.' He gazed at Luksa as he was pulled to his feet. 'Some advice, pal; you keep your fucking mouth shut from now on, and do exactly what Ken Green tells you, unless he's decided he wants no part of you.'

The Glimmer Twins sat in silence for a few seconds after the door had closed behind the prisoner. 'That was good thinking,' said McGuire at last, 'feeding him that nonsense about hidden arterial bleeding. You almost had me believing you; yes, it was worthy of the big fella himself. Are you going to tell him we got more out of Luksa than he did, or will I?'

'I think neither of us will brag about it.'

'Maybe not, maybe not.' The chief superintendent frowned. 'But our friend Arturus really is truly stupid. He fancies himself too. Know who he reminds me of? That Spanish barman in *Hotel Babylon*, on the telly. Mind you, was that description he gave us familiar, or was it not?'

McIlhenney nodded. 'The boy's not a *Dandy* reader, is he? Otherwise he'd have mentioned Desperate Dan too. It's a spot-on match with the one Montell got from the receptionist.'

'Absolutely, and he gave us lots more than that. The letter Desperate showed the managers: the one from Tomas. How did he get that? Assuming it was genuine, that is. Maybe Valdas wrote it.'

'I don't buy that. No, Tomas Zaliukas wrote it, he gave it to Desperate and then went up Arthur's Seat and killed himself.'

'Then get someone back into his house,' said McGuire, 'to copy all the files off his computer then look for one that's in Lithuanian and was created on or before Tuesday evening. If we get a result, find a translator.'

'But how did he know him in the first place? Who is he and what's the connection?'

'Wait a minute, though,' his friend countered. 'We know who the new owner was. It was Laima, Valdas Gerulaitis's wife.'

'And now fellow pork scratching. You're bloody right. And Tomas changed his will in her favour just before he died. So what was her connection to Desperate?'

'Christ knows. Do we know how the will read before that?'

'No,' said McIlhenney, 'but I'm sure we can find out.'

'Have McGurk and Sauce do that; Alex should be able to help them. Meantime that leaves us with this guy Marius. Thanks to our friend we can now have a serious talk with him about trafficking young women for prostitution. He's not going to like that at all.'

'Can we prove it, though? Anna might have identified Valdas and Linas, but did she ever see him?'

'Time will tell,' said the head of CID, 'but right now I just want to find out what he knows. We need to trace the rest of those girls. They're my greatest worry, mate; they might just have become too much of a liability. I'll tell you what; you're on a roll, so you take Marius, but don't delegate it to Becky, you go for him yourself. You're doing that, I'll go up to the Sheriff Court and make sure that our friend Luksa's remand hearing goes according to plan.'

'OK.' The superintendent frowned. 'You know what's liable to happen with him, don't you?'

McGuire nodded, sagely. 'Sure, I can read that script. A good QC will portray him as a frightened man, cornered by police who invaded his home without a warrant, picking up the first thing that came to hand and lashing out blindly. Charlie and Mary will be good witnesses, and the forensic backs them up, but when Luksa's lawyer offers a guilty plea to a charge of serious assault, the Crown Office will take it. Unless Bob leans on them.'

'He won't though; I reckon he'll be more likely to pass word discreetly to the judge, whoever that is, that he's not pleased. In that case Luksa'll still be looking at a right few years inside, and maybe a fine alongside that.'

'Probably,' the head of CID conceded, 'but that's down the road. For now, let's get on with what we've got to do.'

He was heading for the door when his mobile sounded, and vibrated in the pocket of his shirt. He plucked it out, and looked at the number, but it registered as 'anonymous'. 'McGuire,' he answered.

'Mario, my boy.' Professor Joe Hutchinson sounded cheerful, possibly even triumphant.

'Prof. What can you do for me?'

'I have some interesting findings to throw your way. I have a prodigy on my hands. One of my students, a young lady called Kneilands, has excelled herself.'

'How come?' the chief superintendent asked, intrigued, fired up instantly by the pathologist's enthusiasm.

'I told you, I think, that I had left my disciples to complete the detailed examination of the remains of the Gerulaitis couple. Well, Ms Kneilands really got into the detail. She has established that every one of the fingers on Valdas's left hand, and the thumb and index finger on the right were dislocated prior to his death, at the knuckle and at the major joint.'

'And?'

'And?! What do you mean "and"?'

'The guy was trapped behind a locked door, Joe,' McGuire reminded him. 'He must have gone frantic battering it, trying to get out. Surely hand injuries aren't surprising?'

'These are. If he'd done that, I'd have expected fractures, rather than dislocations, or certainly as well as, but there are none, none at all. And why are only seven fingers damaged? In your scenario he'd have been battering so hard that . . .'

Hutchinson stopped, and McGuire heard a sigh. 'OK, I suppose that under oath I'd have to concede that was possible. But there's another thing, his right hand seems to have been slightly larger and more muscled than the left, indicating that he was right-handed. So, if the injuries were sustained as you suggest, why was the left hand more badly damaged than the right?'

'So what are you saying to me? What's your clever student's hypothesis?'

'That these injuries were not self-inflicted,' the pathologist declared.

'Could he have been in an accident before he died?' the head of CID asked him.

'And sat down at the supper table as if nothing had happened? Don't be absurd. He'd have been in extreme pain; he'd have been unable to hold his cutlery. And by the way, neither victim had eaten anything for some time before death. If they were at table when disaster struck, then they must have been saying grace. Mario, this man was tortured; that's what I'm saying to you ... although not to a jury, not without qualification, at any rate.'

'Immediately before death? You are quite certain?'

'Yes. There is evidence of fresh bleeding within the displaced joints.'

'Fuck!'

'Now that's the reaction I was expecting.'

McGuire ignored the professor's exclamation. 'Back to the cause of death, Joe. You said smoke inhalation?'

'Yes. They suffocated. Was the room carpeted?'

'Yes.'

'Then it must have been treated with some sort of compound, for the traces in their lungs were thick and black. Alternatively, was there furniture in the room? Armchairs, sofas, with big cushions? I've seen photographs but I couldn't discern anything.'

'No.' The head of CID hesitated. 'Joe,' he murmured into the phone, 'you realise you're standing everything on its head, don't you?'

'There's nothing I like better.'

'Then why am I not surprised? Report please, Prof, to the last detail. Everything you've just told me, and you'd better give me a statement from the clever Ms Kneilands as well to back it up.'

'Soonest. God,' the old man chuckled, 'I love my job.'

'What the hell was that?' asked McIlhenney, as his colleague ended the call.

'Gold dust, chum. Absolute gold dust. Hang on.' He scrolled through his directory for the fire and rescue switchboard, then pressed his call button. 'Frances Kerr, please,' he said as he was connected. 'Tell her it's DCS McGuire.'

'Be patient,' the investigator said as she came on line, but with a smile in her voice 'You'll have your report this afternoon.'

'I don't think so,' he told her. 'Frances, straight up, what odds would you give me against smoke inhalation being the cause of death in both cases?'

'Honestly? Five to one, but I wouldn't advise you to take the bet.'

'Then don't go into the bookie business, for that's exactly what it was. They both inhaled enough thick black smoke to kill them before the fire did.'

'There was nothing in that room to produce thick smoke of any colour.'

'You sure of that? No treated carpet, upholstery?'

'There was nothing of that nature, I promise you.'

'In that case, it looks as if they were killed somewhere else, and left where they were, before the fire was started.'

'Hold on, I'm dead right about how the fire started.'

'Then somebody's an expert. Did your sniffer dogs do their stuff?'

'Yes,' the fire investigator declared, vehemently. 'They went all over the room; not as much as a bark.'

'Then get them back, and get yourself back along there too, please, soon as you can. If you need help from our people, call them in without bothering to refer back to me. I need you and those dogs to go over the whole damn house. Something else happened there, Frances, something we don't know about. I need you to tell me what it was.'

Fifty-three

'What time do you think you'll be home?' Aileen asked as she slipped her car key into the ignition.

'Not too late, I hope,' said Bob. 'You can still come with me, you know.'

'Thanks, but no thanks; I've got some paperwork to get through and if I can do it tonight it'll free up some time at the weekend. Plus, the kids need some time too. And anyway,' she added, 'you'll have your big kid to keep you company.'

'Are you still going to Glasgow for your constituency surgery tomorrow?'

'I have to, otherwise the voters will be forgetting what I look like.' She looked up at him. 'You did know what you were signing up for when you married me, didn't you?'

'Just as you did with me. We're a popular couple, eh, if you know your classics; politician and policeman, woman of the people and man of the people.'

He closed the door gently, watching her with a smile as she reversed out of the visitor parking space and drove down the slope towards the exit, reflecting on the twists and turns that life can bring. They had met for the first time in the building behind him, when Aileen had been deputy Justice Minister in a previous Scottish administration, before the fall of Thomas Murtagh, MSP, her predecessor as First Minister, and her own rapid rise to the top job. He had been attracted at first sight. His marriage to Sarah had been far down the road to failure at that time, but his secret suspicion, voiced only to Aileen herself, on their brief honeymoon, was that he would have fallen for her even if it had been stable.

'In that case, Skinner,' she had replied, 'you'd have had no chance. I'd my reputation to consider.'

'True?'

'No; not for a second.'

Bob Skinner did not do guilt, as a rule, but he still felt a few twinges over Sarah. He recognised that he had put as many holes in their marriage as she had. If he had made more allowances for the fact that she was an American in an alien world . . . If he had been willing to put her first . . . There had been an occasion when he had been invited to dinner by a friend from the US Embassy, and had been offered, straight out, there and then, a two-year secondment to the FBI with the possibility of a permanent post. That would have put him in a whole new world, but he had turned it down flat, without even mentioning it to his wife.

His fluttering conscience did not stop him from being happy, though. His one concern was that Sarah should find her own contentment and so when he had learned, not from her, but from his son Mark, that she had ended her last relationship, it had set him worrying.

He was still thinking of her, and of what might be in her

mind, as he walked back into the command corridor and saw Superintendent David Mackenzie emerge from Gerry Crossley's room, his uniform military sharp as ever, a folder in his hand. He had seen changes in people over the years, the evolution of Maggie Steele from serious, solitary young detective into an all-round officer destined for a chief constable's chair, perhaps his own when he was done with it, and the growth of McGuire and McIlhenney from knock-about comedians into the most formidable detective duo in the country, but no metamorphosis pleased him more than that of the man formerly known as Bandit. When he had transferred from Strathclyde CID, at Skinner's instigation, he had been brash, occasionally over-confident, but brilliant. His work with the drugs squad had been outstanding. Yet what he . . . but no one else . . . had seen as a failure on a dangerous operation had led him into a crisis of self-doubt, and on to the inevitable crutch of alcohol that had put his career in danger. Skinner had been advised to tip him over the side, to retire him early on health grounds, but he had refused. He had still seen a spark, somewhere deep in the ashes, and so he had brought Mackenzie close to him, and had been rewarded by his complete reinvention of himself, as administrator rather than detective, and as a man of substance rather than of image.

'You after me, David?' he asked.

'Yes, Chief,' the superintendent replied.

'Come on then.' He led the way into his office, with a nod to Crossley, who handed him some internal mail as he passed. He dumped it in his in-tray, dropped into his seat, and motioned Mackenzie towards the one opposite. 'Shoot,' he said. 'What is it?'

'It's about the task Neil McIlhenney passed on to me,' the superintendent replied, laying his folder on Skinner's desk.

'Oh yes. Sorry I didn't brief you myself, but I had a few things piling up at the time. Have you got a result already?'

'Yes.'

'Well done; that's sharp.'

'I had cooperation at the other end.'

'So Jonas Zaliukas has got a record.'

'Yes, Chief, but not the kind you mean. When I put the request to the Lithuanian justice ministry, they came back very quickly and passed me on to the defence ministry. Jonas Zaliukas joined the army as a regular eleven years ago, after graduating from university with an engineering degree. He didn't join the sappers, though; he did officer training and was posted to a front-line infantry regiment. You might think that being a foot soldier in a Baltic nation would have been fairly boring, but five years ago, Lithuania committed troops to a UN force that was sent into the Congo to put down a genocidal civil war, and he was second in command. It got pretty bloody; Zaliukas's CO was killed, he took over and was involved in some very fierce fighting before the rebels were subdued. They stayed there for another eighteen months, before they were withdrawn. A few months after that, Major Zaliukas, as he was then, resigned his commission.'

'On what grounds?'

'He said he'd seen enough blood. He was offered a desk job, but he turned it down. Since then he's been in the property development business; he has a company of his own, and his brother Tomas is listed as a director, but not as a shareholder.'

'So why's he here, I wonder?' the chief constable mused.

'That I don't know for sure. However, he's still an officer in the army reserve, a colonel now; last week, he advised the ministry that he'd be unavailable for an indefinite period, citing family problems as the reason.'

'Family problems, indeed! And a whole week ago. Do we have a physical description of this man?'

Mackenzie nodded. 'Better than that.' He picked up the folder he had brought with him and handed it across the desk. Skinner opened it; the top sheet was in Lithuanian, but the figures '1.79m' and '87kg' were clear enough. He flicked it over and saw a figure of a man in uniform: narrow waist, wide shoulders, a calm face with sharp features and eyes that gave nothing away.

'One thing's for sure,' he murmured. 'This bloke's no cowboy.'

Fifty-four

'Look,' the man barked, as Neil McIlhenney and DI Becky Stallings walked into the interview room at the rear of the ground floor of the Torphichen Place police office. 'What is this? You lifted us last night for no reason. I told you that, and now you've done it again. You turn up with a warrant to search my flat and you bring me here. This is pure harassment.'

'No,' said the detective superintendent, cheerfully. 'We're well short of harassment, aren't we, Inspector?'

'Absolutely, boss. Harassment's when we keep you all night before we get round to interviewing you, and check on you every hour in your cell, to make sure you haven't topped yourself and also to make sure that when we do get around to talking to you, you're well and truly knackered. We haven't got around to that yet, but it could happen.'

'So let's see,' McIlhenney continued. 'The recorder is running, yes?' Stallings nodded. McIlhenney identified both of them, and stated the place, date and time. 'We haven't met before,' he said, 'so for my peace of mind as well as for the tape, you are Mr Marius Ramanauskas, yes?'

The detainee nodded. He was a fat man, but with Popeye

forearms and heavy shoulders that marked him out as potentially formidable. He wore a dark suit, with a pale blue shirt and a matching tie that might have been satin.

'I need you to say it,' the superintendent told him.

'Yes, I am Marius Ramanauskas and where's my fucking lawyer?'

'Lady present, sir.'

'I don't see any,' Ramanauskas muttered. 'Where's my fucking lawyer? Where's Ken Green? I told you to call his office an hour ago.'

Stallings leaned forward. 'We did, Marius. But you should watch less telly. This is Scotland, with its own quirky little system, which I just love, after years in the Met. You have the right to a private interview with a solicitor before you go to court, but you don't have the right to have him in here.'

'And in any event,' McIlhenney added, 'if Mr Green is anywhere right now, he's up at the Sheriff Court representing your friend Mr Luksa, on a charge of the attempted murder of a police officer. Mind you, last I heard he didn't seem too keen to act for him either. Now: let's focus on the business at hand, shall we? Where are the Estonian girls you and Valdas Gerulaitis smuggled into this country?'

Ramanauskas shook his head. 'What's this fairy story?' He laughed. 'What girls are these you're talking about?'

'It's not just me that's talking. Your pal Luksa's been marking our card. About three months ago, Valdas Gerulaitis went to Tallin, in Estonia, and recruited nine young girls, with the usual promises of jobs that pay big money. He drove them down to Holland in a closed van . . . no problem in these days of open frontiers in Europe . . . where they were transferred to a lorry, and driven on board a ferry to Newcastle. We've done some checking up on you, Marius, and it hasn't taken us long to discover that you hold a valid heavy goods licence. When we do some more investigating, we're going to place you on that ferry, in late October, and we're going to identify the lorry you drove. You'd probably taken a legit cargo out and registered the vehicle as empty on the way back, for customs clearance. You and Valdas transferred the girls into another van as soon as you got off the ferry, and he took them on to Edinburgh, where they were shared out, like cattle, among you massage parlour managers. That's what happened; that's what we know.'

'Then prove it,' the man challenged. 'With poor Valdas dead, from what I read in this morning's paper, you'll have trouble.'

'I don't think so. You forgot about Anna Romanova.'

'Who?'

'The girl Linas Jankauskas had. She's under our protection, and I'm bloody sure she'll identify you as the fat man she saw when they switched vehicles in Newcastle. And we can identify you as the man who's been housing the other eight girls for the last three months, in your flat in Scotland Street, while they've been broken in as prostitutes. We haven't finished going over the place yet, but we've found enough female traces on your bedding, in your bathrooms and in the rest of the house to nail you for sure. We've been talking to your neighbours; you couldn't expect them not to notice, Marius. One of them complained to us that it was like living above a girl backpackers' hostel. We're not done either; we're also going to crawl over every one of those massage parlours, so that we can match samples and identify where each girl worked. On top of all that we've found drug paraphernalia in the flat. I'm sure we'll tie that to some of the girls as well. You are done, pal. You would not believe how done you are.'

'Bollocks,' Ramanauskas muttered, but his eyes were fixed on the table.

'I'm impressed by your command of English,' the superintendent snapped. 'Here's what's going to happen, Marius. You're going to sign a statement admitting to being involved in people trafficking, or else.'

'Or else what?'

'Or else I'm going to let you go.'

'Uh?'

'You heard me, I'm going to kick you out of here on your arse.'

'What game are you playing with me?' the man exclaimed.

'No game. It might have escaped your notice, but Lithuanians are becoming an endangered species in Edinburgh. First poor old Tomas, your boss, shoots himself, then somebody very skilled breaks Linas's neck for him. To top it off, somebody kills Valdas.'

'What you talking about? Valdas died in a fire in his house, the papers say.'

'Yes, but not accidentally, we don't think. We suspect that he was murdered, and his wife too. Before I came in here I had a call from my boss, and we now have a new theory that we're running. Goes like this. Jonas Zaliukas, Tomas's brother, with serious combat experience in Africa, is in town, and he is holding you guys, that's to say so far Valdas and Linas, responsible in some way for Tomas killing himself. It looks as if Valdas was tortured before he died, so we reckon that Jonas now knows about your involvement as well. I don't know what he's got planned for you, but I'm damn sure it won't be pretty. So, Marius. What's it to be? Your choice.'

Ramanauskas stared at Stallings. 'He wouldn't do that, would he, lady?'

She threw back her head and laughed. 'So I'm a lady all of a sudden. Oh yes, he would. He'd even issue a press statement saying that you'd been interviewed and released without charge. It would be like tying a label round your neck. Jonas is bound to know by now that you've been lifted. For all we know he's waiting for you to step outside. Do you fancy your chances against him?' The prisoner paled. 'No,' she murmured, 'I thought not.'

'Tell us about Jonas,' said McIlhenney. 'When did you first meet him?'

'Just over a week ago,' the Lithuanian replied. 'Thursday, last week. Valdas told us all to meet him, in Portofino, the restaurant, in the morning before it opens for lunch. When we did, there was this man with him; youngish bloke, cool.'

'Cool?'

'That's best way I can describe him. Together; in control of himself. He was very calm, stood very still, his eyes they were steady, deep blue. He wasn't all that big, but you could not imagine fucking with this guy, not ever. You know what I mean?'

'I reckon I do. Did Valdas introduce him?'

'Yeah. He said that this was his cousin, Tomas's younger

brother, and that he had come over from Lithuania to . . . how he put it? . . . to take care of a few things.'

'And how did he seem when he was telling you this?'

'Seem?'

'Was he relaxed, was he happy, was he nervous?'

'He tried to look normal, but he wasn't. He looked uncomfortable. It was right tense in there, in fact.'

'Did Jonas say anything?'

'Aye. First off, he tell us we could call him Jonas, or colonel, or even Jock since we were in Scotland. One or two of the lads laughed; he didn't. Then he said he wasn't pleased to be here, that he had his own business to run in Vilnius and that was where he should be. But he said that his older brother had asked him for help and he was bound to give it. He said that some of us had been very stupid, and that we had no idea of the bother we'd caused. He told us that because of this he was now in charge of all of us, and that we would do what he said, without question.'

'How did that go down?'

Ramanauskas frowned. 'Like I told you, he's a guy you take seriously. We all sat quiet . . . apart from Linas. He jumped up, got in his face and said, "Why the fuck should we? Tomas never interferes with us, so why should we answer to you?" Jonas just looked at him for a bit, and then he hit him. I don't know what with, for he was too quick; all I know is that big Linas was on the floor gasping for breath like a fish out of water. "Any other questions?" Jonas asked, but of course there were none.' He shuddered. 'If you say he killed Linas, I'll believe you.'

'Was that the end of the meeting?' asked Stallings.

'Not quite. He said the new girls had to go; that we were to get them out of the parlours. He told me to keep them at my place until arrangements were made to move them out.'

'But you didn't take Anna Romanova to your place.'

'I never had her there; I could only take the eight. She always stayed with Linas.'

'Where she was drugged and raped,' McIlhenney said, slowly. 'Did you drug all nine? Was that how you forced them to prostitute themselves?'

'Only the two youngest; they were fresh meat, to fill up the van. The older lassies were all on the game back in Tallin; Valdas found them there and offered them more money to work for him, simple as that. None of them were junkies. Right at the start Valdas said there would be no drugs in the parlours, and that anyone who tried it would be moved offshore.'

Stallings frowned. 'Moved offshore?'

Ramanauskas grinned. 'One of his wee sayings from the old days. About two miles offshore, he meant, weighted down.'

'So when you fed those kids dope you were endangering yourself?'

'No. Valdas told me to do it; he said it was OK. They were always fixed at my place anyway, never at work.'

'So when did Jonas take them,' asked McIlhenney, brusquely, 'and where to? Or are they offshore as well, poor kids?'

'Jonas never took them. On Wednesday morning, about half ten, two women rang my door buzzer. It's got a video camera, ken, so I could see them. I asked what they wanted and they said they were the removal firm.'

'And you let them in, just like that?'

'I guessed they'd come from Jonas. Did they no'?'

'We don't know,' the superintendent admitted.

'So they might have been connected to the other guy?'

'Do you mean the man you all met in Bruntsfield?'

'That's right.'

'Maybe they were, but that's not relevant to this interview. Tell us what happened when you let the women in.'

'They came up the stairs, and told me to tell the girls to get packed. I asked them where they were taking them. The older one told me to mind my own fuckin' business.'

'And you took that from her?' Stallings queried.

'If they were from Jonas, like I thought they were, too right. So I did as I was told. The girls had fuck all to pack, so it took no time at all. Then I'd to tell them to use the lav if they needed. Once they were all sorted, we took them downstairs two at a time.'

'What do you mean "we"?'

'The younger woman stayed upstairs; the older one and I took the first two lassies down and out through the back garden and intae the lane. They'd a mini-bus parked there. She stayed with them, I went back upstairs and took another four down, two at a time, then the second woman took the last pair and that was that.'

'These two women,' McIlhenney asked, 'were they Lithuanian?'

'No, Scottish.'

'Then how did they communicate with the girls.'

'A few of them speak quite good English by now, so no problem.'

'Did they all go willingly?'

Ramanauskas looked the superintendent in the eye. 'These kids do what they're told, mister.'

'Describe the women for us.'

'They were both flashy,' he replied, 'but hard in their eyes. Know what I mean? Dyed blond, heavy make-up. They were lookers though; I'd have seen to the younger one, for sure; maybe even the older one too. The younger one wore jeans and a bomber jacket; the other dark slacks and a furry thing.'

'Ages?'

'I'm no great wi' women's ages, but the older one's probably in her forties, the other maybe ten years younger . . . or maybe more.'

'Could they have been mother and daughter?'

The Lithuanian frowned. 'Aye,' he exclaimed, 'now you mention it, at a pinch they could.' Pause. 'But naw, they weren't. They never spoke to each other much, but when they did, the younger one called the other one "Goldie". She wouldn't have done that if it had been her mammy, would she?'

'Did they give you any clue where they were going?'

'Not the faintest. And I never asked. For all I knew, they might have been moving them offshore. If they were, for sure I didna want to know.'

Fifty-five

'Two women?' McGuire repeated.

'That's what Ramanauskas said,' McIlhenney told him. 'That and a lot more. Whatever went wrong in Tomas Zaliukas's business life happened last week, for that's when he sent for his brother. You know, up to now we've been looking for this Desperate Dan guy for Linas's murder, but now I'm not so sure. When I was interviewing Marius I spun him a line about Jonas having taken care of him and of the Gerulaitases, taking revenge for his brother, but now I'm wondering whether it might just be true after all.'

'But what about the girl's statement? That points to him, doesn't it?'

'The girl was out of her scone, Mario. She might have heard Jonas rowing with Linas, not the other fella. He could have arrived and found him dead already.'

'Would Jonas be capable of killing him, the way it was done?'

'Oh, yes. Ramanauskas saw him in action; the two of them had a run-in before, apparently, and Jonas dropped him like a stone.'

'Mmm,' the head of CID murmured. 'The boss did tell us he has a heavy-duty military background. Let's prioritise him; put out a statement saying that we're anxious to interview him.'

'About the murders?'

'No, let's not blow it up. Just say we believe he's in Scotland and need to talk to him about his brother's suicide.'

'We could get Crown Office permission to issue his mug shot.'

'We don't need it if he's not officially a suspect. Use the picture, but play down the statement. Say we believe he may be in Scotland but may not know of his brother's death. That should stop the press from getting too excited.'

'OK. I'll brief Royston.'

'You better be quick,' McGuire laughed. 'He'll be out the door any minute. The boss doesn't like people whose minds are elsewhere.'

'True. Where are you, by the way?'

'I'm sitting in my car outside the Gerulaitis house. I had a text from Frances Kerr, the fire investigator, while I was in court, telling me she wants to see me on site.'

'Did she say what it was about?'

'She used the word "development", but without the vowels. Whether it's positive or negative, I'm about to find out.'

'How did court go?' asked McIlhenney.

'Routine, as always; no plea or declaration and a remand in custody. No application for bail for us to oppose. Ken Green never showed up, though. The fiscal's office had to get a duty solicitor to represent our man; not that he needed much. After his chat with us he was dead keen to be locked up.'

'Funny, so was Marius. I've left Becky and Jack to take his statement. We're going to do him for possession of heroin for the moment. Once Anna Romanova's fit enough, we'll put him in a line-up. If she can identify him, we'll do him for trafficking as well.'

'Maybe Green will turn up to defend him. I wonder where he's got to?'

'He's probably decided to steer clear of this business. Handling the licensing for massage parlours is one thing; defending a pimp on a police attempted murder charge is something else again. Mario,' McIlhenney murmured, 'given what we know now, should we think about going to the court and having those licences revoked?'

'That's not our decision, mate; it'll be for somebody with "Chief Constable" in their rank. But if we do that, we'll need to be sure we get a result. At the moment, what we know and what we can prove are two different things. The only girl we have in our custody is Anna, and she was kept in Jankauskas's flat.'

'True. In that case we'd better find these two women that Marius told us about.'

'Before they dispose of the witnesses?' McGuire suggested.

'I don't want to think about that. Who do you think they are?'

'Auntie Aggie and Katey; they have to be.'

'Who the fuck are Auntie Aggie and Katey?'

'Did you not read Desperate Dan when you were a kid? Go and look them up. I'm going to pick my way through the ashes.'

The head of CID ended the call, and stepped out of his car. He took a pair of wellingtons from the back seat, pulled them on to replace his moccasins and walked round to the back of the house. Frances Kerr was standing in the garden, smoking a cigarette. 'Jesus,' the chief superintendent exclaimed, 'I thought that would be a sacking offence in your job.'

'Only if it contaminates a fire scene,' she retorted. 'Are you telling me that polis don't smoke?'

'This one doesn't, nor any of his close colleagues. It's not banned, but our boss disapproves, since we're all required to be physically fit.'

'So are we, but smoke's part of our lives.' She took a last draw, then ground the butt into the grass. 'Come on and I'll show you what I've found.'

She led him through the conservatory and into the devastated kitchen, then on, until she came to a door at the far end. It was blackened but intact. She pushed it open; behind it, McGuire could see the remnants of what had been a stair. It had been replaced by a ladder. 'Follow,' said the investigator. She took the lead in descending, into a spacious area, brightly lit by temporary lamps.

McGuire sniffed, and at the same moment felt glass under his feet. 'Wine cellar,' he said, a declaration rather than a question.

'Spot on,' Kerr conceded, 'or it was. Everything's gone now, every single bottle has either exploded or had its cork blown out.'

'But how did the fire get down here?' the head of CID asked. 'The ceiling's almost intact; surely it didn't burn down the way.'

'You're not dumb, big boy, are you? It is possible that sparks dropped through and ignited this area, but that's not what I think happened. Come on and I'll show you.' She led the way across the basement, to a frame where once there had been a door. 'The dogs found this,' she told him, as a preamble. 'They're worth their weight in Pedigree Chum, those two. Look.' She stood back, to let him see inside a small chamber. In the centre of its concrete floor was a shapeless black mass, soaked and stinking.

'This was a storeroom, of sorts,' she said. 'We found odds and ends among the debris, including four lengths of melted plastic . . . only they were just outside the door.'

'Plastic?'

'Yes. They might have been restraints, so your forensic people tell me. Pull-on handcuffs. The one thing I know for sure is that they'd been cut. Now,' she continued, 'see that black stuff? When I went over the scene at first I was a bit puzzled by the conservatory. I found the ashes of chairs, and a sofa, old-fashioned wooden furniture, but I didn't find any upholstery residue. Finally I reasoned that since it was winter, they weren't using the place, and they'd put all the cushions away somewhere. I don't think that now. I believe that the couple could have been killed down here, by people who wanted to make it appear that they'd died in a fire.'

'How? How was it done?'

'The way I see it, they were tied with those restraints, hand and foot, the conservatory cushions were brought in here and ignited with petrol. It's the simplest accelerant of all, and that's what the dogs scented. I've looked at the soot on the walls. It tells me that the material was old, and not flame resistant at all. It would have been lethal. As I see it, Mr and Mrs Gerulaitis were shut in here, hog-tied and helpless. The area would have filled with smoke in seconds and they'd have died within minutes. When they were, the room was opened. They were dragged out, the cuffs were cut off them and left where I found them. The victims were then carried upstairs, placed by the locked door and the main fire was started, in the way I've described. Meanwhile down in the cellar, the original fire was left to burn, to make us think, as we did until you questioned it, that there was only one seat, upstairs. To make absolutely sure, they should have left the door open at the top of the stairs, but maybe they couldn't, maybe there was too much smoke, so they took a chance that the floor would burn through, as it did, although not completely.'

'How did they get out?'

'I'd suggest that they locked the door behind them and went out through the conservatory. We've only found one key, and we've looked all through the house.'

'Jesus. How many people are we talking about?' McGuire asked

'Given that there were two victims,' the investigator replied, 'you'd normally assume that there were at least two of them as well, but I suppose it's conceivable that one determined person could have done it. One thing's certain, though; however many there were, one of them had to have been an expert. The fire upstairs was started in exactly the way I described this morning, by a damp towel placed on exposed wiring. No layman could improvise that. You're probably looking for someone with a degree, or a qualification in electrical engineering, and with a knowledge of chemical reactions as well, given how they were killed.' She paused. 'Or maybe you're looking for a fireman.'

'Any suggestions?'

She smiled. 'None that I know.'

'That's brilliant, Frances,' said McGuire. 'Would it stand up in court?'

'Ah, that I don't know for sure. We can't put the dogs in the witness box, and we can't prove that those plastic ties were used on the victims, but we can identify that smoke in their lungs, and show where it came from. Some of it did come up through the floorboards, though; I've established that too.'

'But can you rule out accident?'

'In my own mind, yes. In the minds of a majority on a jury . . . I'd have to wait and see.'

Fifty-six

The last thing that George Regan wanted was a call-out at five o'clock. He had spent the day in the CID office in Haddington completing an itemised list of goods stolen from the Witches' Hill pro shop in the second robbery, and had just submitted it for circulation to police forces throughout the country. He knew what would be coming his way once it hit the intelligence network: wisecracks and innuendo from all over Scotland. Not that they were needed. None of his senior officers seemed to be blaming him for not anticipating a possible return visit by the thieves . . . a fresh tyre track matching one left the previous day had been found at the scene that morning . . . but he was, for sure. The presence of the Marquis and of Proud Jimmy had made for one of the most embarrassing moments of his professional life, and all he wanted to do was go home to his wife and, whether she was up for it or not, insist that she spruce herself up so that they could take the train to Edinburgh for a meal in his favourite Chinese, the Kweilin in Dundas Street, with a nice bottle of Chablis, or maybe two if he could persuade Jen to share them with him, and afterwards . . .

Or maybe he wouldn't. Maybe the notion of getting your wife drunk in the hope of sex was just too pathetic, repugnant even. Maybe instead he'd ask Lisa McDermid if she was up for a night out; sometimes he thought he saw a look in her eye that suggested she might be. Then again, maybe he'd take the easy option; go down to the Longniddry Inn and get quietly blootered. But that wouldn't get his end away, though, would it?

'Hey, Lisa,' he began.

She looked across their facing desks and smiled. He wondered if she had been reading his mind, or if . . . Christ, he hadn't been thinking aloud, had he? 'Yes, George,' she replied . . . and that was when the phone rang.

He snatched it up, annoyed at the shattering of the moment. 'Yes,' he snapped.

'If that's what it's going to be like, I might as well not bother,' said Marty White, the station inspector.

'Not bother with what?' Regan said, more gently.

'Asking you and Lisa if you'd do me a big favour, one that's going to be a real pain in the arse for you.'

'No, maybe you shouldn't. But go ahead anyway; what is it?'

'I've just had the communications centre on the blower. They've had a call from a member of the public who says he's found a car off the road up behind Garvald, with a guy in it he says is dead. My problem is that all my vehicles are committed elsewhere, and I can't get one from Midlothian or Edinburgh for upwards of forty-five minutes. It'll be well dark before they can get there. I don't have an available uniform. You're my only hope, Obi-Wan Kenobi.'

Regan smiled, for the first time that day. 'You got lucky, Marty; you picked my favourite movie. Hold on while I have a word with Princess Leia here.' He cupped his hand over the mouthpiece. 'Lisa, are you up for helping uniform out of a jam? It could be messy, mind.'

'Why not?' she replied. 'Better than watching you sat there scowling.'

'OK,' said the DI to White. 'You're on. Where is it? How do we get there?'

'Bloody incomers,' sighed the East Lothian native. 'Head south, over the Tyne, towards Gifford at first, but you'll see the sign for Garvald soon. It's only about five miles away. When you get there, head up the hill out of the village, past Nunraw Abbey and on towards the White Castle. Don't go looking for a castle, though; it's an old hill fort, that's all. A bit past that and you'll find it. On you go now, before you run out of daylight.'

The two detectives headed out to Regan's car, parked at the back of the station. The inspector's directions were easy to follow, and the road was quiet once they were out of Haddington. They reached Garvald in less than ten minutes, and drove through, as directed. 'That's the White Castle,' McDermid pointed out as they passed a Historic Scotland sign by the roadside. The DI glanced to his left, but saw nothing, other than a flat hilltop.

'Wow,' he replied, poker-faced.

They had gone no further than a few hundred yards when he had to brake, hard. A truck sat ahead of them, pulled as far up on to the verge as its driver had been able. He stood beside it, a countryman dressed in blue overalls and muddy boots, of middle height and age, slim, and bald, with a narrow moustache. Regan took a torch from the dashboard compartment and switched on his emergency warning lights as they stepped out. 'Are you the polis?' the man asked. 'I'm Joe Leghorn; Ah'm the grieve at the farm just up the road. Some business this. Poor bugger's doon there.'

He stepped aside and the detectives saw that the fence behind him was shattered. Beyond it the ground sloped away for a few feet and then disappeared. 'It's a wee cliff, ken,' Leghorn told them, as he led them to the edge. 'The road's muddy, like, after the thaw the day, but he must have been doing a hoor of a speed tae have gone off like that.'

The DI peered over the edge and saw, in the fading light, the underside of a car; one of its wheels was turning slowly.

'Can we get down there?' he asked.

'Oh aye.' The farmer pointed to a track that led off to the right. 'This used to be a wee quarry, long before my time. You'll need to be careful, mind, cos it's still slippy, but if you walk roon there ye'll get doon. That's how Ah did. Ah switched off the engine, by the way, so it's no goin' tae explode.'

'That's good to know,' said Regan wryly, as he headed down the path with McDermid at his heels.

The car had landed on a rocky bed at the foot of the abandoned quarry. As they approached it they could see that it was a Jaguar, a red Mark II, the model driven by a TV cop whose name the DI could never quite recall. The weight of its underside had crushed the passenger compartment, making it difficult to see how anyone could have survived. He crouched beside it and shone the torch inside. The only occupant was, or had been, a man. His body was squashed between the roof and the steering wheel, which had almost severed his head. Regan looked for long enough to make certain that there was no one else inside, then straightened up, and reached for his phone.

As he dialled Inspector White at Haddington he walked round to the rear of the car. 'The situation's as advised,' he told his colleague as he answered. 'Red Jag, single occupant, white male, dead as last Christmas's turkey. We need a recovery vehicle, a fire and rescue team to cut the body out and a mortuary wagon. You better run a check on the registration: it's G20 KSG.'

'Repeat, please.'

'Golf twenty, Kilo Sierra Golf.'

'I don't need to run a check,' said White. 'I've seen that Jag parked behind the Sheriff Court many a time, and I recognise the plate. That's Ken Green, the lawyer.'

Fifty-seven

Chief Constable Bob Skinner gazed at his bare-chested reflection in the mirror of the bathroom in his office suite. He had almost finished shaving, apart from his top lip. 'Tell me this is all a bad dream, and I'm going to wake up soon,' he said to the man who stood in the open doorway.

'If that's an order,' Mario McGuire replied, 'I'll obey as always. But when you do, the guy will still be dead.'

Skinner scraped off the last of the cream with his razor, and wiped his chin with a hand towel. 'We are sure it's Ken Green himself in the car, are we?' he asked, as he smoothed a men's moisturiser into his face.

'Boss, this is George Regan we're talking about, not some rookie plod making assumptions. He knows Green; he's been cross-examined by him a few times in his career, as most of us have. The body's pretty banged up, so he didn't twig at first sight, but when he was told whose motor it was, he got back down and took a closer look. That's who it is; no doubt.'

'So what are we doing about it?'

'We're treating it as a suspicious death. The man left his office saying that he was coming here, to Fettes, to see Arturus

Luksa, in custody, yet he wound up dead in his car in the wilds of East Lothian. Maybe it was an accident, but after the way the Gerulaitis case is turning out, that's pretty low down my list of possibilities. I've told George to have the road closed off at either end, but there's been no radio chat on this, so I don't expect any press to turn up. From what he tells me, though, it will be a bugger of a job to get the body out of there, let alone the car.'

'That's true,' Skinner concurred. 'I know that area. I take my kids exploring over there sometimes. Anything south of the A1 is another world; you could meet dinosaurs over there and not be surprised. The roads are primeval too; there's barely room for two cars The way you've described the scene, it'll take a crane to lift that Jaguar, but I can't see you getting one down there.'

'That's what fire and rescue say too. They're talking about asking the military for help by lending us a helicopter. The plan will be, get it out of there, transfer it to a lorry on the nearest accessible area and take it to the lab for examination by Dorward's lot.'

The chief opened his wardrobe, in which he kept his uniform and a few items of civilian clothes, and selected a linen shirt. 'And the body?' he asked.

'I've told George to make sure that it's extracted very carefully by the paramedics, once the fire team has cut an exit route, so that there's as little additional damage as possible. Professor Joe and his bright young things did well on Gerulaitis; we'll see what they can tell us about the way Green died.'

Skinner buttoned his shirt, tucked it into the beige jeans he was wearing, selected a soft black leather jerkin from the rail, and closed the wardrobe door. 'What do you reckon, Mario?' he murmured, as he stepped back into his office. 'What's up here? Let's think this through; let's look at things as they happen. Tomas Zaliukas kills himself, less than a week after he brings his brother over from Lithuania, apparently to sort out some trouble. Jonas had a heavy-duty military career, so he's not been imported as a diplomat. Agreed?'

'For sure.'

'What's the first thing he does? He has Valdas, a nervous Valdas according to our witness, call a meeting of the managers, and he says to them that the imported Estonian girls have to be withdrawn from the massage parlours, like yesterday. Linas Jankauskas questions him, and Jonas drops him like a side of beef. What does that tell us?'

'It says to me that Tomas might not have known about Valdas importing the women after all, and that when he found out, he hit the roof.'

'Yes, I agree. But how did he find out? And when he did, why didn't he simply square his cousin up himself? This is still the old Tommy Zale we're talking about, the man who, legend has it, once cut a guy's hand off with a chainsaw just for copying his tattoo. He might not have been hands on in the sex business, but he was still capable of taking Valdas into a small room and beating the shite out of him. Yet he didn't, or if he did, he didn't stop there. No, he called for his brother, a guy formidable enough to reduce a roomful of fairly hard guys to respectful silence. Then there's Desperate Dan. Who the fuck is he? Where did he come from?'

McGuire sighed. 'As of now, we still have no idea,' he admitted.

'Maybe, but we know one thing about him. He had the clout, even with Jonas in town, to call the managers together again . . . before they even knew that Tomas was fucking dead . . .' as he spoke, he stabbed his desk several times with his forefinger to emphasise the point, 'and tell them that he was the new man in authority, with a letter from the newly headless Tomas to prove it. The same day, he took Anna Romanova from Linas's place, over his dead body, and he dropped her off at the nearest surgery . . . and that, my friend is the piece of the puzzle I don't understand. The other eight girls have been made to disappear, yet Desperate Dan dumped Anna Romanova in our lap. Why the fuck did he do that?'

'He could have thought she was too far gone to be any use to us,' the head of CID suggested.

'That's possible, I'll grant you. However, it may also be the case that he didn't care, because he thought that all she could lead us to was Valdas. And if he knew that Valdas wasn't going to be around much longer . . .'

McGuire's eyes gleamed. 'Yes, yes indeed.'

'Look,' said Skinner, 'the way I see it we have two possibilities here. Tomas was in trouble; it got too much for him and he killed himself. Jonas wasn't able to prevent that but he's blaming people, specifically Linas, who's been playing the silly bugger with his girl, and Valdas. So he's been settling up before going back home. He killed Linas, without witnesses, and he tortured and killed Valdas; his wife, being there, had to go with him. I could buy into that; the man has an engineering degree, he'd have known how to set the fire that was supposed to have killed them. He's got away with it, too. Your woman Kerr's theory, it's a good one, I'll grant you. But do we have any witnesses placing Jonas at the scene?'

'No,' the chief superintendent conceded.

'And in a burned-out house will we find any traces of him?'

'No chance.'

'In which case we'll never even get him to court . . . if it was him. As I said, I'd go for that . . . but for one thing, or person, or ex-person: Ken Green. If Ken Green's death was a genuine accident, you could probably persuade me to go with the Jonas theory and close the book on that side of the business. But if it wasn't, then what possible reason could Jonas have had to kill him? Mario, until you can prove to me that Green was going too fast on a dangerous road and skidded off, through that fence and into that quarry, I'm going to assume that he had help. And I'm going to ask, why?' He smiled. 'Specifically, right now, I'm going to ask you why.'

McGuire sat on the edge of the chief's desk. He closed his eyes, and sank into thought. Half a minute passed, more; then he opened them again wide. 'What Desperate Dan said to the managers: he told them that while he's the new guy they report to, he isn't the ultimate boss. There's somebody else.'

'Good, you agree with me. So my alternative to the Jonas option is this. That person, whoever he might be, is very shy. But three people must have known who he was: Tomas Zaliukas, Valdas Gerulaitis, and Ken Green. What did Ken Green do for Tomas?' Skinner asked, but without waiting for a reply, he continued. 'He helped him set up Lituania SAFI, the ·

Uruguayan offshore company. And who was involved in that? Tomas and Valdas we know of, but was there a third person?' He frowned as his mind worked recalling details from briefings he had been given. 'Wait a minute,' he murmured. 'Green told Sauce that Tomas used Regine as a shareholder in the offshore business, because there had to be two. Right?'

'Yes,' McGuire agreed.

'Then he lied to the lad,' Skinner exclaimed. 'Listen, Tomas's original will left his share in the company to his wife. He couldn't have done that if she'd been a shareholder already. So yes! There is somebody else; there has to be, he's listed on the confidential shareholder register out in Uruguay, and Ken Green was so keen to keep the fact from us that he told porkies to a police officer.' He chuckled 'No, before you suggest it, there's no point in you going out there because the names are legally protected from intrusion even by the Uruguayan authorities, let alone us. David Mackenzie checked that out for me yesterday. So what does Green's death mean?' he challenged. 'I reckon it says that there's nobody left alive to tell us who the mystery man is.'

'So any way you look at it,' said McGuire, quietly, 'it's a dead end.'

'Yes, but that's only one road. Let's see what the autopsy on Green shows up, and what our guys can find in his car, but we still have plenty to work on. Look for Jonas; if he turns up back in Vilnius, we need to know. Find Desperate Dan; we've got a solid description of him. And not least find those women and, through them, find the missing girls.'

'If they're still alive.'

'Granted. We can only hope that they are. Mind you, I've got no idea where you start, I admit.'

'With the mini-bus they took them away in,' said the head of CID. 'Ramanauskas told us it was silver, although he had no idea of the make or model. We're looking at street camera footage for Wednesday morning; if we find any possible vehicles we'll show them to him.'

'Good, but something else; we've been thinking locally about this from the off. I want you to check out whether Lituania SAFI has other properties anywhere else in Scotland. You crack on with that, and as you do, I've got business of my own to attend to. The massage parlours are key to the whole business, we're agreed, yes?'

'Yes.'

'Well, that being the case, I'm going to talk to the man who sold them to Tomas Zaliukas in the first place; my old sparring partner, Lennie Plenderleith, the beneficiary of Tony Manson's estate.' He grinned. 'Now bugger off, or I'll be late picking up my daughter.'

Fifty-eight

'I've never been here before,' said Cheeky, leaning against the bar and surveying the function room. 'It's nice. What's it called again?'

'The Grosvenor,' Sauce reminded her. 'It's not bad at all; it's the nearest place to our office that's big enough, so we usually come here for our dos.'

'It's handy for your place too; we could almost walk home from here. I bet you they give you a good deal, considering who you are.'

'I don't know about that. There's a social committee that organises these things, but I'm not on it.'

'How many people are coming?' she asked. 'Will there be seats enough for everybody when they serve the food?'

'About sixty, I think.' He counted the tables surrounding the dance floor. 'Yeah, it'll be fine.' He picked up his drink, and took her arm. 'Come on and meet my boss,' he said, leading her towards the far end of the bar.

'I thought Jack was your boss,' she retorted, nodding towards McGurk, who sat at one of the tables with Lisa Weekes, his partner.

'Jack's my sergeant; that's different. This is our boss; DI Stallings.' He stopped beside a dark-haired thirty-something woman in a dark-blue dress, who stood beside a lean, fit-looking man, with sharp appraising eyes. 'Ma'am,' he said, 'this is Cheeky, my girlfriend.'

Stallings turned. Unwittingly, she blinked as she took in Haddock's partner; the girl would have been beautiful with no presentation at all, but with her perfectly arranged hair and under-stated make-up, she was stunning. *She must have a thing for lads with big ears*, she thought, *or maybe they're a sign of something else*. 'Drop the "Ma'am", Sauce,' she exclaimed. 'This a bloody dance, not an inspection. The name's Becky, Cheeky; I'm not going to ask about your name, but I'm sure there's a story behind it. This is my other half, Ray.'

Wilding's grin stopped a couple of millimetres short of a leer. 'Welcome to our inner circle,' he greeted her. 'Ever been to a policeman's ball before?'

'No,' said Cheeky, 'but I know the punchline. When's the raffle?'

He laughed. 'Ah, we're not having one tonight. We couldn't get anyone to put up the prize.'

'Are all your team coming, Ray?' Sauce asked.

'Sammy Pye and Ruth aren't; he's off on his fast-track course. But Griff and Cowan are coming, possibly even hand in hand, if I read things right.'

'That might be interesting,' Stallings murmured. She nodded towards the door, towards a big grey-haired man in jeans and a leather jerkin, who had just come into the room, accompanied by a tall, slim mid-twenties woman, with big hair and eyes that seemed to command the attention of every man in the room, with the possible exception of DC Haddock.

'Who's that?' Cheeky asked him.

'That's Mr Skinner,' he replied, 'our chief constable. And that's Alex with him, his daughter. She used to go out with Griff; that's Griff Montell, he works with Ray, and with Alice Cowan. From what Ray's saying . . .'

'Don't you believe it,' Stallings laughed. 'That lady left Montell behind a while back. Spat out the bones, I'll bet.'

'You're not from Edinburgh, Becky, are you,' said Cheeky; it was more comment than question.

'No, I'm a newish arrival. I was in the Met when I met Smiler here,' she dug Wilding in the ribs, 'and decided I fancied a spell up north.'

'And you run this lot?'

'Only the CID part, love. Superintendent Chambers, Mary Chambers, is the divisional commander.' She pointed to a table on the other side of the dance floor, close to the spot where the DJ was setting up his lights and his decks. 'That's her.'

Cheeky followed her finger, and saw a chunky, early middle-aged woman, with a square but not unattractive face and dark, close-cropped hair. She was dressed in black trousers that might have been part of her uniform, with her black shoes, and in a black, short-sleeved polo neck that certainly was not. She shared the table with a younger woman, her direct opposite, blonde, slim, with a white shirt, sleeves rolled up, a pale blue skirt and tan shoes with heels so high and sharp that they might have been weapons. They were leaning towards each other, over their drinks, smiling as they talked, their hands brushing. 'Is the other one a policewoman too?' she asked.

'Mmm,' Wilding began, cautiously. 'She's not one that I recognise. That'll be her date, I guess. Superintendent Chambers is discreetly gay . . . or she was discreet about it until tonight.' He stopped as a hand fell on his shoulder.

'Evening, all,' said the chief constable, smiling at Stallings. 'How goes? You all know Alex, yes?' He paused as his eye fell upon the other woman in the quartet. 'Well, no, I don't imagine you do.' He held out a hand. 'I'm Bob Skinner.'

'This is Cheeky Davis, sir,' Haddock interposed, 'my girlfriend.'

'Well done you, Sauce,' said Skinner as he and the blonde shook hands. 'You seem to be doing well on all fronts; people have been telling me good things about you lately.' The DC's face flushed, partly out of pride that the chief not only knew who he was, but knew his nickname. 'This lad has potential, Miss Davis,' he told her.

She smiled. 'I'd worked that out for myself,' she replied, confidently.

The chief laughed. '. . . and don't you be a patronising old bastard,' he added.

It was her turn to go pink. 'I didn't mean that,' she blurted out.

'If you had you'd have been entitled,' he countered. 'I'm sorry, I'm still new at this job and I've always been lousy at schmoozing. My wife can work a room a lot better than I can. Let me simplify things: what are you lot drinking?' He signalled to a barman, and ordered, as each one answered, a

gin and tonic for Stallings, a Bud for Alex, two pints of IPA for
Wilding and Haddock, a Virgin Mary for Cheeky and a bottle
of sparkling water for himself. 'You're not in the force, Miss
Davis,' he said as he passed her the drink, 'so what's your line?'

'I'm on the road to being a chartered accountant,' she
replied. 'It takes a few years, but I'm getting there. I've got my
degree, and now I'm doing on-the-job professional training.'

'On the job? That's a bit close to home for us, Cheeky,'
Wilding chuckled, 'considering the job we've been on for the
last couple of days.'

'Ray,' said Alex slowly, 'is this something that we really need
to know?'

'You do already, don't you? I heard you had a visit from our
boy here on Wednesday.'

'And sent him homeward to think again. Your investigation
doesn't reach into my firm. Let's not talk about it, Ray,
seriously. I still get the creeps when I think about that man
Gerulaitis and his wife.'

The DS nodded, as the light dimmed, then turned electric
blue. 'I forgot that. Sorry, Alex.'

'Gerulaitis?' Cheeky repeated, her voice rising above the
sound of the DJ as he cued in his first play, Santana's 'Samba
Pa Ti', 'Tae get youse up close and personal,' he announced. 'Is
that the man whose house caught fire?'

'With him in it.'

'Accidents happen,' Skinner exclaimed. 'But enough about
our shop. Who're you training with, Cheeky?'

'Nobody you've ever heard of,' she told him. 'A wee firm
called . . .'

'I said, what the fuck is this?' The bellow cut across her reply, and even across Carlos Santana's towering guitar. Every head in the room turned to stare across the still-empty dance floor, at the table close to the speakers. A tall man stood with his back to the crowd, his shoulders massive in a green rugby top with a yellow-gold collar. He was leaning forward, aggressively, ignoring the woman with short blond hair who was tugging at his elbow. 'What are you doing here, Spring? What the fuck is this about, you playing footsie with this fucking old lesbo?'

For a few seconds the room was a frozen tableau, until Ray Wilding broke the spell. He took a few steps across the floor, but was soon overtaken by Bob Skinner. 'Hold off,' the chief said quietly. 'This is one for me.' On the other side of the dance floor, McGurk was standing, but he waved him back down.

He reached Mary Chambers' table in a few strides, just as her companion rose to her feet, her face so pale that it shone blue under the lights. 'Are you telling me you're a fucking pie-muncher too, sis?' Griff Montell shouted. 'Wasn't one in the family enough?'

'Griff,' Alice Cowan pleaded. 'Come on, cool it.'

'Yes,' said Skinner, 'quiet down, now,' putting a hand on the raging man's arm. Montell turned and shoved him, two-handed, square in the chest. He staggered backwards, but only for a pace or two, before reacting by snapping a judo lock on the detective constable's right wrist, then turning him and twisting his arm round, forcing his hand up towards his shoulder blades. 'March,' he whispered in the South African's ear. 'We're out of here now, or I'll put you in hospital. Mary,' he said to Chambers, 'you two start the dancing. Get everyone moving, for fuck's sake.'

Montell had no choice but to obey as Skinner pushed him towards a door behind the DJ's stand. Alice Cowan saw what was happening, and went to open it ahead of them. It led into a small square area, an anteroom for the toilets, on either side. As Cowan closed the door behind him, Skinner released the restraining hold and, as he did so, pushed the South African, driving him hard and face first into the facing wall. 'Griff,' he said, as back in the hall a disco mix of Madonna's 'Ray of Light' replaced the great Mexican guitarist, 'you need to think very carefully about what you do next. You can leave here with a career, or you can leave here under arrest and probably the worse for wear. I don't want to hurt you in any way, son, but you've only got a few seconds to make what's going to be a lifetime decision.' He stood, hands by his side but ready to react, watching as the detective constable turned to face him, thankful as the rage began to leave his eyes, and as the tension left his body.

'I'm sorry, sir,' he said. 'That was unforgivable. My resignation will be on your desk on Monday.'

'And it'll go in the shredder. Now, are you going to tell me why you reacted that way?'

Cowan interrupted. 'His ex-wife, sir,' she said. 'She was AC/DC and he never knew till she left him for another bird.'

He had not realised that she had joined them. 'Quiet, please, Alice,' he ordered. 'Griff needs to talk to me. In fact, give us a few minutes alone. You get back out there and tell

Superintendent Chambers that we're all fine, then stay by the door and stop anyone coming in here until we're done.'

'Yes, sir.'

He waited until he heard the door close. 'So that's your sister partnering Mary,' he murmured. Montell nodded. 'And that's why you blew up?' Another nod. 'You felt she was embarrassing you, in front of your colleagues, was that it?' As the younger man stared at him, Skinner realised that there was far more to it than that. 'Are you telling me you didn't know that your sister was gay?' he asked, unable to hide his surprise.

'Are you telling me you did, sir?' the DC responded.

'Of course I did; it's in your vetting report, man. You don't think I approved your transfer to our CID from South Africa without having you checked out, do you?'

'No, sir, I assumed that would happen. And they knew about her?'

'Yes. So let me get this straight; you and Spring share a house, yet you had no idea, no inkling, of her sexual orientation?'

Montell shook his head, then took a breath and blew it out. 'None at all, sir, honest. We have this deal, the two of us: we never bring partners home.'

'Whose idea was that?'

'Now you ask me, it was hers. But I never thought . . .'

'No, you didn't. Some might say she's been protecting you from your own prejudice.' He shook his head. 'Only you're not really prejudiced, Griff, are you? I know what you did in South Africa; I know where you worked. I looked at your career in your personnel report, and I didn't see the faintest sign of a bigot there. OK, you were hurt in a way you found hard to take. Now you're angry, and you're bitter. But anger and bitterness can be bad for you, as you've just found out.'

The big detective sighed. 'There's something else that's come back to me,' he said. 'Things got pretty acrimonious between my ex and me when we split up, after I found out how she swung. During one of our last discussions she said she fancied my sister more than me. I never read anything into that either. But oh yes, Chief, you're right. I was angry.'

'That's why you never told Alex about your marriage, isn't it?'

Montell nodded. 'Maybe she'll understand now.'

'She'd have understood before, if you'd trusted her enough to tell her, but you were afraid she'd let it slip to me, weren't you?'

'Just a bit. What a bollocks, eh?' He looked Skinner in the eye. 'Where do I go now, Chief? You say I've still got a career, but I've just committed a public order offence. What happens to me?'

'Officially, nothing. Unofficially . . . you were about two weeks away from making detective sergeant. That has to go on hold for a while, until tonight has gone to the back of people's minds, and until the force gossip mill has run out of steam. But nobody's going to get your slot.'

'Thanks, sir. I don't deserve any of that.'

Skinner smiled. 'I'll grant you that another chief constable might take a different view; but you got my daughter out of a very nasty situation once. I owe you, Griff.' He paused. 'Now get the fuck out of here, lad, go on. You know what you've got to do; I'll give you a head start.'

Montell nodded. He opened the door and stepped back into

the hall. The chief constable stayed behind, listening. After around a minute, the music stopped in mid-track, and crackling sounds came through the speakers as a microphone was picked up. 'Can I have your attention, please?' a South African voice asked, then waited until the buzz stilled. 'Most of you here tonight know me,' it continued. 'For the rest of you, I'm a complete wanker who's just proved the fact in the most embarrassing way possible. I'd like to apologise to all of you for chucking cold water all over your evening, and I'd like to pick out three people to express my deepest regret. The first is Alice, who doesn't deserve to be alongside the likes of me. The second is Mary, Superintendent Chambers, who's as good a cop as there is in this room, and as good a person too. And the third is my sister, who I've just learned has been walking on eggshells around me for years, when in truth she never had to, because I love her above all other considerations, and because whatever she's for is OK with me. Finally I'd just like to say that I'm going to leave you to enjoy the rest of the night.' Skinner could hear a few calls of 'No!' from the floor, then a few more, until finally they became general. 'Ah but I have to,' Montell called out, through the mike. 'Alice has just told me that she's never been to the Pompadour Restaurant in the Caley Hotel, and that the only thing that's going to stop her from taking my balls home in her handbag is if she goes there tonight; that's assuming they let me in with this shirt on. So we'll love you all and leave you. Sorry again.'

The chief constable made a mental note to knock a few weeks off the penitent's period of purdah, then stepped back out into the hall. Alex was waiting outside the door. She looked him up and down, as if for signs of dishevelment. 'Did you have to beat that out of him?' she asked. 'Pops, he's twenty years younger than you and bigger. Jack and Ray could have handled him.'

'I doubt if they could, the mood he was in. But even if they had, all they could have done was bounce him, and it would have become a disciplinary thing. As it is, it's history. Come on, let's get back to the bar. This is a police do; some bugger will have nicked our drinks.'

Sauce and his girlfriend, in the middle of a group of dancers, watched them as they skirted the floor. 'She's quite a looker, your boss's daughter,' Cheeky commented. 'I reckon she could pull any bloke in here, if she wanted.'

'Not this one.'

'Aw, that's nice.' She glanced around the room, looking towards the main door, just as Montell and Cowan were leaving, then laid her head on his chest. 'I've got a confession to make,' she murmured.

'What's that?' he asked, a little anxiously.

'That business has put a bit of a damper on the night for me. I don't like upsets, Sauce.'

'Then we'll go somewhere else. What do you fancy?'

'You, big boy. Let's just go back to yours and take up where we left off the other night.'

'Suits me.' He frowned. 'I've got a golf tie tomorrow, midday; fancy pulling my trolley?'

She grinned up at him. 'That's the best piece of innuendo I've heard in a month of Sundays. I'll pull anything you like, lover. Come on, let's head.'

Alex watched them, over her father's shoulder, as they headed for the door. 'She's a nice kid,' she remarked, as she raised her Budweiser bottle towards her lips. 'Young Sauce has done all right for himself.'

Bob grinned. 'That takes a bit of getting used to, you know.'

'What does?'

'Hearing you refer to somebody as a kid.'

'Hey, I'm a long way off being the youngest person in this room,' she pointed out, glancing towards the entrance, just as Sauce and Cheeky made their way out, his arm around her shoulders. And then her expression changed. The laugh left her eyes and the smile left her lips, as her gaze locked on to a man who stood just inside the door. He was in conversation with Ray Wilding, but had the look of someone who wanted to escape. He was around six feet tall, heavy-shouldered, with blond curly hair and green eyes that she knew only too well. 'Oh fuck,' she hissed, as he left the detective sergeant and headed in their direction. 'Just when the night was taking a turn for the better. Pops, I'm out of here.' Bob stared at her, dumbstruck, as she laid the bottle on the bar and slung her bag over her shoulder.

'What . . .' he began, as she started to leave . . . only to be forestalled by the newcomer's arrival.

'I'm sorry, Alex,' said Andy Martin. 'I'd no idea you'd be here, but I need to speak to your dad.'

'Sure,' she snapped. 'Well, the last thing I need is to be the sandwich filling between you two.' She glared up at Bob. 'Did you know he was coming here?'

Skinner turned to face the new arrival. 'I promise you I

319

didn't,' he said, grimly. 'You wouldn't have been here if I had, but neither would he. Who told you about this?' he demanded.

'A source who will remain nameless,' Martin replied. 'But it isn't exactly a secret, is it? Bob, I'm sorry, but I really do need to talk to you. Since you're never available when I try your office, I haven't been left with much option but to waylay you.'

The chief constable looked him in the eye, as he weighed up the situation. 'OK,' he decided. 'There's a table in the corner. Let's go over there before we draw too much attention and you can say what you have to. Alex, this won't take too long. Hang around and I'll take you home when we're done.'

She shook her head. 'You take as long as he needs, Pops. Don't worry about it; I'll grab a taxi. See you, Andy. How's the baby, by the way?' She turned and walked away before he could answer.

'I don't reckon what's broken between you will ever be repaired, Andy,' said her father, looking after her. 'Nor should it be.'

'I'm not trying,' Martin told him, as he led the way towards the empty corner table.

Mary Chambers started towards them as they sat, but a quick look from the chief constable warned her off. 'So,' he said, coldly. 'Why do you need to talk to me? Are you going to tell me who tipped you off that I'd be here, so that I can gut the bastard?'

'First off, thanks for the gift you sent for Robert. I appreciated it.'

'It has fuck all to do with you. It's for the boy, just as Danielle's investment bond is all hers. They're tied up till each of them turn eighteen. Now stop prevaricating; what's this about?'

'Bob, I'm sorry, heart sorry, about what happened between me and Alex, and the way it all went public.'

'It didn't go public, remember. My kid doesn't work for the best law firm in Scotland for nothing. And the guy who took those candid camera snaps is in a place where he can't try to flog them to anyone else.'

'As well for him,' the other man said. 'I'd have fucking killed him myself if I'd found him.'

'You'd have been in a queue. But this has nothing to do with why you're here. So tell me why the deputy chief constable of Tayside has chosen to by-pass his boss in making contact with me directly. Your opposite number is Brian Mackie, not me.'

'Not any more,' said Martin, quietly.

Skinner's eyebrows rose. 'You haven't quit the force, have you?'

'No, but I'm on my way out of Tayside. I assume you saw the circular a few days ago, advertising the deputy director post at Serious Crime and Drug Enforcement.'

'Yes. Are you telling me you've applied for it?'

'No, I'm telling you I've got it. I was approached on Wednesday and told that the job was mine, there and then, if I wanted it. There are new circumstances. Arnie Vardy, the director, is on long-term sick leave; he's been diagnosed with motor neuron disease, so the Justice Secretary told his department to fill the deputy job fast. They came to me, I said yes. It was effective immediately, so as of Monday I'm acting director general of the agency.'

'Lucky for you that Aileen's lot are no longer in power,' Skinner growled, 'or I'd have squashed that.'

Martin smiled. 'No you wouldn't, Bob. You and I might have fallen out big time, but you wouldn't have let that affect your judgement. Without being big-headed, out of all the candidates for the job, I'm the best qualified, given that no currently serving chief would apply for it. We both know that, and if you'd been asked for an opinion, you'd have said so.'

The chief constable glared at him, eyes narrowed. 'You think?'

'I fucking well know. You might be a hard-headed, hot-tempered bastard and you might have a down on me for the rest of our lives, but I know you too well to believe that you'd ever let any of that get in the way of your integrity, or make you act against what you knew to be in the public interest.'

'So now you want me to congratulate you?'

'That would be nice, but no. I want you to accept that you and I aren't on different sides of a territorial fence any longer. My remit covers the whole country. By definition most of the agency's work is in Strathclyde, since that takes in half of Scotland, but there will be occasions when I'm active on your patch. Professionally, we have to get along.'

'We always did professionally, chum,' the chief constable conceded. 'The job transcends personal issues; you don't have to tell me that.'

'So, is there any chance of you burying what's between us, and being civil to each other again?'

Skinner threw back his head, and drained his bottle of formerly sparkling water in a single swallow. 'Christ, son,' he said, 'we were always more than civil with each other. You were my best mate once. You were going to marry my daughter before the pair of you messed that up. And it's Alex that's the problem. I'm joined at the hip to my kids . . . not just to her, to the younger batch as well. If we get close again, you might get close to her. And that could be a disaster. That's the real reason why I built the wall between you and me, that's why I ostracised you, even after I'd cooled down from the stuff that happened six months ago: to protect my daughter, to protect your Karen as well, and maybe even to protect you. You and Alex, you need to stay apart. You're like nuclear particles. When you collide, any fucking thing can happen. All three of us know that, and to be honest, its potential scares the crap out of me.'

'Not just the three.'

Skinner frowned. 'No?'

'No, Karen knows it as well, and she's not about to live with it; with that and quite a few other things. She's binned me, Bob; we stayed together while the baby was on the way and to see him through the first few months, but now it's over. As you know, my new base will be in Paisley; I'm going to move closer to it, but Karen's not coming. She's staying in Perth. She likes it there; she's even talking about rejoining the police when the kids are a bit older.'

'Aw, hell,' Bob exclaimed, as his reserve and his recrimination dissolved. 'Andy, I'm sorry. For both of you . . . what am I saying? . . . for all four of you.'

'Thanks,' Martin replied, 'but we've talked it through, and we're agreed it's for the best. We recognise that we got together for the wrong reasons, on both sides. It's civilised, honest.'

'But your kids . . .'

'They're very young. I'll be a good absentee dad, and it'll be more or less what they've always known.'

'Where are you going to move to?'

'As a first step, back to Edinburgh. You'll remember that I never sold my place in Dean Village; I kept it as an investment and rented it out. The tenants moved out a month ago, so I'm going back in there; this weekend, in fact. I'll commute by train most of the time, and see how that goes. I might wind up stopping there. But I'll stay away from Alex, I promise.'

'Andy, make me no promises that you can't keep. As the Tartan Army would put it, que sera, sera.'

He smiled. 'Sera, indeed. That reminds me, sort of; I had an email from your ex the other day, completely out the blue.'

'From Sarah?'

'It would hardly be from Myra, would it?'

Bob smiled; Martin's levity in using the name of his dead first wife reminded him of the way it had been between the two of them, before their lives had become so complicated. 'What's she saying to it?' he asked.

'Nothing, really, just hello, and that she's looking forward to seeing me again.'

He stared. 'Eh? Are you going to New York, with this new job on your hands?'

Martin looked back at him, blankly. 'No, she's coming here, in May. You didn't know?'

'It's the first I've heard of it. What is that woman up to?'

'Oh dear. Foot in it, sorry.' He paused. 'I suppose there's something else I should get off my chest.'

'Go on, then, clear the decks.'

'I've pinched your press officer.'

Skinner beamed. 'Is that supposed to upset me?' he asked.

'I thought it might.'

'Not a bit. Alan Royston needs a move; you'll be fine with him.' He rose, extending his hand; they shook. 'I have to go,' he said. 'Do you want me to tell Alex about this?'

'That's your decision. I'm not going to knock on her door; don't worry about that.'

'Hell, Andy, I don't know anything any more. I'll tell her though. Like we said, what will be, will be. I'm off; you hang about here, if you like, catch up with some old chums.'

He waved goodbye to Mary Chambers, then headed for the door. As he stepped through it, he came face to face with Maggie Steele. 'Bob,' she exclaimed, 'sorry I'm late. Stephanie took a while to settle tonight.' She smiled. 'Have I missed much?'

Fifty-nine

George Regan willed himself not to shiver in the cold evening air; he stood as close as he could to the floodlights that had been set up, hoping to absorb a little of their energy in the form of heat. The old quarry seemed to be a magnet for mist, adding dampness to the list of his discomforts. His new old Crombie coat was hanging on a peg in the Haddington office, ornament perhaps, but certainly no use to him at that moment, and he cursed his lack of foresight, no, his idiocy, in forgetting one of the tenets of policing, that every time you went on a call, you were partly blind in that you could never be quite certain of what was waiting for you out there.

But he kept his mouth shut, his hands in his pockets and his expression as close to normal as he could manage. He had no intention of letting Lisa McDermid know what a clown he had been, Lisa wrapped up in her parka, with the furry hood that she had pulled over her head. No, he stood, impassively, watching as the fire and rescue team worked away, cutting away the roof of the Jaguar, which had been righted and sat on all four wheels, on the uneven rocky ground. They had been at it for three hours, and still the late Ken Green was jammed in his death trap as tightly as before.

Beside him McDermid sighed, her exhaled breath showing clearly as a cloud in the harsh silver light. 'Why are we taking such care with this guy?' she asked.

'Because the big guy McGuire, our headquarters boss, told us to. That's reason enough for me.'

'Is he involved in something?'

Regan looked at her. 'Ken Green's sort,' he replied, 'are always involved in something or other, but I don't know of anything specific.'

'But this is an accident. I mean look at it; it's absolutely clear what happened.'

'Sure it is. But the head of CID hasn't seen it, so he doesn't know that. He's also a detective, like you're supposed to be, and so his job, and ours, isn't just to determine what happened, it's to determine what made it happen.'

'Fine,' she retorted. 'Well, this is Detective Sergeant McDermid telling him that what happened was that Green was going too fast in bad light and bad road conditions and instead of zigging, he zagged; instead of taking this corner he went straight on. You came damn close to doing the same thing yourself.'

'Fine,' said the DI, 'but don't tell him until you can prove it, not that one.' Finally a small shiver escaped him.

'George,' McDermid exclaimed, 'you're freezing.'

'I'm fine,' he insisted.

'Like hell you are. You'll catch your death.'

He laughed. 'If I do you'll be able to prove to McGuire exactly how it happened. I won't though. I've been out on many a worse night than this.'

'Maybe, but there's no need for both of us to be here. You could go and I could get a lift back to Haddington with one of the emergency vehicles; they have to go that way. Go on, get yourself home.'

'It's a fucking sight colder there,' he muttered, under his breath but not as far under as he had thought.

She looked at him. 'Problems?' she asked.

He nodded. 'Jen's not good; she's withdrawing from life, while I'm trying to go in the opposite direction.'

Silence grew between them, until Lisa broke it. 'Earlier on,' she began, 'just before we got this call, you were going to ask me out, weren't you?'

'Not exactly. For a drink, maybe . . .'

'And then a Chinese, maybe, and then see how it went . . . I know how these things play out.'

'And?'

She checked her watch. 'With a bit of luck the Chinky in Haddington will still be open when we're done here. But that would be it. I'm not a social worker, George, I'm not a bereavement counsellor. I'm a work colleague, plus I'm a woman, which puts me on Jen's side. Anyway, you wouldn't want me to shag you because I felt sorry for you, would you?'

'Right now, I wouldn't be so sure of that.'

'That's your dick thinking. Let me tell you something about me. Two years ago, my mother died of pancreatic cancer. She was a fine, big, fit woman, then she was diagnosed and she was dead in six months. My father was devastated, and he still is. He's been through all sorts of phases; my brother and I have seen them all. First, immediately after Mum died and he was left alone, we had him drinking too much, until he realised that wouldn't help. Then we had him spending all the hours God sent on the golf course, even though he's no fucking use at the game and can't stand it really. After that we had internet dating; that led him to meet a succession of randy middle-aged women, some of them married . . . I checked them out if I could . . . all of them with an eye for the main chance. Each of those encounters left him feeling a wee bit emptier, a wee bit lonelier and, as well, guilty; for he couldn't shake the idea that he was betraying Mum.'

Regan shivered again, more fiercely than before. 'What are you saying to me, Lisa?' he whispered.

'I'm saying that there is no cure for him. He tells me that he dreams about Mum, and that in those dreams she isn't dead, she's just away for a wee while. That's good, George, in a way, but for the eighteen hours or so that he's awake, she is dead, and there's no escape from that. It's how his life is and even though it's unbearably sad for him, it's how the rest of it will be. We can't help him, my brother and me. He has to live it. It's the same with you and Jen; that's how it is, that's the hand you've been dealt. You have to get on and play it. You say she's withdrawing. I look at you and I see you going in the opposite direction, dressing like a wannabe fashion plate, thinking about getting across me, or any other woman in your immediate vicinity.'

'Hey,' he joked, weakly, 'I really like my Crombie.'

'It's a disguise, George, that's all. You're still the same wounded man underneath.'

'So what do we do?'

'I told you I'm no counsellor,' she pointed out, 'but from what I've learned from watching my father, it seems to me that you simply have to face up to it and bear the unbearable pain.'

'What's he doing now?'

'My dad? He paints. He does landscapes, beach scenes, and even the odd still life. He's not bad; he sells them through a gallery. He does portraits too, but they're not for sale. They're always of my mum.' She reached out and touched his cheek, feeling its cold.

'Neither Jen nor I could paint the kitchen door,' he said.

'No, but I'm sure you'll find something if you look for it. You're better off than Dad. You've still got each other . . . unless you drift too far apart. Go on, man; I really can handle this scene on my own. Get yourself home.'

Regan looked at her. 'Are you sure you're not a social worker?' he asked, then turned up the collar of his silk blend jacket and headed up the path that led towards his car.

Sixty

'Mario,' said Professor Joe Hutchinson, 'you really must stop doing this to me. You people have sent me four bodies this week already, three of those in pretty poor condition. That was bad enough, but I managed to pick my way through all of them; indeed I venture to suggest that I've done a bloody good job. In the wake of that I was looking forward to putting my feet up this weekend, listening to some music, and playing with my grandchildren. I stress the word "was", for I've just had a call from the manager of the mortuary telling me that you've dumped a fifth on me, and you want him dealt with as soon as possible. My friend, I have a fee structure which I believe is fair to both of us, but if you want me in that examination room before Monday morning, it's going to be doubled. Not just my cost, but that of my assistant. If you're not in a position to authorise that, you can find somebody else.'

McGuire's smile at the pathologist's tirade drew a quizzical look across the breakfast table from his partner Paula. 'What's up?' she mouthed, but he put a finger to his lips.

'You're a fucking old extortionist,' he said.

'I'm so wounded by that ageist remark that I have a notion to make it treble time, but I'll give you ten seconds to accept my original offer . . . unless you feel you have to seek authorisation. If that's the case I'll feel that my ability is being called into question and it'll be four times.'

'It's a deal, Joe. Just you send me an invoice and it'll be paid.'

'Who's the client?'

'He's a solicitor called Ken Green.'

'I know that name.'

The chief superintendent chuckled. 'That's probably because his clients have sent you a few customers in your time. He was a defence brief, high profile, with one of those numbers that hoodlums commit to memory.'

'That's the chap. What happened to him? Disgruntled defendant catching up on release?'

'No, he was killed in his car yesterday evening, on a back road in East Lothian, up past Haddington. It took four hours to extract him from the wreckage; from what my DS told me he was pretty bendy when they did.'

'A road traffic accident?' the professor shouted into his phone. 'You're sending me a blinking RTA on a Saturday morning?'

'That's what I want you to tell me, Joe. Whether he was an RTA or whether he was assisted.'

'Have you any reason to believe that he was?' the pathologist asked, more quietly.

'He had a business relationship with Tomas Zaliukas, and we believe that Valdas Gerulaitis was involved in it too.'

'I see. My day is brightening up. This one sounds like a bit of a challenge. If he was rendered as flexible as you say, it may take me a little while, but I'll give you a provisional report as soon as I can. Keep your mobile charged and ready.'

'Will do, Joe.' He hung up.

'Is that the one you didn't want to talk about last night?' Paula asked. 'The thing that made us late for the disco?' Mario nodded and reached for the slice of toast that she had buttered while he was on the phone. 'Even I've heard of Ken Green,' she said. 'There wasn't a week without his picture in the *Evening News*.'

'They wouldn't use the latest one, I promise you, going by what Lisa McDermid told me.'

'Why would he have been in East Lothian? Is that why you think it might be iffy?'

'That was a consideration at first, but apparently he did have a cottage there. His secretary told us about it last night.'

'So he would have been on his way there?'

'I suppose he must have been.'

'Maybe it really was an accident.'

'Honest, love, I really hope it was. My crew are getting stretched.'

She laughed. 'You might not get too much out of some of them today, if you have to, given the state they were in at the end of the disco. That woman Becky likes a drink; she and Ray Wilding were made for each other. It was good to see Maggie out and about too.'

'It was,' Mario agreed, 'although I nearly fell over when I saw who she was talking to.'

'The special guest star? Yes, what about that? Jack McGurk told me that when he arrived Alex Skinner walked straight out the door. Then he and her dad went and sat in a corner and had a long chat. I wonder what that was about.'

'Andy's new job; it's being announced on Monday, so Maggie told me, and she got it from him. He's going to SCDEA, to run it, in effect.'

'What does that mean?'

'It means that Andy's going to be a part of our working lives again. So it's just as well that he and the boss were talking. They hadn't spoken for six months.'

Paula shrugged. 'Well, they seem to have parted friends last night, according to big Jack.' She refilled his mug from the coffee pot and looked at him across the table. 'But as for today,' she continued, 'what have you got planned for us?'

'How about,' he replied, 'we get the fuck out of this city and head up to Stirling? Visit the castle, the tourist thing, do a bit of shopping, then book ourselves into Gleneagles Hotel for the night. I'm sure they'd appreciate the business.'

'I'm for all of that,' she declared.

'That's good. Let's pack a bag. And on the way there we can call in at the police lab. There's a banged up Jaguar that should be there by now, and I'd like to take a look at it.'

Sixty-one

By the nature of their profession police officers can be regular prison visitors. During his career Bob Skinner had visited most of the Scottish estate, but HMP Kilmarnock was a new experience for him. It had been in operation for eleven years, since its controversial construction as the country's first privatised jail, and to the best of his knowledge had been as incident free as any institution of its type could ever be.

It had been easy to find too; he had headed down the M77/A77 from Glasgow, turned on to the A76 and there he had found it, only a minute or so down the road. The car park access was barred, but he announced himself into a microphone contained in a metal box, and his way was cleared. He found a space in the visitor section, then stood for a moment by the side of his car, surveying the site, and contrasting it with other, older places in which a difficult job had been made worse by the demands of an expanding population and a general recognition of prisoners' human rights. As he walked towards the entrance he noted that the complex was smaller than he had expected, given that it housed over five hundred men, explaining possibly why it lacked the air of menace that hung over the likes of Barlinnie and Peterhead.

The gate opened as he reached it, and a security officer stepped out of a doorway just inside. Skinner showed him his warrant card; the man inspected it, nodded and said, 'Follow me, please,' without the merest suggestion of a smile. He led him out into a courtyard. The complex was made up of several buildings, most of them accommodation, but his escort took him into the first. He stopped in a reception area. 'Chief Constable Skinner, Sadie,' he told the woman seated at its only desk. 'The director wanted to know when he arrived.'

'Thanks, Willie,' she said, rising. She smiled at the visitor. 'I'll let Mr Elgin know you're here.'

Skinner had not been expecting an official greeting, but he nodded acquiescence and watched as Sadie opened a door behind her and leaned inside it. 'Come this way,' she told him as she turned back to face him.

The man who stood waiting for him looked more like a television presenter than a professional custodian of human beings. The first prison governor he had ever met had been a red-faced slab of a man who had worked his way up from hall duty in top security jails, a hard-line veteran who had seemed to take grim pleasure in describing executions that he had witnessed earlier in his career, strengthening in the process Skinner's own natural aversion to capital punishment. 'James Elgin,' he introduced himself, as they shook hands. 'It's an honour to meet you, sir.'

'This is well off my patch,' the chief constable told him. 'I'm surprised you've heard of me.'

'We're colleagues, in a sense,' Elgin said. 'The police are my suppliers, with the prosecutors and courts as the middlemen; I make it a point of knowing who's who in each camp. You have some very interesting hits on Google, you have a fan page on Facebook and your Wikipedia entry is extensive.'

'You're kidding me,' Skinner retorted, taken by surprise. 'If it wasn't for Mark, my older son, I wouldn't know what Wikipedia and Facebook were.'

Elgin chuckled. 'This place is on Wiki as well, but its entry is only a stub, and out of date. Yours is carefully maintained. Does your press office do it?'

'I've no idea, but if I find that he has been, my press officer will be even happier that he's just resigned. I confess that I'm uncomfortable with some of the modern media.'

'Maybe, Mr Skinner, but it's not going to go away. The man you're here to visit, he's on Wikipedia too. It's the home base for all sorts of fascinations.'

'So it seems.'

The director looked at him, hesitantly. 'Actually,' he continued, 'I'd like to ask you about him. He's only been here for three months, and the governor in Shotts, where he came from, told me no more than that he was a model prisoner. So far, I have to agree with that; he has been. But I like to know my people as well as I can, and to anticipate things before they happen. The fact that you, of all people, have asked to see him, and at such short notice, that concerns me. Your encyclopaedia entries are cross-referenced to each other; they say that you were his arresting officer. Is that correct?'

'Yes. I did Lennie; I charged him with three murders, and he pleaded guilty to them all. There was a fourth killing, out in Spain; he did that too, but there was no evidence to corroborate his confession, so the book's closed on that one.'

'Your visit . . . can I ask you this . . . does it mean that he's still criminally active?'

Skinner laughed. 'No, absolutely not. He's got no family, and no friends to speak of from his old world. I've visited him a couple of times a year since he went inside.'

Elgin pursed his lips. 'My colleague in Shotts didn't think fit to share that with me either.'

'Nor should he have. Those visits aren't on any record, and nobody in the prison population ever knew they happened. It'll be the same with this and future calls I may pay on him, for reasons that you'll understand. "Lifer talks to chief constable." If that ever got out into the prison population or, worse, into the tabloids, it would be disastrous. That's why Rab McGonagall at Shotts always cooperated with me and it's why I trust you will too. When I come here I'm visiting you, and nobody else, not even your staff should ever see Lennie and me in the same room together.'

'I don't know if I can,' Elgin replied. 'I'm responsible for your personal security.'

'You're the second person who's made that mistake in the last couple of days. I go where I want; I can look after myself.'

'But this man is a multiple murderer, and you put him away. Doesn't that worry you?'

'It's never bothered either of us before. Big Lennie and I had our head-to-head years ago and we're both still around. He's no threat to anyone any more, and least of all to me.'

'Tell me about him, his background, please. There are gaps in my knowledge.'

'OK,' said Skinner. 'You know that Lennie Plenderleith is a very clever guy. He's blossomed in prison. But you may not know that he's also very wealthy. As a young man, he worked for a criminal, a guy called Tony Manson, who virtually adopted him. Manson was successful, so successful that I never managed to lock him up. When he died, he left his all to Lennie, including a trust fund in Liechtenstein. The big man has no interest in any future criminal activity; indeed his interests lie in avoiding it. You can trust him absolutely, as I do.'

'I see.'

'So we understand each other?'

Elgin nodded. 'We do. I'll go and get him.' Skinner rose, but the director held up a hand. 'No, stay there,' he said. 'You can use my office. It's the most private room in this place; I have it swept for bugs every month.' He left by a second door, not the one that led from his outer office.

The chief constable waited. He glanced round the modest room, noting that the pictures on the walls were cheap, mass production prints. If Elgin had chosen them, he was still in his early Vettriano period. If not, whoever had decorated his office had been cost conscious. As he sat, he felt his phone vibrate in his shirt pocket, then heard the ring tone. He took it out and saw 'Alex home' in the window. He flipped it open. 'Hi, daughter,' he said.

'Can you speak?' she asked as she usually did when calling his cell phone.

'Briefly.'

'What happened last night? I've been expecting you to call to tell me.'

'I've been busy. More happened than I have time to discuss. Andy and I are fine now, but you and I need to talk. Not now, though. You doing anything tonight?'

'Movie with Gina and Genevieve Cockburn. I could come to Gullane tomorrow.'

'We're having Maggie, her sister and Stephanie for lunch. Come and join us; you and I can grab a minute in private.'

'No, I'll drop out of the movie; the girls won't mind, if I say it's family business.'

'It will be, for we'll all eat together, something we don't do often enough. Head on out whenever you like. Aileen and I probably won't be back till after five, but Trish and the kids will be pleased to see you. See you then.' He ended the call, and had just switched off the phone when the door opened.

The man who came into the room was massive; six feet seven inches tall, according to his file . . . and according to his Wikipedia page, as Skinner discovered later . . . although that could have been an inch or two short of the truth, and with shoulders that seemed as wide as the entrance he had just used. His hair was lustrous, with more grey in it than the chief recalled from their last meeting, and although it was still winter and he was in prison, his skin was ruddy and healthy. He was forty-five years old, but looked half a decade younger.

'Hello, Bob,' he said as he sat in the second visitor chair. 'Good to see you. I thought my new digs might be a bit far away for you to visit.'

'Nah. There's a new road out of Glasgow that wasn't finished when you went inside. It cuts the journey down. My wife has constituency business in Glasgow today, so this visit fitted in. I dropped her off, and I'll pick her up on the way back. How are you doing? How does this new place compare with Shotts?'

'It's warmer in the winter, I'll tell you that. Plus, the air's cleaner and it doesn't smell of piss. That's the single worst thing about being inside, even now that nobody has to dump their leavings in the morning.' Lennie Plenderleith smiled. 'Congratulations, by the way, twice. On the new job, and on getting married. Mind you, after the things you've said to me about politicians over the last few years, I can't get my head round you having married one.'

'Seven,' said Skinner.

'What?'

'Seven years. That's how long I've been paying private visits to you in the nick. And you know what happens in one more.'

Lennie nodded. 'Oh yes. Thanks to that very generous judge who fixed the punishment period of my life sentence at eight years, on the basis of advice that I never saw, I can apply for parole.'

'Are you going to?'

'I don't know.'

'Why not?' asked Skinner, taken aback.

'Honestly? Because I don't know that I've done enough time. If I get out next year two things could happen. The right-wingers might use me as a great big club to beat the system with. That might have an effect on other guys coming up for release; it might make the parole board more cautious. On the other side, the huggies will depict me as a poster boy for the system, and that won't be fair either. No other prisoner has my resources; they'd all be held back.'

'Then why don't you help them?'

'What do you mean?'

'Tony Manson left you filthy rich, man. You've got more money than you know what to do with. Have you ever thought about using some of it to set up a foundation to fund Open University study by long-term prisoners with potential? Len, you're a fucking poster boy already, for more than just the huggies as you call them; while you've been inside you've picked up degrees in criminology and psychology and combined the two in a PhD.'

'No,' Plenderleith admitted. 'I never have thought about it. But I will. I see one problem right away. Who's going to assess applications for grants?'

'You are.'

'Not on my own. You can do it with me.'

'I couldn't, not in my job.'

'Then how about your wife? She was Justice Minister once, wasn't she?'

'I'll ask her. As for the parole thing, if you apply, I'll be asked for a view. I'll back you, and I'll even offer you a job.'

'You're kidding! As what?'

'As a consultant, a profiler. There is a need for people with your qualifications, and let's face it, your background gives you the edge on anyone else out there. Think about it.'

Lennie frowned. 'OK, I will; I promise.'

'While you're doing that I could probably get you open prison status, if you want.'

'I don't.' The response was swift. 'I'm in jail for murder, Bob. I came to terms with that fact the day I was sentenced, and I'm happy to stay in a closed prison.'

'You don't have any problems?'

The huge prisoner chuckled. 'What can you bench press these days, in kilos?'

'Twice my age, plus VAT.'

'Mmm. That's about a hundred and fifteen, yes? I can do two hundred, still, and I make sure that there are plenty of people in the gym to see me do it. I've followed that practice since I've been inside, so I've never had any problems. I am courteous to staff, I am civil to my fellow prisoners, but I am aloof. I have no friends, and I have no enemies. I'm sorted, Chief.' He gazed at his visitor. 'Now what do you want to ask me?'

'Why should I want to ask you anything?' Skinner exclaimed.

'I'm a graduate psychologist, Bob. I can read body language. You're not quite at ease; you've come to see me, but you've got an ulterior motive and you're guilty about it.'

The chief constable grinned. 'You're going to tell me next what it is.'

'No, I'm going to guess. Something to do with the Lithuanian disease that seems to be gripping your city, from what I've been reading in the papers.'

'I am definitely employing you, maybe even before you get out. Yes, you're on the mark. Remember those massage parlours of Tony Manson's that you sold?'

Lennie nodded. 'To that psychopath Zaliukas, yes?'

'Psychopath?'

'He was trying to suppress it, but in a guy like him, it's incurable. I'm not one, by the way. I never was. Every person I killed was for a reason, all but one of them out of what I saw as my duty to Tony, and I always felt remorse afterwards. I still do, especially for that stupid wife of mine. She's the main reason why I'm not sure I've served enough time.'

'You can do penance on the outside, Lennie,' Skinner told him. 'Now; that deal. Was Zaliukas the sole buyer?'

'As far as I know. His was the only name my lawyer mentioned, and his was the only signature on the papers. Why do you ask?'

'Because the Lithuanian disease, as you call it, seems to be related to them. Something's been happening that shouldn't have, and there's been a falling out over it. The way I see it, Zaliukas wasn't the only one involved in that deal, but we can't get a sniff of anyone else who might have been. His lawyer said that Tomas listed his wife as the second shareholder, but I believe he lied about that.'

'I don't think I can help you. I wasn't long inside then, so all I had to do with it was agreeing to the money and signing the deeds. What about the lawyer who acted for him? I remember his name as a witness to Zaliukas's signature on the things . . . there were eight of them, so it stuck in my mind. Ken Green; a pushy man. When I was arrested he came to see me in custody, without me asking for him.'

'I remember.'

'He told me he had a fair chance of getting me off. I told him he had no chance, because I was guilty as charged. I didn't like him, so I told him to fuck off and I instructed Frances Birtles instead. I liked her from the off; she impressed me as straight, whereas Green . . . didn't. If there was money being laundered for somebody, he'd have known about it. Yes, go and talk to him, Bob.'

Skinner looked at him straight-faced, but a corner of his mouth twitched. 'He's under detailed examination even as we speak.'

'There you are then.'

'Unfortunately it's by Joe Hutchinson, the pathologist, and his helpers. He was found dead in his car last night.'

Plenderleith whistled. 'In his garage? Are we talking suicide like Zaliukas?'

'No, we're talking accidental, like Valdas Gerulaitis and his wife were supposed to be.'

'Only they weren't?'

'We don't think so. Naturally, that makes us sceptical about Green's death.'

'I can see that. So you've got three accidental deaths, that probably weren't, and a suicide . . .'

'That undoubtedly was. We've also got eight trafficked Estonian prostitutes gone missing, en route to yet another accident for all we know, and a guy who showed up the day after Zaliukas died, at a meeting he had called the night before, with a note from Tomas saying that the business was under new management and he was it. Not the owner, though, a front man.'

'Can you describe him?'

'Heavy built, big chin, forty-ish; my crew are calling him

345

Desperate Dan. We think the same man dumped a ninth Estonian lass in a doctor's surgery. She'd been drugged and abused by the one stick-on certain homicide that we know we have.'

'The man Jankauskas that I read about?'

'That's him. Does that description ring any bells?'

'Sorry; there's a dozen guys in here look something like that. Anything else?'

'The hookers were moved by two women. We don't have a clue who they are either, but we assume they're connected to the bloke.'

'They must be,' said Plenderleith. 'One thing, though; I reckon those girls are safe enough. Your man seems to have been concerned enough about the other one to make sure she got help. Plus they will know by now that you'll be putting the pieces together. I'm sure they'll move the other eight on, get them out of your reach, so you'll never be able to prove anything, not even that they were here. But kill them? Eight of them? No. These people, from what you've said, sound like very smart professional criminals. They might be ruthless but they're not unreasoning. They'll have worked out that it's better the women turn up alive somewhere far away and out of your reach, than dead in Scotland to get you really excited. Yes, they'll move them out, probably with a few quid in their pockets.'

'How?'

'Same way they brought them in, surely. It should be easy. What resources do the police devote to tracking women being trafficked out of Scotland, rather than in?'

'Good thinking,' the chief constable conceded. 'Do you have any other insight, Dr Plenderleith? Seriously,' he added. 'I'm not taking the piss.'

'Just this. Two women, and a man involved with a degree of caring in his make-up; I think you're looking for a family.'

'You reckon? That's a good start. If you're right, and they were operating within my force's area, I believe I'd know about them. I may need to broaden this investigation.'

'Good luck,' Lennie told him. 'Other than that I can't help you. From the sound of things I'm the only guy who's made out of this business, having sold off those seedy places and bought a very nice flat with the half million I got for them.'

Skinner stared at him. 'Half a million,' he repeated. 'Our information is that Zaliukas only paid half that amount for them.'

'Well, he didn't, I promise you. You can check the public registers, or save time by calling Frances Birtles. She's still my lawyer. Looks as if you have proof, Bob. Zaliukas did indeed have a partner.'

Sixty-two

'I can't believe they painted it magnolia,' Paula Viareggio exclaimed as she gazed at the Great Hall of Stirling Castle from the western ramparts.

'It's not magnolia,' Mario laughed. 'It's . . . it's . . .' He gave up the search for an alternative. 'Although I'll grant you it's pretty close.'

'Whatever it is, it's garish.'

'Maybe so, but if you take a look at the guidebook, you'll see that they reckon that's how it looked when it was built.'

'When was that?'

'About five hundred years ago.'

'They had magnolia paint five hundred years ago? Did they have builders' merchants as well?'

'I suppose they must have, of a sort. I'll tell you what they did have, for sure, in the fifteenth and sixteenth centuries: pretty much constant wars. This place wasn't built for show. It was a citadel, even more so than Edinburgh Castle. It was besieged so often they probably had greasy spoon carts down below, flogging bacon rolls to the enemy while the Stuart kings went hungry inside.'

'You know, for a detective, you've got a vivid imagination.'

'Only off duty.'

She took hold of the lapels of his car coat, pulled his face down towards her and kissed him on the forehead. 'Mario, love of my life,' she murmured, 'you are never that.'

'I try, honest.'

'I know you do. Don't worry, it's what I knew I'd be in for, the day I decided that what the rest of the world thought didn't matter, set against you and me. Anyway, I'm not exactly a lady of leisure either.' She took his arm and led him towards the hall. 'Did you spot anything interesting in that car you looked at?'

'Nothing that caught my eye.'

'Was it all bloody?' she asked, with a mock shudder.

'Surprisingly not; considering that the guy was crushed in it, there wasn't a hell of a lot of blood. There wasn't a hell of a lot of anything.'

'What were you hoping to find?'

'Hoping? Nothing specific. Expecting? Maybe some indication that there was somebody else involved; the accelerator wedged down, Green's foot tied to it. But there was nothing like that, nothing to suggest that it was anything but an accident.'

'Wife?'

'No, he was divorced; for the second time. Our Ken had a reputation with the ladies.'

'I wonder how many will turn up at his funeral?'

'Not as many as there'll be polis reading the name on the coffin plate to make sure he really is dead.'

'Not one of your favourites, then.'

'No. There was always a whiff about Green. Most of us couldn't see much difference between him and his clients.'

They stepped inside the Great Magnolia Hall, and as they did, McGuire's mobile sounded. 'Sorry, love,' he said, taking it out under the disapproving stare of a castle custodian. 'Yes, Joe,' he answered.

'God, Mario,' the pathologist exclaimed, 'you're good.'

'Top notch,' he agreed, 'but caller ID helps. How are you doing?'

'I'm doing fine. However, the Humpty Dumpty on my table is not. I had him X-rayed. His skeleton's like a jigsaw puzzle, consistent with the photographs that were taken at the scene. All his major organs are crushed, and his heart and lungs are torn by rib fragments. If you're looking for a specific cause of death, one that couldn't be challenged under cross-examination, I don't think I'm going to be able to help.'

'That's in line with what out lab people are saying too. The car wasn't tampered with in any way.'

'So I hear. You asked me to tell you that this wasn't an accidental death, chum. I'm afraid I can't.'

'Fair enough. Thanks for making the effort, Joe.'

'My financial pleasure,' the professor replied. 'That said . . .'

The pause grabbed McGuire's attention. 'What?'

'There is one head injury that seems slightly different, in that there was a little more bleeding there than in other injury sites. It might have been caused by Mr Green's head hitting the window frame on impact, but then again, it might not.'

'So you are saying . . .' the head of CID began.

'No, I'm not. For me to make an absolute determination, I'd actually need to take his head off and fit it into that section of the vehicle. Unfortunately, I can't do that. I had images emailed to me by your people, and they show that in getting him out of there, the crucial area was cut through when they took the roof off, and twisted beyond recovery. Anyway, it was only an outside chance, unlikely to be definitive.' He sighed, frustrated. 'So, the verdict has to be that our Green died in the act of proving that Jaguars can't fly.'

Sixty-three

Alex frowned as she looked at her father, sat in a chair in the garden room. 'What do you want me to say, Pops?'

'Nothing that you don't want to,' he replied. 'I'm just telling you what happened after you stomped off last night.'

'I didn't stomp off!' she protested, indignantly.

'It looked like a stomp to me, kid, but I'm not blaming you for it. Andy was pushing his luck in showing up where he did, although I concede that his gamble paid off.'

'I wonder who told him you'd be there.'

'She's in the kitchen, helping Seonaid make the supper.'

'Seonaid's four, Pops; I know you think she's a prodigy, but not even Jamie Oliver started that young. Are you serious? Aileen told him?'

'Yup. She confessed as soon as I got home last night. Andy called her and asked for her help to put things right between us. She suggested that he just turn up here, at the house, but he didn't want that, in case there was a row in front of the kids. So she told him about the Torphichen office disco.'

'Are you mad at her?' his daughter asked.

'She was afraid I would be . . . but I'm not. I couldn't be, ever. The truth is she was right; apart from the professional side of it, he and I needed to sit down together. There are times when I need to be protected from myself.'

'Maybe I do too.'

'What do you mean?'

'I've done some daft things in my life,' she pointed out, 'almost invariably involving men, the daftest of all being that which caused the bother between you and Andy in the first place.'

Her father smiled, gently. 'If that's true it's in the blood. You're talking to a three times married guy who's had a couple of indiscretions himself. I'd prefer to say that most of the time you've been unlucky. I'm the one who's been stupid, and a bloody sight more indiscreet than you.'

Alex winced. 'You've never broken up anyone's marriage, though.'

'Nah.' Bob shook his head. 'I know it's easy for you to accuse yourself, and in part you're right. You knew Andy was married and yet you and he . . .' He left the sentence unfinished. 'Karen would have been within her rights to slam the door on him there and then, but she didn't. She took time to think the situation through properly and when she had done, she came to the conclusion that the easy thing to do would have been to forgive him for the one slip he ever made in their marriage, but that the right thing was to face up to the fact that there was more fundamentally wrong with it than that. She wasn't happy before the thing with you muddied the waters. And neither was Andy. When they got together, they were both wounded people, for different reasons, and they were good for each other's recovery. But they got married far too quickly; if they'd taken time to let the icing harden on the cake, they might not have. Then the family came along, Andy got deputy chief rank, and . . . they drifted apart. You might have been a catalyst, but all you did was spark a reaction that would have taken place anyway.'

She looked at him. 'Andy told you all this last night?' she asked.

'No. Karen did. I phoned her as soon as I left the disco, before I drove home. We had a long chat, and she told me everything she was feeling. She doesn't blame you, not any more. In fact . . .' He stopped short.

'What?'

'Nothing.'

'It's out of the bottle now; tell me.'

'She said,' he continued, a little reluctantly, 'that the two of you should never have split up in the first place.'

'Is that what you think too?' she challenged.

'What I think doesn't matter. All I know is that a relationship counsellor could write a bestseller on the emotional history of you and Andy Martin. It's what you and he believe that counts.'

'I can't speak for him,' she said. 'I'm not even sure I can speak for myself. What I do know is that when we did break up, acrimoniously, the underlying cause was a lack of communication. We were engaged, I got pregnant by mistake, and I had a termination without telling him. He went crackers, and I told him where he could shove his ring. We didn't talk to each other, before or during the disaster. He had his assumptions about me and motherhood, that he never put into words, but they were wrong. I knew enough about him to realise that if I'd told him I was expecting and what I planned to do about it, the row would have been just as big as it eventually was. I couldn't take the chance that he'd pressure me into having the baby, so I had the abortion without telling him.'

'And now?'

'Now? I'm more mature than I was then; in the same situation I'd tell him, and then go ahead and do the same thing whether he liked it or not. Look, Pops, I know you're getting round to asking me whether he and I are likely to get together again, but don't, please don't. The truth is that apart from that specific, just as there was something else wrong between Andy and Karen, there was another problem with the two of us, the same thing that went wrong between you and Sarah. He and I were both far too career-obsessed at the time to have been even thinking about domesticity. Well, I still am, and from what you've told me about the way his marriage has worked out, so's he. I might be strongly attracted to him, I might love him, but where we were before, I'm not going back there, no way.'

'I don't imagine he'd fancy that either.'

'I'm not going to call him, Pops,' she vowed.

'And he says he's not going to call you. So there you are, it can stay in the past.' He shrugged. 'You're both going to be living in the same city, but it's a big place.'

'It'll need to be. OK, you've told me. Thanks. Now, how's today been?'

'Interesting. I went to see an old acquaintance, in the nick, somebody who once did business with your firm's late client,

Mr Zaliukas. What he told me makes me all the more pleased that Mitch had the sense to move you off that account. We are going to have to look at those companies, to check on the amounts that moved out of there and into Tomas Zaliukas's pocket.'

Alex's eyebrows rose. 'Indeed?' she murmured. 'Mitch is going to love that.' She paused. 'But you won't find anything; nothing that you shouldn't, at any rate.'

'Maybe not,' Bob conceded, 'but we're going to have to look. There are some numbers that don't add up.'

Sixty-four

'That was a real tragedy about Ken Green, wasn't it, Jack?' said Frances Birtles, looking across her desk at her first visitors of her early starting day. 'A sad loss to the legal profession. I'll bet you lot'll miss him too.'

McGurk studied her face for signs of irony, and found them in plenty. 'I couldn't possibly comment, Frankie,' he replied, deadpan. 'He'll be one less rival for you at court, though. You won't be shedding any tears.'

'No, but purely because I never could stand the man. I could never quite get my head round the fact that he and I were members of the same profession,' she confessed. 'Ken's main skill as a defence lawyer lay in bullying scared and vulnerable witnesses into uncertainty in their testimony and in putting the seed of doubt in the mind of enough jurors.'

'I thought that was what you all did,' Sauce Haddock ventured.

'Who's your monkey, Jack?' the fair-haired solicitor asked, without even a glance at the DC.

The DS smiled. 'I use him for bullying scared and vulnerable defence briefs. He had Ken Green falling over himself to give him information last week. Unfortunately, not quite enough information. Sauce won't be that gullible again; once bitten, much less shy.'

'I'd better take you two seriously then, given what happened to Ken.'

'You always do, Frankie. You wouldn't be selective with what you tell us, like he was.'

'Don't be so sure. You know the rules; it would depend on what's privileged and what's not.' She smiled. 'Fortunately for you, in this instance, I've been instructed by my client, Dr Plenderleith, to offer you full cooperation, and to answer your questions as best I can.'

She looked at McGurk, appraising him as he sat awkwardly in the red leather chair with the squab that was far too short. 'What?' he exclaimed.

'I'm just trying to work out who's the taller,' she told him, 'you or Lennie. The only thing I know for sure is that I'd like you both in my basketball team. Now,' she continued, before McGurk could retort that as a former rugby player he considered basketball a game for Jessies, 'you want to know about the sale of eight,' she paused and gave a light cough, 'massage parlours, left to my client as part of the estate of Mr Tony Manson, of which he was the principal beneficiary.'

'Correct. I know it's a few years ago, Frankie, but . . .'

'My firm's records go back a few years, Sergeant McG, and so does my memory. Selling a consignment of eight quasi-legal brothels is a one-off for me, and it'll remain so. What do you need to know?'

'How was the money paid?' Haddock asked. 'In what form?'

'In two tranches, simultaneously,' she replied. 'There was a certified cheque for a quarter of a million drawn on the personal account of Mr Tomas Zaliukas. The balance, the other half, was paid in Eurobonds.'

'What was that source?'

'I have no idea. Eurobonds are wonderful instruments for preserving your anonymity.'

'Where did Ken Green say they came from?'

'He didn't; to be honest I've always assumed that Zaliukas funded the lot. He asked if that form of payment by his client would be acceptable. I had no reason to decline. If it had been cash, sure, I'd have needed rock-solid assurances that it wasn't laundered money, but Eurobonds are as good as currency, better in that they don't attract the attention that a suitcase of readies would. No, Constable Haddock, don't look at me like that. You have to remember that when Ken Green made an approach to buy the properties he was acting on behalf of an offshore company. I didn't know who its principal was, and he wasn't obliged to tell me. The first I knew that Tomas Zaliukas was involved was when I saw that transfer coming from his account, and his name as authorised signatory on the deeds.'

'But weren't you suspicious?' the DC persisted.

'No. And why should I have been?' she challenged. 'Offshore companies exist; they're not banned by international law, or by ours for that matter. My client wanted rid of those places as quickly as possible; that was his instruction to me. I thought it was going to be a long and tedious job, and that I was going to have to sell the places off one by one, so when Ken Green turned up offering to buy the whole lot at property valuation, I practically tore his arm off. My brief was to help my client dispose of some iffy property for a decent price and invest the proceeds in something blue chip. I did a good deal for Lennie, end of story.'

'Nobody's disputing that, Frankie,' McGurk conceded.

'Then why are you here?'

'Because these places connect to the trail of deaths across the city last week. Zaliukas, his cousin Gerulaitis and his wife, are all out of the picture.'

'A suicide and an accident, I read.'

The DS raised his eyebrows. 'That's how it looked. But the managers have all been told to close temporarily and there's a new owner in place already. We're wondering if he's always been there. That's why we're interested in that quarter million in Eurobonds.'

'Can't you check the offshore company?'

'No. The late Ken was smarter than you give him credit for. It's based in a jurisdiction where we can't get access to its records. Uruguay's tighter than Switzerland. We're going to Green's office next, hopefully with a warrant, if our boss can talk a sheriff into giving us one. Maybe we'll find something in Green's files. I'm not raising my hopes too high, though, so think back, please; when you and Green did the deal, who else did you meet?'

'I never met anybody else,' Birtles told him. 'I advertised the portfolio, Ken phoned me, and said that he wanted to talk about the properties, all of them. We had one meeting. I showed him my surveyor's valuation, and I invited him to think about it and let me know. He called me a couple of days later, offered me half a million . . . I'd quoted him six hundred thousand. I told him to put it in writing, he did and I accepted. That formal offer was the first time I'd ever heard of Lituania SAFI.'

'Did you ever ask him who was behind it?'

'Of course I did, Jack. I was curious; no argument about that.'

'Did he drop any hints?'

The lawyer frowned, her eyes narrowing as if she was trying to place herself back in a conversation that had taken place seven years before. 'No,' she murmured. 'When I asked him, he just smiled and said, "Men of substance and influence, Frankie." That was all. But he used the plural; he definitely said that there was more than one.'

'What do you know about Zaliukas?'

'I never acted for him. I met him, though, early in my career, when I defended his cousin Gerulaitis on an assault charge.' She smiled. 'I got him off, but it wasn't down to me really. When the victim went into the witness box and was asked to identify the man who attacked him, he pointed to one of the guys in the press box.'

'Could Valdas have been a partner in the acquisition?' Haddock asked.

She looked at the young detective. 'Not a chance. That guy was a chronic gambler, and a bad one. He was perpetually skint in those days; Tomas even paid for his defence. He told me he wasn't sure that it was money well spent. When I asked him what he meant, he said that it might have been kinder to let Valdas go to jail for a bit, and here I quote, "to give him a break from that fucking wife of his". He was a funny guy; too bad he stopped seeing the joke.'

Sixty-five

Normally, Bob Skinner enjoyed the first day of the working week after recharging his batteries by spending quality time with Aileen and the children. Although their Saturday had been curtailed, their Sunday had been one of the best, thanks to the lunchtime visit by Maggie Steele, Bet Rose, her sister, and an increasingly boisterous Stephanie, who was developing facial features that promised to owe a lot to the father she would never meet.

There had been a further highlight, when the family had been gathered round the table for their evening snack. Bob had mentioned, casually, his accidental discovery that he had a page on Wikipedia, and that he would be interested to know who had posted it and who was keeping it up to date. His older, adopted, son Mark had said nothing, but a slight flush in his cheeks, and a touch of uncertainty in his eyes had combined to betray him.

'You, Markie?' Bob had said. 'You're my public affairs consultant?'

'Yes, Dad,' the boy had replied.

Skinner always made a point of spending at least as much

363

time with Mark as with any of his siblings. His determination was that while the boy should always remember and respect his birth parents, both dead, he should feel that he was as much a father to him as to his natural children. And the responsibility was growing, with the approach of his teens. From his early years, Mark had shown a prodigious talent for mathematics, and for physics. There had been a time when Bob had been determined to develop it by sending him to Fettes College, with James Andrew, and eventually Seonaid, but when he had proposed it, he had been faced, for the only time in their lives, with a united rebellion by both of his sons, who had pleaded to be allowed to move on to the local high school when the time came. Being a secret soft touch for his children, he had yielded, and found Mark the best private tutor he could find, to allow him to develop his talent at its natural pace, and not be held back.

'Didn't you think to ask me?' he had murmured.

'No.' The boy looked him in the eye. 'I didn't start it,' he said. 'Somebody else put it up. I found it and it was full of cra . . . nonsense, so I logged on and edited it, made it accurate. Now I just keep it up to date. I do the same thing for Mum as well. Her page was rubbish too.' The three children had two mums, Aileen in Gullane and Sarah in America, and managed to make it invariably clear to which they were referring.

'My page was started by the Labour Party,' Aileen had laughed.

'But they don't know you. Neither did the guy who started your fan page on Facebook. I've taken that over too.'

Skinner was still smiling inwardly over the revelation as his senior colleagues left his room at the end of the Monday morning meeting, but none of it worked through to his expression. There had been no progress on any of the deaths of the previous week. Tomas Zaliukas was still, unshakeably, a suicide, and none of the specialist teams were prepared to say, unshakeably, that the deaths of the Gerulaitases and Ken Green had been caused by anything other than misfortune, or in the lawyer's case, recklessness. Only Linas Jankauskas was listed definitely as a murder victim, and there had been no progress in finding the comic book lookalike who had rescued Anna Romanova from his flat. He had been testy with Mario McGuire at the staff gathering, and the atmosphere had been strained, since the head of CID had never been one to meekly bare his bottom for the headmaster's cane.

His door opened after a faint knock, and Gerry Crossley stepped half into the room. 'David Mackenzie's here,' he began.

'OK,' the chief grunted. The superintendent replaced Crossley in the door frame, looking a little hesitant. *Word must have got around*, he thought. 'Come on in, David,' he said, 'and relax. I've had my red meat ration for the morning. What can you do for me?'

'Brighten your day?' Mackenzie suggested.

'Please try.' He offered a seat, but rose himself. 'Want a coffee?' he asked as he stepped across to his filter pot on its warming plate. 'I think I'm having withdrawal symptoms.'

'I'll give it a miss, boss.'

'Fire away, then.'

'It's that job you gave me, to see if I can locate any property owned by Lituania SAFI outside our area. I got a result, and then some. Over the past six years or so, the company's been pumping money into acquisitions, in the same or related fields to its Edinburgh holdings. It owns three premises in the Dundee area, one in Perth, one in Inverness and four in Aberdeen, all licensed massage parlours. It also owns a sex shop in Dundee and bingo halls in Montrose and in Aberdeen.'

Skinner whistled as he resumed his seat. 'Does it, by Christ,' he murmured, his first morning smile lighting up his face. 'Who are the licence holders?'

'Individuals in each case, as is the pattern here; the people who're actually running the places. I only suspect that for the moment but I'll keep digging. That's all there is, though, all the company owns.'

'That's good work, David. Hold off on the digging for now. I'm sure you're right, but I may spread the load a bit. These licence holders,' he continued. 'Do their names sound, how shall I put it, funny to our Celtic ears?'

Mackenzie grinned. 'Do you mean are they Lithuanians, sir? No, nary a one. There's a Patel running the Montrose bingo hall, but the rest are all Anglo.'

'Well, isn't that interesting. Here in Edinburgh where Tomas was the player, he put his own kind into everything the company owned. But in the other areas of the country . . .'

'. . . somebody else was placing the people. Is that what you're saying?'

'That's where I'm heading.'

'Do you want me to bring the Tayside and Grampian forces into this?' the superintendent asked.

'No. I want you to leave it with me for now. There's someone else I think I'll consult first. Thanks, David.'

He watched his visitor as he left, then picked up the phone as the door closed behind him. 'Gerry,' he said to his assistant. 'Call the HQ of the Drugs and Serious Crimes Agency, through in Paisley, and see if you can get the acting director on the blower for me.'

He sat and waited, sipping his coffee, letting thoughts run through his mind. Finally the phone buzzed. 'I have Mr Martin on the line for you, Chief,' Crossley announced. 'Now that was a surprise.'

'Not just for you, chum. Thanks.' He waited until he heard the clink of the call being connected. 'Andy,' he exclaimed, 'isn't life a funny bugger? I go six months without speaking to you and on your first week in your new job, something drops in my lap that I need to talk to you about.'

'Funny indeed,' Martin agreed, 'but are you sure you need to talk to me? I'm not being precious or anything, but I don't want my people thinking I'm hogging stuff for myself, or that I haven't read my job description.'

'I know that, man. I'm under the same constraints.' He chuckled. 'Although . . . your job description says that you're the boss, so if you chose you could do whatever you fucking liked . . . until you screwed up, of course. But this call might be to Andy Martin, rather than to the acting director general. This thing I've got has developed a decidedly Tayside feel, and since you've still got the dust of the place on your shoes, you're exactly the guy whose brain I need to pick.'

'OK, but right now? I'm just about to go into my first department heads meeting. I'm expecting it to go on well into lunch.'

'Then that's your top priority,' Skinner agreed. 'Where are you laying your head tonight?' he asked.

'Like I told you; Edinburgh, tonight and every night. I can meet you later if that's all right. If I catch the four-thirty train, I can be with you by half five.'

'Then do that. I might have a couple of people sit in on our chat, if that's OK.'

'Fine by me.' The chief constable heard a quick intake of breath. 'Bob,' his friend said, 'it's good to be back. Know what I mean?'

'Yeah, Andy,' he sighed, 'I know. Same here. You sure there's no chance for you and Karen?'

'None. I'm rarely certain about relationships, but I am this time.'

'Too bad. See you later.'

He ended the call and leaned back in his chair. His coffee was well on its way to being cold, but he finished it nonetheless. He closed his eyes and went back to the musing he had begun while waiting for the phone call, poring over the events of the past week, probing for holes in the investigation, flaws in the procedure. Suicide? He had to believe that. Accidents? No danger. Someone had cleaned out the Zaliukas camp, for sure, and had silenced Ken Green because he knew . . . what? The name of the other player in Lituania SAFI, presumably, and with him gone, that was . . .

He sat bolt upright, his eyes opening wide. 'Shit!' he whispered, as he pushed himself out of his chair and headed for the door. He strode past Gerry Crossley without a word, out of the command suite and along the corridor that led to the head of CID's office. McGuire was at his desk as he entered; he made to rise, but the chief constable cut him off with a wave of his hand.

'Mario,' he boomed, 'we've been fucking negligent, and I include myself in that plural, for I'm supposed to be the top gun around here. We've been so obsessed by what's been happening here that we've ignored the broader picture. Tomas is dead, and so's his cousin; their wee brothel empire's been taken over. But it was bigger than we thought; the company owns another twelve businesses. There is a partner, and we reckoned that Ken Green was probably our last means of proving who he is . . . but he might not be. There's somebody else, and we've been ignoring her as this thing's developed. Regine Zaliukas. She's sitting in a wee French village with her kids, and she could be in danger. She could also be an important witness; we need to get to her, we need to talk to her and we need to keep her safe. This isn't something that can be left to a sergeant and a DC. We need to get somebody over there now, somebody with weight enough to impress the local police, and that, my friend, means you.'

'Wow,' McGuire whispered, 'you're the boss, but . . . You said yourself that when Alex spoke to her she wasn't in any hurry to get back. We could get out there and find she's shacked up with a toyboy, and that's why Tomas offed himself.'

'If that was the case, Tomas wouldn't have "offed himself".

He'd have taken the other guy's head off with his fucking chainsaw. I'm serious; I want you on your way to France, soonest. I can't go with you, but you will need someone. Given who you're going to see, it had better be a female officer, with rank.'

'Stallings.'

'She'll do. Where's your passport?'

'Here, in my drawer. I always keep it handy.'

'Good; that's a start. Call Becky and tell her to go home and pick hers up, assuming that she needs to, and to pack a bag, enough for a couple of nights. I'll make the arrangements, flights, a hire car if you need it, and I'll get Regine's address from Alex. I know she has it. If I can get the two of you there today I will, so tell Stallings to be ready to leave soonest. How are you off for clothes?'

'I keep an emergency bag here too, and a couple of hundred euros.'

'Right: tell Neil what's happening, and get ready to leave for the airport. We've left that woman and her kids unprotected for too long.'

Sixty-six

'M s Wisniewski,' said Sauce Haddock, 'we appreciate that you're still in a state of shock, but we have a job to do.' As he looked at the woman, he remembered his imperious reception on his first visit to the firm of Grey Green, only a few days before, and noted the contrast. Gladys Wisniewski gave the impression of someone who was standing on a rug without being certain whether there were floorboards under it. Bereft of Ken Green's presence, his room seemed much larger, and his secretary that much smaller.

'But I don't have the authority,' she blustered. 'I can't just let you walk in here.'

'We've got the authority ourselves,' Jack McGurk told her, holding up the sheet of paper that he had shown to the grim-faced receptionist a few minutes before, 'in the form of this warrant from the sheriff, which allows us to search these premises, unless you voluntarily supply us with the items we require. So, with Mr Green gone, who's the senior partner? Would that be Mr Grey?'

'There is no Mr Grey,' she murmured.

'Don't prevaricate, please,' the sergeant snapped. 'If it's Miss or Mrs, where is she?'

'No, you don't understand. There are no partners in the firm. Mr Green was a sole practitioner. We do have legal staff, but they're all employees, mostly doing court work.'

'Fresh out of university?' Haddock speculated. 'On minimum salaries to maximise the firm's profit from its legal aid clients?'

Mrs Wisniewski nodded. 'You get the picture,' she acknowledged, as she began to recover both her poise and her accent of the previous week. 'There's nothing wrong with that. It's common practice across Scotland. This firm provides valuable training for young lawyers. Quite a few of the people who started with us are advocates now. A couple of them will be QCs quite soon.'

'Save us the PR speak, please, lady,' McGurk sighed. 'We're not here to question Ken Green's scruples or his business practices. If they were OK with the Law Society, they're OK with us. What we need to talk about is his relationship with the late Tomas Zaliukas, and with a company that he set up for him called Lituania SAFI, registered in Uruguay. Are you familiar with all that?'

'I've met Mr Zaliukas,' she admitted. 'And I've heard the name of that company before.'

'So who were its principals?'

'Mr Zaliukas was.'

'We know that, but under Uruguayan law, an offshore company has to have at least two shareholders. So there must have been someone else involved in the transaction. I'm wondering, could it have been Mr Green himself?'

'No,' she replied firmly. 'That would have been against the Law Society rules, and Mr Green was a stickler for those. Why don't you ask the Uruguayan Embassy?'

'We have done. Their law allows SAFI shareholders and directors to keep their names secret, so they aren't about to help us. We need you to tell us.'

'But that would break client confidentiality.'

'That's not what the sheriff thought when she signed this warrant. So, will you please bring us all the firm's files relating to Mr Zaliukas, and to the company.'

'I can't.'

McGurk drew a deep breath and seemed to grow even taller as he towered over the woman. 'Ms Wisniewski,' he threatened, holding up the first two fingers of his right hand, and stopping just short of pressing them together, 'you are that close to being charged with obstructing us. Do yourself a favour and get those records, now, or we will take this place apart until we find them.'

'I tell you I can't,' she shouted. 'They're not here.'

'What do you mean?'

'I'm trying to tell you that Mr Green didn't keep them here. Some files, the Lituania SAFI papers among them, weren't stored here. None of the meetings relating to those parts of the business took place here either.'

'Hold on,' said Haddock. 'If this is a one-man firm, why would it have a second office?'

'It doesn't, not as such. As far as I know, Mr Green used his cottage in East Lothian for that purpose. That's where he met those clients and that's where their files were kept.'

'What would the Law Society think of that?' asked McGurk, drily.

'There's nothing to prevent a lawyer from working at home,' the secretary retorted.

'How will we get access to the cottage?'

'With another warrant, if I had any say in the matter.'

'Which clearly you don't. So who does? Who's Mr Green's heir?'

'He has a son from his first marriage, Kenny junior; he inherits everything. I know, because I witnessed the will. He's only fifteen, so his mother is the executor. She's remarried and her name is Marianne McKean now. She lives in Uphall, but I doubt if you'll find her there just now; she works at Curle Anthony and Jarvis, as a partner's secretary.'

'We'll head up there,' said McGurk to Haddock, 'just as soon as we've searched the premises.'

'What do you mean?' Gladys Wisniewski screeched indignantly. 'I've told you there's nothing here.'

'Yes, you have, ma'am,' the sergeant replied, coolly, 'but in the circumstances, I'm afraid we can't take your word for it.'

Sixty-seven

'What are you two doing here?' Alex Skinner asked the two detectives as they stepped into the reception area of Curle Anthony and Jarvis, just as she was passing through. 'If you want to talk to me about the Lietuvos companies, you're wasting your time. Mr Laidlaw's holding the reins on that business now, and he will be until a new chief executive's appointed.'

'Close,' said McGurk, 'but no cigar. We need to talk to one of your staff, Mrs McKean.'

'I don't smoke cigars, Jack, only good quality skunk.' She smiled at the flash of alarm that showed for a second on Haddock's face. 'That was a joke, Sauce. Chief constables' daughters do not smoke anything. Why do you want Marianne?'

'It's to do with her former husband.'

She frowned, quizzically. 'Who's that?'

'Wrong tense,' Haddock told her. 'Was. Now deceased; Ken Green.'

Alex's eyes widened. She gasped, and the young DC experienced another momentary flash, of lust. 'Ken Green the lawyer?' she repeated. 'Marianne was married to Ken Green? No wonder she never talks about her private life.'

'Does that mean you don't know she has a son?'

'It's the first I've heard of it. Ronnie might know, but she's never mentioned it to me.'

'Ronnie? Who's he?' McGurk asked.

'She. Ms Veronica Drake, the partner she works for. Well, well, life is a never-ending run of surprises.'

'Yeah,' the DS drawled, 'and we had a few of those on Friday night, didn't we? First Montell having to be huckled off by your old man, then Andy Martin turning up.'

'Don't push your luck, big boy,' Alex warned him, not wholly in jest. 'I'm surprised you noticed anything, the way you and Lisanne were all over each other.' She turned to Haddock. 'And as for you, Sauce,' she added, 'you looked like all your Christmas days had come at once when that gorgeous piece of eye candy of yours whipped you off for an early bath. What did you say her name was again?'

'Cheeky.'

'I didn't mean to be; it was a straight question.'

'That's her name, Alex . . . at least it's the name she goes by.'

'Of course, how could I have forgotten that? How long has she been on the scene?'

'About a week.'

'My God,' she exclaimed, 'and you're barely out of breath. You're obviously smitten, the pair of you.'

The young detective grinned. 'Early days yet,' he said. 'I'm seeing her again tonight.'

'If you're finished in time,' McGurk pointed out. 'Our boss

is on her way to France, so our shift might run on a bit, especially if we take any length of time out in Green's cottage.'

'That's all right. I'll text her if we look like running late.'

'Green's cottage?' Alex repeated. 'Where is it?'

'East Lothian,' Haddock volunteered. 'A couple of miles south of Garvald.'

'My home county. My dad and I went on a car treasure hunt when I was a kid, and the clues took us out that way. If we'd found an undiscovered tribe I wouldn't have been surprised. You'd better get your inoculations before you head out there.'

'We'll need to get permission before that. That's why we need to see Mrs McKean. We found a holder with a lot of keys among Green's personal effects, and we're hoping that one of them is for the cottage, but we need her OK as executor to open it.'

'Then let's find her.' She turned to the firm's receptionist. 'Sonia, would you call Marianne McKean and tell her that the police are here and would like a word.' She waved the detectives a quick farewell and walked off towards her office.

McGurk and Haddock waited as Sonia picked up her telephone and made a call. 'Marianne will be with you directly,' she told them, as she replaced it in its cradle.

They stood, looking in the direction in which Alex had gone, only to be surprised when a questioning voice came from behind them. 'Yes, gentlemen?' They turned to see a small woman with burnished auburn hair, wearing a grey trouser suit, walk through the door they had used. She caught their confusion at once. 'I work in the other section of the office,' she explained. 'The corporate departments are over here; the rest of us in the overflow area. We call ourselves the peripherals. Is this about Ken?' she asked.

'Yes, I'm afraid so,' the DS replied. 'We're sorry for your loss.'

'He isn't my loss. He never was, in fact. The day I signed the divorce papers ranks as one of the best of my life.'

'How's your son taking it?'

'Kenny's shocked, naturally. It's his first experience with death, so my husband and I are keeping an eye on him, but so far he's bearing up. I gave him the option of staying off school, but he chose to go.'

'Had you heard from Mr Green recently?'

She seemed distracted for a second. 'What? Sorry. No, not for a while, not for ages. Since the divorce our only contact has been to do with Kenny. In the early years, his dad used to take him to rugby internationals and the odd football game, but that fell away.'

'Who's organising the funeral?'

'Why?' she retorted. 'I don't see the police sending a wreath.' She smiled, briefly. 'Sorry, I shouldn't talk like that, otherwise you'll be thinking I fixed his brakes. The sad fact is that even though he's acquired another ex-wife since we split up ten years ago, I'll have to organise it, or at least instruct the undertaker, since I've been informed that the bugger made me his executor, without even asking me. That Polish witch of a secretary of his called me about half an hour ago to tell me. I don't mind, though; it's better I look out for Kenny's interests than anyone else does.' She looked up at McGurk. 'So what do you want?'

'We'd like your permission to go into your hu ... Mr

Green's cottage,' he told her. 'It's in connection with a current investigation. We want to see certain papers and we have reason to believe they might be there. We've got a sheriff's warrant, but it only covers his office.'

'The cottage, eh,' Marianne McKean said, a gleam in her eye. 'God knows what you'll find in there. I didn't know the place existed until my lawyer did the property inventory for the divorce, and he was forced to own up to it. As soon as I found out, everything fitted into place. The meetings away from the office, the papers that should have been there but weren't, the clients whose names . . . actually more often their initials . . . were in his phone book and his diary but never appeared in the practice accounts, the money held in the clients' account for people who were totally fictitious, like we didn't even have their addresses or any record of services provided. I was Ken's secretary until I split up with him; I was always asking him about that stuff, but he always fobbed me off. I knew he had to have somewhere.'

'Are you saying that Mr Green was bent?' asked Haddock.

She looked at him. 'Ken? Bent?' She laughed. 'Bear? Woods? Shit? In business, he liked to give the impression that he was one of those guys who sailed close to the wind but never against it. He sat on Law Society committees, he kept a high media profile, and he never broke the rules in court, for all that he had a reputation as an aggressive cross-examiner. But all the time . . . Bent, no, no: that word doesn't come close to describing him. Don't even think of corkscrews either; that wouldn't do him justice. He was the dodgy client's lawyer of choice. The only thing that was straight about Ken was that he was resoundingly heterosexual. That place of his was a fuck-pit as well, not just for him, but for his pals. One of them confessed as much to me years afterwards.' She nodded. 'Yes, you can have my permission to enter the cottage. I'll give you it in writing, just in case another Ken Green ever questions your right to have gone in there. Good luck; I hope you find what you're looking for. In fact, since it's going to be Kenny junior's, if you want to clear all his dad's crap out of the place you'll be doing me a favour.'

Sixty-eight

'This is all a bit sudden, sir, isn't it?' DI Becky Stallings ventured, looking at Mario McGuire across the low table in Edinburgh Airport's executive lounge.

'Welcome to Bob Skinner's world, Inspector . . . and don't call me "sir" when there's just the two of us about. I've been answering to Mario all my life and I can't break the habit. When the big man does decisive, nothing gets in the way. Still, this sets some sort of record, even for him; less than two hours after he gave the word, here we are waiting for our flight to be called.'

'I don't even know where we're going,' Stallings pointed out. 'I know who we're going to see, but when Ray asked me where, I couldn't tell him. And I still couldn't: you've got the boarding cards, remember.'

'So I have, sorry.' He took four slips from an inside pocket, and handed two over. 'You'll see that we fly to Charles de Gaulle and from there to Bordeaux.'

She glanced at the cards. 'Business class?'

'David Mackenzie does all the chief officers' bookings through a travel agency. They get us a good rate, plus an upgrade, 'cos we're polis. It doesn't cost the taxpayer any extra, if that bothers you.'

'I'll take it if it's going,' she said cheerfully. 'I've never flown in the posh end of the plane before.'

'It won't be that posh. A few extra chips with the meal and better wine . . . for you at any rate.'

'Don't you drink?'

'McIlhenney would fall over laughing if he heard you ask that. It's not that. When we get to Bordeaux, about five thirty if we're on time, we pick up a hire car and drive down the autoroute as far as Agen, about an hour, hour and a half, then across country to the place we're going. It's called Mezin.'

'Won't it be dark by then? French time's an hour on from ours.'

'No problem. The car will have satnav.'

'How's your French? Mine couldn't order me a sandwich.'

'Not as good as my Italian, but it'll be OK for our needs.'

The DI sipped her coffee. 'This might be an obvious question, but does this woman know we're coming?'

'Obvious but fair. The answer's no, she doesn't.'

'Then how do we know she's going to be there?'

'The chief has checked that out, indirectly. He asked Mitchell Laidlaw, Alex's boss, to call her and ask whether she'd be available tomorrow morning to receive some papers he has to send out to her. She said she would. It wasn't a lie,' he added. 'He genuinely does need to send her some documents.'

'I see. She's there, but she's not expecting us. I wonder how she's going to react when we ring her doorbell, and flash our warrant cards.'

'We can't be flashing anything in France, officially. We should be checking in at the local gendarmerie, but until it has to be official, and let's hope it doesn't, we're not going to do that. We're just going to pay a private visit to the woman, that's all; to check that she's all right. How'll she react? Regine's a cool lady. She'll handle it.'

'You know her?'

'I know her from seeing her around at Indigo; we've spoken a few times. There's no reason why she should remember me though; that place is always packed.' He glanced up at the information board. Their flight still showed 'Wait in lounge'. 'But what do you reckon, Becky? You're a woman, what's your take on her state of mind?'

Stallings frowned. 'Never having met her, or even heard of her until all this lot started, I'm not sure I'm the person to ask. We're not like bees, us gals, we don't have a swarm mentality. But based on what I've read up about her . . . She and Zaliukas were more than husband and wife, she was an important part of the entertainment side of his business. There doesn't seem to have been any hint of marital problems . . . Jack and Sauce haven't come across as much as the whiff of a scent of a bit on the side. Yet the week before last, she took herself off to France, back to her old home village with their kids. She flatly denied Gerulaitis's story that there was a break-up, but a few days later Tomas shot himself, leaving a note on his computer, saying, "I couldn't live without Regine and my kids." Sounds like they had indeed fallen out. Then, when she was contacted and told that he was dead, she didn't quite say, "So what?" but she didn't do what you'd have expected either, that is, jump on the first available plane and go home. It's a reasonable assumption that whatever had happened between them, she was pissed off with him big time, to let it carry on beyond the grave.' As she spoke, the information screen changed, telling them that their flight to Paris was ready for boarding.

'But could she really have been that mad at him?' she continued. 'Apart from the suicide note, all we know about the separation came from Valdas Gerulaitis, not the most trustworthy witness. But what if that was all a smokescreen? We know that there was trouble in the massage parlour business. What if that got so big it made Tomas get her and the kids out of the way, before it all blew up. If that was the case,' she said, as she finished her coffee and rose to her feet, to follow McGuire out of the lounge, 'did the danger end with his death? That's the question that's sending us over there, isn't it? It could be that when she opens that door and we're there, she's going to be very pleased to see us.'

Sixty-nine

'I'm surprised we can get a mobile signal out of here,' said Jack McGurk. 'Alex Skinner wasn't kidding when she told us this place was in the back of beyond.'

'You're in, though?' Neil McIlhenney asked.

'Oh yes, no problem about that. There's just the one key, for a Chubb five-lever lock; not hard to match from the lot we took from Green's office.'

'What's the place like?'

'It's quite a nice wee place. It's called Moor Cottage. There's a letter box on the road at the start of the drive that leads up to it, otherwise you'd never know it was here. The original building has two bedrooms, kitchen, bathroom and a living area, with a conservatory on the back, but he's built it out at the back, with another bedroom, en suite ... complete with mirrored wardrobes, and a steam room, would you believe ... and an office. That's where we are just now.'

'Have you found what you're looking for?'

'Not so far. We've been through his desk, but there's nothing of interest there, apart from a photograph we found tucked away in a drawer of Green with a bird.'

'Ex-wife?'

'It's not Marianne, that's for sure. Can't say about the second Mrs G. Sauce thinks it might be his receptionist, but it's a pretty bad image.'

'Bring it back with you anyway. Did he have a computer there?'

'No, but there is a broadband connection, so maybe he had a laptop that he used when he was out here.'

'It wasn't in his car,' said the superintendent. 'I've seen the inventory. It could be in his Edinburgh house, I suppose.'

'No,' McGurk replied. 'I spent a good chunk of my Sunday going through that. I'd have found one if it was there.'

'Well, what else have you got?'

'Old technology,' the detective sergeant told him. 'There's a four-drawer filing cabinet, stuffed with papers, sorted in a way that might have made sense to Green but makes none to us. Sauce is still going through it, for the second time, but so far he's found nothing that relates to Lituania SAFI, or to Zaliukas.' He chuckled. 'It is a fucking treasure trove, though. We've found some very interesting names in there. It's like a who's who of Edinburgh criminal society, and more than that. He's been involved with other people, names you'd recognise but wouldn't imagine associating with Ken Green. From the quick look we've had, offshore companies in out-of-the-way locations seem to have been a specialty of his. I can almost smell the laundered money.'

'But there's nothing on Zaliukas's company,' McIlhenney repeated.

'No, sir, not yet.'

'Even though there must be. Jack, are there any signs of forced entry?'

'Not that I can see. The first thing we did was check the security of the place. The front door was double locked when we opened it, most of the original windows are painted shut and everything at the back's fairly modern and looks pretty much burglar-proof.'

'Somebody's been in there, though. I can feel it. Have you looked in any of the other rooms yet?'

'Sure. We eliminated everything else before we started here. We've found his coat, his condoms, a vibrator, some ladies items, including exotic underwear, and two pairs of wellies, size ten and ladies size thirty-seven. All the business stuff is in the office.'

'Are there any outbuildings?'

'There's a wooden shed. There's nothing in it but folding garden chairs, a lawnmower, electric trimmer and some other implements.'

'Take another look, there and outside. An uncle of mine had a place like that, away up in Ullapool, miles from anywhere. He had a fixation about getting there and finding that he'd forgotten the key, so he planked one in the garden. You might find that Green did the same thing. From what you say, everything in the shed's summer stuff, so look for signs for something having been moved recently that shouldn't have been, there and around the house.'

'I'll do that, sir, while Sauce finishes going through the filing cabinet.' He paused. 'What about these other papers? Can we take these with us?'

'Are they evidence of crime?'

'I suppose they could be. But we won't know until we've studied them, will we?'

'No,' McIlhenney conceded. 'In that case I'm not sure that we've got a legal right to remove them. I'll need to take advice on that.'

As he held his phone to his ear, a broad smile spread across McGurk's face. 'No, you don't,' he said. 'We do have the right. Marianne McKean, Green's executor, told us we could clear his stuff out of the cottage. She said we'd be doing her a favour.'

'In that case . . .' McIlhenney exclaimed. 'But just to be certain, give her a call and get her to say it again. If she gives you the all clear, shove the lot in your car and bring it back. We can look at it at our leisure. You're right, we might have got ourselves a bonus. It's still second prize, though, behind something to identify Tomas Zaliukas's partner in the massage parlour business.'

As he listened, McGurk was aware of hand signals alongside him. 'That's Sauce finished now,' he said. 'There's nothing.'

'Bugger!' the superintendent swore. 'Still . . . even that tells us something. There should have been a file on Lituania SAFI, but there isn't. Somebody has beaten you to it, I'm certain. Jack, I want the two of you to wait there. Dorward's going to love this, but I'm going to ask him to send a team out there. I want that place gone over. If there's even a single trace there, and we can match it . . .'

Seventy

'Thanks for the car pick-up,' said Andy Martin, as Skinner greeted him at the main entrance to the police headquarters building. 'It's a bugger trying to get a taxi at Haymarket Station at this time of night.'

'It's just as well your place is walking distance,' his host noted. 'You won't have to bother with that most nights. Do you think the train commuting will work, long term?'

'I reckon so. I don't have to tell you how much reading the job's going to bring with it. I'll be able to do quite a lot of it on the move.'

'I'm glad you got it,' Skinner confessed. 'Tayside was too small for a guy like you. And as for coming back here as my deputy . . . this force is too small to contain both of us these days. You're best off in the agency.'

'I think I agree with you.' He shivered. 'Bob, can we get inside? It's bloody freezing out here. The cold weather seems to be on its way back.'

'Sure.' The chief constable led the way through the revolving door, and up the stairway behind the reception desk.

At the top, instead of heading left for the command suite he turned right. 'Where are we going?' Martin asked.

'Neil's office. He's pulled all the relevant files together.'

'Neil? Not Mario?'

'Yup. The McGuire is in France, for reasons that we'll get to later.' As he spoke, they arrived at the superintendent's door. He gave it a quick, unnecessary rap, then opened it. 'Guest's arrived,' he said.

McIlhenney rose from behind his desk, extending his hand. 'Hi, Andy,' he greeted him, like the old friend he was. 'Good to see you. Congratulations on the new job. And commiserations,' he added, 'on the other thing.' Martin frowned in sudden alarm. 'It's OK,' the superintendent assured him. 'The boss told me so that I didn't put my foot in it, but it's not general knowledge.'

'Good. We don't plan to issue a press release. Those who need to know, will. Those who don't . . . can mind their own fucking business.'

'I'm his unofficial PR adviser on the subject,' Skinner told McIlhenney, 'having been over the course myself. Are you ready to start?' he asked him.

'Yes. I've got all the files here.' He waited until the two senior officers were seated. 'Andy,' he began, 'from the days when you were head of CID here, do you remember Tomas Zaliukas?'

'Tommy Zale? Sure; Lithuanian, minor hoodlum as a youngster, never convicted, gone straight, so he says, and doing very well for himself in the pubs and clubs business, then more recently in property development and management.'

'And in another sector.'

Martin nodded. 'Massage parlours, or licensed brothels as some call them. He bought Tony Manson's properties from his estate. Good investment, but the downside was that it soured his reputation among the city establishment. He was on the point of joining the New Club and the Royal Burgess Golf Club, but he was blackballed for both. Regine, his wife, wasn't too pleased either, but Tommy assured her that the places would be run as clean as he could manage. To ensure that he installed his own people as managers; all Lithuanian, all loyal to him.'

'Jesus wept, Andy,' McIlhenney sighed. 'See that memory of yours. Is there anything you don't know about Zaliukas?'

'I know that he and Regine have two kids, that she runs Indigo, their top place, personally, and that she's as important as he is to that side of their business. But that's it.'

'Then you know everything about him,' said Skinner, 'save one important fact. He's dead.'

'What?' Martin looked at him, incredulous. 'How?'

'In the early hours of Wednesday morning he climbed to the top of Arthur's Seat with a sawn-off shotgun that must have been a souvenir from the old days, and shot himself.'

'That's news to me,' Martin confessed. 'Mind you I was pretty busy from Thursday on, with one thing and another, so I can claim that as an excuse for missing it. Plus the fact that he wasn't under the eye of my new outfit, so it wasn't flagged up when it happened.'

'Maybe you should have been watching him,' McIlhenney suggested. 'We believe . . . no, we're bloody sure that he had a partner in the massage parlour business. Frances Birtles, who acted for the vendor of the Edinburgh places . . .'

'That would be Lennie Plenderleith?'

'Spot on again. The places were bought by an offshore company set up by Ken Green. He told us that it was owned by Tomas and Regine alone, but we know he lied about that. We're certain there was a partner involved, and we know that when they completed the deal Zaliukas put up half the money personally, and the rest was paid in untraceable bonds. With me?'

'Of course.'

'Let's go on, then. The night before Tomas died . . . get that, the night before . . . his brother Jonas, who'd only arrived from Lithuania a few days before, told the managers to close up. Next day they were summoned to meet a guy none of them knew. He showed them a letter from Tommy, saying that the businesses were under new direction, and he said that he was the director.'

'Do you know what triggered this?'

'You're bound to remember Tomas's cousin,' McIlhenney grinned, challenging.

'Valdas Gerulaitis? Yes. Slimy character; he does Tomas's books, in theory, but that's just to keep him employed and out of trouble. Of all Zaliukas's home country crew he's the only one who's family, and that's why he was tolerated. He's a bad bastard and he's not too clever with it either.'

'You're not wrong on either count,' the superintendent told him. 'A few months ago he decided on a wee bit of private enterprise. He imported nine girls from Estonia, hidden in a lorry, and put them to work on their backs in the massage parlour; more profit per shag than the local talent, so he thought. That seems to have been the catalyst.'

Martin's eyebrows rose. 'Indeed! Now that's something the SCDEA is interested in. Traffickers of women for prostitution are among our key targets. I've got a dedicated team on it. Have you made an arrest? If you have I'd like them to sit in on the interview.'

'You've been very busy, Andy. You've missed another chapter. Gerulaitis is dead too, and his wife; they were caught in a fire in their house last Thursday.'

'Jesus, this gets better. Where are you holding the women?'

'We've only got one of them.' McIlhenney explained how Anna Romanova had been found, and how she had been treated. 'She's still in hospital, and she'll be taken into care after that. The other eight were being kept at a flat in Scotland Street, but they were moved from there on Wednesday, by two women. We've no idea who they are.'

'Can my people talk to this Anna girl?'

'Sure,' said Skinner, 'but you won't learn anything. We believe this was a one-off piece of private enterprise by Valdas, and now he's dead. This is our reasoning. Zaliukas let Valdas run the Edinburgh massage parlours, and he pulled this daft stroke behind his back. Somehow, the unknown partner found out about it before Tomas did, and the stuff hit the ventilator. The pressure on him was so great that he killed himself . . . and he did; there's no other possibility. But something strange happened after that. In his will, he left his stake in the offshore company to Valdas's wife, Laima, a fucking horrible woman by all accounts.'

'She was,' Martin agreed. 'As I recall, the Lithuanians all called her the Gorgon.'

'Ironic: she wound up being more or less turned to stone herself. Anyway, the following evening, she and he went to the bad fire, and about twenty-four hours later, Ken Green, who'd set up the company, was killed in a car crash, on his way to a cottage where he kept details of the parts of his business that he didn't want anyone else to see. We can't prove otherwise, not to jury standards, but we don't believe for a fucking minute that these deaths were accidental. They were loose ends being tied off. On top of that, Green's files on Lituania SAFI have vanished from his cottage hideaway. Jack McGurk's out there just now, with a forensic team. Jack's found a key hidden under a plant pot in the garden . . . and there were recent marks in the soil beneath it that make it look as if it was used and then replaced. Someone's been in before them.'

'I can follow all that,' Martin told him. 'So Tomas's partner's made a hostile takeover for the business, and you're stuck.' He grinned. 'I'm flattered to be asked for help, but what makes you think I can?'

'Because we're not entirely stuck. We've got a description of the man who dumped young Anna at the doctor's. Also . . . and this is where you come in . . . we've discovered that Lituania SAFI has property interests outside Edinburgh. It owns a sex shop, nine massage parlours and a couple of bingo halls, and six of these places are in your old patch, Tayside.'

'I can see why you're clutching at this straw, Bob,' his colleague replied, 'but I doubt if I can add anything. I take it these places are all owned by the offshore company and licensed by someone else?'

'Yes.'

'OK. If you give me a list of the managers I'll see if they've got form, but other than that . . .'

'We've already checked that. They've got nothing more than a few speeding charges among the lot of them.'

'Then I don't see what else I can do. Yes, we took an interest in these places in Tayside, but in truth, in my time there we never had any complaints about any of them. We had a woman in Perth who skulled her husband with the steam iron when she found some credit card payments to the parlour there, but that's the only occasion I remember any of those places coming to the attention of the police.'

Skinner sighed. 'Fuck it,' he muttered. 'It was a forlorn hope, I suppose.'

'Look,' Martin offered, 'if you tell me you think this is serious organised crime, I will put a team on it, but to me it looks like a fairly localised turf war over some brothels. Even if you're right, what can we do? We could interview each licensee or manager; but if they are working for a guy who's serious enough to have had three people killed to protect his identity, do you think they're going to tell you who he is? I'm new in post, and I cannot send my people off fishing for guppies when their job is to catch sharks.'

'No; I understand that,' the chief constable conceded. 'Too bad. We'll just need to keep on looking for Desperate Dan. He's the last hope we have.'

'Who?'

Skinner chuckled. 'Ah, it's just a nickname, for the guy who delivered Anna to the surgery, and who might well have done for Linas Jankauskas, her pimp ... although I'm still not convinced Jonas Zaliukas didn't take him out. The witness who gave us his description said he's a dead ringer for the old comic book cowboy.'

'Bloody hell!' Martin exclaimed. 'Why didn't you tell me that before?'

'Why?'

'Because I reckon I know who he is.'

Seventy-one

'I'm glad we had the satellite navigation,' said Becky Stallings. 'This place is further off the motorway than I'd thought from looking at the map. And it's not very big either.'

'We'd have found it,' Mario McGuire assured her. 'My mother lives in Tuscany. Compared to some of the in-country villages there, this Mezin is a metropolis.' As he spoke, the mellifluous female voice from the box told him to take a right turn into Place Armand Fallières. When he obeyed, it told him that his destination was straight ahead. He drew the car to a halt at the kerbside, in what appeared to be, in the faint light just after nightfall, a square, bounded on two sides by shops and a pizzeria, on the third by a church, and on the fourth, in the direction in which they faced, by houses, with a street opening to the left. 'That must be Rue St Cauzimis,' he murmured.

'What time is it?' Stallings asked. 'I can't find it on this display.'

'It's down there in the corner, see,' he replied. 'Bottom right. It's seven, on the dot.'

'Will we go straight there?'

'No, let's check into the hotel and dump the motor. According to the map, it's just behind the church.' He engaged gear, and drove slowly towards the foot of the square. There he found, as he had expected, a second road beside Rue St Cauzimis, that led into a large manor house with a sign that read 'Hotel de Ville'.

He parked the car at the side of the main entrance, and led the way inside. The receptionist smiled as they entered. 'Our late bookings?' she asked.

'That's us,' said Stallings, cheerfully, pleased to be addressed in English for the first time since they had arrived at Charles de Gaulle.

They completed the check-in formalities, for one night with an option on a second, and went to their rooms, agreeing to meet back in the foyer at seven thirty.

When they did, McGuire was still in his travel clothes, black chinos, a red Ralph Lauren polo shirt, and a sports jacket, but the DI had changed from her jeans into a light pleated skirt, with a white blouse and a short, elegant, brown suede coat. She caught his glance. 'I know I'm here as the obligatory female, Mario,' she told him, 'so it's best that I dress like one. How do we play this? Do we call her first?'

'No. We march right up to number one-oh-five and knock on the door.'

'Now?'

'It's why the boss sent us here. Let's go.' He led the way out of the hotel, and down the drive.

The temperature had dropped by a few degrees in the time

they had been in the hotel. Stallings pulled her coat tight. 'This is France,' she muttered. 'Should it be this cold?'

'In the winter it can get a lot worse than this.'

They stepped into Rue St Cauzimis, a cobbled street that sloped downwards from the square, checking the numbers as they walked, 'One zero nine,' the detective superintendent muttered, 'one zero seven. One hundred and five,' he announced. 'This is it.'

The house was on a corner, old like those around it, and built in stone that an unthinking owner had decided to ruin by painting white. A light hung over the blue front door, showing a brass knocker in the centre. McGuire seized it and rapped three times, hard. 'God,' Stallings whispered. 'Anyone, anywhere in the world would know that's the police.'

'That or the rent collector.'

'I wonder how much the rents are around . . .'

She was interrupted by the opening of the door, not by the woman they were expecting, but by a tall man, McGuire's equal in height if not width, dressed all in black, trousers and a crew-necked sweater. He looked a year or so short of thirty; his dark hair was close cropped and his tan looked out of place in February. A couple of yards behind him stood a second man, identically dressed, a clone of the first, save for a neatly trimmed beard.

The doorkeeper said nothing; he simply stared, unsmiling.

'We'd like to see Mrs Regine Zaliukas, please,' the head of CID told him.

The man replied in a language that neither police officer understood.

McGuire repeated his request, but in French.

'She's not available,' he said, in the same language.

'Would you like to ask her whether she is or not?'

'Just go away, will you?'

His French is OK, the detective thought, but his accent's odd. 'We can't do that,' he said. 'We've come a long way to see the lady, from Scotland. We're concerned about her welfare.'

'That's what we're for,' the man retorted.

'Now why doesn't that reassure me?' McGuire murmured, in English.

The man edged forward, until the Scot made him pause with a shake of his head. 'Don't do that, soldier boy,' he said, quietly. 'I've been to the same school as you. And think on this. As long as you're standing in that narrow doorway, it's just you and me.'

'That might not worry me.'

The guardian's hand moved, reaching behind his back . . . but like others before him, he had underestimated McGuire's hand speed, and was unprepared for the power of the fist that slammed into the pit of his stomach, and upwards, in a surge of agony that drove the breath from his lungs. The detective grabbed him before he could fall and spun him around, making his body a shield against the second man's advance and, as he did so, snatching the pistol he had sought from the holster that was strapped to his belt, against his spine. 'Just stop now,' he ordered. He had reverted to English again, but his message got across.

'*Oui*, Zaki; *arretez.*' The woman's voice came from the foot of a stairway to the left of the entrance hall. '*Je connais cet homme. Il est police, mais il est un ami . . . je pense.* Is that right, Mario, are you a friend?'

He laughed. 'I'm surprised you can recognise me in the daylight, Regine. We usually see each other under those UV lights of yours in Indigo. Yes, I'm a friend all right, don't you worry. We're not police here, though. We're no more official than these guys are, but somehow we didn't think you'd want us to turn up with the local plod behind us.' He released his hold on the doorkeeper, who was still gasping from his punch, slipped the pistol back into its place, and patted him on the shoulder. 'Sorry about that, Zaki,' he said.

'No,' said Regine Zaliukas. 'That's Max. Zaki's the other one.' She stepped out into the hall. She wore an outfit that was a cross between a tracksuit and pyjamas, and pink fluffy carpet slippers.

'Then tell them both I'm sorry, and that I hope there are no hard feelings.'

She did as he asked, adding a lecture for their heavy-handedness. Max nodded, muttered, 'I sorry,' in strangled English and offered his hand.

'Come in,' she said, turning towards a door at the rear of the hall. 'Come on through to the living room. We can talk there; I've just put the kids to bed. Who's your colleague?' she asked as the officers caught up with her.

'DI Becky Stallings,' McGuire told her. 'And who are yours?'

'Friends of Jonas, my brother-in-law. They served under him in the United Nations army, in the Congo, hence their jungle French. They're here to protect us. We weren't expecting you, though.' Her laugh was quiet, but there was sadness in it. She led them down a few steps into an elegant room, as modern as the exterior of the house was old. 'Take a seat. Would you like a drink?'

'To be honest, I could slaughter a beer.'

'I can do that. I've even got Perroni. That's what you drink, isn't it? And you, Inspector?'

'Becky, please. Any sort of white wine would be lovely.'

The widow nodded and disappeared up a second short stairway, shuffling in the backless slippers.

'Nice house,' Stallings murmured. 'I fancy this furniture: cream leather, very nice.'

'There's a very good shop in Bordeaux,' said Regine, returning with a bottle of Italian beer, another of Chenin blanc, and two glasses, all on a tray.

'Is this your house?'

'It's my parents' place. But they're not here just now,' she added, as she handed McGuire his beer and poured two glasses of wine. 'They have an apartment in Marbella, in the south of Spain. Too cold for them here in winter now.' She sighed. 'And for me.'

'I'm deeply sorry, Regine,' McGuire told her. 'You must still be in shock.'

She looked at him. 'Mario, I honestly don't know what I'm in.'

'But you are safe? We need to be sure of that. Things have been happening back in Edinburgh since Tomas died.'

'I know. But yes, I'm safe now.'

He took a slug of his beer, straight from the bottle. 'Are you implying that you haven't always been?'

'I'm implying nothing. I'm saying nothing; not just now.'

'Regine, what's going on? This story about you leaving Tomas: nobody believes it for a second.'

'As I told Alex Skinner, I didn't leave him; that must have been what Tomas told people. He made me take the kids and come over here, for safety, he thought.'

'But why? What was the threat?'

She shook her head. 'Mario, please, not now. Honestly, I can't tell you any more tonight. Maybe tomorrow. Yes, you come back tomorrow, and if everything is as it should be, I will talk to you then.'

'Seriously?'

'Yes, I promise. If I feel that I can, then I will. You come back at midday. In the meantime, don't worry: I'm safe with Max and Zaki.' She smiled again, weakly. 'Maybe not from you, if you were an enemy, but from everybody else. Where are you staying?'

'Hotel de Ville, across the street.'

'Good. If there is a problem I can call for you. But there won't be, I'm sure.'

'OK.'

They sat for a while in silence, finishing their drinks. When they were done, the police officers rose to leave, and Regine stood with them. 'Valdas and Laima,' she began, as they walked to the door. 'They died in a fire, I was told.'

'That's what we're saying, but we believe they were killed before it was started. There's evidence that he was tortured, but why, we don't know.'

'But they were dead before the fire . . . reached them?'

'Yes.'

She shuddered. 'That's a sort of kindness, I suppose. He was a greedy, vicious fool, and she was a deeply unpleasant woman, but they didn't deserve to . . .'

'That's one way of looking at it, I suppose,' said McGuire, as she opened the door. 'Good night. See you tomorrow.'

'What was that about?' Stallings exclaimed, once they were outside on Rue St Cauzimis.

'God knows. And hopefully so will we after our next meeting. Something heavy's happened, that's for sure. Regine is not a woman to be scared easily, but she has been.'

'So what do we do now?'

McGuire shrugged. 'Well, I don't know about you, but I'm heading for that wee restaurant up in the square. Right now, a pizza and a few more beers seem to be the only show in town.'

Seventy-two

'You're having us on!' Skinner exclaimed.

'Not about this. The man you're after is called Henry Brown; I'm sure of it. The joke in Dundee is that he was the model for Dan's statue in the High Street. Henry's forty-six years old, and he runs a metal recycling business on the outskirts of the city. He's been doing that for the last sixteen years, since he married a woman called Daphne McCullough, the younger sister, by fourteen years, of one Cameron McCullough, known in and around the Silver City by the affectionate nickname of Grandpa. Except there's nothing affectionate about Grandpa; he's as cold-hearted a bastard as I've ever met.'

'You told me about him, didn't you?' said McIlhenney. 'Last year you had him in the High Court on murder and drugs charges.'

'That's right. The only charges that have ever been laid against him. And he walked on both. The witnesses to the murder disappeared, and he suborned a Polish clerk to steal the heroin we were going to do him for, out of our own evidence store. The clerk vanished as well; he was supposed to have gone back to Krakow, but he never showed up there.'

Skinner nodded. 'I remember that. Graham Morton had the piss ripped out of him at the next chiefs' association meeting. Phil Davidson, Lady Broughton, was the judge, wasn't she?'

'Yes. She was as angry as me after it all collapsed.'

'Are you taking it personally, Andy?' the chief murmured.

'Too fucking right I am. Is that unprofessional? Yes, and I do not care. The day that Cameron McCullough goes down will be the highlight of my career. I've taken a copy of the Tayside file on him to my new office.' He scowled. 'It's not going to be easy, though. Grandpa has run things at second, third and fourth hand for the last twenty years and more, hiding behind his legitimate businesses, and with every year that passes it becomes harder to nail him.'

'Why?'

'Because his cover is absolutely uncrackable, because he operates behind clever people who are absolutely ruthless, and because when it comes to it he's more ruthless than any of them. He doesn't take risks of any sort. Since he had his close shave, he's become even more elusive. He's says that he's getting ready to retire, and he spends most of his time on the golf course. There's some evidence that he has backed off on the criminal side; drugs are a wee bit harder to come by in Dundee these days. But that could just be his people jacking up the price.'

'What's he supposed to be?' McIlhenney asked. 'His legitimate cover?'

'Grandpa's a group: CamMac Enterprises PLC, that's the parent company. It operates in quite a few areas. For example, construction. CamMac Homes builds houses; on spec, and more recently for housing associations, since they're the only people with money just now. CamMac Projects is a commercial contractor, tendering for stuff like factories and offices. He tends to win most of the projects he offers for in the Tayside region. People seem to work out that it might just be best to give him the job, even if he isn't the lowest bidder. Still, not even he's immune to the current market, so that company is just ticking over just now. CamMac Metals is still doing fine though. That owns the yard that his brother-in-law Henry runs, as well as a big metal-broking business. CamMac Leisure has a couple of country house hotels in Perthshire and Angus, with leisure clubs attached, and it owns a few city centre pubs in Dundee. To all outward appearances the group is legit: its legal business is handled by Lionel David, one of the top firms in Dundee, its auditors are Deacon and Queen, a small but prestige accountancy firm, and to put a final layer on its veneer of respectability, last year it appointed a new public affairs consultant. Guess who that was?' Martin challenged.

'Tommy fucking Murtagh,' Skinner growled.

'You knew?'

'I know just about everything that little bastard does. I saw the appointment at the time, but I didn't look into the background of his client. The name meant nothing to me.'

'You won't nail Murtagh through the connection,' Martin told him, 'or even embarrass him. These companies are all profitable, and although we are quite certain that they were started with the proceeds of crime, no one will ever prove it. If you're thinking that McCullough might be using them to launder drug money, forget it. He's way too clever for that.'

'What else has he got?'

'There's a farm; he owns one up in Angus, a few hundred acres of arable land and some slopes where he has cattle.'

'If he's that successful in business, why is he . . .' Skinner began.

'Because he is, simple as that. Look, all three of us have known recidivist criminals, all through our careers, the Dougie Terrys, the Moash Glaziers, the Kenny Basses. OK, they're all small time, and McCullough's at the other end of the scale, but he fits into the same category. It's what he does, it's what he is, and he's better at it than anyone I've ever met.'

'This Henry Brown,' asked McIlhenney, 'what does he do for him, apart from running the scrap business?'

'Everything, mate. Cameron's great strength is that he keeps it in the family. Those witnesses who disappeared last year? You can bet that Henry either organised it, or he made it happen himself.'

'How could he have done that? Weren't they protected?'

'In theory, yes, they were; in practice, sadly, no. They were under twenty-four-hour police observation up in Aberdeen; there was always a car in their street, and they had an Alsatian in their back yard. But one night, the cops who were keeping an eye on them were called away to a major incident that turned out to be a false alarm. When they got back, the dog had been fed a poisoned steak and two women had vanished.'

Skinner frowned. 'What did Brown do before he married McCullough's sister?'

'He was in the army for a few years; he fought in the first

Gulf War, in a special demolition unit that operated behind enemy lines; real close quarters, no mercy stuff. When he left he became a fireman for a couple of years . . .'

'A fireman? Now that's interesting, given what happened to Gerulaitis and his wife.'

'That is a thought, indeed. Anyway, he was in the fire service when he got hitched to Goldie, and after that he was made.'

'Goldie?' McIlhenney repeated.

Martin smiled. 'Apparently Daphne's never been too keen on her given name. Everyone calls her Goldie.'

'Including the woman who was with her when she collected those eight Estonian girls from their hideaway last Wednesday,' the superintendent told him. 'We have a witness, Marius Ramanauskas, one of Zale's men, who heard her.'

'Is he in custody, this witness?'

'No,' the superintendent replied. 'We didn't have grounds to hold him, although we know he helped Valdas bring the girls in. We released him on bail, until we can stick him in a line-up for Anna Romanova to pick out. Even then, we'll be struggling to prosecute him without a second witness.'

'If he's out there,' Martin retorted, 'and he can tie Goldie Brown to these girls, you'd better bring him in for his own safety. Meantime . . .' He looked at his companions. 'Do you guys fancy some overtime, and some activity completely unbecoming to your rank?'

Skinner smiled. 'I'm always up for an away day.'

'In that case, why don't we head straight for Dundee? I'm not having anyone else pick up Henry Brown, or his lovely wife.'

Seventy-three

'You do know where we're going, Andy, yes?' Bob Skinner asked, as he drove up the Kingsway, the dual carriageway that skirted Dundee to the east.

'Of course I do, Bob. I have all the McCullough family addresses committed to memory.'

'I would doubt that of anyone else,' Neil McIlhenney murmured, 'but not you.'

'Left at this roundabout,' Martin instructed, 'then right, about half a mile along.' The three officers sat in silence as the chief constable followed his directions. 'That's fine,' he declared, as they made the second turn. 'The Browns' place is the fourth on the left, the one on the double plot.'

'Chunky pad,' the superintendent commented, as they drew to a halt. 'Has it got a name?'

'Would you believe South Fork?'

'It was either going to be that or the Ponderosa. That's fucking gangsters for you.'

'Not really; all the house names have TV themes. CamMac homes built this place, and the rest; it's owned by CamMac

Metals and Henry and the wife pay a market rent. But you're right in a way. This street's becoming a compound. Tommy Murtagh lives in the last house on the right.'

'What about the Bentley Continental there in the driveway?' Skinner asked. 'Is that a company car?'

'That's Goldie's; a birthday present from her big brother.'

'You know a lot about these people, Andy.'

'I know everything about these people, Bob. I looked at going the Al Capone route; you know, setting the Inland Revenue on them, but Grandpa's accounting is always immaculate, and everyone always pays their taxes.'

'Is there a Grandma McCullough?'

'No. She died ten years ago; throat cancer.'

As Martin spoke, McIlhenney's mobile sounded. He snatched it from his pocket, almost as if he was fearful that the sound would alert those in the house. 'Yes? Jack, hi. Have you got him?' Pause. 'Fuck. Have you talked to the neighbours?' Pause. 'Not since then? Did you look for his passport? Of course, sorry. Them too? Ah Jesus . . . Listen, Jack, check with DVLA, for a car registered in his name. If he's got one, look for it parked locally. Then check with the other Lithuanians. Who knows, they've maybe got a regular Monday card school; the bugger might be there.' Pause. 'Sure, but do it.' He ended the call and turned to his colleagues. 'McGurk,' he said. 'He's at Scotland Street; Marius Ramanauskas isn't there. He hasn't been seen since Friday night. Jack kicked the door in and went through the place. There are dishes in the sink, and a bottle of turned milk on the work surface beside the kettle. No sign of recent occupation, though.'

'Surprise, surprise,' Martin drawled. 'The cleaners have been.'

'Just because he could identify this Goldie woman?' McIlhenney exclaimed.

'Absolutely because, I'd say. These are very efficient people. The best we can hope for is that they've scared the shit out of your man Marius and told him to disappear for good. The worst is that they've made him disappear for good.'

'Not in my back yard,' Skinner growled. 'Let's go and see this man Brown and do some scaring ourselves.' He took his key from the ignition and stepped out of his car into the street.

'How are we going to play it?' the superintendent asked.

'With no subtlety at all. Come on. Andy, you with me. Neil, keep out of sight at the side of the house, in case our man thinks of slipping out the back.' He led the way up the ungated driveway, towards the big floodlit villa. A few drops of rain were falling, with the temperature low enough to offer the threat that they might be followed by snowflakes, but the front door was set back in a covered porch which offered some shelter. He rang the bell. As they waited, he noticed a spyglass just above it. He held his thumb against it, cutting off the view from within.

'Who's the comedian?' said a female voice, as the door opened.

'Nobody's joking, Goldie,' Andy Martin replied, stepping into the light.

'Jesus!' the woman snapped. 'Not you again. I heard we'd got rid of you.' She was blonde and high-breasted, barefoot but dressed in a tight-fitting leotard. Her cheeks were pink, glistening with a light sheen of perspiration.

'Technically not till the end of the month, but even then, you won't be rid of me.' He glanced at her, and sniffed. 'You're a bit sweaty.'

'I was in the gym,' she retorted, 'and I want to get back there.' She stared up at Skinner. 'Who's your pal?'

'I'm a police officer from Edinburgh,' he told her, unsmiling. 'You'll be Daphne Brown, I take it.'

'Take what you fucking like, as long as it's not liberties. What do you want?'

'In due course I want to talk to you about eight missing Estonian girls, but right now, we want your husband.'

'What for?'

'We plan to charge him with at least one murder, maybe more. That's for starters. Please tell him we're here, or we'll go in and get him.'

'You'll have a job. He's no' in. See for yourself; his car's no' there.'

'Where is he?'

'Why the fuck should I tell you that?'

Martin leaned against the door frame. 'Why doesn't come into it, Goldie. You're going to talk to us, either here or along at Tayside police headquarters, after as much exhausting questioning as it takes. If you don't tell us now, we're going to arrest you in connection with harbouring illegal immigrants, maybe abduction, and also for the murder of a man called Marius Ramanauskas. You know him; you visited his flat in Scotland Street, in Edinburgh, last week, and relieved him of some guests; you and another woman that I believe was your niece Inez.'

'What do you mean murder? He's . . .' She stopped in mid-sentence. 'I'm saying fuck all to you, here or in the polis station.'

'That's not how it's going to be,' said Skinner quietly. 'You know my friend here, but you don't know me. Your family seem to think that they can invade my city, cause however much mayhem they like, then walk away from it.' Goldie Brown looked away from him, but he seized her jaw and twisted it, forcing her to meet his gaze. 'You focus on me when I'm talking to you, lady, because I'm here to tell you that however clever you think you are, however far above the law you believe you and your crowd are, you have got it fucking wrong. I have a team of very capable people who have built a cast-iron case against your husband. We are here for him, and every second that you refuse to tell us where he is makes it ever more likely that you'll be charged as his accomplice. So . . . where is Henry Brown?'

She stared at him even after he had released her from his grasp, realising just how serious he was. 'He's . . .'

Whatever she was about to say was cut short by the noise from within, of a loudly creaking door. 'Is he in there after all, Goldie?' Martin barked. 'Enough of this.' He barged past her, just as a dishevelled figure in his shirtsleeves, his jacket held in his hand, dashed down a wide staircase, swung himself round the post at the foot and bolted through a door at the rear of the hall.

As Skinner held on to the woman, tight, not joining the

pursuit, a strange smile spread across his face. 'Is your gym upstairs, Goldie?' he asked.

Before she had time to reply a shout came from outside, followed by the sound of a brief struggle. Skinner turned, pulling his captive with him, just as Neil McIlhenney and Andy Martin came into view with theirs. 'Well, well,' the chief constable laughed. 'Christmas in February. If it isn't my old friend Tommy Murtagh. What is it you do for the CamMac group, Tommy? Public Affairs Consultant, is it? Or should that be Private?' He stepped into the house, still with a firm grip of the woman's arm. 'Come on, guys, let's take this away from the neighbours.' He looked at Murtagh, as the former politician gave up the futile, and painful, struggle to free himself from McIlhenney's armlock. 'Of course you are the neighbours, Tommy, aren't you?' He turned to Goldie Brown. 'Let's all behave now,' he said, as he let her go. 'The dynamic of this situation has changed just a bit.'

She said nothing; instead she led the way into a sitting room, switching on the light as she did so. The superintendent kept Murtagh restrained until Martin had closed the door behind them, then pushed him firmly down, on to a sofa. Grim-faced and chewing at her bottom lip, the woman took a seat beside him.

Skinner beamed. 'How long has this been going on?' he sang, doing a passable Paul Carrack imitation.

Murtagh glared up at him. 'Just fuck off,' he hissed. 'Fuck off back to that bitch of a wife of yours.'

The smile vanished. With one hand, the chief constable picked the man up by his shirt front, raising him up on his toes until their eyes were level. 'Mention Aileen once more, in any way, and what happens after will be very painful. That's a promise.' He threw him back on to the couch, like a doll. 'OK,' he continued. 'This is going to work out in one of two ways. Either you're going to tell us right now, Mrs Brown, where we can find Henry, or . . . we are indeed going to fuck off, all three of us. Very soon after that, Henry's going to get an anonymous phone call, advising him that you and Mr Murtagh have been doing the horizontal mambo whenever his back's been turned. You might get off with a simple tanking, because of who your brother is, but Tommy . . .' he shook his head, '. . . his tea will be out, as we used to say in the west of Scotland when I was a lad.' She stared up at him, eyes working as if she was assessing the threat. 'You think that's a bluff, Goldie? Ask your boyfriend whether I'd baulk at throwing him to your old man.'

She looked to the side; the slight trembling of Murtagh's pencil moustache, and the naked fear on his face, told her all she needed to know. 'OK,' she sighed. 'He's gone to the farm.'

'Long gone?'

'About three hours ago, maybe a bit more.'

'When do you expect him back?' Andy Martin asked.

'He said he'd be a while. Probably not much before midnight.'

'Why has he gone there?'

'I don't know. He got a call on his mobile, but I don't know who it was from, or what was said. He had his back to me while he took it. All I heard him say was, "I'll see to it", just as he was finishing. Then he stuck it back in his pocket.'

'Did he tell you what it was about?'

'He said there was a wee bit of bother up at the farm, and that he'd need to sort it out. I asked him what it was; he just laughed and said there was a bull loose up at the byre, and it needed taking care of. But he wasn't laughing on the phone.'

Curious, Martin frowned. 'Does Henry often go to the farm?'

'No, never. There's a manager.'

'Does he live there?'

'The manager? No, nobody lives there. There's a house, but it's not occupied; our Cameron goes there for the weekend sometimes, but that's all. That's not where he'll be, though. He'll have gone to the sheds, like he said.'

'Do you know how to find the place, Andy?' Skinner asked.

'Of course I do. We drove past it on the way here. It's just past the Friarton Bridge, on the Perth road.'

The chief constable turned back to Goldie Brown. 'Those Estonian girls; are they safe?'

'Yes, as far as I know.'

'What do you mean . . . as far as you know?'

'I just helped to pick them up. There was nobody else tae do it. When we got back, Inez dropped me at the foot of the road. I don't know where she went after that.' Her eyes narrowed. 'I'll deny all this after, mind.'

'As long as those girls are all right, and as long as we round up your old man, I don't give a bugger. That phone call,' he asked, 'could it have come from your brother?'

'If it was a problem, no chance of that. Cameron wouldn't be that direct. Ask your pal there, he'll tell you.'

'I'm sure he wouldn't,' Skinner told her, 'but I don't want

him making an exception this time.' He turned to McIlhenney. 'Neil, I want you to stay with these two while we sort this out. I don't want them to get anywhere near a phone. Andy, can you arrange for a car to pass by Cameron McCullough's house, quietly, and check that the lights are on?'

'Sure, I can do that. I can have somebody pick up Inez as well.'

'Fine. While that's happening, you and I will go and see how Henry's getting on rounding up his bull.'

He was at the door, in the act of opening it, when Goldie called out to him. 'Mister, wait a minute. Henry's in enough bother as it is, so there's something else you'd better know. When he left, he took a gun with him.'

'Fuck!' Skinner snapped. 'That changes everything. Andy . . .'

Martin cut it off. 'You don't need to say it. It's time for me to tell my colleagues that we're here and what we're up to. I'll get an armed response team to meet us at the farm.'

'Try not to hurt him,' the woman called out, a trace of fear in her voice for the first time.

'That'll depend,' the chief constable told her, 'on whether he tries to hurt us.'

Seventy-four

'Do you think this is a punishment detail?' asked Alice Cowan.

'Not even informally, according to what the chief said to me last Friday night,' Griff Montell told her.

'Amazing. You called a divisional commander a "fucking old lesbo" in a room full of people and you're getting off scot-free. I gave my police inspector uncle a harmless tip-off last year and I got bumped off Special Branch.'

He grinned. 'Yeah, but it's worked out, hasn't it?'

'You reckon?' She frowned for a few seconds as if considering. 'I suppose the Pompadour might be called "working out",' she conceded. 'And all that sweaty stuff at my place on Saturday night, that was OK too.'

'OK?'

She laughed. 'See you guys? My mother's always saying that there are only two things no man will ever admit to doing badly, and the other one is driving. But, if you want me to pat your ego, big boy, I'll score you better than just OK. You are officially very good at shagging, Montell, no worse than eight out of ten on the Alice-ometer.'

'When am I going to get a chance to improve my score?' he ventured.

'Try offering to feed me again. You might find there's a correlation there. I can never get randy on an empty stomach.'

'How about if I cook for you at the weekend?'

'You can cook? Let me guess; burgers and lager?'

He raised an eyebrow. 'Hey,' he asked, 'have you been out with a South African before?'

'An Aussie, a few years back. You're much the same animal. This cooking,' she murmured. 'Where would it be happening?'

'My place.'

'I thought that was off limits.'

'Not any more,' he told her. 'Spring and I had a long talk when she got home yesterday.'

'Yesterday? Sunday?'

He nodded. 'She stayed away for two days to let me cool down.'

'At Mary's?'

'Yup. Anyway, we had a chat and we're square. She's my sister, and I love her however she is. The "no partners" rule was her idea; now I know why.'

'So you two are fine. That's good, but how about you and Chambers?'

'I think we're OK too. I went to see her yesterday afternoon and apologised. She told me she understood how it must have been a shock to me, since she kept herself a secret for years.'

'Will she be there at the weekend?'

'Dunno.' He glanced at her. 'Would that bother you?'

She smiled, in a way he had either never noticed, or had

failed to understand, before. 'As long as the queue for the bathroom isn't too long, not one bit.'

'I'll tell Spring; maybe they'll give us a clear field.'

'Do you think we'll have a clear field tonight . . . work wise?' she added.

'I've got no idea,' he admitted, 'but I hope not. I'd rather see action than spend a night shift sat on my arse.'

'What's this about anyway, Griff?'

'Robberies, I'm told. The bosses want a CID response team on duty all night, in each area, in case a situation arises. That's what Ray said; but he didn't explain what that situation might be. We don't need to know that, apparently . . . until it happens, of course. The load's being spread; we drew the short straw for this week.'

'And we don't work on anything else?'

'Nope.' He reached into his man-bag and tossed her a book. 'Try that,' he said. 'It'll pass the time.'

She looked at the cover. '*Inhuman Remains*,' she read. 'A woman detective: yes, that's my kind of hero.'

Seventy-five

'Maybe the gun was for the bull right enough,' Detective Chief Superintendent Rod Greatorix ventured, with a half smile on his face.

'Maybe it was,' said Martin to his Tayside colleague, 'but after the mayhem that Henry's caused in Edinburgh over the last week or so, we don't feel like taking a chance on that.'

'Are you dead certain it was him?'

'We've got a physical description that convinced Andy,' Skinner told him. 'Then there are the Gerulaitis deaths. We still can't prove to prosecution standard that they were murdered, but we're sure. They were killed by someone with specialist knowledge, an arsonist who knew how to set a fire and make it look accidental.'

'There's just one thing I don't get, Bob,' said Martin. 'The pathologist thought that Valdas was tortured before he died. Henry's a ruthless guy, and we suspected him of a few serious assaults and even a couple of murders, but he's practical too. Why would he do that?'

'Punishment, maybe. Gerulaitis was importing his own whores to work in the massage parlours and skim the profits, or . . .' He paused and for a few seconds his eyes seemed to lose focus, as if they were fixed on something in another place. 'Of course,' he murmured. 'Less than a day before he killed himself,' he went on, 'Tomas Zaliukas changed his will. Instead of leaving his interest in Lituania SAFI to Regine, along with everything else, he left it to Laima Gerulaitis. Now why would he do that? He couldn't stand the fucking woman; nobody could apart from Valdas, and we're not even sure about him. Think about this, bright boys. What if he was meant to leave it to somebody else? And who else would that person be but his partner, your target, Cameron McCullough?'

'So why would he leave it to the woman?' Martin asked.

'Because he guessed what would happen. After all, Tomas had a wicked sense of humour, hadn't he? Remember the guy who copied his tattoo? The story was that he thought what he did to him was hilarious.'

'Are you saying that Valdas was tortured to get Laima to sign away her interest?'

'Let's say I'm offering it as a possibility.'

'But how would McCullough even know for sure that he had changed his will?'

Skinner's expression darkened. 'Now that is a hell of a good question. But he did, because Henry had a meeting with the managers the very next morning, and told them that the old order was gone for good, and that new hands were on the tiller. Who was his source? Well, the SAFI lawyer was Ken Green. Marianne McKean, his ex-wife, is Tomas's lawyer's secretary. We can't ask Ken any more, but tomorrow my guys are going to be having another word with her. She's the obvious likeliest. How he knew what was in it, that may be another question, but equally it might not be. The McKean woman may have typed it. I hope she did, for selfish reasons. That's our Alex's firm, and if the information has leaked from there, the partners need to identify the source and shut it off.' He turned to Greatorix. 'Can you see any movement up there, Rod?' he asked.

The Tayside detective leaned against the gate behind which they were concealed. His car, and Skinner's, were parked on the farm track a hundred yards further back. He put a pair of heavy night glasses to his eyes, and surveyed the buildings once more. 'Not a sign,' he whispered. 'Henry's car's still there, driver's door hanging open. But he must be still in the cattle shed. Likely he'll have shot the fucking bull and he and the manager are butchering it.'

'In the dark? There are no lights showing. Andy,' he asked, 'how about the check on McCullough?'

'He's at home. When our car drove past, the curtains weren't drawn. They could see him in his living room.'

Skinner shifted impatiently. 'Where is this team of yours?' he said to Greatorix.

'They'll have had to get ready first, sir,' the detective replied, defensively. 'We don't have twenty-four-hour armed patrols. Our guys have to be brought in.' He swung the glasses round and looked back down the track. 'That's them now,' he announced in a tone that might have been satisfaction, or relief.

There were four people in the firearms unit that approached them, quickly but silently. Skinner saw sergeant's stripes on the black uniform of the slightly built leader, female, he realised as they drew close.

'What have you got, sir?' she asked, speaking directly to the chief superintendent, as if the others were spectators.

'Henry Brown,' he told her. She whistled. 'He's wanted for questioning in a murder investigation in Edinburgh. His wife says he's armed. He told her that a bull was causing trouble up here, but since Henry wouldn't know a bull unless it was medium rare and on his plate, we're not convinced. He came up here to meet somebody; that's all we know for sure. It's been quiet, though.'

'So you can't actually say that he's in there?'

'No, Doreen, that's what we want you to find out. Challenge him, tell him to come out and if he does, secure him. If he refuses, or if he doesn't respond . . . in either circumstance, you're the trained officer so you're in charge of the incident. What happens next will be your call.'

'And if he offers armed resistance . . .'

He cut her question short. 'That's why you've got guns, Sergeant. We'll back your judgement.'

Seventy-six

'How's the book?' Griff Montell asked.

'Not bad. I like this woman. She's got balls.'

'Why's it called *Inhuman Remains*?'

'I don't know yet. I haven't got that far.'

'Come on, Alice,' he challenged, 'you're a detective. You're supposed to work things out for yourself.'

'Well,' she ventured, 'I've got one idea, but I'll need to wait and see.' She laid down the book. 'Do you fancy making some tea?' she asked. 'It's your turn.'

'What time is it?'

'Eleven twenty. The night is yet young.'

'Too bloody young. OK. But I'll have coffee: I suspect that the hardest thing we'll have to do on this shift is stay awake.' He walked across to the small table against the wall, picked up the kettle to judge by its weight whether it held enough water, then switched it on.

He was watching it boil when the phone rang. Cowan snatched it up. 'CID, Leith,' she said, trying to keep her surprise from her voice.

'This is ACC Steele,' a calm female voice replied. 'We have reason to believe that a robbery is in progress at Joppa Golf Club; it's right on your doorstep. We've got lucky. We have a car in position opposite the entrance right now. You know where it is?'

'Yes, ma'am, exactly. My Uncle Jock's a member.'

'Then you and Montell get along there, now.'

'How many at the scene?'

'Us or them?'

'Them.'

'One vehicle, we believe. Now stop asking questions and listen. We could apprehend these people there, but we're not going to. If they leave before you arrive, our car will follow discreetly and guide you to a rendezvous. You will take over pursuit, at a safe distance, and you'll follow. The game is to have these people lead us to where they live. Understood?'

'Yes, ma'am; we're on our way now. We'll check in with the comms centre as soon as we're on the move.' She put the phone down, picked her jacket from the back of her chair, and snatched a key from Montell's desk. 'Forget the tea, Griff,' she said. 'Arse in gear; this is our lucky night.'

They ran downstairs and out through the back door of the old police station, into the yard. Their car was a black Mondeo Cosworth, innocuous to anyone other than an expert, but capable of keeping pace with any other saloon on the road and with all but the most exotic sports models. 'Gimme the key,' Montell demanded, as they reached it.

'In your dreams,' Cowan replied, as she opened the driver's door. 'One, I know where we're going, two, I know what the orders are and three, I've done an advanced driving course. Do you tick any of those boxes, big boy?'

He smiled and slid into the passenger seat. 'I like it when you call me big boy,' he murmured as she started the engine.

'All boys do,' she replied, enigmatically, 'regardless.'

She pulled out of the car park and headed for Salamander Street, then on to Seafield Road. As she drove, Montell took the radio microphone and called the communications centre to report their position and to be patched through to the patrol car in position at the golf club entrance.

'Anything happening?' he asked his nameless colleague, once contact had been made.

'No,' came the reply through the speaker, 'but they're still in there. Where we are we can see the top of their vehicle. It's one of these pick-up things, four seats in front and platform behind with a hard top over it.'

'Any chance they can see you?'

'Nane. We're tucked up a wee side street wi' no lighting. How far away are you?'

'Less than a minute,' Cowan shouted for the mike to pick up. 'We're crossing the bridge in Seafield Road.'

'Roger,' said the patrolman. 'Here, they're moving. They'll be coming out into Craigenside Drive. If they go left, they're heading for you. If they go right, you'll need to catch them up. We won't show ourselves. Hold on, here they come. It's a white vehicle, registration Sierra Lima zero six X-ray Charlie Oscar, and it's turned . . . left, heading your way.'

'Copy that,' said Montell.

'Shit,' Cowan hissed. They were almost upon the junction

of Craigenside Drive and Seafield Road. 'Choice to make.' She drove straight on, and as they passed the junction, they saw a white extended pick-up approaching the turn, indicating left. 'Sorted,' she murmured. 'Keep an eye on them, Griff, let me know when they're out of sight.' She slowed her speed, checking in her rear-view that they were clear behind.

'OK. They're gone.'

She swung the car in a violent u-turn then tramped on the accelerator, retracing their steps.

'Heading west,' Montell told the communications centre, as they cleared the bridge and the target vehicle came into view once more, 'and in pursuit.'

'What's your bet, Alice?' he asked as they cleared a green light, and as Seafield Road became Salamander Street.

'I don't have one yet. They could be local; we'll have a better idea soon. Look,' she said, glancing at a woman standing on the pavement as they passed, 'the massage parlours are shut, so the hookers are back on the street.'

'Ladies of negotiable affection,' he corrected her. 'Sounds more refined.'

They drove on, up Constitution Street and along Great Junction Street, lucky with the lights until the pick-up was stopped by a red at its end. 'Bugger!' Cowan cursed. 'I'd rather not be directly behind them.'

'It's OK,' Montell reassured her. 'They can't see us for the top on the load platform. They don't even know we're here.'

As the signal changed to red and amber, the vehicle's left indicator came on and it turned into Ferry Road. 'I'll place that bet now,' she declared. 'They're not from Edinburgh. If they were heading for Glasgow they'd have gone right at Seafield. Assuming that the driver knows where he's going, I reckon he's taking us across the Forth Road Bridge.'

'To infinity and beyond,' Montell drawled.

'Wherever, Griff,' said Alice. 'When he gets there I'll still have him in my sights.'

Seventy-seven

'There's no response from inside the barn, sir. You probably heard us giving him the megaphone warning to come out. There's been not a whisper.'

Skinner and Martin could hear Sergeant Doreen McSeveney's report on the radio that Greatorix held.

'Is the rear secure?' he asked.

'There's only one entrance; the big sliding door at the front. It's open wide enough to admit one person.'

'So Henry could be in there, waiting?'

'If he's gone, it wasn't in his car,' she pointed out. 'Anyway, I'm not going to get any older wondering. We're going in.'

'Take no unnecessary risks, Doreen,' Greatorix warned.

'We won't. We've got a high intensity light with us. The plan is we shine it through the opening. It'll blind anyone who's looking into it for long enough to let three of us roll inside.'

'How about stun grenades?'

'We're not the SAS, sir. Besides, it's a big space in there; they'd be less effective.'

'OK, go for it.'

Skinner and Martin could see little or nothing in the

moonless night, only the dim outline of the barn and the shape of Brown's car in front of it. They watched nonetheless, waiting, in silence. Then suddenly they saw a burst of bright light, and heard the sergeant's sharp command, 'Go!' through the radio.

They tensed, ready for the sound of shots, but none came: only the sergeant's voice once more, but different, much less in control. 'Oh fuck, oh shit, oh fuck! Get up here, sir. Henry's here all right . . . at least I think it's him.'

Seventy-eight

'I win,' said Cowan, as they cruised round the long curving bend and on to the slope that led down to the mighty, but decaying, Forth Road Bridge, the only direct road connection between Fife and the Lothians. She had followed the white truck carefully on the way out of Edinburgh, varying the distance between the two vehicles, even letting her quarry out of sight on occasion on stretches where she knew there was no turn-off available.

'Too bad for you we didn't have money on it,' Montell pointed out.

She ignored his reply. 'He's watching himself,' she murmured. 'He hasn't been over the speed limit at all, but he's never far short of it either. This is a guy who doesn't want to take any chance of being pulled over. Once he's over the bridge, he'll probably think he's free and clear. Out of our area.'

Her companion picked up the radio mike. 'Control, we're on the point of crossing into Fife,' he said. 'What's our status? Do we hand over to them?'

'ACC Steele again, Griff,' a voice crackled through the speaker. 'Maintain pursuit; repeat, maintain pursuit. This is a joint force operation; Fife are aware of your presence and of the orders in relation to the target. They won't interfere, or attempt to stop it under any circumstances, but they'll be available to assist if you request it.'

'Understood, ma'am. Just as well you said that, for we're in Fife now.'

'And the pick-up is speeding up,' Cowan added. 'Doing eighty as we join the motorway.'

'We've done a check on the number. No help there; it belongs on a red Dodge Caliber; the owner lives in South Shields. Don't let him lose you, Alice,' Steele cautioned. 'We've no way of tracing him if you do.'

The constable laughed. 'Ma'am, Nigel Mansell couldn't lose me in what I'm driving.'

'Any feel for a destination?' the ACC asked.

'He's ignored the turn-off for Dunfermline, still heading north. There's nothing significant between here and Perth or St Andrews. What's he got in the truck?'

'Seventy grand's worth of top of the range golf clubs and clothing, we're told by the club pro. He's on site now. That probably rules St Andrews out. It's the last place you'd go with knocked-off kit. The town's full of that stuff as it is. Check in when you know for sure, and I'll let Tayside know you're coming.'

'Understood, ma'am,' said Montell. He returned the mike to its holder, and looked across at Cowan. 'Jesus, Alice, did you hear that? Seventy thousand in stolen goods and we let them drive away from the place. We'd better recover this stuff or the top brass are going to be in shit as deep as the crew in front of us.'

Seventy-nine

Skinner slammed on the brakes, skidding slightly as he pulled up alongside Henry Brown's abandoned car. The beam of his headlights picked up one of the armed response team; he was doubled over, throwing up as if he was never going to stop. And it found something else; a dark trail on the ground leading into the barn.

The chief constable and Martin stepped out, just as Greatorix pulled up beside them. 'What's that?' he asked, following their gaze.

'It's a blood trail.' Skinner's voice was matter-of-fact. 'You've seen one of them before, Rod. Let's follow it and find out where it goes.'

'It goes here, sir,' said Doreen McSeveney. She stood in the open doorway. 'We've got our light on a stand. Maybe you shouldn't step inside,' she ventured as the three approached her. 'Contamination of the scene.'

'You've contaminated it already, Sergeant,' Martin pointed out. 'We know what not to do.'

'Then prepare yourselves,' she warned.

Skinner patted her on the shoulder. 'I gave that up years ago,

Doreen,' he told her, 'when I stopped being surprised by the things that human beings can do to each other.'

He stepped into the barn. It was flooded with brilliant light, centred on a fearful tableau. Two men hung there, no more than ten feet away, suspended by their rope-bound wrists from a steel beam that ran from wall to wall. Their feet were bare and bloody. The top of each man's head was missing. What was left lolled backwards, and the ground beneath their feet was stained red for yards around.

'Ohhh,' Greatorix moaned as he took in the carnage.

'Don't vomit in front of the other ranks, Rod,' Skinner whispered. 'Bad for the image. You don't want anyone telling the story at your retirement do.'

'Is that how you keep it in check?' The chief super-intendent's words were mumbled, as he wiped his mouth with the back of his hand.

'Absolutely.' He took a step towards the dangling bodies, and pointed towards the one on the left, the one with the massive lower jawbone. 'This will have been Henry, I take it.'

'It could be no other,' Martin confirmed. 'You only need that chin to identify him.'

'Who's the other one?'

'I'd guess that would be Dudley, Brown's sidekick.'

'Sidekick now, all right. Except nobody's kicking any longer.'

His friend nodded. 'Deadly Dudley, the drug dealers call him, out of fear rather than respect, after what he did with a pair of them who were caught flogging their own stuff. The rumour was he took them to a pig farm, shot them, chopped them up and fed them to the livestock. Dudley was pure pond life.'

'Was he on McCullough's payroll as well?'

'Officially he was a site agent with the building company. And in another way; Dudley was shacked up with his daughter Inez. He was family too.'

'A lousy night for the McCullough ladies, then.'

'And for Grandpa,' Martin added. 'For him it'll be like losing your right and left arms at the same time.' Pause for thought. 'Unless they upset him badly enough, that is; badly enough for him to get involved himself.'

Skinner shook his head. 'No, no. Your man wasn't responsible for this. Not directly, at any rate.'

'I suppose you know who was.'

He nodded. 'Sure I do,' he whispered.

'Then shouldn't we get people looking for him?'

'They'd never find him. How long have these guys been dead?'

'Given when Goldie said that Henry left home,' the recovered Greatorix suggested, 'it could be four hours or more.'

'Then your man is well gone.'

'Man?' he exclaimed. 'Are you telling me that one man took care of these two monsters?'

'Yes. Henry's phone call, the one that brought him here might have been from Dudley. If you find a mobile in his pocket that'll confirm it. But by the time Henry got here, Dud was deid, so to speak. Look at Henry's legs . . . they're in tatters. That's where the blood trail came from. As soon as he stepped out of his car, he was shot, hit over the head, maybe . . . we'll never know . . . then dragged in here and strung up, ready for his execution. Not that he was killed right away. Look at the ground beneath the two of them.'

The chief superintendent peered, at several shapeless red objects. 'What the fuck are those?'

'Their toes.'

'Oh my God!' He retched.

'I know,' said Skinner, 'you're going to tell me that this sort of thing doesn't happen in Dundee. Well, it does now.' He took his colleague by the elbow and tugged him, stumbling, towards the exit. 'You need to waken up your crime scene people and tell them to get here.'

'We have to ask them, now they're a central service.'

'Bollocks to that. Dorward in Edinburgh still jumps to it when my people call for him. I don't care whose damn payroll he's on; he's a police resource.'

The three officers stepped outside. 'You and your team can stand down now, Doreen,' Martin told the firearms squad commander. 'We'll be calling in the cavalry.'

'We'll wait till they get here,' the sergeant replied.

'If you wish.' He turned to Skinner. 'Who's going to tell Goldie?' he asked.

'Neil, if he wants. I'll give him a call on his mobile, and tell him what's happened here. We've got no reason to hold Murtagh now, so he can turn him loose. If he wants to tell Daphne she's a widow, he can, but maybe somebody should find this Inez woman and let her know that she'll have an empty bed tonight.'

'What about her dad?'

'The women can go and cry on his shoulder, get it softened up for us when we call on him.'

'We're going to see him? You and me?'

'Too fucking right we are. Not tonight, though. There's a few things to sort out before we do that. Meantime . . .' He fell into a contemplative silence.

'What?'

'The farmhouse, the one that's only occasionally used: can you reach it from here?'

'Directly, no. You have to go back out on to the main road.'

'Then do you fancy taking my car and having a look at it for signs of entry? Rod's a bit flaky; I should stay here and give him support. I suppose it's possible that the guy who did this checked it out, to make sure there was nobody there to disturb him. This scene's such a mess that it'll be a miracle if we find traces of him here, but if he's been in there, you never know.'

'Yes, I'll do that. The way things have turned out tonight, anything's possible.'

Eighty

As he turned into the roads that led to the Hillside Mains farmhouse, Andy Martin felt a hand grip the pit of his stomach. He had to will himself to defeat the urge to pull his car over and follow the example of the response team constable. If it had not been for the fact that he had not eaten for almost twelve hours he might not have succeeded. Bob Skinner had the apparent ability to switch off all feeling when confronted with the aftermath of the most violent of crimes, but it was something that he had never mastered. *Of course,* he recognised, *who knows what's really going on inside another person's head?*

The deaths of Henry Brown and his henchman Dudley . . . the question, *What the fuck is a hench?* ran, uncontrollably and unanswered, through his mind, making him realise that he was not very far away from hysteria . . . these deaths had left him with what had become already an indelible memory, yet another that he would carry to the grave, unless Alzheimer's or some other affliction erased it first.

Martin was shaken by his own weakness. Although he knew that he was regarded as a hard guy, as international-class rugby flank forwards invariably are, he did have a soft side and he was quietly proud of it. Nonetheless his CID career had developed under Skinner's tutelage, which tended to work on what he called Billy Ocean principles; as the song went, when the going got tough, the tough got going.

For sure, something had knocked him off kilter, and he knew what it was. There were two people in the world that he loved totally, simply and without complications, and their names were Danielle and Robert Martin, a toddler and an infant. For all that he was presenting the break-up of his marriage as an agreement to part by two mature intelligent people facing up to the truth, and for all his talk of having been an absentee father all along, he had been keen to lead his friends in their pursuit of Henry Brown simply because it postponed the moment when he would have to go back to his empty house in Edinburgh, knowing that in Perth his daughter would be asking why he wasn't in his appointed place at her bedtime, talking to her and reading her a chapter from her chosen book. And when he did go home, what a picture he would be taking with him, in his head . . .

He glanced at the dashboard clock; it was showing five minutes after midnight. The household would be quiet, Robert permitting. He smiled at the thought but felt his eyes moisten. 'Go back, Andy,' he whispered in the darkness, but he knew that there was no way. There were too many obstacles between him and Karen.

And then there was the job. It had all happened very quickly; vacancy circulated, applications invited, and then, before he had even completed the form, a direct approach. He had accepted on the spot, but after one day in his new office he found himself wondering whether his enthusiasm had been based in part on its fortuitous timing, and the opportunity it had given to put up a smokescreen to conceal from the world the truth about his break-up. But that notion had gone as quickly as it had arrived. He had never taken a job without one hundred per cent certainty that it was right for him, and the SCDEA post was the destination for which his entire career had been headed.

The sharp bend took him by surprise: he jerked the wheel violently to stay on the narrow drive. 'Focus, man,' he said aloud, chiding himself.

The road straightened, he crested a rise, and there it was, in view, silhouetted against the sky, the farmhouse, a substantial stone building with two storeys and an attic floor above. If it had been for sale, an estate agent would probably have described it as a mansion. And it was in use. On either side of the main entrance there were two huge bay windows. They both seemed to be in darkness, but as he eased closer, Martin could see that the curtains in the one on the left were drawn. They were heavy, but a slit of light was showing. He looked up; in two of the four windows set into the roof, there were signals of occupation.

The drive opened out into a garden, and forked. He took the branch to the right; and parked, in sight of the house, but well to the side, engine ticking over, but lights off. He reached out for his mobile, which was set in a dashboard socket, found Skinner's number and called it.

'Andy.' The chief constable's voice filled the car through the Bluetooth speakers.

'Bob,' he told him, 'this place is not empty. Is Rod sure Grandpa's tucked up?'

'Hold on.' He heard muffled voices. 'Yes,' Skinner told him as he came back on line. 'They did another check twenty minutes ago. He's watching TV and having a beer.'

'I don't know whether that's a relief or not. Do you reckon there's any chance the shooter's holed up here?'

'And advertising the fact?'

'Maybe not.'

'Do any obvious alternatives occur?'

'Ah,' Martin exclaimed. 'What did Goldie say? "Our Cameron goes there sometimes." I'll bet she wasn't talking about her brother; she meant her niece.'

'I'm not with you.'

'There are two Cameron McCulloughs. That's why the first is called Grandpa. The other one is Inez's daughter; she was named after him, and she's the apple of his eye, his only soft spot. It's probably her. I'll go and check.'

'Don't do that,' said Skinner sharply. 'Yes, you're probably right, but it's not impossible that we could both be wrong and there is a man with a gun in there. The memory of Stevie Steele is still fresh in my mind. I'm not having you knocking the wrong door unprepared. Hold on while I send Doreen's team round to join you.'

'Fucking hell, Bob, don't babysit me. I can take whoever's in there.'

'Andy, I don't know if I can give you orders any more, but this is one anyway. Do not move out of that car until back-up gets there. We're going to be hosing brains off the roof of this barn. I don't want the same to happen to you.'

Before Martin could reply, the fist grabbed his stomach again, without warning, squeezing the adventure out of him. His mind was filled with a vision of the nightmare in the barn, and he started to tremble. 'OK,' he whispered, 'I'm convinced; we'll do it your way.'

'Are you all right?' his friend asked.

'Yeah. It's just that I can't shake this daft question from my head.'

'Google it while you wait. I'll send them now. You let Doreen ring that bell.'

The mobile went dead. Martin sat in the dark, feeling un-manned by his weakness. Still thinking of the horrors, he threw his head back and looked at the grey roof lining, but he seemed to see the two ravaged forms there, as if it were a cinema screen. He closed his eyes, but it made no difference. He thought about calling Karen; he reached for the phone once more, but when he opened his contact list and saw the first name and number that came up, he went no further. He pressed the call button and waited as the car was filled with the two-tone sound.

'Andy,' said a sleep-filled voice, 'd'you know what time it is?'

'Yes, sorry. Are you alone?'

'Of course I'm bloody alone.'

'Sorry, I meant, can you talk?'

'I'm not sure I want to. I was dreaming about Granada. I've just read a book that's set there and so I've booked to go. It was a good dream.'

'Sorry again. Mine was a nightmare. I won't tell you what was in it. Alex, what the fuck is a hench?'

'A what?'

'You know. A hench, as in henchman. What the fuck can it be? I can't get the question out of my head and it's driving me crazy.'

'Andy. Are you all right?'

'You're the second Skinner to ask me that in the last five minutes.'

'I hope you gave my dad a proper answer.'

'No. The truth is I think I've lost my bottle. I'm just a wee bit confused. I'm not saying I don't know who I am any more, but I don't think I'm quite the same guy.'

'Are you drunk?'

'Hell, no.'

'Where are you?'

'Sat in my car in Perthshire, waiting for a woman with a gun to make me safe.'

'You're not making a lot of sense.'

'Not even to me, kid.'

'Have you been in a stressful situation?'

'You could say that. So has your old man, but he's like a rock, while I've got the shakes. That's never happened to me before.'

'Welcome to the human race, love.'

'What did you call me?'

'Slip of the tongue. Let me tell you about my dad. Whatever it is you've seen that's shaken you up, if he's seen the same thing, then at some point over the next couple of days, he will get quietly hammered. It won't be too noticeable, for he's got hollow legs for the drink, as you know, but he will. The next morning, he'll either go for a run or he'll go to the gym and he'll knock ten bells out of himself. That's his way; but you've never lived with him so you're not to know that. As for the Glimmer Twins, I spoke to Paula the other day; she told me that when Mario came home last Thursday, from that fire scene, he drank two bottles of Albarino then started to cry. I'm glad you've got the heebies, Andy. To tell you the truth I used to be slightly scared that you never did before.' She waited, filling the car with the sound of her breathing. 'And you miss your babies,' she added, finally.

'Yeah,' he conceded. 'There is that.'

'That's the road you've chosen. That'll be a lot tougher than looking at dead things. But you'll make it, because you're Andy Martin, and he's OK.'

'So're you, kid.'

'Too damn right.'

He laughed, properly, for the first time since he had left his family behind. 'Yeah well; Alex . . .' He was cut off short as the beam of two headlights speared across the lawn lighting up the front of the house. 'What the . . .' he exclaimed.

'The woman with the gun?'

'No, she doesn't make that much noise. Alex, I have to go. Something's happening here.'

Eighty-one

'Where's he heading now?' Montell asked.

'Depends. If it's Perth, he'll take the turn-off he's just approaching.'

'I don't see an indicator flashing.'

'No,' said Cowan. 'And he's past it. He's taking the Dundee Road, over the Friarton Bridge.'

'Another fucking bridge? Is it as high as the last one?'

'You won't notice in the dark. Don't tell me you've got a thing about heights.'

'I don't even wear cowboy boots.'

'That's all right. I wouldn't fancy the spurs.' She stared ahead into the night, focused on the red tail lights that were all she could see of the vehicle they were following. 'OK, my boy,' she murmured, 'where are we bound?'

'What's in Dundee?'

'Lots,' Alice replied. 'It's our fourth city; used to be famous for the three Js, jute, jam and journalism. The last one's still hanging in there, but the other two are pretty much rubber ducked.'

'Nice turn of phrase.' Montell paused. 'And talking about turns . . . is he slowing down?'

'Yes he is indeed,' she said, excited. 'And, thank you very much, indicating like the good driver he is, to the left, and there he goes. We'll just back off a bit, though.'

'Why?'

'Because there's no through road up there. We'd have seen a sign by now if there was.' She let the Mondeo slow right down as she approached the turn. 'There's one, though, but not a proper road sign. Hillside Mains Farmhouse,' she read. 'That looks like our destination. I'm going after him; you can call it in.'

She made the turn. The road was narrow, barely wide enough for two cars to pass each other. 'We've got him, Griff. Get some orders.'

Even as she spoke, Montell was on the radio, reporting their position. 'Don't lose them now,' Maggie Steele's voice boomed. 'You're off the highway and they know the territory. Close in and apprehend.'

Cowan smiled. 'Lovely,' she hissed. She put her foot down, unleashing the power of their vehicle. Within seconds they were closing on the pick-up. She snapped her headlights on to full beam, then pressed a button to start the flashing blue lights that were hidden in the front air grille.

The driver in front swerved, but corrected and accelerated. They could see a house ahead, then an opening. The pick-up raced through it, then braked hard, and spun through a hundred and eighty degrees until it was heading back towards them.

'No danger,' Cowan muttered. She swung the Cosworth around, blocking the exit.

The pick-up made to turn again, but before it could complete the manoeuvre, another car, another Mondeo, appeared out of nowhere and drove across its path, leaving it no space to move further.

Montell snapped his belt free and jumped out of the passenger seat. 'Police,' he shouted.

'Me too,' another voice replied, as the occupant of the other car reached the driver's door of the white truck and tore it open. The detective constable saw the man's eyes widen. He looked through the passenger window. Inside were two figures, each dressed in black jumpsuits, and wearing black woollen hats, from which strands of blond hair had escaped. 'Bloody hell, Inez,' the man on the other side exclaimed, 'what have you and your daughter been up to?'

'Robbery,' said Montell. 'We've tailed them from Edinburgh.' He opened the door on his side, took the older woman by the arm and pulled her firmly, but not roughly, from her seat.

The younger of the two stepped out unaided, tugging off her hat and shaking her hair loose. She glared across the top of the vehicle, not at him, but at his captive. 'Mother,' she snapped. 'You are a complete tit.'

'Mr Martin?' Cowan exclaimed, as she reached the scene. 'Alice?'

'Hello, sir. This is DCC Martin,' she told her colleague. 'He was one of us before your time. He's just been appointed to run the SCDEA. What are you doing here, sir?'

'I just happened to be passing,' he replied, casually. 'Who's in the house, Cameron?' he asked the younger woman.

'Search me.'

'DC Cowan may have to, but we're not there yet.'

'Look, I have no idea, honest. I haven't been here in weeks.' She nodded at her mother. 'You'd better ask her.'

As the truth dawned, Martin's smile almost lit up the night. 'Let me guess, Inez,' he laughed. 'There's eight of them, they're female and they speak Estonian.'

Eighty-two

'I was out by one,' he said. 'It turned out that there were nine people in the house, the Estonian girls and the guy you told me about, Marius Ramanauskas. He couldn't wait to talk; he told us that he's entirely innocent, and that he was only there because Inez told him to come and look after them while she arranged transport home.'

'Did Inez say anything to that?' Skinner asked. They were at the murder scene. The whole area had been floodlit, but they stood to the side, in the darkness, as crime-suited technicians made their way across the ground.

'As it happens, she backed him up, in a way. She said that since his crowd had got the two youngest ones on drugs, it was down to him to help them get clean.'

'Have you searched the house yet?'

Martin nodded. 'Your two did that. It has a bloody enormous cellar, mostly filled with golf clubs . . . Callaways, Titleists, TaylorMade, Ping and a few other top-of-the-range makes . . . and expensive clothing, Hugo Boss, Ashcroft and so on. We'll have to consult the manufacturers to work out the total value. As for returning it to its owners, that'll be a nightmare. How will we know whose is whose? It looks as if they've been stockpiling. My guess is they weren't going to sell it in Britain; it was all going south in a container, to France, Spain . . .'

'Or east, to Scandinavia,' Skinner suggested. 'Russia even; they've got the golf bug. Where are the women now?'

'I've had everybody taken to Perth. The Estonians will be kept in a youth hostel, under guard. Inez, Cameron and Marius are being locked up for the night, and Goldie will be taken there in the morning, to be interviewed. According to Neil, she's in shock. He decided to tell her about Henry, after Murtagh had gone, and she cracked up. I've sent a woman DC to stay with her overnight.'

'And what about Grandpa? What are you doing about him?'

'Nothing tonight, for sure. Inez is declaring loud and long that her dad knew nothing about the robberies or the stuff that she and Dud were keeping there. She said it was all Dudley's idea, and that Grandpa was never involved. I'm going to back off now and leave it to Rod, but my view is that the next time we lift Cameron, it's got to be for good.'

'So how's it going to pan out?' the chief constable asked.

Martin scratched his stubbled chin. 'Good question, with more than one answer. I think Inez is fucked; we've got her for the robbery in Edinburgh, and as a minimum for possession of the stuff in the cellar. But we can't lay a glove on Goldie for any of that, or for trafficking. The most we can do her for is harbouring illegal immigrants, and I would not dream of asking the fiscal to proceed with that charge. The state itself knowingly harbours illegal immigrants, for fuck's sake. She'll be released. I don't know about Marius, though.'

'He's bailed on minor drugs charges that won't even make court, so you'll have to cut him loose too. But,' Skinner frowned, 'couldn't you do Grandpa for possession? The gear was in his cellar, after all.'

Andy chuckled. 'Ah, but that's the beauty of it,' he exclaimed. 'I know I said earlier that he had a farm, but technically, he doesn't. The name on the land register is Cameron McCullough, all right, but it's not him. It's his granddaughter. She's his heir; everything he does is for her eventually.'

'And is she worth it?'

'She is to her grandad. She might be only a kid, but he's closer to her than anyone else. As soon as she turned twenty-one she was appointed to the boards of CamMac plc and all its subsidiaries. She's well smart; it's as if all the female brains in the family by-passed her mother and her aunt and went straight to her. Put her and Alex in the same business, and they'd rule the fucking world in five years.'

'Speaking of my daughter,' Bob murmured, 'I had a call from her, about an hour ago. She asked me if you were all right. Are you?'

'I wasn't then: I am now. Thanks to her.'

'Good. Now, young Cameron,' he continued, quickly. 'What's she saying?'

'Apart from telling her mother that she and Dud make Fred and Wilma Flintstone look like intellectuals, she's saying nothing at all. She's cool. My suspicion is that she expects her grandfather to reach in and pull her out the fire.'

'He'll have a job. She took part in a robbery, and she was followed from there to here.'

'Yes, and I'm having difficulty understanding why. She's much brighter than that. How many of these robberies have there been?'

'This was the tenth. The pattern was the same until tonight; patrol cars diverted by fake calls, so there was nobody to respond.'

'What was the difference tonight?'

'According to Maggie, the earlier calls were made by a man; these were by a woman. By the way,' he added, 'when can she have them?'

'What do you mean?' asked Martin.

'When can she have Inez and Cameron? They're hers. This was her operation, they committed the robbery in Edinburgh and that's where they should appear in court. Maggie deserves the credit, and so does Alice . . . and Griff: he could use a gold star on his record right now.'

'I can appreciate that, but we have to charge them here, in Tayside, with possession.'

Skinner looked at his friend. 'We're not getting into a turf war here, are we, Andy?'

'Not at all; you know I'm right. I'll tell you what; we'll charge them with what we've got and stick them up in court tomorrow. We'll have them remanded in custody, then hand them over to you.'

'Fair enough. Cowan and Montell can interview and charge them after that.' Skinner broke off as Rod Greatorix approached, looking haggard and exhausted. 'What's happening?' he asked him.

'They're just getting to work. The door of Henry's car's

peppered with heavy gauge shotgun pellets, so that'll give them a starting point, but. . . they've looked out round the back and found a bin. There's a lot of stuff been burned in it, paper underneath, files and the like, and something else on top. They reckon it's a suit like the ones they wear. Meticulous, eh?'

'We've seen something similar,' the chief constable remarked, 'in an investigation we had long ago. A guy dressed himself up in protective clothing for his kills.'

Greatorix brightened up as he clutched at a straw. 'Any chance of a link?'

'Not unless he's risen from the grave.'

The light was extinguished. 'Damn it. For a minute there . . .' He sighed. 'I'm inclined to believe these are contract killings. What do you two think?'

'I'm not going to knock that on the head, Rod,' Martin told him. 'But I've never seen a professional murder that's as messy as these, or one that involved torture, for that matter.'

'It happened in Ireland often enough,' Skinner pointed out.

'But those were political.'

'Are there any "buts" with murder?' He looked at the chief superintendent. 'Yes, Rod, logically you might be right. But if you are, there's a follow-up question, isn't there? Who ordered it?'

'Someone with a grudge against Grandpa, I suppose; sending him a message.'

'From what I've seen, it would have been easier to kill McCullough himself than to take out these two.'

Greatorix sighed. 'So you're as much in the dark as me?' he

blurted out, his voice full of frustration; 'Is that what you're saying?'

Skinner shook his head, and checked his watch. 'The only thing I'm saying, Rod, is that unless we can help you in some other way, it's time that Andy and I picked up Neil McIlhenney and headed back to Edinburgh. What I'm thinking is this: you guys have gone on for years knowing that Cameron McCullough has done, or ordered, things, but you've never been able to prove it. Right?'

The other men nodded, simultaneously.

'Well, he didn't do this one, but it's going to fall into the same category. Get ready to list it as unsolved, or to keep the file open for a long time.'

'Are you telling us you do know who did it right enough?' the chief superintendent asked.

'I knew who did it as soon as I walked into that barn.' He beckoned to Martin. 'When I'm ready, I'll tell you. Come on, it's the middle of the fucking night and I think I'm going to have a very early start.'

'Why?' his friend asked. 'Where are you going?'

'France.'

Eighty-three

'If you don't mind me saying so,' said Jack McGurk, 'you look a bit bleary-eyed.'

'Yes I mind,' Neil McIlhenney growled. 'My wife minds. My kids mind. And everybody around me will mind about irritating me by the time this day is done. I got in at three thirty, wakening the wee one in the process, and thus the whole household, then I was back in my office by eight. And now the mountain has to come to Mohammad and his mate because you don't have a DI. In fact, with Sammy off on his course and Becky on her travels, there's hardly a fucking DI left in fucking Edinburgh. Have you done that thing I asked you?'

'When you phoned me from the road at quarter to three?'

'That's right, and you're not bleary-eyed at all.'

The DS grinned. 'Yes I've done it. I called on Mrs McKean pretty much as soon as her office opened. She wasn't going to tell me anything, at first; she even tried to hide behind legal privilege until I pointed out that she isn't, in fact, a lawyer. Eventually I said that if it wasn't her it must have been her boss and could I speak to her please, and that's when she gave up. I let her off light; I took her out and bought her a coffee, and let her take her time. She admitted that Green called her out of the blue, on Tuesday of last week. He asked her to do him a simple favour, and confirm that Tomas Zaliukas had been in the office that afternoon to change his will.'

'And she told him, just like that?'

'She says she refused, at first, but he pleaded with her. He said it had nothing to do with any of his clients; that this was a matter of his personal security, and if she didn't want to get caught up in it herself or, worse, get young Kenny involved, she'd tell him. So she did.'

'Was that all he asked her?'

'No, he asked if she could get him a copy of the new will. She said she couldn't, because it had been drafted, printed and witnessed by Veronica Drake. The copy was in her safe and Mrs McKean doesn't have access.'

McIlhenney frowned. 'She didn't know what was in it?'

'She said not, and I believe her. Does that make a difference?'

'It might, if the boss's theory is right: that the Gerulaitises were killed by Desperate Dan and his mate Dudley, after Laima had been forced to sign away her inheritance from Tomas, the interest in Lituania SAFI. If they didn't find out he'd left it to her from Ken Green, through his ex-wife, then who the hell did tell them?'

'Who the hell knew?' asked McGurk.

'Veronica Drake knew. And, eventually, we did.'

'And who else?'

'That's what we need to find out.'

'Do you want me to go back up to the law firm and interview Drake?'

'No. Because somebody else knew too, the day before the couple died.'

'Who was that?'

'Who told us about the contents of the will?'

McGurk winced. 'Alex Skinner.'

'Precisely. No, Jack, you will not go charging into CAJ. If anyone's going to take that further it'll be me, and it'll be with her dad, not with Alex.'

'Thanks, sir,' said McGurk, sincerely. 'You go and get some sleep now,' he added, as the superintendent headed for the door.

'Fuck off, Sergeant,' he replied, as his mobile rang. He took it out and checked the incoming call; the number showed 'unknown'. 'McIlhenney,' he grunted.

'Neil, it's Andy.'

'Where are you?'

'In my new office, but I've just had a call from Rod Greatorix, up in Perth.'

'Oh yes? Did he say when we can pick up the women?'

'Yes and no. At half past eight this morning a lawyer turned up at the office where they were being held, saying that she'd been instructed to defend them. Not any old legal hack either; no, it was Susannah Himes.'

'The Barracuda?'

Seated at his desk, Sauce Haddock's eyebrows rose at the mention of the name; he had met her before, and been impressed.

'That's right. She asked for a private interview with her clients, and of course that had to be allowed. They went straight into court when it was over. When they were called, Himes told the sheriff that her client, Inez McCullough, would be entering a plea of guilty to the possession offence, and that she'd be cooperating with police in Edinburgh and around Scotland over several other current investigations. But she also said that Inez had told her that her daughter Cameron had no involvement in any of these, and that she'd gone along last night thinking that she was helping her mother pick up stuff that the golf club had agreed she could have.'

'What?' McIlhenney shouted. 'Did the sheriff swallow that crap?'

'From the Barracuda? Hook, line and sinker. She applied for bail; we opposed it, but it was useless. As they left, Susannah told Rod that if you want to interview either of them, you'll have to do it through her. The fiscal reckons it's the start of a bargaining session. Inez will plead to the lot if there are no proceedings against Cameron. Otherwise, it's a trial.'

'You know what the outcome will be, don't you?'

'Sure; the Crown Office will take the deal. I know where Inez's orders came from too: her father's mouth to her ear, via Ms Himes.'

'The boss is going to love that, I don't think.'

'Do you think I fucking like it? I'm going to talk to Grandpa, at the first opportunity. Bob might want to come with me. Where is he?'

'Gone. Red-eye flight this morning. McGurk says I look half dead, so Christ knows what state he's in.'

Eighty-four

'I'm sorry we're later than arranged,' said Mario McGuire as Regine Zaliukas opened the door; 'but as I said when I called you earlier, someone wanted to join us, and we had to wait for him.'

'That's no problem,' she replied. She was dressed casually, as she had been the evening before, in slightly more formal day wear, but with the same fluffy carpet slippers on her feet. 'What happened to him?' she asked. 'Didn't he turn up?'

As she spoke, a figure stepped into view from the side of the doorway, to stand alongside Becky Stallings. His face was lined with tiredness and his clothes were creased from travel, but his eyes were clear and alert. 'No, I made it,' he told her. 'It was a bit of a rush, everything ran to time.'

She peered at him for a second or two. 'It's Mr Skinner, isn't it?' she murmured.

He nodded, smiling as he extended his hand. 'It's been a while, Regine. You look barely a day older; I wish I could claim the same.'

She shook his hand, and stood aside. 'Please come in.'

'Where are Mork and Mindy?' McGuire asked, as he stepped into the hall, after Skinner and Stallings.

'Max and Zaki?' She laughed softly. 'They've taken the girls to Agen, to the cinema.' She looked at the chief constable. 'Why are you here, Mr Skinner?'

He ignored her question. 'How old are they now?'

'Aimée is eight, and Lucie is newly six.'

'Have you told them about their father?'

'No, not yet. I need quiet time with them before I can break that kind of news. Too many things have been happening.' She moved towards the sitting room, and beckoned them to follow. 'Come through and sit.' The three police officers followed; McGuire and Stallings took seats on the sofa facing the widow in her chair, but Skinner stood, beside the garden door.

'OK, Regine,' he said. 'It's time to tell us what happened.' He stopped abruptly and frowned. 'But first,' he continued, '. . . you're not alone in the house, are you.' Statement, not question. 'Yesterday evening you felt unsafe, so Mario and Becky told me, yet this afternoon your bodyguards have gone out with the kids . . . and left you alone? No, you feel safe now, don't you?'

She shrugged. 'I should. You're here.'

'It's nice to know we have your confidence, but I reckon you've got a little added insurance. Come on, call him, or do I have to go looking?'

'No, you don't.' The accent was thick, but the words intelligible. The voice came from the opening that led to the kitchen, at the top of the steps, where its owner had appeared, a man in his early thirties; clean-shaven, dressed in jeans and a fresh white T-shirt with a caricature image of Nicolas Sarkozy on the front. He was smaller than either police officer, but the definition of his musculature said that he was no less formidable.

'You'll be Jonas, I take it,' said the chief constable. The newcomer nodded. 'In that case, Regine will be fine.' His eyes narrowed, imperceptibly. 'But she'll be fine now anyway, won't she, Colonel?' The surviving Zaliukas brother returned his gaze, but quizzically, suggesting mystification.

He turned back to the woman. 'OK, let's begin. In your own time. There is no pressure on you here. We need to know the circumstances that led to Tomas's death, but be sure, lass, that we regard you, I regard you, as a victim too.'

She nodded, and seemed to relax a little. 'Where do I begin?' she murmured.

'Let's start with the massage parlours, and the company known as Lituania SAFI. How did your husband come to be involved in that?'

'At the time, I never knew he was involved,' she replied. 'He didn't tell me when he did it, even though we were supposed to make all the business decisions together. I only found out a couple of years later, not long after Lucie was born, when we were at a party, a business thing, and one of the women there, a banker's wife, I think, made a nasty remark. She called him a pimp. I didn't know what she was talking about so I punched her.' She tapped the side of her nose, and smiled, very faintly. 'Right there,' she whispered. 'It bled all over her blue satin dress. There was a scene, of course, and Tomas had to take me home. Once we got there I made him tell me what she had been talking about.'

'You made him?'

'Oh, I made him, all right.' She looked at Stallings. 'Imagine, he thinks I couldn't stand up to my husband. Tomas might have been ... what he once was ... but I was no pushover either.'

'I know that well enough,' Skinner chuckled. 'No one ever took you for a softie, Regine. So what did he tell you?'

'He said that not long after Tony Manson died, he was approached by a man he called Dudley.'

'Eh?' Skinner's eyebrows rose. 'How did he know this man?'

'From his time in the merchant navy. Dudley was on the crew of his ship.'

'But he's Scottish. On a Lithuanian ship?'

She nodded. 'He joined in Amsterdam, after some men defected and left them short-handed. He and Tomas sailed together for a couple of years, and when Dudley left the ship in Scotland, Tomas went with him ... unofficially. He deserted, and he was allowed to stay.'

'I know that. When he approached Tomas, what did he want?'

'He thought that Tomas had been left Manson's massage places,' she explained. 'It was known that Tony had left everything worth having to an associate, and Dudley assumed that it was him. He told him it wasn't and he thought that would the end of it, but Dudley came back. He said that he had someone who was interested in buying the places, and that if my husband could help, he would cut him in for half of the deal.

Tomas thought why not, and so he approached the lawyer who was acting for Lennie Plenderleith . . . he was in jail by then.'

'How did Ken Green get involved?'

'When Tomas asked Mr Conn at Curle Anthony and Jarvis to act for him in the deal, he said he'd rather not. Green was introduced by the other man in the deal.'

'This partner, this other man. Who is he?'

'I don't know that. Tomas wouldn't tell me. He never did tell me, ever.'

'Do you know if the two of them ever met, or was all the business done through Dudley?'

'Oh yes, they met. When the company in Uruguay was set up, they went there to sign the papers. Four of them went. Tomas took Valdas, because he was going to be looking after the places, and the other man had someone with him too. Not Dudley, though; a man Tomas called Henry.'

'Was that the trip when he had the tattoo done on his shoulder?' McGuire asked.

She nodded. 'He said that they all did.'

'Excuse me for a moment.' Skinner stepped out into the garden, took out his phone and called McIlhenney. 'Neil,' he said as the superintendent answered, 'no time to chat, but call Greatorix and tell him that his pathologists should check for a tattoo on Henry Brown's shoulder. They'll find one, and when they do, they should photograph it. Then check the photos that were taken at Tomas's autopsy, and at Valdas's; you should find two the same, although Valdas's will be a wee bit singed.'

He went back inside. 'Sorry about that, Regine,' he murmured. 'So Valdas knew who the man was?'

'Yes.'

He looked at Jonas Zaliukas, who had come down the steps and was standing behind his sister-in-law's chair. 'What about you?' he asked.

'I was in the army when this shit happen,' the man replied.

'That's not an answer, but we'll go back there later. For now, do you know, Regine, if Tomas put any more money into that company?'

'No, he didn't. He was paid a dividend on his investment, fifty thousand every year, twenty per cent of his capital, but he didn't put any more in.'

'Where did the money go?'

'Into a bank account he opened in France, for the girls. I doubt if he paid tax on it; it was always in cash.'

'We don't really care about that,' the chief constable told her. 'Why don't you bring us up to date now?' he invited. 'When did all this business begin?'

'Two weeks ago,' she replied, and as she did, the tension seemed to grab her once more, tightening her shoulders, and narrowing her mouth.

'How?' the chief constable asked quietly.

'Tomas came home from the office on Wednesday night,' she replied, 'the week before last. He told me that there was big trouble in the massage parlours, that Valdas had done something very stupid, and that his partner was very angry.'

'Did he tell you what Gerulaitis had done?'

'No, but he said that it was criminal, against the law. You see, those businesses are sensitive, what happens there is . . .' She paused, frowning. 'How do I say it?'

'What happens there is tolerated,' Stallings prompted her. 'Men go there, and to places like that all over Britain, and they pay for sex. We all know it happens, but there's an unspoken agreement that nothing will be done about it. Our society can never eliminate prostitution, but it can't be seen to make it legal either. So we compromise; we turn a blind eye to women selling themselves in places like that, because it's a hell of a lot safer for them than doing it on the street. As long as the business is properly run, and the women aren't exploited; if they were, that couldn't be overlooked.'

'And that's what Valdas was doing,' Skinner added. 'He had smuggled in a squad of girls, youngsters, some of them under age, from Estonia, and put them to work. Some were willing, and those that weren't were drugged.'

Regine stared at him. 'That's what he did?'

He nodded.

'Tomas didn't tell me that. Now I know, I'm even more glad that he's dead.'

'How did his partner find out?'

'Through Dudley, Tomas said. From time to time he would go into the places as a customer, to check that they were being run properly.'

'And when he did that a couple of weeks ago,' McGuire murmured, 'he saw the new talent.'

'Just so,' Jonas Zaliukas growled. 'Valdas!' he spat. 'What's your word in English for someone who is very stupid?'

'Idiot, dimwit, moron . . . take your pick.'

'I take all of them. My brother made not many mistakes, but he was one. And it kill him.'

'Regine,' Skinner whispered, 'go on. Tomas sent you here, didn't he?'

'Yes. He said he would have to deal with the trouble, but that his partner was a very serious man, and there could be danger until it was all made clear. He told me to take the children and come here to Mezin. He said he would come for me when it was safe. But it never was for him.' Her eyes filled with tears, but she kept her self-control. 'We left the very next day; I drove and we got here on the Friday afternoon. Everything was fine over the weekend. Tomas called me several times, and I told him we were OK. On Saturday he told me that Jonas had arrived from Lithuania, and also that his partner seemed to understand that what had happened was not his fault. I was going to go back, but he told me I should stay here for a few more days.' She stopped. 'I'm sorry. I need something to drink.'

Stallings rose to her feet. 'I'll get you some water.'

'Thank you,' said Regine. 'A very little water, please, with a lot of whisky in it. You'll find both in the kitchen.' She looked around. 'Would anyone else . . .?'

The three men shook their heads. 'Nice shirt,' Skinner remarked to Jonas Zaliukas, as the inspector left. 'It looks brand new. Bit tight, though; maybe you should take it back and get a size bigger.'

The Lithuanian shrugged. 'It's OK,' he murmured, with evident disinterest.

They stood in silence until Stallings returned, carrying two glasses, the whisky and a sparkling water for herself. The widow thanked her, and sank half of her drink in one swallow. 'Where was I?' she murmured. 'Yes, the weekend. On Monday morning, just after ten o'clock, the doorbell rang. I thought nothing of it. I assumed that it was the postman, or maybe the friendly Englishman who lives a few doors up. But no, it was two other men, and they were not friendly. One was Dudley; I met him once a long time ago. The other was bigger, big strong man, with big chin. They pushed me into the house, then came in and closed the door. I told them to go or I'd call the gendarme, but Dudley just laughed. He told me we were all going, them, me and Aimée and Lucie. He was going to take us straight away, but the other man . . .'

'Henry,' said McGuire.

'His name is Henry? Ah. He is not a nice man either, but he's nicer than Dudley; he let me take clothes for the children, and some toys and books. I asked him where we were going, but he wouldn't tell me. They took us outside . . . there was nobody in the street, but there never is . . . and put us into the back of a car, a hire car with the label still hanging from the mirror. We drove for a while, until we arrived at a cottage on the far side of Agen, in the country, with nothing around it. There was another car parked outside, just like the first. When they took us inside, I saw they had food in bags on the table. I asked how long they were going to keep us there. Dudley said that would depend on Tomas. He said that if he did what he was told we would be home in a couple of days. If not . . . He didn't finish, but the way he looked at me, and the girls, made me very frightened.' She shuddered, and winced, as if in pain. 'Dudley is a very bad man.'

Skinner looked at her and sensed renewed hesitancy. 'Tell

us, please,' he asked. 'I think I know but we need to hear it from you.'

She nodded, and finished her whisky in a second swallow. 'They gave us a bedroom and left us there. The girls wanted to know what was going on. I told them that these men were friends of Daddy's and that they were going to look after us for a little while. I checked the window, of course, but it had been screwed shut. I thought about breaking the glass and maybe using a piece as a weapon, but with two of them that would have been hopeless. After an hour or so, they came back. They made us all sit on the bed. I asked the other man, Henry, how they had known where we were. He looked at me, and he said, "Valdas's wife doesn't like you. She knew where Tomas would have sent you. We only had to ask her the once." That bitch Laima,' she hissed. 'Even if he hadn't told me I'd have guessed quickly enough. Then Dudley took out a mobile telephone. "We're going to make a wee movie," he said, and he smiled, but in a horrible way. He pointed the phone at us, and he began to speak, in Lithuanian, very bad Lithuanian. I was surprised at first, but I remembered those two years at sea.'

'You speak it yourself?' Stallings exclaimed.

Regine stared at her. 'Lady,' she replied, 'if you marry a man and you don't learn his language, then you are a fool.'

'Of course,' said the chief constable. 'But go on.'

'When Dudley spoke, it was as if he was speaking to Tomas. "Here we are," he said, "us and your three treasures. And this is what's going to happen." The other man stopped him there. He asked me if he could take the girls for a walk. Looking back,

I took a big risk trusting him. He could have been a paedo-phile, anything, but something in his eyes told me that I could, and that I should get the children out of there. So I said yes, and I told them to go with him.' She sighed. 'And that left Dudley and me alone.' Once again, pain flashed across her face. 'As soon as they were gone, he switched on the phone again, and he began to speak again. "Tomas," he said, still in his terrible Lithuanian, and I remember every word, "the big man says there's a price for the crap that's happened, and it's you that has to pay it. Tomorrow, you're to go to your lawyer and make whatever arrangements you need to, to transfer your holding in Lituania SAFI to another company, Scotland SAFI. Don't you worry, we'll know when you've done that. When you have, you'll go to a public place . . . and we'll be watching you, don't you worry . . . and you will kill yourself. That's what the man wants. If you don't do it, then we'll send your wife and your kids back to you in as many boxes as it takes, but it'll be at least a dozen. And you know, the man always keeps his promises." And then he stopped.' She looked up at Skinner. 'That's why Tomas killed himself,' she said. 'To save our lives.' She sat silent for a few seconds. 'As soon as he'd brought the girls back,' she continued, 'Henry left in the other car, and he didn't come back. Dudley locked us in our room, brought us food and let us out to go to the toilet when we asked, but he didn't say any more to us. I didn't want him to, because I was terrified. Two days later on the Wednesday he drove us back to Mezin and let us out of the car on the edge of the village. When he did that, I knew that Tomas was dead.'

Skinner nodded. 'Yes,' he murmured, 'that's what I thought.'

As he looked at Regine once more, he seemed to share her pain. 'But that's not all, is it?' he added.

The woman's face twisted; her eyes screwed up tight. 'It's all,' she cried, quietly.

'Ah, but it isn't,' the chief constable went on, as his colleagues' attention switched to him. 'Dudley didn't stop where you said, did he?'

Very slowly, Regine Zaliukas shook her head, and drew her right foot out of its fluffy slipper. Its middle toe was missing, the stump covered by a white bandage.

A small scream escaped from Becky Stallings; from McGuire a low animal snarl.

'He set the phone,' the woman told them, her voice almost a moan, 'so that it filmed him as he did it, with a pair of garden clippers. When I had stopped screaming, he told me that if I did not give him Tomas's number, he would cut off another. I did, of course. He sent the video to Tomas, and then he waited. After a few minutes his phone rang and it was Tomas. He put it on speaker so I could hear. He yelled at Dudley; he promised that he would take all ten of his, one by one, before he killed him. But Dudley said, "You won't be able to do that, will you, because you'll be dead." And now he is.' She slumped back in her chair, looked at Stallings, and held out her empty glass. 'Please.'

'I'm going to eat that bastard when we catch him,' McGuire swore, as the DI headed for the kitchen.

'My sentiments entirely,' Skinner concurred. 'Or they would be if Dudley was still fit for consumption. Somebody strung him up last night, in a barn,' he put his wrists together

above his head, 'like that. Then he cut off all ten of his toes.
When he was finished he put a shotgun in old Dudley's
mouth and pulled the trigger. When Henry Brown came
charging on to the scene, like the Seventh Cavalry, armed
with a big Colt handgun, he shot the legs out from under him,
and then did the same to him.' He looked at Jonas Zaliukas.
'We found them maybe sooner than you expected,' he said.
'But it was still too late for us to trace your flight. You were
back in France by that time. There's a late evening service
from Edinburgh to Carcassonne on a Monday,' he explained
to McGuire, and to Stallings as she returned with a refilled
glass. 'David Mackenzie found it when he checked all
possible flights for me first thing this morning. Its passenger
list shows a Colonel J. Zaliukas, travelling on a Lithuanian
passport. Let me guess, Jonas,' he said. 'You bought the shirt at
the airport when you landed.'

'Yes, I did,' the man admitted. 'But I know nothing of the
other things.'

'You know everything, Colonel. You also know that we'll
never place you at that crime scene in a month of wet
Sundays.'

'Maybe,' McGuire exclaimed. 'The shirt he wore
yesterday . . .'

'You can have it if you want,' the Lithuanian offered.

Skinner smiled. 'Don't bother, Mario. He wore a sterile
tunic, and then he burned it in a bin behind the barn . . . the
same bin, I reckon, that was used to burn Ken Green's files to
ashes. He and his clothes will be clean as a whistle. But that's
why Regine wouldn't talk to you last night. She had to wait

until Jonas got back, to tell her it was OK. Did he tell you what he was going to Scotland to do?' he asked her.

'I tell her nothing,' said Zaliukas quickly. 'Only that she should stay with Max and Zaki and say nothing to anyone until I got back.'

'So why did you go to Scotland?'

'I go to make arrangements for Tomas's funeral. You can check if you like. People called Scotmid will do it.'

'And it'll be safe for Regine to go back?'

'Yes.'

'Are you sure? A man called Cameron McCullough might have a different view.'

'No. That man, you will find, is a realist. If he did think to do harm to Regine, or rather order it, for he does nothing himself, he would know that while he may have a few hoodlums left, I have an army.'

Skinner stepped slowly across to him, feeling his eyes sting with weariness as he looked down at him. 'Let me tell you something, Jonas. If any of your soldiers set foot in Scotland, they will be on the first plane home . . . if they're lucky. Regine will be safe because I will make it my business to ensure that she is. As for McCullough, I still have to make his acquaintance. But I will.' He tapped him on the chest. 'And you? As soon as your brother is in the ground, Colonel, you should go back to Lithuania. And you should fucking stay there.'

Eighty-five

'You don't think Tayside will be able to build a case?' Aileen asked her husband. He was beside her, sprawled on the sofa in the garden room. On a table by his side lay three Corona beer bottles, two of them empty, and a plate, on which lay a small piece of crust, the last relic of a pizza that he had picked up from the takeaway on his way home.

'Not against Jonas. We can track his movements, no problem. He flew to France on the evening before his brother died. He did tell me that Tomas insisted on it. He wanted him to be ready to look for Regine and the kids if those two bastards didn't keep their word and let them go, but I think also he was afraid that Jonas would try to stop him carrying out their last instruction.'

'To kill himself?'

Bob nodded. 'When he got to Mezin, Regine and the kids had just been released. He treated her injury . . . which, incredibly, she'd managed to keep from her daughters . . . and he brought his two ex-soldier pals across to make sure they stayed safe while he took care of business. That may well have been his last order from his brother, but we'll never know that. What we do know is that he flew back to Edinburgh on Sunday. We know as well that he visited the Scotmid Funeral Service on Monday morning. But we can't place him anywhere else until he caught that late evening flight to Carcassonne. And there is no chance that we ever will.'

'Does that bother you?'

He looked at her, sideways on the couch, considering her quiet question. 'I wouldn't say this to many other people,' he began, 'but during my career there have been a very few occasions, just one or two, when I've seen someone get away with a crime, and even though I've done my best to nail them, I haven't been too upset by my failure. This is one of them. We have Tomas Zaliukas's mobile phone among his possessions. That video's on it. I've seen it, and honest to God, if it had turned out differently and we had that guy Dudley in our custody . . .' His voice tailed off.

She laid a hand on his chest as he picked up his bottle. 'You've had a hell of a couple of days, my love.'

'You could say that,' he conceded, 'and probably another one to come tomorrow. Andy's taking me to meet this Grandpa McCullough.'

'You know,' Aileen confessed, 'when you told me about this I couldn't help laughing at the thought of Tommy Murtagh, caught *in flagrante* with his client's sister, the wife of a ruthless killer to boot.'

'Yes, that was a beauty; I gave in to a small smile myself. Yet lucky wee Tommy's free and clear. Goldie's a widow now, so who knows how that relationship might develop.' He killed his third Corona.

'I'll get you another,' his wife offered.

'You are an angel of mercy in the darkest of worlds.'

'How nice.'

'So don't just bring me one, bring me a six-pack and an opener. Don't bother with the lime.'

'Are you sure? About the beer, not the lime.'

'Honey, I dropped off to sleep on the flight home. I had a nightmare. Apparently I started to shout some very scary things about toes. Mario had to waken me.' He waved the empty bottle. 'I'd like to put a few more of these between me and my next dream.'

When she returned with six more Coronas, he was staring out of the window, into the night, so still that for a moment . . . He stirred, looked up at her and smiled. 'Thanks, angel mine,' he said, as she uncapped one and handed it to him. 'Every little helps.'

'But don't overdo it.'

'I never do. I'll work it off tomorrow anyway.' The smile left him. 'But I've got more on my mind than gory crime scenes.'

'Such as?'

'A couple of things. This whole damned inquiry for a start. I've been reviewing it and I see great big glaring holes in the procedure. For example, the girl Anna Romanova was a direct link to the investigation of Zaliukas's death, she was found hours after it and yet it took a full day for us to tie her in, and we only did that when two of our CID teams turned up on the same doorstep for different reasons. A shambles, a total . . .' He sighed. 'If we'd got our act together quicker, through proper interchange of current information, Valdas Gerulaitis might have been in custody on Friday evening, instead of being tortured and killed. If someone had tried to find out where Ken Green was when he failed to show for a client interview, maybe he wouldn't be dead now either, and we might have found evidence in his cottage to tie Mr Murtagh's prize client into this whole business. I doubt that, mind you; everything that man does seems to be invisible.'

'Maybe he doesn't really exist.'

'Oh, he's real, all right, as I'll find out tomorrow.'

'The cottage,' Aileen exclaimed. 'If Green was killed, how did they know about that?'

'They'd probably been there. He probably used it for meetings that he couldn't have in his office. My guys found a key under a plant pot. There were signs that both had been used, fairly recently.'

'You can't blame anybody for that.'

'Hey, listen, I'm not blaming anybody but myself.'

'For what?'

'For a fundamental management mistake I've made. The problems we've had flowed from a lack of clear, single-minded thinking, at the top of the CID tree, starting with me when I put the present structure in place. The Glimmer Twins: having Mario as head of CID and Neil as his deputy, it just doesn't work. They didn't get their nickname by accident; they are genuinely like brothers. They're both brilliant detectives, outstanding police officers, but they're too close and neither ever questions anything the other does. I'm going to have to separate them . . . but without either of them ever knowing it's happened, for I don't want either one thinking that he's failed in any way.'

'How are you going to do that?'

'At this moment, I haven't a bloody clue. That's next week's problem.'

'What's this week's?'

'A leak. I've still got one question that's unanswered. Tomas's last show of defiance: he was told to transfer his share in the massage parlours to another company. But he didn't. Instead he left it to Laima Gerulaitis.'

'A horrible woman, from what you've told me.'

'Yeah, which makes me sure that he didn't pick her name out of a hat. He did it knowing what might happen to her when Henry and Dudley found out. But how did they? Green's ex-wife was able to confirm that he'd been to see Veronica Drake and that he'd changed his will, but that was all she could do. After Tomas was dead, Alex asked Drake about the contents; Drake told her, and she told us, via Jack McGurk and young Haddock.'

'Which makes you think, again?'

'Which makes me fear . . . that the McCullough clan has a mole in my force.'

'What are you going to do about it?'

'What else? Trap it. I don't know how, but when I do . . . would you like a pair of moleskin gloves?'

Eighty-six

'You've been looking distinctly fresher the last couple of mornings,' Jack McGurk remarked.

'What do you mean by that?' Sauce Haddock retorted, bristling. 'Did Neil McIlhenney not cure you of that terminal smugness yesterday?'

'It'll take more than that. Anyway, you know damn well what I mean.' The DS peered at Becky Stallings as she came into the room. 'You, on the other hand, look bloody knackered.'

'If I'd the energy to be offended,' she told him, 'I would. But I don't, so somebody be kind to an old woman who does their performance reviews and get me a coffee.'

'Put like that, how could Sauce refuse?' he replied. 'Good to see you back, by the way. Are you going to tell us where you've been?'

'Once I'm sat behind my desk with that coffee, and possibly a choccy biscuit to go with it, I'll be happy to.'

He followed her into her small, theoretically private, room, taking a seat as she hung her coat on a hook behind the door, watching as she tidied an accumulation of paper from the previous day, waiting for Haddock to join them. When he did, he was carrying two mugs. He set one before the DI, produced two KitKats from his shirt pocket, and handed one to her.

'Where's mine?' McGurk complained.

'You, Sergeant, can fuck off and get your own.'

'Settle down in class, now,' said Stallings. 'Thanks, Sauce. You were asking where I've been, Jack. I've been with the head of CID on a whirlwind trip to France.'

'You've been to see Regine?' Haddock's eyebrows rose.

'Yes I have. And by the time we got to see her, there was someone else in our party: the chief.' She frowned at her two-man team. 'Was there any talk yesterday about two homicides, up in Perthshire?'

The DS shook his head. 'No, but there was some other news from there. The sensation of the day was Montell and Alice Cowan tracking a truck from a robbery in Edinburgh and catching the driver and her mate. And in the process guess what they found as well?'

'Eight missing Estonian girls,' she shot back, 'being looked after by Marius Ramanauskas.'

'You know about that?'

'Yes, and here's the rest of it.'

The pair sat in silence as she told them of the interview of Regine Zaliukas, and of her story. By the time she finished, the mood in the room had changed. There was no more banter, only shock. 'Mr McIlhenney has Tomas's phone, with the video on it,' she said. 'He called me as I was driving in. He says it's pretty horrible.' She paused. 'But only one-twentieth as horrible as what was done to Henry and Dudley, before they died.'

'Serves them fucking right,' McGurk whispered.

'We all think that, Jack.' She crumpled the paper from her biscuit and threw it in her bin. 'That's the story, lads,' she concluded. 'On to the next. After . . . Mr McIlhenney says that we have all to be available for interview this afternoon, by the deputy chief.'

'About what?' asked Haddock.

'I don't know. He didn't tell me the agenda, but from his tone, I don't think he's going to ask us if we're happy in our work. We'll find out when it happens. On you go, now; and close the door behind you. I want some peace and quiet.'

'Any ideas?' McGurk murmured, as he and Haddock returned to their desks.

'Me? None.'

'That's not like you: you've usually got a theory for every occasion.'

'Not this time.'

'Too busy thinking about your baby?'

'Knock off the Marvin Gaye. Remember what happened to him.'

'Is that it, though? Are you chucked? Seriously; I'm not taking the piss.'

Haddock sighed. 'Maybe. I tried to call her all day yesterday, after she no-showed on Monday night. I left messages on her voicemail, but nothing.'

'Ain't too proud to beg?' the DS murmured as he switched on his computer, a broad grin spread across his face.

'Aw, not more fuckin' Motown, Jack. Look, it's down to her to call me now, end of story.'

Still smiling, McGurk watched his screen and waited as his terminal booted up. As soon as it was ready, he checked his box for email. Finding it empty, he turned to the force's private network, and saw an intranet message waiting for him. He opened it and read it. 'Yes!' he exclaimed. 'Another box ticked.'

'What's that?' Haddock muttered, as he waited for his own connection to complete.

'That key we found under the pot at Green's cottage. Forensics found a print on it and they've got a match. It belongs to one Dudley Davis; he had several assault convictions on his record . . . but no more, Dudley, no more.'

'Say that again.'

'What?'

'That name.'

'Dudley?'

'No not fucking Dudley. The other one.'

'Davis. That's his surname.' The sergeant looked at his young colleague. 'Why? What's up?'

'Probably nothing, Jack. It's just that coming from a police family, I was brought up to believe that most coincidences aren't.' He reached for his phone, then stopped. 'No,' he said, to himself. 'Do something for me, please,' he went on. 'Get the number for an accountancy firm called Deacon and Queen, then call their office and ask if you can speak to one of their trainees, a Miss Davis. If they say yes, just hang up.'

At once McGurk was as serious as the detective constable. He took Yellow Pages from his drawer, found the number and dialled. 'Hi,' Sauce heard him drawl. 'Council here, finance department. I wonder if you could connect me with one of your postgraduate trainees. She did some work for us, and there's a query. Miss Davis.' He paused, listening. 'Sorry,' he continued. 'My mistake; I must have my firms mixed up.' As he hung up, he whistled. 'They don't have a Miss Davis,' he told Haddock. 'In fact they only have one female trainee, and her name is Cameron McCullough.'

Eighty-seven

'Do you agree with my diagnosis?' Skinner asked.

'About Mario and Neil as a command pairing? Yes, I do. Truth be told,' Andy Martin continued, 'I wondered about it when you made the two appointments, but the guys had worked their way there. Sometimes you find things out by trial and error.' He raised an eyebrow. 'There might be a solution soon, though.'

'What's that?'

'There are going to be two jobs coming up in Tayside; mine and the chief's. Graham Morton told me he's going early.'

'Really? First I've heard of it.' He frowned. 'I doubt if Mario would fancy a move to Dundee, though, and he's not eligible for the top job anyway. And Neil couldn't apply for either.'

'No, but Brian Mackie could. He'd be a perfect replacement for Graham. Right age, right experience.'

'By God, you're right,' Skinner conceded. 'I don't want to lose him, but he deserves the step up. I can't prompt him, though, Andy.'

'No you can't, but I can mark his card. Leave it with me: this conversation never happened.' He glanced around the great hallway in which they stood. It was Victorian, reminiscent of much of Edinburgh's New Town, he thought, but grander than any building he could recall. 'First time I've been here,' he remarked. 'I hate to admit it, but McCullough runs a very impressive hotel.'

'What's it called? I missed the sign when you drove in.'

'It's doesn't have one, not on the road; very discreet. Its name is Black Shield Lodge.'

'Sounds Masonic.'

'That's your Motherwell origins showing.'

'Maybe,' he paused as a figure approached them from the right of the stairway, 'but I tell you one thing. It takes more than a building to stamp class on a place. The staff have a lot to do with it too.'

Martin turned, and laughed softly when he saw who was coming to greet them.

'Gentlemen,' said Thomas Murtagh. He was dressed in a five-hundred-pound suit, and immaculately groomed, his hair the customary shade that everyone who saw it assumed was a dye. 'Welcome to Black Shield.'

'Nice to see you in a jacket and tie,' Skinner retorted, 'and with your fly zipped. You can stop faking nice, though. You hate our guts, and we don't like you either.'

'I try to be professional. My client is ready to see you, but there are a couple of ground rules I want to get clear.'

'What?' the chief constable roared. 'We're police officers, and you're nothing. You hear me? Nothing!'

'I'm Mr McCullough's adviser,' the former politician countered, 'and the only way to see him is through me.'

'Our pleasure,' Skinner growled, then felt Martin pull gently at his sleeve, as if he was tugging at a leash.

'Go on, Mr Murtagh,' he said. 'Say what you have to and we'll decide whether we're staying, or whether we're going to arrest your client.'

'I don't see that you could. My advice to Mr McCullough is that we should all be clear that this is a private visit, not an official one, and that he should be sure that it isn't recorded.'

'Oh for fu . . .' the chief sighed. 'If we were going to tape him, we'd be doing it at our place, not his. As for it being official, just get out the road or it will be.' Murtagh's nostrils flared. 'Now!' he barked.

'Very well. Follow me. My client's in the leisure club lounge. There's no one else there just now.' He led them through the hall, out of the building by a back door and across the lawn towards a glass annexe, built to enclose a swimming pool. They followed Murtagh inside, then through it, past the pool and into the area beyond, a gym, with exits marked 'Spa' and 'Relaxation Room'. Their escort opened the door of the second, and ushered them through.

As he looked at Cameron McCullough, Bob Skinner had a very strange reaction. For the first time, he felt every one of his fifty years, a birthday he had decreed would pass by with no recognition by anyone other than his wife and older daughter. He knew that the man was eight years older than him, and yet he realised that anyone walking in on them would take him for his junior. He had a full head of silver hair, and skin that although tanned was smooth and shining with health. He wore a black tracksuit, narrow-waisted, broad-shouldered, and he stood with his thumbs tucked into the pockets of the trousers.

'Welcome to my world,' he said, in a voice that seemed to have no accent, and certainly no hint of Dundonian. 'I understand you want to see me.'

Skinner nodded, then pointed at Murtagh. 'He leaves.'

'Oh no I don't,' the man retorted.

The chief ignored him, looking McCullough in the eye. 'In that case, we do. I've seen you; job done.'

McCullough smiled, showing perfect white teeth. 'Tommy, excuse us, please.'

'But Cameron . . .'

'It's all right. I'll pull the panic alarm cord if they get rough with me. Go on, now.' He laughed. 'I'll take it as read that you've searched them for hidden microphones.'

Murtagh's face flushed; he left the room, avoiding the police officers' eyes as he passed them.

'He tries,' McCullough chuckled, as the door closed. 'I'm sorry about all that crap about recordings; I like him to think I take his advice seriously. He's useful to me. By the way,' he added, 'this room isn't bugged.'

'He's got no influence in politics any more,' Skinner murmured. 'You know that, don't you?'

'Of course he hasn't, nationally, but he's still got some sort of name on Tayside. He knows the councillors, so it's worth having him on the payroll. I've got other political consultants, of course, but they like to stay in the background.' He picked up a fruit bowl from a table in the centre of the room and offered it. 'Would you like an apple? Or there's smoothies in that fridge in the corner if you'd prefer.'

'We're fine, thanks. We had lunch in Perth on the way up.'

'You could have lunched with me, if you'd said.' The smile again. 'But maybe not. You know why Tommy was so keen to stay, don't you? He's worried you'll tell me about catching him with my sister.'

'You knew about that?'

'Please, Mr Skinner! Surely you know what's going on in your family?'

'I don't have any sisters, my kids are all youngsters, apart from my adult daughter, and she'd kill me if she caught me spying on her.'

'Your daughter's a bright girl, I hear. A coming force in Edinburgh legal circles.'

Skinner felt his eyes narrowing, and realised that it was obvious when McCullough raised a hand. At the same time, he sensed Martin stirring beside him.

'Gentlemen, gentlemen, gentlemen; please, no,' their host exclaimed. 'I'm a businessman, and I keep myself abreast of what's happening in Scotland, and beyond. I like to know who the top talent is, in case I ever need to add to my team of advisers. I promise you I haven't been checking up on the young lady specifically.'

'You'd better mean that,' Martin murmured.

'Of course I do.'

'My friend has this fixation,' said Skinner. 'He dreams about putting you in jail. He thought he had you too, only you managed to walk away from it.'

'There were no witnesses to the alleged murder.' He

grinned. 'There wasn't even an alleged body. And the police couldn't produce the alleged drugs that they alleged were mine.'

'No, they couldn't, could they. But there were witnesses. They couldn't be produced because they'd vanished, but they existed. Their bones probably still do, unless you had them fed to pigs too.'

'Here,' McCullough protested 'if you're going to start that, maybe this should be formal, and maybe I should have Susannah Himes here.' He relaxed once more. 'But no, let's keep this as a quiet chat. I'll say this, just the once: you'll never find anything, never, that links me to any enterprise other than those that I own and of which I'm a director.'

It was Skinner's turn to laugh. 'Oh Christ, I know that. We never will, and not least because there's been a disease that's taken all the witnesses out. Tomas Zaliukas, Ken Green, the Gerulaitis couple. You know what? I think Valdas would have died in that fire anyway, even if Tomas hadn't pulled his trick of leaving his shares in your offshore company to his nasty wife.'

'There you go again,' McCullough sighed.

'Yes I do,' the chief retorted, as he lowered himself into a chair, 'because this is a private meeting like you wanted, and we're going to talk. I'm going to tell you what we know, and you're going to listen.'

The man shrugged. 'OK.' He took a seat beside the window as Martin walked across to the fridge and chose a soft drink. 'Shoot.'

'I've been known to, but not today. That's not something

your people are much into either, not recently at any rate. They've used other methods. I want to show you some stuff. Andy, have you got that netbook?'

'Yes, it's here.' Martin opened his attaché case and produced a small computer. He hit the space key and it awoke from slumber.

Skinner took it as he rose and crossed to sit beside McCullough. 'Let me show you some photos, Cameron.' He clicked a folder and a grotesque image appeared on screen, naked flesh, gore, bone. 'That's Tomas Zaliukas on the mortuary slab . . . before they started to carve him up, but after he had done what he was compelled to do to save the lives of his wife and children.' He clicked again and a slide show began. 'That's a man called Linas Jankauskas, after your brother-in-law broke his neck.' Pause. 'That's Valdas Gerulaitis, after the fire.' Pause. 'That's his wife.' Pause. 'That's Ken Green, dead in his car, after Henry and Dudley had finished with him. We know they were in the cottage, by the way; we'd have them if they were alive.' Pause. 'Only they're not. This is them as they were found, on Monday night, after Jonas Zaliukas had finished with them.' Skinner held the photograph and zoomed in on it. As he looked at it, McCullough gave a short gasp, his first reaction. 'See those things on the ground?' the chief asked. 'Jonas played a game before he killed them. This little piggy went to market, this little piggy stayed at home, and so on. He played it four times, once with each foot, and then he put them away. Did he tell you he was going to do that when he came to see you, Cameron?'

The man's eyes locked on to Skinner's. 'What do you mean,

came to see me?' he snapped, but a second too late. 'Pure fucking fantasy.'

'Fantastic but true. Jonas paid you a surprise visit, at home, on Monday. You had no idea he existed, did you, or what he was. You and he had a chat, just like this one, and after that, probably in exchange for him agreeing to stop at the two of them, you set up your brother-in-law, and Dudley. You're a seriously hard man, I know, but so's Jonas. And you're both realists, so you did a deal, the two of you. Why do I say this? Because Goldie told us that Henry took the call that sent him to the barn on his mobile, his shop-bought pay-as-you-go, no contract, anonymous mobile, the same as Dudley had, and the same as you've got so that we can never trace certain calls you might not want us to. Your privacy means everything to you, Cameron; you kill to protect it. Henry took your call, he put his phone in his pocket, he took a gun . . . he must have sensed something was off, or you slipped him a signal in your instructions . . . and he went to his death. How do I know that's what happened? Because we never found their fucking phones, man, and we know for sure that Henry had his on him. Jonas took them away from the scene, and destroyed them, along with the legally held shotgun he took from his brother's house and the shears he took from his garden shed. That was part of your agreement, no doubt. But no, Jonas never told you about his plans for their toes, did he, and he didn't tell you about this.'

He closed the netbook, laid it aside and took a cellphone from his pocket. 'This was Tomas's.' He found the video folder, hit the 'play' key and held it close to McCullough's face.

Neither he nor Martin could see the movie, although they had before, and they had heard the sound, the strange, unintelligible words, and then the endless, endless scream. As it continued the man seemed to press himself further and further back into his chair, his eyes becoming smaller and smaller as they screwed up tight. 'I would like to believe,' said Skinner when it was over, 'that you didn't order Dudley to do that. Otherwise I will have to consider very seriously letting Jonas know that you did, and then not giving a fuck when he comes back for you. If that happens, I doubt if he'll stop at toes.'

'That Dudley was a fucking animal,' McCullough whispered. 'Greedy, ambitious and a fucking animal. Henry might not have been too nice, but he had a soft side.' He caught Martin's incredulous stare. 'Oh yes, and he showed it, losing it and killing that guy when he found what he'd done to that girl, then taking her to the doctor's when she was supposed to go to the farm with the rest. A big mistake, as it turned out. But Dudley . . .'

His face twisted, and in that expression Skinner and his colleague saw the heart and soul of Grandpa McCullough, the man within that he had determined to hide for good, at whatever cost. 'My daughter actually wanted to marry the pig,' he growled, 'but I told her that would happen over his dead body.'

'Your granddaughter took his name, though,' Skinner countered. 'She used it when she went to a club where everybody knows that a lot of cops hang out off duty, and picked up one of my young officers. She fucked him so enthusiastically that he thought nothing of telling her all about his day's work, pillow to pillow, including the bit about the disposal of Tomas's share in Lituania SAFI to a woman neither he nor anyone else could stand. His inspector brought him to see me this morning, after he'd discovered who she ... "Cheeky Davis", she called herself . . . really was.

'Poor lad was in tears,' he continued, 'not because he thought his career was over . . . which it isn't . . . but because he really did believe that she was the only woman he'd ever love. When you asked her to get close to the police in Edinburgh if she could, to check whether we'd bought the story of Tomas's suicide, and the other accidents, you couldn't have imagined that she'd pick up that piece of information, but what a bonus when you did. It meant that Dudley could torture Valdas to get Laima's signature on a piece of paper signing her inheritance over to you.' He smiled. 'Yes, she's a smart lass, all right. She was nearly rumbled last Friday, when Andy here turned up at a dance she was at with her lad. He'd have recognised her, of course, but she had the presence of mind to get them both out of there before he spotted her.'

'My granddaughter is an independent young woman,' McCullough murmured. 'She makes her own choices. I've called her Cheeky all her life, and as for using the name of her mother's partner, nothing unusual about that.'

'No more unusual than driving robbery vehicles,' Martin said. 'And getting away with it, this time. The Crown Office have accepted Himes's bargain. We can guess whose idea it was, too. You're sending your own daughter to jail to keep her clear.'

'Serves Inez fucking right, the idiot, for getting Cheeky

involved in it. She's going to blame Dudley though; she won't get that long. And it was his idea; she told me the clown knew an assistant pro in the Czech Republic. They were going to send the stuff out there in a crate and he was going to flog it in his shop. Not to France, mind, not Germany, not Spain, where they've got real money. No, to the Czech Republic, where they've hardly got any fucking golfers. He might have been good at thieving, but when it came to business, brainless . . .' his eyes gleamed, '. . . and now literally so, now that I come to think about it.'

Suddenly, McCullough sat upright, as if he was coming to attention in his chair. 'That's it, gentlemen,' he announced. 'This conversation's at an end. I have another meeting.'

Skinner stood. 'It's not quite over. Do something for us, please. Take your tracksuit top off.'

The man laughed, grimly. 'Why don't you do the same and we'll have a pose-down? You look like a chunky guy.'

'Maybe, but that's not the issue. When Tomas and his partner went to Uruguay with Valdas and the partner's minder to set up Lituania SAFI, they all got tattooed, to celebrate. So please, humour us.'

'Fine,' McCullough agreed, affably. He unzipped the jacket and slipped it off; beneath it he wore a red Nike training vest, sleeveless, so that his arms were completely exposed. Just below his right shoulder, where Tomas Zaliukas had sported his tattoo, a square of skin was red-raw and blistered. 'A wee accident,' he said, as the police officers stared. 'Silly me, I spilled some fucking acid on it.' He put the top back on. 'Now, if that's us done . . .'

The chief constable shook his head. 'No, no, there are two more things. First, the massage parlours.'

'But they're not mine, so there's no point in asking me to sell them, if that's what you're going to do.'

'No, I wasn't going to. Instead, I want you to get word to the owner, whoever he might be, that I want those places to be run impeccably. No noise, no nuisance to the neighbours and absolutely no illegality going on in there, other than the thing we know about and ignore for the greater public good.'

'I couldn't agree more,' said McCullough. 'After all, wasn't that what this whole business was about?' He smiled. 'And your other concern?'

'Regine Zaliukas. She's coming back, and she's going to be running Lietuvos Leisure and Lietuvos Developments. You do not even look in her direction. If you approach her in any way, then what I said about Jonas applies. Someone will call him, and turn him and his army loose on you. Not me, of course. I stand apart from such things, just as you do.'

He nodded. 'I always regarded Mrs Zaliukas as a better business person than her husband. I wish her all good luck in her future endeavours, but I have no desire to extend the CamMac group holdings into Edinburgh. The fact is,' he added, 'I doubt if that city's big enough for both of us.'

'No,' Skinner concurred. 'You can be sure that it isn't.'

Eighty-eight

'He wasn't talking about himself and Régine, you know,' said Martin as he drove on to the motorway from the slip road. 'That bit about the city.'

'Neither was I,' Skinner snorted.

'What did you think of him?'

The chief constable leaned back in the passenger seat and reflected on the question. 'I think he's one of the most dangerous men I've ever met in my life. It's not so much his physical menace, although he has that in plenty. It's his ruthlessness and his complete thoroughness that sets him apart. He'll never feel your heavy hand on his shoulder again, or anyone else's for that matter. He's way, way too clever. I hope Murtagh never upsets him, though.' He smiled. 'What have I just said? Maybe I do. If I was him I'd steer clear of Goldie, though, given what happened to Grandpa's last brother-in-law.'

'What about your boy Haddock?' Martin asked.

'What would you do with him?'

'I think if it was possible to pat his head and kick his arse at the same time . . .'

'It was. Becky Stallings did the kicking and I did the patting.

The kid has learned. In fact the kid learns something new every day, and that's what makes him so damn good. I don't want his self-belief damaged by this. In fact, I won't let that happen.' He dipped his fingers into a bag of chocolate M&Ms that Martin kept in his central console, and took as many as he could grab. 'What about you?' he said. 'What did you think of all that?'

'Do you really want to know? Seeing you and Grandpa McCullough in the same room was the most surreal experience of my police career.'

'Eh?' he laughed. 'Why?'

'Bob, remember what I said about Alex and young Cameron ruling the world? Well, I understand where that came from now. You and he, you could be fucking clones. You're two peas, if not from the same pod, then pods grown on the same branch. You know what McCullough's dad was? He was a lawyer, like yours, only he worked for the council rather than in private practice. What was it you said? Physical menace, ruthlessness and complete thoroughness. You could have been describing yourself, man. I watched the two of you in there and I thought, thank God one of them's on our side of the fence, otherwise we'd all be fucked.'

'Are you serious?'

'Absolutely.'

Skinner picked up the bag of chocolate pills and emptied its remaining contents into his open hand. 'In that case,' he said, just before he swallowed them, 'I'll take it as a compliment.'

Eighty-nine

'Jack,' said Sauce, 'it's a nice thought, by both of you, but I'm OK. Maybe we'll go to Indigo on Friday, but I'm not in a boozing mood tonight. I'll stay in, watch a couple of miserable French movies and cry my eyes out. Failing that, I'll put on the Motown twenty-fifth anniversary CD and think of you. See you tomorrow.'

He hung up and walked across to his DVD collection. He almost settled on *In Bruges* but passed it by, because he found the finish heart-rending at the best of times. He looked at his CDs. *Motown Twenty-fifth Anniversary* was not a starter for the simple reason that he did not possess it, nor was Tom Waits' *The Black Rider* because it was so weird that it was positively creepy, nor *The Travelling Wilburys* because Roy Orbison was dead. Finally he settled for the Foo Fighters' *Skin and Bones*, turning the volume to just below neighbour intolerance level, and maybe even a shade beyond.

The sound was so loud that he almost failed to hear the buzzer. When it broke through, he turned the level down and stepped into the hall.

She was standing there when he opened the door, her

500

carefully cut blond hair casually disarranged, her make-up simple but perfect and her lips that soft shade of red that he liked so much. 'Hi,' she whispered.

'Miss McCullough, I presume,' he replied, coldly.

'Sauce, I'm sorry,' she began. 'I should have told you my real name, but with my grandpa being a wee bit notorious, and you being a cop . . .'

'I didn't tell you I was a cop until after you'd told me your name. I'm a fucking detective; I can work that out. You also left out the bit about you being a fucking getaway driver.'

'That was all a misunderstanding. That was my moron mother's fault. They've dropped the charges against me.'

'Yes, and what I told you, gullible idiot that I was . . . God, a woman died.'

She flinched, and he thought he saw real pain in her eyes; for sure he saw tears. She put her arms around his neck and buried her face in his chest. 'I didn't know that would happen,' she sobbed. 'My mum asked me, for that bastard of a man of hers. But I never thought . . .'

He heard a neighbour's footsteps on the stair below, and drew her inside. She ran her fingers through his hair, and kissed him lightly. 'I'm sorry,' she whispered, 'so sorry.'

'Sorry doesn't make it right.' He looked into her smoky grey eyes. 'You realise I'll never be able to believe another fucking thing you tell me?'

She nodded.

He kept on looking. 'Can I still call you Cheeky?' he asked.

Ninety

In another part of the city, another door chime sounded. Andy Martin thought very seriously about ignoring it as he continued to gaze at the photograph on the sideboard. Karen had taken it: Robert, held in the crook of his arm, with Danielle looking at him with sisterly pride.

The chime summoned him again. 'Bugger,' he whispered, but trotted downstairs to street level, and swung the door open.

She stood there, in jeans and an open-necked white shirt, oblivious to the chill of the evening. She held a bottle in her hand, up beside her shoulder, with its label turned for him to see: Siglo Gran Reserva rioja, one he recognised from another time. Behind her he caught a glimpse of a taxi as it disappeared round the curve in the road.

'To answer your slightly crazed question of the other night,' she said, 'there is no such thing as a hench. If it's a word at all, it's an adjective, but no one really knows.' She smiled, and in spite of everything, his heart sang. 'And now that I've answered the security question . . .' she continued, '. . . can I come in?'